Soulsight

SEEING IS NOT ALWAYS BELIEVING

H. Paine

instant
ap☐stle

First published in Great Britain in 2016.
Instant Apostle
The Barn
1 Watford House Lane
Watford
Herts
WD17 1BJ

British Library Cataloguing-in-Publication Data

A catalogue record for this book is available from the British Library.

This book and all other Instant Apostle books are available from
Instant Apostle:

Website: www.instantapostle.com

E-mail: info@instantapostle.com

ISBN 978-1-909728-49-3

Printed in Great Britain

Chapter 1

Flickering light woke him, alternating bright, then pitch black, glowing through his closed lids. As he opened his eyes tentatively, the glare of the early morning sun hit him full in the face, only immediately to be extinguished again. He lay under his thin cotton sheet, watching the pastel blue sky of the new dawn flash intermittently. On... off, dark... light... until his fascination turned to irritation.

Forcing his way into wakefulness, he cleared his throat sufficiently to speak.

'House?'

'Good morning, Silas,' trilled the computer, in its high-pitched and chirpy 'morning' voice.

'The window is faulty,' Silas complained, grimacing as another flash of sunlight momentarily blinded him.

'I am working to rectify the problem.' There was a brief pause before the computer announced, 'The problem has been rectified,' and Silas was plunged into darkness once again.

'I'm awake now, stupid machine, there's no point leaving me in the dark... House?' he grumbled.

'Yes, Silas?' came the unsuitably happy response.

'Set window to one-way,' he requested grumpily, and a subtle pink hue stained the glass, turning the sky pale purple. A few wispy clouds hovered high in the atmosphere, marring the otherwise unblemished canvas.

'Time?'

'06:50,' the computer answered.

Ten minutes, he thought, definitely not worth trying to doze off again. Instead he remained still, trying to recapture his dreams. It had been the recurring dream, he realised with disappointment… a vast featureless wasteland, with nothing to break the monotony, no sounds to hear, and no colour to see… just an endless stretch of grey. It left him with an utter sense of emptiness.

Disturbing the silence, the house began its automated daily spiel.

'Please present yourself for assessment. The time is 07:00; the current temperature is 17 degrees centigrade, 10 per cent cloud cover with a light breeze. The appropriate UV filter uniform has been selected.'

Resigned to the inevitability of a new day, Silas shambled into the Biocubicle next to his bed. The door automatically shut behind him and infrared beams criss-crossed his body.

'Percentages,' continued the voice. 'Muscle… 36 per cent… Fat… 10 per cent. Blood pressure… 110 over 60. Heart rate… 60 beats per minute. Weight… 47 kilograms.'

As the machine made its assessment, Silas studied himself in the stainless-steel wall opposite. What he saw did not impress him. At 15 he still had the look of a pre-pubescent child. His biceps and abs were there, but only just. There was not an ounce of fat on him, but neither, it seemed, was there any muscle.

Thick, curly brown hair fell across his forehead in an untidy tangle, and he ran his fingers through it, pushing it off his face. Without a fringe to obscure them, his green eyes looked peculiarly large. They were a striking colour; an iridescent, multilayered green, flecked with gold, like sunlight breaking through the trees, deep and rich.

'The eyes are the window to the soul,' was what his mum had said, and Silas reckoned that if there were such a thing as a soul then his would be permanently bathed in a greenish glow.

'Recommended protein shake dispensed,' burbled the synthesised voice. 'Lunch requirements have been forwarded to the nutrition engineers at your clinic.'

He sighed but dutifully picked up the glass of viscous liquid from the dispenser. However much shake he drank, it didn't seem to have any discernible effect. After downing the glass of the liquid breakfast in a few gulps, he threw on some shorts and a vest and went into the health suite.

His brother, Marc, was already jogging on the treadmill, maintaining a decent pace. Silas glanced at Marc's muscular legs, and then down at his own, and sighed again.

'Hey! Silas, Stay-last,' Marc jeered. 'What has she got you doing today?'

Wincing at the distortion of his name, Silas turned his attention to the screen by the door. Based on the Biocubicle assessment, the house would recommend the most appropriate exercise, and Silas was unsurprised to see... 30 minutes of muscle-building exercises... again. He wandered over to the weights machine blocking out the snorts of derision from Marc.

'Maybe when you've put some meat on those matchsticks, Still-last, she'll let you try out some of the other equipment.'

The door to the health suite opened, preventing Marc from launching into a more aggressive verbal attack, and their father walked in. He was already dressed for work; the dark green of his suit rippling into black with every movement of his lean body as he purposefully strode towards Marc. Had his father overheard Marc's comment and was he now stepping in to defend his youngest son? Silas wondered hopefully.

'Good, Marc! Great speed! And you are *well* above your targets! That's my champ! Looking good, feeling great, eh, son?' Their father paused. 'Oh, and morning, Si. Still on the weights, hmm?' His words tailed off as he silently watched Silas settle himself at the machine. He looked like he might say more, and Silas waited expectantly for some further acknowledgement or even encouragement, but instead his father turned back to study Marc.

'Good work, good work,' he said, nodding his head approvingly. 'I've got time before I need to go in today, so why don't I match you on my machine and let's see if we can't push your speed up even more.'

Silas watched his brother's face light up at the challenge. Squashing down his own sense of failure, he emptied his mind, as his body went through the apparently futile motions of building muscle.

Later, standing in the shower, with hot water pounding against his skin, he felt his shoulders relax. Having his father hovering around the workout suite always increased the agony of the session. He was usually out of the house before the boys had even got out of bed.

His father was a legend: 'Anton Corelle – inventor of the Biocubicle – Saviour of the Nation.' Of course, that had all taken place before Silas was born, and now the Biocubicle was a fixture in nearly every home. Yet Bio-health Laboratory, with his father at the helm, was still pushing forward, always striving for excellence.

Over the last few months, his father had even been called to attend regular meetings with the Flawless Leader, Helen Steele. What had been his father's description of her? Something along the lines of 'the pinnacle of human perfection', and he had seemed completely in awe of her.

Silas had never met her in person, but he had seen countless Viva party updates, and Helen Steele deserved the title of Flawless Leader. She was completely faultless.

From what Silas could gather, she wanted to invest government money into Biocubicle research and upgrades until *every* citizen, young or old, Seen or Unseen, had a personal cubicle. With the support of the Viva party, business for his father had never been better.

To be the son of such a great man should have made him proud, but instead Silas only felt his shortcomings more keenly. He could see it when he looked at his own reflection, he could see it when he looked at Marc and most prominently, he could see it etched on his own father's face… disappointment.

'Clinic commences in 30 minutes.' The voice cut through Silas's reflections, and he reached to turn the shower to dryer. Seconds later he was pulling on his pre-selected summer uniform. The smart-fabric was equipped to filter out any damaging levels of sunlight but allow the optimum amount for vitamin D production.

Emblazoned across the back were the words 'Vitality Private Clinic', and then, underneath, in slightly smaller letters ran the clinic motto, 'Achieve Perfection, Achieve Success'. The pale blue leggings and shirt fitted like a second skin, and this time Silas avoided looking at his reflection.

It was considered an excellent advert for the clinic that the uniform would cling to, and define, every toned muscle. However, in Silas' case, it meant everyone could see exactly what he *didn't* have.

He made it to the front door in time to see Marc sprint down the garden path and, with one beautifully timed stride, hurdle the front gate. Without breaking step, his brother fell into an easy pace with a group of Vitality kids as they jogged and joked their way to clinic. They radiated beauty and health – the top students at the leading clinic in Prima, the nation's principal city.

Silas shoved his feet into his clinic trainers and stumbled after them.

Chapter 2

The buzzer sounded one long clear note, indicating the start of clinic, as Silas panted his way up the white stone steps and through the grand front entrance. The familiar cocktail of sweat, hormones and disinfectant filled his nostrils.

'Out of my way, Gold first, and don't forget it.' Marc's voice rose above the hubbub in the corridor.

Following the sound, Silas saw him near the Gold warm-up room, tormenting a puny boy half his size. Marc stepped left, then right, to ensure his victim couldn't escape.

'You seemed so keen to get in my way; now you have to wait for my permission to leave. Tell me you understand.' Marc towered over the boy, oozing aggression from every pore.

'I understand! I'm sorry ...' the kid was desperately looking for a way past Marc's bulk when, effortlessly, Marc grabbed him by the shirt front and pinned him against the wall.

'Say, "I'm sorry, Gold Standard!"'

'I'm sorry, Gold Standard! Truly, I'm sorry, I'm sorry ...' With his feet dangling uselessly beneath him, the kid was squealing out apology after apology until, suddenly tiring of his sport, Marc dropped him. Landing awkwardly but without pausing to recover, the smaller kid shot off in the direction of the Bronze warm-up rooms. With a turn of speed like that, Silas could see how he had got a place at Vitality.

The other Gold students laughed and followed Marc into their warm-up room, doing impressions of the high-pitched whimper, 'Sorry, please put me down, I won't do it again...'

As the door swung closed behind them, cutting off Marc's self-satisfied laugh, the highly polished sign bearing the words 'GOLD 1' glinted in the light.

Marc had been in Gold 1 from his first day, blazing a glorious trail of success. This was his final season at clinic, and in recognition of his outstanding physical abilities, he had recently been crowned with the highest award any student could achieve, that of 'Male Gold Standard'.

'Male Gold ...' Silas wracked his brains to think of an appropriately belittling term, '... Stupid,' he muttered under his breath, staring with loathing at the shiny door sign. I can't even come up with a half-decent insult, he thought, frustrated with himself, and brimming with resentment towards Marc.

Another Gold student, perfectly toned and proportioned, went through the door, and before it swung shut, Silas saw them all... like gods and goddesses... so far out of his reach...

Before he started Vitality Clinic he thought that he would be just like Marc and be a Gold student from the moment he joined, and it had come as a bitter blow to him to be streamed into the bottom ability level, Bronze 5. He vividly remembered his father's confused expression when he had brought home his initial assessment. It was almost like he was looking at Silas without recognising him, as if to say, 'Whose child are you?'

But Silas had worked hard, and over the last five years he had clawed his way up to Bronze 1. He reckoned he would move up to Silver 5 at the next trials. Maybe then his father would be pleased.

Usually Bronze students were the butt of every joke, but because Silas was Marc's brother, the Silver and Gold students didn't pick on him. It was the only perk of being a Corelle as far as Silas could see. But even that had a downside. The other Bronze students then resented his special treatment, and therefore punished him in their own way, by ignoring him.

He spent his days surrounded by people and simultaneously alone. It didn't bother him; well, not much. The less people noticed him, the less they compared him to Marc. They stayed away from him, and he stayed away from them.

Suddenly realising he was going to be late for his own warm-up, Silas darted along the now deserted corridor and round the corner to the door labelled 'BRONZE 1'.

Most of his level was already following the routine of Coach Regan, and Silas stepped into place and began stretching each of his muscle groups. The coach was not a woman to mess with and so he tried to stay focused. She had been a world-class wrestler before she came into training, and each of her thighs were as thick as Silas' waist. Rumour had it that she had once dislocated a kid's shoulder using only the pressure from her index finger. No one knew for sure if that was even physically possible, but the anecdote was enough to keep the students in line.

As they stretched and limbered up, the coach barked out a register of attendance.

'Yes, Coach Regan,' the students responded in turn.

She gave a few routine announcements regarding the upcoming end of season, Inter-Clinic Trials, and then added, 'As of tomorrow, a new student will be joining Bronze 1.' That too was fairly routine, and Silas let the information wash over him. It was unlikely to impact him; he knew that from past experience. Kids were occasionally moved up or down the levels in the middle of the season as their bodies grew and muscles developed. Bronze and Silver levels saw the most movement. Gold kids tended to remain in Gold. Once exceptional students, like Marc, were discovered, they generally stayed exceptional.

'This student is a little ...' the coach paused and narrowed her eyes. Silas homed in on her words, as she eventually said '... special.'

It was a well-known fact that the coach had no particular love for the Bronze level students, but she really seemed annoyed about this particular student and made little attempt to conceal her displeasure.

14

'The student's admission assessment was only just a Bronze 5,' the coach continued, enunciating each word slowly as, with uncharacteristic openness, she shared the reason for her anger. There was a collective gasp from the class and most completely stopped their warm-up routine.

Silas was as stunned as everyone else. He had worked so hard to move up from Bronze 5 to Bronze 1. It had taken five years of intense training, and this newcomer – this fraud – was going to just stroll in as a top Bronze! Where was the justice in that?

The sound of low-grade muttering and cursing bounced around the room. Silas looked apprehensively at Coach Regan, but she seemed as disgruntled as everybody else, and the noise of complaining voices rose.

'You've got to be kidding …'

'Not fair!'

'What a cheat!'

'Enough!' bellowed the coach, making everyone jump and resume stretching. 'For some reason, this student has been fast-tracked by the manager. We in Bronze 1 will soon lick them into shape. I will not allow the standard of this level to be dragged down to a Bronze 2!'

'Yes, Coach Regan!' came a chorus of incensed voices, united in their outrage.

Silas felt hope rising in his chest at the sound. Maybe Vitality would not be so grim if someone else was the most despised kid in clinic.

The conversation was all about the newcomer when they were released from warm-up and made their way to history.

'Why would the manager do that? What if our level falls?' a girl called Edie piped up, talking across the top of Silas' head to her friend on the other side of him.

'I'm getting my parents down here tomorrow. They won't stand for it!' Dexter cut across their conversation. Silas could recognise his nasal voice anywhere. He thought he was so

15

important. As if the manager would take any notice of the parents of a Bronze kid!

This could all work out well for me, though, Silas thought with growing satisfaction, and he allowed himself a tiny smile at the notion that his life may just be getting a little bit better.

The complaints from the others were cut short as they entered the history room where Coach Atkins was waiting for them.

'Set your learning stations to moderate, Bronze 1. We have a lot to cover this morning, and I want everyone concentrating.'

Silas reluctantly moved to his usual place, as near to the back as possible, and sighing inwardly ran his hand across the screen. '*S. Corelle – Bronze 1 – history. 60 minute, moderate speed.*'

He pointed to the 'accept' icon, and the learning station treadmill took him from a walk to a slow jog and then to a comfortable, steady run.

'Bronze 1, why do we study history?' Coach Atkins started every lesson with this question, his dull monotone draining all interest from the words.

'To achieve perfection by learning from our mistakes; to achieve success by never repeating them,' the students intoned. Silas could never fathom whether the coach was reminding the class or reminding himself that his subject was even worth studying.

'Correct. Without looking at your notes, can anyone recall which mighty historical blunder we are going to be learning from this term?'

'Yes, Coach,' a blonde girl at a learning station near the front of the room immediately responded.

'Sara?'

'The peri-millennial obesity epidemic and its contributing factors,' she volunteered confidently, sounding like she was actually enjoying herself.

'Good,' he answered, without a measure of fluctuation in his tone. 'What were those contributing factors?' Coach Atkins' eyes skimmed around the room. 'Silas?'

Typical! 'Um ...' Silas stalled while hurriedly looking through his notes from the previous week's lesson. He really hoped he had put something down. His mind tended to wander during history. All those pointless facts and figures from over a century ago... yawn, yawn... his worst subject and, unquestionably, his worst coach. The perfect storm of boredom!

Phew, yes he had recorded it. 'Lack of exercise and poor nutrition,' he finally said.

'Surprises never cease, Corelle. You do pay attention occasionally,' Coach Atkins remarked drily. 'Although the word "poor" implies not enough nutrition, for the people living in this country between 1980 and 2050 there was continual *over*-nutrition. The eating style known as "fast food" arose.' He paused, 'Standing rest.' The students obediently halted their treadmills and started taking notes.

'Fast food,' the coach continued, 'was inexpensive and readily available. It contained high levels of fat, salt and sugar. It seemed our ancestors considered it as a type of treat, and yet records show they were fully aware of its negative health impact. One fast food meal would often exceed the kilojoules per day requirement of an average adult. Combined with their incredibly sedentary lifestyle, this resulted in rapidly rising obesity levels. This was also a major contributing factor to the catastrophic drop in fertility and a vastly shortened lifespan, leading to a population implosion. Resume treadmills and watch your screen.'

What followed was a series of images of round-faced children and adults. They were eating what Silas assumed must be the dreaded 'fast food'. Some were putting thin yellow sticks daubed with red into their mouths. Others were stretching their mouths open as far as they could go in order to insert tall, layered, circular, greasy towers into them.

The students gasped with disgust at the revolting consumption of the unregulated food.

'Idiots… no wonder they all died out,' Dexter said in his superior tone.

Silas couldn't help but agree – there was an obscene grotesqueness to the images, which made him feel queasy. However, he also couldn't help noticing that all those kids from the olden days looked genuinely happy as they ate themselves into their own personal extinction.

The morning meandered through the timetabled lessons. Biology had been more interesting than usual. They had been asked to dissect a variety of animal muscles for microscopic examination. When Coach Evans had been called out of the room, the students had flung bits of frog and worm tissue around. One large lump became stuck to the ceiling, and Silas watched with fascination as it slowly unpeeled and hung above them, suspended by a fine, sticky thread.

By the time the coach returned, however, they had their heads down. The biology coach was frightening in a different way to the rest. His detentions were so physically gruelling that they would make your body ache for a week after.

Towards the middle of the day, all levels converged in the nutrition hall for a chance to rest and refuel. The room was large and phenomenally noisy. After punching in his ID code, Silas joined the queue. An immaculate nutrition engineer passed a tray through the hatch to him with an efficient movement. '9075?' she asked, her perfect fingernails tapping down a checklist on the screen in front of her.

Silas nodded in acknowledgement.

'Two protein bars, a multivitamin drink and a dish of slow-release carbohydrate.'

He took his tray and looked across the sea of blue uniforms in the hope of finding somewhere to sit. Carefully avoiding the Gold students, who loved nothing better than to 'accidentally' knock your tray out of your hands, he spotted a space at a table of other Bronze 1 students. However, as they noticed him approaching, they spread out along the bench to make a solid wall of bodies with no room for him. He wasn't about to demean himself by asking them to move up. As he walked by he heard them snigger among themselves… yet again he was being laughed at.

Eventually he found a seat near a group of Silvers who, after briefly glancing his way as he sat down, continued with their conversation as if he didn't exist.

As he swallowed down his food, a commotion from the other side of the hall caused him to raise his head.

'It's the Gold Standards,' one of the Silver students said to his group of friends. 'Marc Corelle and Taylor Price.'

At the mention of his brother's name, Silas shifted in his seat. He could just see Marc strutting into the hall. What amazing thing was he doing now?

The Silver kids climbed on the bench to get a better look.

'They've made it official… aww,' one of the Silver girls giggled, 'they are *perfect* together.'

Reluctantly, Silas stood to his feet to see over the heads of the crowds in front of him, and immediately pure, red-hot jealousy bubbled through his veins.

Marc's arm was casually draped around the shoulders of Taylor Price, the Female Gold Standard. She was giggling and smiling at the admirers around them. Her shiny black hair spilled smoothly over her shoulders as she lifted her faultless face to Marc's. He lowered his head to kiss her, and the hall erupted in cheers and whistles. His brother really did have it all… it was so unfair!

Silas suddenly couldn't bear watching any longer, and grabbing the last of his food, he swiftly left the hall.

Chapter 3

A fine cloud of white dust billowed out from his hands as he brushed off the excess chalk. He was ready.

An hour of Rejuve had left him feeling relaxed, and all his earlier annoyances had been massaged away. He gazed up at the immense wall looming over him. This was what he was best at; this was where being skinny and light was an advantage. His speciality sport – climbing.

Not as glamorous as some of the other specialities, admittedly, but Silas loved it. Also, this was possibly the only sport in clinic that Marc hadn't achieved a medal in. That in itself made it all the more precious to Silas.

Vitality boasted a magnificent climbing wall, and he had easily managed all of the ascents except one. He took a small step back and assessed the massive artificial overhang that he had yet to master. It was his intention to conquer it before he reached his final year at clinic, and today felt like a good day to try.

'Coach! I'm ready,' he called out.

Coach Hunter wandered over and took his time testing the knots on the rope and belay. He tightened Silas' harness and walked slowly around him, inspecting him from every angle.

'All safe, go ahead, Corelle,' he eventually declared.

At last! I swear he gets slower every time, Silas thought as he started working his way up using his favoured route.

Handhold, foot steady… pull. Left hand reach, pull. Steady… Letting go with one hand, he pulled the slack through the belay.

By the time the other specialisation climbers came into the room, he was already halfway up the wall. Ignoring them, he remained focused, clearing his mind of the noise and distractions.

Why couldn't the rest of life be as straightforward as climbing? Right foot, steady, pull… Reduce rope slack, pull…

He was approaching the overhang and tightened his grip. He could do this.

The barked instructions from Coach Hunter reached him, but he couldn't spare the effort to listen properly. He angled his body and clung to the wall. His muscles were screaming as he defied gravity and held fast.

Then, unbidden, the image of Marc kissing Taylor sprang into his mind, and he felt his concentration slipping. Someone like Taylor was so far out of Silas' reach. None of the girls in his own level even gave him a second look. Why did it always have to go so well for Marc? He always had to be the best at everything – get the best girlfriend, be the best student, be the favourite son…

'Focus!' he hissed. His breathing had become rapid now and sweat was beading on his forehead. Craning his neck to see the next handhold, he desperately reached for it, already sensing that he wasn't going to make it. Holding on for that last desperate second, he strained again with his arm, missed the hold, and his destabilised body fell from the wall.

The safety line attached to his harness caught him and left him dangling in an undignified fashion with his feet pointing up to the ceiling. He slowly spun around on the end of the rope before straightening up and lowering himself with angry jerky movements.

'What happened?' The concerned face of Coach Hunter hovered in Silas' peripheral vision.

'I nearly had it, Coach. I can do it. I lost concentration, that's all. I'll try again now. I'll prove it!' Red with anger and feeling tears pricking at the back of his eyes, he swallowed down his frustration. He would never live it down if he started to cry!

Coach Hunter nodded in approval and put his hand on Silas' shoulder.

'I like your determination, Corelle, but I'll not have you climbing when you are not at your best. That leads to mistakes and further falls. Climbing is about pushing our bodies but staying safe. If you take risks you will cause yourself damage. I want you in good condition for the Inter-Clinic Trials next month. Go and clean up and get changed. You can try again tomorrow.'

Coach turned away to deal with another climber.

'I could try again now,' Silas muttered, but he obediently went to the shower room and wished he could wash away his jealousy of Marc, and his anger at himself, as easily as he washed away the sweat.

The journey home was the best part of the day. No buzzers, no treadmill, no time limits. There would be no one at home expectantly waiting for his return, either, so like a feral creature, Silas was free to wander and explore the routes around his neighbourhood; short cuts, alleyways, abandoned houses and gardens left to ruin.

Inevitably, all his exploring would eventually lead him into the heart of the Uninhabited district where, hidden down a narrow dirt driveway, was a tiny derelict cottage. The roof had caved in decades ago, and weeds and shrubs were growing inside the house, but towering over the crumbling bricks and mortar, like a guardian angel, was an immense tree. The colossal trunk rose solidly upwards. The canopy gently swayed, beckoning with a promise of freedom from the mundane.

With a well-practised run and jump, Silas scrambled up into the lowest branches. The familiar knots and twists of the trunk guided him, like signposts, to a branch halfway up the tree. He settled onto his perch with his back resting against the trunk and looked out over the city. This was his hideaway and his refuge.

Silas had found the tree by chance. It was soon after his mother had died that he had taken to wandering the streets. His father was so consumed by grief that he had failed to notice the comings and goings of his two boys.

While Marc busied himself by joining up to every pre-clinic training scheme he could, already starting to make a name for himself, Silas just wandered aimlessly.

For a while he became so overlooked by his father and brother that he decided he must have developed special powers and had actually become invisible. It was during one of these times he had found the tree, and with it, a temporary peace. The tree was solid and enduring. It became his safe and reliable sanctuary, his place of retreat.

'There won't be any here, Nana. I'm sure it wouldn't grow in the city. The conditions aren't right.'

The girl's voice, loud and close by, interrupted his thoughts.

Silas nearly fell off his branch with shock and outrage. He had never caught even a glimpse of another person here! Nobody bothered with the Uninhabited areas. Why would anyone else come here? And what right did they have to enter his domain?

He tried to peer through the thick foliage but could make out little more than flickers of colour and movement. A flash of red cloth and dark hair passed beneath him, but Silas couldn't see any more without moving lower and giving his presence away. Instead he just held his breath and listened.

'Yes, yes, dear, but I wanted to check,' a second woman answered; her voice was deeper and sterner. Silas shifted stealthily along the branch, trying to work out how many trespassers were stamping around his tree. This time as he looked down he caught a glimpse of grey hair. 'I tried planting seedpods here, but you are right, it's far too dry. They won't grow. Let's head home now, but we'll have to go to the Community before the end of summer to get supplies.

23

Although I'm sure you won't mind a trip up there... maybe during the season-break? It'll give you something to look forward to.'

A rich, husky laugh of surprise and delight filled the air.

'That would be amazing! Can I seriously come with you? You'll have to run it by Mum. She might take a bit of convincing, after what happened last time.'

'I'll talk to her about it,' the other woman reassured her. 'You are older now, and hopefully wiser.'

'Maybe Mum will come too.' The girl sounded optimistic.

'Hmm...' The older woman took her time to answer. 'I don't think she will. Not now she's got a new assignment. You know what your mother is like. Work, work, work ...'

The voices became fainter, and soon Silas could hear nothing more than the gentle rustling of the thick, concealing leaves. The unwelcome visitors had gone, he was sure of it. However, he struggled to shrug off his unease. It was obviously just bad luck that they had come to his tree. They hadn't found whatever they had been looking for in the overgrown cottage garden, and he sincerely hoped they would have no reason to return.

When he was sure the coast was clear, Silas nimbly clambered down from his vantage point and headed home. The evening was drawing in and, although he would never admit it to anyone, he didn't like being out at night. The Unseen started work then and they spooked him. It was the flowing shapeless cloaks and hidden faces that triggered some primitive fear. Who knew what disfigurements lay under their long robes?

When he arrived at his house, he opened the front door and padded in as quietly as possible. His dad wouldn't be home yet, but Marc would be bursting to gloat about his new girlfriend, and Silas really, really didn't want to hear about it. It seemed that, for Marc, it wasn't enough to be the best at everything; he also needed to make sure that *everybody* knew that his younger brother was the worst at everything. Everything except for climbing, Silas thought, consoling himself with his little achievement. Climbing is mine!

Peering into the Image room, he could see Marc lifting weights as he watched highlights from the day's competitions. He seemed transfixed by the projections surrounding him, so Silas risked tiptoeing past the doorway into the nutrition area to see what had been allocated for him to eat, then silently carried his plate and glass to his room.

Chapter 4

'Can I speak with you?'

Silas broke off from his daydream and looked up. His father was standing over him, watching him. Silas hadn't even heard him come into the health suite. Giving a guilty start he tried to make it look like he was putting some effort into his morning workout.

'Dad?' he gasped, feigning breathlessness.

'Stop that a minute and let's talk.'

'Er, sure.'

His father led the way out of the health suite and towards the front door. Silas hurried after him, intrigued as to what could be important enough to interrupt his exercise routine.

'There are some exciting developments with my work and the Flawless Leader has been paying special attention to the next stage of Biocubicle development. You know that, don't you?' Silas nodded as his father continued. 'Flawless Leader Steele has brought in a specialist to collaborate with me – Dr Esther Veron, a biochemical engineer – an absolute genius in her field.' His father was staring intently at him.

A confused frown flittered over Silas' brow, and he looked back at the health suite. He still had 20 minutes of his workout to complete before clinic.

'Dad, I don't get what …?'

'Don't interrupt, Silas,' he reprimanded. 'I don't have long; I'm meeting with Dr Veron first thing. This partnership is incredibly important for the future of Bio-health. With Dr Veron's help we could be looking at eradicating all disease…

no more sickness... even among the Unseen... can you imagine?'

His father clearly could, as his voice thickened with emotion at the importance of his project.

'That sounds great, Dad,' Silas said, still uncertain why he had chosen that particular moment to tell him about it. 'Is that what you wanted to talk to me about?'

'No, not just that... I need your help.'

Silas looked at his father properly this time. This is a first, he thought wryly.

'Dr Veron has a daughter, Zoe, who is about your age. I have spoken personally to the manager at Vitality and have been able to persuade him to allow this girl to be placed in your level. Silas, I need you to make this girl feel welcome. Look out for her and maybe try to befriend her ...'

'What?' Silas interjected. 'But Dad ...'

'Listen, Silas, her mother is absolutely crucial for this next stage of my work, but she has made perfectly clear that she will only stay in Prima if her daughter is settled here. She was quite adamant about it. She is concerned that her daughter may struggle to adjust to life in the city.

'I don't ask a lot of you, but this is important to me. Make every effort with this girl. Make friends with her; make sure she is happy at Vitality. You'll do that, right?'

'Dad... I don't think hanging around with me is going to make this Zoe girl happy!' Silas paused, about to add, 'Or me happy!' but his father was already snatching up his running bag and opening the front door.

'Thanks, Si, I know I can count on you. I've got to go; I'm going to be late.'

He closed the door behind him without looking up, so missed the look of horror plastered across his son's face.

'This is a nightmare!' Silas thumped himself on the head with a balled-up fist. 'Wake up! Wake up!'

'Hey! So-last! I can do that for you.' Marc had finished his health suite session and was walking past him. 'What did Dad

27

want? It must have been important. Don't tell me you're dropping down a level?' He stopped and then stepped closer to Silas. A head taller, and twice as broad, he shoved Silas in the chest, forcing his back up against the wall. Silas tried to stay calm. Marc wouldn't do him any serious damage. He wouldn't risk it. The punishment would be too severe. Injuring another person might even be enough to get him kicked out of Vitality.

But a seed of doubt formed in his mind when Marc raised a balled fist, poised ready to smash into Silas' face. Marc was getting more and more unstable recently. Silas tensed his body, waiting for the unavoidable impact, but then Marc suddenly relaxed and smirked down at him.

'I had you there! You should have seen your face. Like you were going to pee yourself. Ha!'

Silas kept quiet and tried to inch towards the stairs, but Marc grabbed his arm roughly, digging his fingers into Silas' flesh.

'Seriously though, Sad-last, are you dropping down a level? You better not be! Having you stuck in Bronze makes me look bad too, you know. Like I've got weak genes or something.'

Giving Silas a final hard smack on the top of his head, Marc suddenly lost interest in tormenting his brother and sauntered nonchalantly into the nutrition area.

Silas took his opportunity and, rubbing his bruised arm, swiftly ran upstairs. Marc was becoming a problem. He would have to keep away from him; maybe reset his wake-up call and get out of the house earlier. Yes, Marc was avoidable.

What, however, was unavoidable, and was making him feel sick with anxiety, was his father's request. This daughter his father was forcing on him, she must be the new kid that Coach Regan had explained about yesterday. Everyone already hated her for being unfairly advanced four levels. If the other kids found out that it was so she could be in a level with him – he could feel his protein shake threatening to make a reappearance – it would make his life more of a living hell than it already was.

28

No wonder he was late. With every step to clinic, he had fought the rising urge to run and hide. What was his father playing at? He knew nothing about life at Vitality. Silas almost felt sorry for this girl. If he was her only hope for welcome and acceptance at clinic, what chance did she have? He felt overwhelmingly sorrier for himself, though. He was not going to make friends with her... this wasn't pre-clinic any more! His safest bet was to ignore her and keep his head down.

As he reached the ornate front gate of Vitality Clinic, Silas heard the starting buzzer sound. Growling with irritation, he broke into a half-hearted run, knowing that he would get a detention if he missed warm-up.

'That would be just my luck,' he muttered bitterly, increasing his pace. He could probably still slip in... as long as there wasn't a coach patrolling the hallway.

Taking the white stone stairs two at a time, he ran into the deserted entrance hall. He was about to turn the corner to the Bronze corridor when he heard voices.

Coming to an abrupt halt, Silas leaned against the wall and listened. From around the corner came a suppressed gasp of horror and then a giggle. It certainly didn't sound like a member of staff – he couldn't imagine any of them giggling – so maybe he could still safely get to his warm-up. He peered around the corner...

'Revolting!' The loud, confident tones of Taylor Price echoed down the corridor. She was flanked by two of her perfect friends. They had their backs to Silas. From the corner where he was lurking, he couldn't see past them to glimpse what they were looking at.

'Oh, I feel sick!' one of the girls squealed.

From the disgust in her voice, Silas assumed it must be something rotting, or a dead animal. Perhaps it was something from the biology labs... maybe a load of worms from yesterday's dissection.

'What is it doing here?' Taylor asked, looking around her as if she might find a likely culprit.

Silas pulled back behind the corner, before risking another glance. The only way to get to his warm-up room was to go past Taylor, but he didn't want her accusing him of moving stuff from the labs around clinic. Everyone would automatically believe her, she was the Female Gold Standard after all, and Silas would be landed with a month of detentions from the feared biology coach.

'Move!' Silas muttered under his breath, watching them again. They really seemed intrigued by whatever they had found and seemed in no hurry to go.

All of a sudden, Taylor seemed to get an idea into her head, and she turned to whisper in her friend's ear, causing them both to giggle again. Then, with lightning speed, she leaned forward and, like a magician, flamboyantly pulled a sky-blue cloth up into the air and flung it over her head.

It landed on the floor near the corner where Silas was still hiding. He jumped back in horror, thinking that some lump of animal carcass was being thrown at him. Looking down with trepidation at the blue fabric, he could make out the crumpled logo of the clinic written across the back of a Vitality shirt. What disgusting thing had been wrapped up in a Vitality top, he wondered?

'Let's see all the gory details, then!' Taylor said, causing Silas to peer from his hiding place once more.

Taylor and her two friends had separated now, and formed a loose circle around what Silas could now clearly see was another girl. He could not stop staring. She was so unlike any of the other students at Vitality. No wonder Taylor was fascinated… and repulsed.

The girl was short, and her dark hair was cropped so that it only just covered her ears. She had a round, plain face with small dark eyes set in pale brown skin. Her lips were pressed together with concern, and her expression was wary as her eyes darted from one tormentor's face to another.

Without her Vitality shirt she was left exposed, wearing only a blue bra-top and her uniform leggings. What was so unusual about her appearance was that any normal muscle definition was lost under a layer of fat.

Silas had never seen as much fat on a real person. Instead of the sleek straight lines of the other female students at Vitality, this girl seemed to be made up of bulges and curves. Her bra-top strained across her oversized chest and the elastic cut in at the sides underneath her arms. Her body tapered in again lower down towards her waist but then a squishy line of flesh almost hung over the waistband of her leggings. Her navel was distorted into a flat line and her thighs were actually touching in the middle even though her feet were spaced apart.

She remained totally still, her arms by her side.

The girls started circling her, squealing with disgust as they prodded her.

'It wobbles!'

'It's sickening! It's making me feel unhealthy just by looking at it. Who let something like *this* in?'

Taylor gave another vicious prod, leaving an indent of her perfectly manicured nail on the girl's stomach. Her two friends immediately copied Taylor and dug their own sharp nails into the soft, exposed flesh, gasping with revulsion at the sensation.

The girl endured it silently, although Silas saw her wince.

'It doesn't feel pain!' Taylor announced. 'All that fat must get in the way. It's unnatural! Stay out of my way, Blob.'

Linking arms with her friends, Taylor strode up the corridor towards the staff rooms. Hastily the girl sidestepped to avoid being knocked over, but Taylor's final remark drifted down the hallway. 'I'm going to talk to the manager about this. It can't stay here; it's polluting the environment!'

Silas couldn't tear his eyes away as he watched the girl cover her face with her hands. He expected her to start crying... any normal person would after that spiteful attack. I probably would, Silas thought, except I'm so used to Marc being vicious.

Marc and Taylor... so well suited, he thought with a bitter smile.

Just then, the girl took a long, deep breath. There was no hint of a sob as she pulled her shoulders back, let her hands drop to her sides and opened her eyes. Her gaze locked with Silas'. She had seen him watching!

He felt colour flood his face, and nearly turned and ran away. But then the new girl actually smiled.

Silas was frozen to the spot. He couldn't understand why she was smiling. Maybe she was odd in the head; maybe she didn't understand what Taylor had said and done. Silas continued to stare, open-mouthed, until the girl raised a hand in greeting, finally breaking the spell.

'Er... hello? Are you OK?' she asked, pronouncing her words carefully.

She thinks I'm simple, Silas realised, embarrassed by his slack-jawed appearance. Snapping his mouth closed, he briskly stepped around the corner, stooping to pick up the clinic shirt.

'Um, this is yours, I think.' He kept his eyes averted as she took the shirt and pulled it over her head in a rush, obviously attempting to cover her body as quickly as possible.

'Thanks,' she said, as he tried not to stare at her.

It wasn't much of an improvement. The enhancing cut of the Vitality uniform was not designed to cope with a figure like hers, and the bulge of her stomach seemed even more obvious under the tight-fitting top.

'Are you enjoying the show?' she asked drily, noticing his assessment of her.

Startled, Silas looked into her eyes. She smiled at him again, as if she were trying to put him at his ease. Her voice was low and had a husky quality. It seemed familiar, but he didn't know why.

'Sorry... it's just... I've never ...' Words failed him. He nearly asked, 'What are you doing here?' and, 'Who let you in?' before realising those were the same questions Taylor asked, and they wouldn't sound any less aggressive coming from him.

'It's my first day here,' she said brightly. 'Do you think I'm going to fit in?'

Silas did his best impression of a fish as his mouth opened and closed silently.

'I'm joking,' she finally said. 'I know it's going to be horrendous.' She seemed strangely resigned to the fact, and Silas shook his head in confusion.

'How are you are able to joke about that?' he asked, looking warily along the corridor in case Taylor had decided to return and resume her vicious harassment.

'Bleugh! They're not going to hurt me with words …' She stuck her tongue out in the same direction. 'Anyway, it's what's in here that counts,' she said tapping her forehead and looking unblinkingly at Silas. 'Or in your case, it's what's in here… I see you,' she added, letting her hand drift towards his face and nearly touching him. Silas jumped back as if he had been stung, and the new girl smiled ruefully and turned the movement into the formal extended hand of greeting.

'Hello, it's nice to meet you.'

'Um, sure… yeah …' Silas wiped the sweat off his palm and briefly grasped her soft, podgy hand, the requirement for politeness overruling his aversion to this unusual, misshapen girl. 'Si Corelle.'

'No way! Anton Corelle's son? Our parents are working together. Did you know that? I'm Zoe Veron… I'm in the same level as you!'

Silas felt his heart sink as the penny finally dropped. He could hardly believe it! *This* was the daughter of his dad's genius colleague? No wonder the mother was concerned her precious child wouldn't settle in the city. What were they thinking of, sending her to Vitality? She should be in one of the mediocre clinics like Everfirst or Purehealth. This was far worse than he could have imagined. Why did his dad have to get him involved?

'Come on,' he said grumpily, fuming at finding himself stuck in this situation. 'We are late for warm-up. I'll show you the way.'

As he turned on his heel, he suddenly remembered where he had heard Zoe's voice. It had been the day before. She had been the one traipsing around his hideaway at the tree, disturbing his peace! This was perfect, he thought sourly. There was no way he was going to make any further effort to welcome her here, not even to please his father. Zoe Veron would have to stay friendless and unwelcome.

Chapter 5

There was no possibility of sneaking into the warm-up room unnoticed, and all heads turned his way as Silas opened the door.

'Corelle! Lunchtime detention!' shouted Coach Regan.

Today was going from bad to worse, thought Silas as he slunk to the back of the class and stood in line with the other students, who sniggered at his punishment.

Then a stunned silence fell over the room as Zoe walked in. Coach Regan recovered first and, shaking her head from side to side, strode across to tower over Zoe.

'You must be our new student,' she said, with a dangerous level of sweetness in her voice. Zoe nodded once.

'Yes,' she answered.

'Yes, *Coach*,' Coach Regan corrected her.

'Yes, Coach,' Zoe repeated nervously as Coach Regan looked her up and down with an expression of distaste. Then she leaned forward, bending at the waist so that her face was intimidatingly close to Zoe's.

'What has happened to the standards of Vitality to let a creature such as you in?' Coach's voice had dropped to a furious undertone that carried clearly in the stillness of the room. Every consonant was exaggerated, causing a fine mist of spittle to float gently around Zoe's head. 'You belong to the Unseen! This clinic is for the best of the best. It is for the purest of the pure, and you are like floating excrement on the surface of all this health and beauty. You belong in the sewer. You are an affront to my eyes! You also will be in lunchtime detention, today, for your lateness, and for the rest of this month for your obscene fatness!' Coach Regan's voice had reached shouting pitch, but Zoe meekly withstood the verbal assault.

'Yes, Coach,' Zoe responded, lowering her head and quietly stepping into place at the front of the room. All eyes followed her.

'Level dismissed!'

The students seemed transfixed by Zoe's appearance and didn't move.

'I said, level dismissed! Move! Now!'

Zoe looked nervously over her shoulder at Silas, who pretended not to see. He really didn't need the extra negative attention, so he tried to lose himself in the body of students as they made their way out of the door.

Thankfully, Zoe's learning station was on the other side of the room from him during geography and she was set behind him for mathematics, so during both lessons he could avoid her. The rest of Bronze 1 remained completely fascinated by her appearance and jostled to get a good view of her when she started running on the treadmill.

The comments and questions from the other members of staff were as barbed as Coach Regan's as they took every opportunity to humiliate Zoe. Much to Silas' surprise, though, she didn't get upset, and kept her answers clear and concise. By the end of the lesson, the maths coach had even seemed to warm to her slightly, as Zoe had understood and completed the complex algebra in a fraction of the time of the other students.

The next time he saw her was at their lunchtime detention. Zoe was standing outside the detention room, and she looked exhausted. Clinic was hard work for the physically fit; it must be agony for someone like her, he thought. Despite the promise he had made to himself, Silas found he couldn't just ignore her. It wasn't her fault she'd been sent to Vitality. No; he decided that like him, she was at the mercy of thoughtless and self-obsessed parents.

Despite the growing pity he felt for her predicament, his need for self-preservation still held strong. Checking there was no one else watching him, he quickly walked past her and into the detention room. Thankfully the room was empty, and he closed the door behind her as she warily followed him in.

'Hi, Silas,' she said, mustering up a faint smile.

'Hi,' he answered reluctantly.

'I've been wanting to speak to you all morning,' she said, 'to apologise. You were late because of me, weren't you? That's why you're in detention.'

'Yes,' Silas said bluntly, but as her smile faded, he immediately felt bad. It had been Taylor tormenting Zoe that had caused him to be late. He took a deep breath. 'No, Zoe,' he finally said. 'It's not your fault, it was... well, I was just late. Look, let's get this over with, and we may have time for a break before specialities.'

'So how does this torture chamber work, then?' Zoe asked, looking around.

Coach Regan had set their detention in the circuit training room. A series of stainless-steel machines lined all four walls.

'You type your ID number in here,' Silas pointed to the screen by the doorway, 'and then work your way round the machines. If you don't complete the tasks in the given time, you get punished. It *is* a torture chamber, you are right there.' It occurred to Silas that even though for Zoe this may seem like torture, letting her loose in the nutrition hall would be more like a gladiatorial arena. Maybe it was for her protection that she had been given a month of detention.

'Punished?' said Zoe, her face incredulous. 'How?'

'Well, nothing makes you work hard like the fear of pain. If you don't complete the task fast enough, you get an electric shock.'

He saw the look of horror on Zoe's face.

'Oh, it's only little to start with. Just to get you moving faster. Although the shocks get bigger the slower you go,' he admitted. 'Look, just do what I do.'

Feeling increasingly sorry for her, Silas tried to smile encouragingly as he stepped up to the first machine. It was similar to the standard treadmill but with a set of five moving steps. He started walking up them at a fast pace, and after a few minutes the machine beeped and slowed to a stop.

'Your turn now, but watch what I do on the next machine while you are using this one.'

Next was a rowing machine, and Silas settled in the seat and started pulling on the metal handles. He watched Zoe on the step machine. Every movement caused her flesh to ripple like a miniature earthquake. He was mesmerised by the wedge of fat that sat above her trousers. Every time she placed a foot down, the bulge jumped up slightly.

'Ow!' He suddenly pulled his hands off the rowing machine handles, then quickly grabbed them again and started rowing faster.

'I got a shock, stupid machine.'

Zoe breathlessly let out a bark of laughter. 'Just do as you do, right?' She turned her head and caught his eye and involuntarily, he smiled back.

The machines beeped, and they obediently moved around the room. Silas started on the moving climbing wall. Easy, he thought as it gently scrolled down and he grabbed the handholds.

'What was your last clinic like?' he asked. He was becoming more and more curious about Zoe. She didn't seem to know how any of the equipment worked. What kind of clinic didn't have a circuit room? And what kind of place would allow Zoe to become so unfit without expelling her?

'I wasn't in a clinic,' Zoe said breathlessly as she took Silas' place and began rowing steadily.

'But I thought you had just been transferred.'

'Oh, well, sort of. My mum was working on a research ship in the Mediterranean. We lived in the middle of the ocean. She taught me. It was amazing out there,' Zoe said wistfully.

'Why did she agree to move here, then?' Silas asked, thinking what kind of clueless mother would inflict Vitality Clinic on someone like Zoe.

'She'd made an incredible discovery about the immune system of the common brittlestar ...'

'What's a brittlestar?' Silas asked, and reached up with his hand for the next hold.

'It's a sea creature,' Zoe explained slowly, as if surprised by his ignorance. Silas picked up on it immediately.

'Not all of us get to live on a boat!' he said defensively, climbing with renewed vigour.

'Of course not,' Zoe said in a placating tone. 'It's a type of starfish... Anyway, Bio-health labs – your father – has seen a way to take her research and, with her help, manipulate it to use on humans. It's cutting-edge science.'

Silas heard the same edge of excitement in her voice as he had heard in his father's earlier that day. 'Dad sort of mentioned it,' he admitted. 'A way to make us all healthier?'

'Something like that – though I doubt I'll get to see her to talk about it now we're in Prima. Once she gets started on a new project I seem to lose her for a while. Do you know what I mean?'

'I know that feeling,' Silas muttered, thinking he had lost his dad years ago – just about the same time as he had lost his mum.

'Don't get me wrong,' Zoe added, 'she's an inspiration. She taught me more science during our time on that boat than most Upper Clinic students get taught on their entire course. It's just, when she gets excited about some part of her work, she forgets about everything else.'

They moved onto the next machine, and the conversation faltered as Zoe focused all her attention on climbing, and Silas lay on the bench and started lifting weights.

'Ow! The wall gave me an electric shock!' Zoe said crossly.

'It's nearly time to change, just a few more seconds,' Silas said through gritted teeth. He had droplets of sweat across his brow as he lowered the weights back into their cradle, only to tense his muscles and slowly lift them again.

'Ow!' She let go of the wall completely this time and dropped to the floor, rubbing her hands together. A beep sounded, and they moved positions again. Zoe's mouth had narrowed into a thin line, and she pushed her jaw out.

She is determined, I'll give her that, Silas admitted to himself as he watched her lay on the weights bench. She may even manage a full day here... but I doubt she'll make it to the end of the week.

The detention lasted 40 minutes, and Zoe was shaking by the end of it. She had been shocked a further four times. She slumped on the floor by the door as a nutrition engineer appeared with two trays.

'9075 and 9408?'

Silas had recovered and, nodding, accepted the trays from her hands. He pushed Zoe's tray across the floor to her and wordlessly she shoved the protein bar into her mouth and leaned her head against the wall, eyes closed, chewing rapidly. She grabbed her drink and gulped that down too. Her breathing was beginning to slow as she looked up into his face. One large tear had formed in her eye. It rolled over the chubby curve of her cheek and dropped onto her top, leaving a dark blue stain.

Chapter 6

'This week will be spent focusing entirely on speciality sports,' Coach Regan announced one morning at registration.

The excitement in the room was palpable. This was it; this was the final build-up to the Inter-Clinic Trials.

Over the last month, the Clinic had undergone a major overhaul because it was Vitality's turn to host. The trials were always broadcast live across the nation and were yet another way to showcase the excellence of the clinic.

Silas guessed that teams of Unseen had been recruited to clean the buildings and make the grounds ready. There was even a huge new external climbing wall that had been installed in the middle of the arena. He was itching to test it out, but it was firmly out of bounds until the day of the trials.

'All of you will receive your schedule through your screen, and for newcomers among us …' Coach Regan paused and looked pointedly at Zoe, her blatant disapproval of Zoe's placement in Bronze 1 still evident on her face, '… how you perform in the trials not only affects where Vitality ranks among the clinics, but also your personal placement in a level, as well as the ranking of your level as a whole. Any weak link could cause you to *all* be stuck with me, in Bronze 1, for another whole season!'

By now everyone was looking with pure animosity at Zoe, who wisely kept her head down and her eyes glued to her screen. She was, without a doubt, the weakest link in the level, and if anyone were going to pull the results down, it would be her.

Contrary to Silas' prediction, Zoe had remained at Vitality for over a month now, and she didn't show any sign of quitting. All the students and most of the staff remained hostile to her very presence at clinic, but still she persevered.

Her fitness levels remained far below target, but she did have one strength. Her time living at sea had ensured she had become a strong swimmer. She wasn't fast, but she seemed tireless as she powered up and down the pool.

No one celebrated her minor success, though. Instead, it had become a source of entertainment to the Vitality students, to try to get a glimpse of her in her sky-blue swimming costume. Her time in detention had shaved off a little of the excess weight, but her body shape was still quite unique among the toned athletic physiques that paraded around the poolside.

Coach Regan allowed the silence and the staring to drag on, until Zoe was in no doubt at all how unwelcome she was at Vitality. Silas saw a film of sweat break out on Zoe's forehead before Coach Regan finally spoke. 'And if your results are bad enough, you will be expelled.'

He thought he could detect a flicker of longing in Zoe's face when Coach Regan spelled out her final threat. She must really hate it here, he realised. I bet she is desperate to leave. How she tolerated such open aggression from students and staff utterly amazed him. Silas had experienced his fair share of unpleasantness, but at least the coaches were keen to accommodate Anton Corelle's second son, even if he didn't come close to the first-born.

Marc's girlfriend Taylor seemed to have developed a loathing for Zoe that bordered on obsessive. Since their initial encounter in the hallway, Taylor had taken it upon herself to try to break Zoe and get her to leave Vitality Clinic. It had started with a petition for Zoe to be expelled, as her presence was detrimental to Vitality's reputation as a top organisation.

Everyone had signed it, including Silas. He felt bad about it, but people would have noticed if he had refused to add his name. He had even seen Coach Regan's scrawl on the list.

Manager Gilroy had dismissed it, though, and the matter had been dropped.

Taylor's next scheme was to humiliate Zoe so much that she had to leave. Somehow she had managed to get posters made of Zoe in her blue swimsuit, fat bulging out of every gap and the legend 'Flawed Loser' splashed across it in large letters. They had been put up next to every image of the Flawless Leader that the clinic possessed. The manager had started a lengthy investigation into that particular episode, but nobody would betray the Female Gold Standard, so the posters were removed and no more was said about it.

Yet Zoe remained stoically unmoved. Silas was beginning to see that though on the outside she was flabby and weak, on the inside she must be made of steel.

Zoe was also clever – exceptionally clever. Advanced programmes had been provided for her in all academic subjects, and while everyone else learned the basic facts, Zoe tapped away on her screen. Unfortunately for her, this just added to her image as a freak.

Silas had developed his own fascination with Zoe. She intrigued him. Although he still hadn't done as his father asked and befriended her, he tried at least to not join in with the general Zoe-abuse that amused the other students. A few times he had spotted her walking home after clinic and he had followed her. She seemed oblivious to his presence, and he watched her enter a big old house on the edge of the Inhabited area. It was a few streets from his tree, which went some way to explain why she had been there the first time he had seen her. He felt guilty that he hadn't really spoken to her much, but he had honestly thought she wouldn't have lasted at Vitality for so long. Anyway, Silas decided, it was too late for that now. When the trials were over, she would be expelled, and he would never see her again.

The day before trials began was the only chance that Silas and the other Vitality climbers had to study the new climbing wall and talk tactics with Coach Hunter. They were forbidden from attempting to scale it as that would provide them with an unfair advantage over the visiting clinics, but looking at it was a pretty helpful start.

The wall was 15 metres high and eight metres wide. It was divided into four vertical 'lanes' by three white stripes running from the base to the top. Each section had the twin safety ropes for the individual climber. The handholds were identically reproduced across the four lanes, but it was for each climber to ascertain the best route.

Ten metres up, the wall jutted forward at a 15-degree angle that slanted outwards for the last five metres, thus creating a sustained overhang. That would be the most challenging part of the climb, and Silas craned his neck to study this highest portion.

Coach Hunter was drilling the assembled climbers.

'Remember, keep your hips close to the wall, especially on that last five metres. Keep that rope taut. Even if it takes time to remove the slack, don't be tempted to rush it. Points will be knocked off for perceived recklessness. Now, go back to the indoor walls and practise, bearing in mind what you have seen here.'

The climbers broke off into small groups and headed towards the gym. Silas took one last long look at the wall and followed after them.

The next morning, he was wide awake before the house computer called him. The day had dawned bright and clear, and there was a bubbling excitement rising up inside him. He felt good; he felt ready.

After impatiently enduring his Biocubicle assessment, he assumed his position at the weights machine. His father had just finished his workout and stood mopping the sweat from his brow.

'I've rearranged some of my schedule so I'll be able to come and watch you boys compete today,' he said.

Silas looked up at him.

'Really?'

'Yes.' He nodded. 'I've been so caught up with this project recently that I've barely seen you and Marc. You do want me to come?' he asked, suddenly sounding unsure.

'Of course, Dad, that would be great.' Silas was amazed his father had even realised that trials were today, let alone rescheduled so he could be there.

'Really, really great.' He smiled as his father walked off to shower. This was going to be a brilliant day; he just knew it.

Vitality Clinic was a hive of activity as teams of students from the other competing clinics arrived, each proudly displaying their colours.

The team from Everfirst walked through the gates, sporting the green and yellow uniform of their clinic. Despite their name, they usually came last in the trials and were derisively known as Neverfirst.

Purehealth were dressed in black, and the Quality Clinic team were in purple. But it was the deep red, iridescent uniforms worn by the students from Active Clinic that really drew the eye. Active was Vitality's closest rival for the position of top clinic and Silas studied the competition carefully. They looked impressive, even fitter than last year. But then so did Vitality, he thought, catching sight of Marc and the other Gold students and feeling a genuine sense of pride in his clinic.

Across the crowds, Silas spotted Zoe heading towards the swimming pool. Silas felt a pang of sympathy for her. If Coach Regan's assessment was accurate, then this was probably going to be her last day, and she had to spend it being stared at by a load of students from other clinics.

Then he noticed that Zoe wasn't alone. She was walking next to a straight-backed grey-haired woman. Silas didn't think he recognised the older woman, but there was something about seeing them together that jogged a memory. Then it dawned on Silas who she was. When Zoe had been 'trespassing' in the Uninhabited district, near his hideaway in the tree, Silas had heard *two* women talking, and he had distinctly seen grey hair as he had peered through the foliage.

He hadn't seen or heard either of them there since, but he couldn't help wondering who the grey-haired woman was and why she would have been in the Uninhabited area at all. Curiosity got the better of him, and he jogged over and caught up with them before they reached the door.

'Hi, Zoe,' he called out. She looked over her shoulder, and her eyebrows shot up in surprise.

'Silas... hi!' Hearing the amazement in her voice, the older lady turned around and peered intently from one face to the other. There was an uncomfortable silence, as neither of them knew what to say. He suddenly realised how odd it must seem that he had spent a month barely talking to Zoe and now, out of the blue, he was chasing after her. He felt himself beginning to blush.

'It's a big day ...' he started to say, in an attempt to justify himself, but Zoe started speaking at the same time.

'This is my... sorry.'

'No, you first...' Oh earth, swallow me, he thought, as he felt his cheeks grow even redder.

'I was going to introduce you to my nana,' Zoe said, also blushing now. Silas turned to the old lady. He could see she was thoroughly enjoying their discomfort, but when she spoke her voice was warm and affectionate.

'I know who you are, young man,' she said. 'You are Ellen Corelle's youngest. You look just like her.'

He felt tears suddenly prickle under his eyelids, and his heart did a strange flurry of extra beats. He hadn't heard his mother's name spoken out loud for years.

'You knew my mother?' he gasped.

'Oh dear, forgive me.' She looked deep into his eyes and shook her head sadly. 'I've upset you. I am so sorry. Ellen was my good friend, and I still miss her very much, as I'm sure you do too.'

'I'm not upset,' he lied. 'It's fine.' He blinked rapidly to clear his vision. 'It's just no one even mentions her any more. Not Dad, not Marc. It's because her death was declared… well…. you know, self-inflicted.' Silas suddenly stopped talking. He was sharing far too much with this total stranger, and all in front of Zoe. He took a step backwards but the old woman reached her hand out and placed it reassuringly on his shoulder.

'I know you will do well today, Silas, and tonight, after the trials are over, come and visit us. We can talk some more. I think you may already know where we live?' She nodded knowingly and Silas saw the ghost of a wink. He gave a guilty look in return. Oh no! She's seen me following Zoe, he thought. She must think I'm really odd. Or perhaps she thinks I want to go out with Zoe… Yuck!

The old lady looked at her granddaughter and smiled. 'Come on, Zoe, show me where I need to sit to watch you swim.'

Zoe opened the glass door and ushered her grandmother through. She looked at Silas with an apologetic smile, and whispered, 'Sorry about Nana… she's a bit intense. She means well, though. You don't have to come tonight if you don't want to.'

'My dad's going to be here today, and he might have organised something, so I don't think I'll be free,' he muttered back. He had no idea if that were true, but there was no way he was going to miss any after-trials party to spend an evening with Zoe and her nan. He felt unnerved and shaken by the encounter with the unusual old woman and was sure that he did not want to repeat it.

'I understand,' she said diplomatically, giving him a small wave goodbye, as the door to the pool complex closed behind her. Automatically, Silas waved back, then quickly lowered his hand again, surreptitiously looking over his shoulder to see if anyone else had noticed. There's no point trying to be her friend now, he firmly reminded himself.

47

Chapter 7

Silas sat on his favourite perch, staring sightlessly out over the city. He was consumed by an impotent rage that threatened to swallow him.

It had all been looking so good. The wait for his turn to climb had seemed interminable, but it had been valuable to watch the routes taken, and mistakes made by the other climbers. He had seen his father arrive and take his place in the VIP viewing box and had felt a massive surge of adrenaline. His dad had actually made it. The box was elevated and gave a bird's eye view of the whole external sports arena.

Finally it had been his chance to climb, and he had felt on fire. After glancing at the competition, his focus had been only on the task ahead. The climb had been incredible. He felt he had floated, lighter than air, up the first ten metres.

Out of the corner of his eye he had seen the shiny red uniform of an Active Clinic climber gaining on him, but hadn't panicked. He had reached the overhang first, and kept his hips level and close to the wall. The red climber slipped and lost precious seconds in regaining his grip, so Silas had pushed himself up the last few metres. Suddenly his hand was on the top rail. He swung his leg up and over, and he was standing, king of the world, breathing heavily and grinning from ear to ear.

From this vantage point he could look down into the VIP box, and he had sought his father's face so they could share his moment of victory. Eventually, Silas saw him, but his father's attention was elsewhere.

Tracing his line of sight, he turned to see the final seconds of the inter-clinic 100-metre sprint. Clear to make out was Marc in his sky-blue kit; chest thrust forward, pounding first across the finishing line.

There was a Sports News crew, and as crowds of Vitality fans surged around him, Marc was shaking hands with the reporter and posing in front of one of the many drone cameras. Silas had watched his father leave the VIP box and rush across the arena and then realised that the other climbers had already begun to abseil down and Coach Hunter was calling up to him to get off the wall.

Silas had been deaf to the congratulations of his teammates. It wasn't fair! His one tiny chance of success and glory and his brother had stolen it. Even from across the arena, he could see the press of people around Marc.

They'd lifted him high onto their shoulders and were parading him around like he was some kind of god.

There was no way he was going home to pay homage to the Almighty Marc, so he had left the trials as soon as the afternoon had ended, not even bothering to wait to hear which clinic had won. Instead, he had done what he had always done... run away and sought solitude.

That had been three hours ago, but now the sun had commenced its steady descent below the horizon and the shadows were lengthening. There was no avoiding going home; he couldn't stay out all night.

After being still for so long, his arms and legs felt stiff so he rubbed his thighs briskly to loosen his muscles, and then started to slowly climb down. It was time to go home and pretend. Pretend to be pleased for Marc, pretend his father cared, and pretend he wasn't insanely jealous.

He reached the bottom of the tree. This was where he had first set eyes on Zoe and her peculiar grandmother. That was an alternative, he thought. The old lady's invite; she claimed to have known his mother... and she'd seem to recognise him straightaway.

Suddenly his anger was eclipsed by loneliness, but had it really come to this? Either to go to the house of a virtual stranger and her oddity of a granddaughter, or go home and have his tiny speck of success eclipsed by mighty Marc? He knew the answer.

Knocking loudly on the white front door, he saw movement through the thick frosted windowpane. The glass distorted the figure so much that Silas couldn't make out if it was Zoe or the old woman.

This option had seemed the less dire of the two. He just didn't feel ready to hear his father going on about how wonderful Marc was. His own disappointment was still too raw. Yet now, as the figure approached, he wasn't sure if this visit was such a good idea. He knew so little about Zoe's grandmother. She said she had met his mother... been good friends, even... but if that were true, then surely Silas would have some memory of her?

He looked up and down the road and contemplated running off.

On first glance the street seemed deserted, but in the gathering gloom he could make out two cloaked shapes emerging from a side alley. The Unseen! With a shudder he turned to face the door, keen to be safely inside and not exposed and vulnerable. Light spilled out as the front door opened and relief flooded through him.

'Hi!' It was Zoe.

'Hi,' he gasped, struggling to bring his sense of panic under control, and steady his breathing.

'You're here!'

'Yes.'

They stood staring at each other for a couple more seconds, and then Zoe swung the door wide open.

'You'd better come in. Nana will be unbearably smug. She's spent the whole afternoon insisting you would come. She

50

always seems to know stuff like that. She's been cooking for you.' Zoe was babbling but Silas didn't mind. It was preferable to awkward silence.

'Cooking? For me?' Silas was surprised. He didn't know anyone who cooked. All nutrition was supposed to come from the Nutrifarms, to ensure that everyone received an appropriate nutritional intake.

She closed the door behind him and led the way down a dimly lit hall. He followed, glad to be in a house – any house – rather than be outside in the darkness.

'Yes. Stew, I'm afraid. It's always stew.' Zoe sounded blithely dismissive of her nana's unusual skill.

'What's stew?'

Zoe gave him a sideways glance as she opened another door. A cloud of white steam billowed out and with it, the most incredible aroma. The air was suddenly alive, textured with warmth and luxury, with colour and intensity.

Silas inhaled deeply and, as if waking from a prolonged hibernation, his stomach let out the most almighty growl. Clutching at his belly in embarrassment, he walked through the door.

The room he entered was small and furnished with a wooden table with four chairs spaced around it. Cupboards of all shapes and sizes ran around the edge, and towards the furthest end stood Zoe's grandmother. She had her back to them and was leaning over a large metal pot. That was the source of the beautiful fragrance.

'Just in time, the food's ready. Sit down, Silas Corelle, and... relax.'

Without turning round, Zoe's grandmother waved with one hand in the direction of the table and chairs while her other hand continued stirring the mixture in the pot. Zoe collected three bowls from a tall brown cupboard and set them on the table.

Feeling very ill at ease, Silas sat rigidly on a chair as Zoe set spoons by the bowls and then sat next to him. Her nan carried

51

the pot to the table and started ladling out the stew. He looked at the mess being spooned into his bowl: brown liquid with chunks of orange, yellow and beige bobbing about in it. As unappetising as it looked to his eyes, his nose was still telling him a different story, as miniature clouds rolled up into his nostrils, and the delicious smell set his insides grumbling again.

'Thank you, um, Mrs ...' His words tailed off in embarrassment as he suddenly realised he didn't know Zoe's nan's name.

'It's a pleasure, dear. Anyway, it is a celebratory meal, and you are the guest of honour! I saw you climb. You won, didn't you?'

Silas nodded, frowning slightly. Why had she watched him climb?

'I knew today would be a great day for you. Eat, my dear, try the stew. Oh, and just call me Nana, like Zoe does. I'd prefer that.' Nana smiled at Silas and then started eating.

He turned his attention back to the bowl in front of him, unsure whether or not to refuse the food. It hadn't been processed and cleansed; what if it made him ill?

'It is safe to eat, Silas. I wouldn't give you anything that would harm you,' Nana said.

Silas gave a guilty start, discomfited by his transparency and Nana's forthrightness, and quickly dipped his spoon into the mixture.

Experimentally he sipped a bit and let the taste linger on his tongue. It was rich and velvety, meaty and earthy at the same time. It tasted like the smell of the sun on the soil after the rain had fallen. He closed his eyes as he took another spoonful and then another. Small chunks of yellow disintegrated in his mouth with a peculiar bittersweet taste. He opened his eyes to see Zoe and Nana staring at him.

'What's the matter?' he asked, suddenly feeling defensive.

Zoe laughed. 'Nothing... but its only stew, and you look like you are eating food for the first time in your life!' She closed her eyes in imitation of him, adopting a dreamy, transported look of delight, swaying gently from side to side as she pretended to eat.

Self-consciously, Silas lowered his spoon as the heat of a blush crept up his neck and across his cheeks. His over-full stomach churned and unexpectedly felt heavy and unpleasant. He hated being laughed at. He was already ridiculed enough by Marc.

The desire to say something hurtful back overtook him, but before a word passed his lips, he caught sight of Nana's expression.

She was smiling, but it was such a sad smile, and her grey eyes were bright with unshed tears. 'You look so much like her,' Nana said, searching his face with her sorrowful eyes, 'on the outside. And you are becoming more like her in here too.' Nana passed her wrinkled hand over her eyes before gently pointing at Silas' face.

Forgetting his irritation with Zoe, Silas shifted his attention to Nana. He didn't need to understand all she was saying to know she was talking about his mother. Nana didn't look away and somehow her prolonged study of him was soothing rather than unsettling; as if her recognition of Ellen in Silas' features made his mother less of a distant memory.

'How did you know her?' Silas asked eventually. From what he could remember, his mother had hardly any friends, and he was convinced he had never met Nana before.

'We met before your brother was born,' Nana said, then paused and turned to her granddaughter. 'I think we may need tea, Zoe. Will you pour some? It's already brewed, but it will need heating through.'

'Of course,' Zoe said, clearing the table as she got up. Taking Silas' bowl, she whispered, 'I'm sorry for teasing you earlier. I made you cross… I was clumsy.' She gave a rueful smile. 'Friends?'

In surprise, Silas nodded his acceptance of her apology and even managed a small smile in return. Of course she had only been teasing; why had he been so quick to take offence?

53

'Friends' may be too strong a word, though, he thought, as he watched her broad body move across the nutrition area; he still couldn't risk being known as Zoe's friend.

'I guess Ellen was lonely,' Nana said.

Turning back to the old lady, he leaned across the table, eager to hear more about his mother.

'Your father had started working on the Biocubicle project and his hours were long. He was hardly ever home.'

'No change there, then,' Silas muttered to himself.

Nana shot him a sympathetic look, but continued talking. 'Your parents lived a few houses further up this street; that was before the business really took off and they could move into the heart of the Inhabited district.

'We got chatting one day, your mother and I. She would visit me here, and I would sometimes cook for her. I was busy back then, though; most of my time was taken up with the work I was doing among the Unseen – health clinics and provision of nutrition and so forth.'

Silas frowned. He had never heard of Seen going near the Unseen, let alone helping them. Seeing his confusion, Nana explained, 'Before you were born, and before Biocubicles and the Nutrifarms, there was no government aid for the Unseen. There wasn't any work for them, either. No one wanted to risk being associated with the Unseen, and almost nobody would support them. As far as I recall, the general opinion was that because the Unseen couldn't meet their Health Targets they didn't even deserve any help. It was an awful time,' Nana said slowly, shaking her head. 'There were, however, others of us who didn't hold that view at all. We could see the suffering going on around us, and we wanted to do something. Your mother was one of those people. She had a kind and generous heart and cared enough for those who couldn't help themselves, so she and I cooked together, in this very house. We made a lot of stew – but for some reason she always went into raptures over mine.'

'She worked preparing nutrition? Cooking? With the Unseen?' Silas nearly laughed at the idea. 'Are you sure we are talking about the same Ellen Corelle? From what I can remember of her, she barely left the house. She certainly wasn't making stew to feed the creepy Unseen!'

Nana smiled sadly. 'You may not have known this, but Ellen was still involved in helping the Unseen right up to the day she died.'

Silas suddenly felt angry. 'That can't be right. How come she found the time to care for *them*,' he spat, 'but couldn't be bothered to care about herself?' He found he was shouting now, furious with his mother for dying, and infuriated with Nana for knowing more about her than he did. 'If she'd looked after herself properly then she wouldn't have died, and left me and Dad and Marc. Why couldn't she have cared more about us?' Letting his rage spill out he pointed an accusing finger at Nana. 'Why couldn't you have done something? If you were her friend!'

His outburst was met with calm silence, and Silas turned away, struggling to get his emotions under control. He was shocked by the intensity of the feelings that the old woman had provoked in him.

He heard Zoe rejoin them and looked up as Nana pushed a glass of translucent green-brown liquid towards him. He wrapped his hands around it, drawing comfort from its heat, and as he inhaled the soothing scent of mint he felt his anger soften. He let the warm vapour travel across his face, and took a small sip.

'She cared for you so much.' Nana spoke softly, seemingly untroubled by Silas' angry words. 'She loved you utterly. Ellen was very proud of you, Silas. You were her second-born. Among the healthiest of the Seen, infertility still persists, and not many people can easily have one child, but she considered you as her special gift. You were the apple of her eye.'

Silas sighed heavily. His brief flare of anger had completely diminished and what replaced it was a sadness, a mourning for the mother who had loved him, and yet who he had so few memories of.

'I miss her,' Silas said, realising he had never spoken this out loud to anyone before. Her death had been hidden under a cloak of shame that prevented anyone from ever mentioning her. It was a release to finally talk about her freely. His mind was immediately flooded with a hundred questions.

Here at last was someone Silas could trust to be honest with him. Nana wasn't ashamed or embarrassed to talk openly about Ellen, but at that moment Nana stood up.

'I miss her too. Her death was a shock to us all.' She swayed slightly, lost in thought for a moment. 'Don't be deceived by the label of self-inflicted; Ellen valued her health and life ...' Her gaze seemed to become slightly unfocused. Eager to hear more, Silas also got to his feet.

'What do you mean by that? Her death *was* self-inflicted; the bio-records proved it. She'd stopped all bio-assessments and hadn't maintained her targets in months... Nana?'

The old woman seemed to buckle with a weight of sadness before his eyes, and Zoe leapt up to hold on to Nana's arm.

'Other things took up our time,' Nana said simply, though Silas couldn't imagine what could be more important than maintaining your health. 'There are many memories... and much loss. I am aware that I let Ellen down. She was giving too much of herself... I should have seen it.' Nana's voice tightened with emotion, and her eyes shone over-brightly as tears collected, ready to spill down the frail skin of her cheeks. 'I don't mean to spoil our evening, but I need to be alone for a bit. Sorry, Silas. I know there must be more you want to know... and I will tell you... but not tonight.'

'Are you sure you are all right, Nana?' Zoe asked, her worried gaze meeting Silas' behind Nana's back. 'Can I get you anything?'

'No, Zoe, leave me for a bit. I'll be fine.' Nana turned to Silas. 'Don't feel you should leave; in fact, promise me you'll stay. Just for a while. Keep Zoe company; she can show you around the house. She doesn't have any friends in the city ...'

'Nana!' Zoe objected, her brown cheeks glowing red.

In her embarrassment, she couldn't even look at Silas as she firmly ushered her grandmother upstairs.

Silas remained standing alone in the nutrition area, the amusement of witnessing Zoe's discomfiture warming him for a brief moment. However, that pleasure was soon replaced with a gnawing hunger, not for food, but for information.

His body remained motionless, rooted to the spot, but his mind was doing somersaults. He needed to know more, to understand about his mother's life and death. Was his limited recollection of her a distortion of the truth? He had chosen to remember her as a selfish, careless creature that had left them motherless through her own neglect. But his memories were those of a hurting nine-year-old boy.

He realised he understood nothing about the woman who was Ellen Corelle. Nana's glowing words and raw grief had challenged him. Maybe there was a good deal that was not as it seemed. Yes, he needed to know much more – and Nana had promised to tell him. He would hold her to that, he decided, but while he was here he wanted to see the rest of her house, and maybe find some hint of his mother that still lingered in this old and unusual home.

Chapter 8

Shelves filled with faded old books and untidily stacked cases lined the walls of the first room they entered. Zoe briskly led the way, as if she were keen to get the tour of Nana's house over with as quickly as possible so that Silas could leave.

Two cushioned chairs were haphazardly arranged in the centre, each with ancient, yellowing books in them, some resting precariously over their arms. There was dust, not enough to give an air of abandonment, but sufficient to make the room smell inviting and cosy. A large black box occupied one corner. It reached chest height and was long and narrow.

Silas ran his hand along the smooth top, inadvertently leaving a faint trail in the fine dusty layer. He wiped his fingers on his shirt. 'What's the box for?'

'Oh, it's an old-fashioned music maker. It's called a piano.' Zoe sounded impatient, but Silas wanted to glean as much from Nana's house as he could and refused to let her hurry him.

'Wow! I've never seen one up close before. Can I look inside?'

'Sure, you just fold this part up.' Zoe lifted a thin lidded section and Silas looked down at the row of black and white lines.

'Does it work?'

'Yes, it still works. Nana can play on it a bit. I think her grandfather taught her. She's shown me a few notes.'

Silas moved out of the way to let Zoe stand in his place.

'Will you show me?' he asked politely, so Zoe could do little else but comply.

Zoe pressed down on a white rectangle with her index finger and the piano obediently produced a sound. Her fingers moved up a couple of keys and different notes joined in. The noise was soft and echoed inside the instrument briefly before fading away entirely. Zoe's hand wandered up a few more keys and a simple slow melody filled the room.

'It's a nice sound, isn't it?' Her fingers continued to drift over the keys, repeating the line of melody over and over. 'Nana said that in olden times lots of people would learn to play the piano. You know how we use music beat programmes on the Pace-Setters to keep us moving? Well, they used music to help them to stop moving. Would you like to hear some?' Zoe asked, encouraged by Silas' interest in the piano. 'I think Nana's managed to transfer some onto her Pace-Setter.'

'Sure,' Silas said as Zoe gently closed the piano lid and turned her attention to the more familiar silver Pace-Setter that sat on one of the cluttered shelves. There was a buzz and a click and then a barrage of tumbling notes filled the room, making Silas jump. It was deafening, and he slammed his hands over his ears while Zoe fiddled with the machine.

The cacophony subsided to a less painful level, and he lowered his hands. The notes were hurrying and tripping over one another, clashing and bashing and then resolving only to pick up and start scurrying chaotically around once more. To him it was an undifferentiated clamour, and reminded him of the ebb and flow of the din in the nutrition hall at lunchtime.

Zoe carefully shifted the books off one of the soft chairs and settled down in it, so Silas followed her example. The music had slowed, and he could discern a simple melody running over the top of deeper notes. It was the same tune Zoe had played on the piano earlier, but richer and softer. It was compelling to listen to. Zoe closed her eyes and rested her head back. She sat perfectly still and seemed in a state of utter peace. The music flowed, and he studied her face, properly, for the first time.

Her lips were a little apart as she drew gentle steady breaths; her skin was pale brown with a smattering of darker freckles over her nose and forehead. With her eyes closed, her black eyelashes rested on her cheeks, and he could see her eyes moving under the paper-thin skin of her lids. As he watched, an almost imperceptible change came over her and gradually, she seemed to alter. Somehow she was growing... beautiful. He blinked a couple of times.

Physically she looked the same as always: dumpy nose, and short hair, round face, chubby body... and yet she emitted beauty. How had he not seen that before? He couldn't stop staring at her. What was different? Nothing was... and yet everything was.

The sound of the music faded into insignificance as he observed her, trying to understand what he was seeing. She seemed more alive, more vital. The colour of her dark hair and brown skin was incredibly vivid. It was as if he had only seen a flat two-dimensional image of her and now, here before him, was the real deal in three dimensions.

He was still gazing at her, transfixed, when the music finished. Zoe drew a deep breath in and out and opened her eyes. She held his gaze for a moment, then her eyes widened fractionally. Silas knew he was behaving oddly, but he not only couldn't tear his eyes away from her face, he found he didn't want to. How had he been so blind to Zoe's beauty?

Her expression suddenly darkened, like a shadow had fallen over her face. She was angry, Silas realised, as he tried, and failed, to look away from her. In fact, she was more than angry, she was furious.

Books scattered everywhere as she leapt up from the chair. Silas made a half-hearted attempt to stand as well, but his legs felt unsteady beneath him. All he wanted to do was stay in that room with Zoe, drinking from her beauty, drawing from the radiance that she exuded.

'What has she done now? Si, stay there!' Zoe barked at him and slammed out of the room and ran up the stairs. He sank back down into the chair, still marvelling at what he had just witnessed. There were more doors slamming and the sound of raised voices, or more accurately, *a* raised voice – Zoe's.

'Why would you do that? You added it to the tea, didn't you?' She was shouting, so although her voice was muffled, Silas could still make out every word. 'I wondered why you made him stay around. I'm doing fine, Nana. I don't need your help!'

Nana's response was much quieter and indistinct through the layers of floor and door.

'You should see the way he's looking at me now, and it's not like a friend... more like a homeless puppy! You shouldn't have interfered!'

Then Silas could hear more mumbling, followed by a firm tread on the stairs. The door opened, and Zoe was standing there, looking flushed and angry. Even so, as much as he tried not to stare at her, he found his eyes magnetically drawn to her face.

'You have to go now!' she said abruptly.

Surprised, and hurt, he stammered. 'B... but... can't I stay a bit longer... with... you?'

'No!' She was physically pushing him out of the room and towards the front door, and deftly opened it while still propelling him forward. When he was standing on the doorstep, he turned to face her and put his foot in the door to stop it closing. How could he make her understand that he didn't want to go, that he needed to stay?

'What have I done wrong? I really like being with you. You make me see things in a new way. Like the food and your music ...' He nearly added, 'and your beauty' but held back at the last minute, knowing he sounded foolish. 'Please let me stay just a little bit longer.'

Zoe's demeanour softened, and Silas realised he must have looked as forlorn as he sounded.

'Look, *you've* done nothing wrong, but you need to go home now and recover – I mean, rest. I'll see you tomorrow, at clinic.

Now, go!' She shut the door firmly in his face, and he stood watching through the glass until she switched the hall light off. The house inside and the steps outside were plunged into darkness.

With his mind so full of the events of the evening, he barely noticed the walk home. Although it was night, he felt none of his usual fear. He even passed a couple of Unseen and found himself unperturbed by the robes and the sinister shapes underneath. Tonight they held no terror for him. They, of course, left him well alone, for to even speak to a Seen without first being spoken to would result in severe punishment. The Citizen-Safety Monitors were set at every corner to ensure his security.

The house was deserted. As he closed the front door behind him, the familiar melodic tones of the computer greeted him.

'Good evening, Silas, a message awaits you.'

'Play message.'

There was the background noise of cheering and laughing and then his father's voice.

'Hey, Silas, I couldn't see you at the award ceremonies. Have you heard? Marc won! Fastest 100-metre sprint ever recorded at an Inter-Clinic Trial! Can you believe it? 9.24 seconds. Yes! What a champion!'

There was more loud background cheering and shouting. 'Oh, and guess what? The Flawless Leader has invited us to a big event at the Spire tonight! She wants to meet Marc and congratulate him in person. Come and join us when you get this message. It's going to be a night to remember!'

'Message end,' the computer chimed.

'Yeah, right! Thanks, Dad, but no thanks.' Kicking off his trainers, he padded up to his room. His clothes tumbled into the laundry chute, and he stepped into the shower room. At that moment, he caught sight of his face in the mirror over the basin. He stopped and moved forward for a closer look.

From somewhere he could hear the sound of a high-pitched scream, and it took a second to realise the noise was coming from his own wide-open mouth. He stood for another couple of seconds maintaining eye contact with a reflection, which was both his, and yet, terrifyingly, not his, until the room began to spin and tilt sideways and blackness consumed him.

Chapter 9

'Good morning, Silas. Please present yourself for assessment.'

'Whaa …?' He opened one eye experimentally. His brain started an assessment of its own. Who am I? OK, I know who I am. Where am I? Cold. Floor. Shower. My room.

His relief at working out his location was immediately replaced with the horrified realisation that he was naked and freezing. He tried to sit upright, and in rebellion his brain chose that moment to introduce him to a whole new set of sensations. Lights flashed before his eyes and the pounding of a sledgehammer started inside his skull. He gently prodded his scalp, and his fingers discovered a huge, tender lump behind his left ear.

'Present yourself for assessment.'

'Dad! Marc…!' His voice sounded feeble and croaky. He was absolutely parched with thirst. 'Dad, Marc…!'

Using the sink to pull himself to stand, he managed to stay upright enough to stagger to the Biocubicle. The door slid shut.

'Increased sodium level detected. Calibrating dietary alterations. Scalp contusion detected. Do you require Health Emergency-Life Preservation?'

Alarmed, he croaked out 'No!' then cleared his voice and repeated his answer. The first and only time he had seen HE-LP in action was six years ago. Having found his mother lying slumped on the floor drooling and grunting, he had rushed to the Biocubicle and turned the Emergency key. HE-LP had arrived in the form of four efficient silver-uniformed workers. After accessing the Biocubicle data, they had lifted his mother onto a stretcher and taken her away. That was the last time he had seen her.

No! He definitely did not require the ministrations of Health Emergency today.

Tottering over to the dispenser, he removed his pre-prepared shake.

'Water.' The machine clicked, a cup appeared and was automatically filled with water. Gratefully, Silas swallowed the contents in one go. 'Water,' he said again. Three cups later he was beginning to feel more human and started to sip on his shake. Being careful not to aggravate the hammering inside his head, he gently pulled his shirt and leggings on. He sat on his bed trying to piece together the previous evening's events. He remembered his rather unusual time with Zoe. The music they'd listened to, and then, how she became different and somehow radiant; her beauty had been mesmerising. He recollected his rather abrupt expulsion from her house and then arriving home and then... yes... he had looked in the mirror... and seen his reflection.

Standing up too fast and reeling slightly, he returned to the mirror in the shower room. Staring back at him was his familiar face, a bit pale and tired-looking, but otherwise as normal as ever. Trailing his fingers over his right eye, he could feel the prickle of his lashes, and the skin of his eyelid crinkled under his touch. The firm ball of his eye yielded fractionally to his probing digits.

Suddenly he remembered, and his stomach rolled as a wave of nausea washed over him. Yesterday when he had looked in the mirror, his eye socket had been empty. Just a gaping hole with flickering shadows, like black flames, crawling over the skin around his lids. His image had repulsed and terrified him. He must have fainted and, as he fell, cracked his head on the edge of the shower. His hand wandered again to feel the jelly-like bruise on the back of his head.

I've had some kind of hallucination, he thought. Maybe the stress of the trials or the whole Marc thing has really got to me.

Yes, that's it! I'm fine; it was an optical illusion, a trick of the light, he rationalised to himself.

In reality, he still felt shaky and weak, but today was the last day of the season. Personal and Level results from the trials were announced, and he wanted to see if he had moved up.

Also, he was worried about Zoe's results. Yesterday he had been so wrapped up in himself that he had completely forgotten to ask her how the swimming had gone. In fact, up until last night he hadn't even cared about it, but now his throat felt tight with anxiety. What if she *was* kicked out of Vitality? He might never see her again.

Voices could be heard coming from downstairs... Dad and Marc's, he guessed. 'Si? Are you there? Come and hear this!' His dad sounded unusually excited so Silas tried to pull his expression into something resembling happy, then made his way downstairs.

What greeted him was the bizarre spectacle of Marc, dressed in a shiny white, skintight jumpsuit and matching calf-length running boots, admiring his reflection in the mirror. Meanwhile his father flittered around him like a bee around a flower, every now and then coming into land to brush away an imaginary speck or flatten a non-existent crinkle and all the while buzzing away, 'I can't believe it, such an honour... so proud...' buzz... buzz... buzz...

'Hi,' said Silas cautiously. 'What's going on? Why are you wearing that?'

His father paused in his frantic movements and looked around. 'Si, you *are* here. Where did you get to yesterday? I can't believe you missed the biggest day of Marc's life.'

'Yeah... sorry... friends...um.' But he knew he wasn't really being listened to. His father had already turned back to marvel at Marc, who was marvelling at himself.

Marvellous! thought Silas bitterly. 'So, Dad, are you going to tell me what this is all about?'

'Last night, after the trials, we were all invited to a celebration at the Spire. It's a remarkable place; it's a shame you missed it.'

'Yes? How does that explain the shiny monkey suit?'

Choosing to ignore the comment, his father ploughed on, 'We met the Flawless Leader, and she was so impressed with what she saw in your brother that, starting from tomorrow, he'll be working at the Spire, with her! With Helen Steele!'

'She made the right choice! I knew I'd get to the top! Did you hear what she said, Dad? About me being the future of Prima... and all that?' Marc chipped in, flexing his impressive biceps at himself in the mirror.

'Great,' Silas said as enthusiastically as possible. 'Congratulations, Marc. So... why the special outfit?'

'It's my new uniform. The Flawless Leader has created a department for the elite from the city's top clinic. She has hand-picked the best of the best. Governmental Health Advisor.' He puffed out his chest a bit more, and the shiny white fabric glistened in the light. Silas saw the black lettering forming the initials 'GHA' move as the muscles on Marc's shoulders and arms rippled as he posed again. 'And I advise you to get out of my way, if you want to stay healthy!'

Laughing heartily at his own joke, Marc swaggered into the workout suite, deliberately shouldering his younger brother and muttering 'Stuck-last' as he passed him.

Silas was too drained to respond to his brother's jibe and instead headed for his room. Perhaps he should miss his workout this morning. His dad probably wouldn't even notice, not with the awesome Marc in the house.

'Silas, just quickly before you go,' his father called after him. Silas turned expectantly. Just maybe his dad *had* seen his climb yesterday after all, and was going to congratulate him. 'Have you thought about what you are going to do over the next few weeks? Season finishes today, and Marc will be occupied with his new duties.'

'Oh, Dad,' Silas winced; this wasn't the conversation he was expecting. 'I was so busy with preparing for the trials, I hadn't thought much about it. Maybe I could stay in bed?' Actually, with his aching head that was all he wanted to do, but his clouded brain had forgotten that he shouldn't make comments like that to his father.

'I hope that is a joke!' he growled, scowling at his son. 'Decide today and let me know. If you don't want to join up to a training camp, then you can come with me to work. There is always a need for volunteers to help out in the under-tens pre-clinic.'

'Yes, Dad, all right. I'll sign up to something, don't worry. Message received and understood. Look, I'm going to sort it out now!' He jogged out of the door, waving at his father's still-glowering face.

At a point where he knew he couldn't be seen from the house, he stopped running and plodded to clinic, thinking about his options for the season-break. Going to help out at Bio-health with the training camp for the pre-clinic brats was definitely not going to happen! He had been there and done that two years ago. Let someone else handle the little…

'Hey! You're early.' The voice, so close behind him, startled him, and he whirled round.

'Zoe!' The initial surge of joy at seeing her was replaced with a sense of confusion. He clearly remembered feeling incredibly drawn to her last night, yet in the cold light of day, he felt none of that intensity. She looked at him closely for a moment and he held her gaze.

'Look, I'm sorry about kicking you out last night,' she said.

'Nah, it's fine. From what I remember, I was behaving like an idiot anyway. I don't think I was very well. I had some odd visions, like hallucinations… I think.' He didn't know how else to describe it.

Zoe looked at him sympathetically. 'I'm sorry,' she repeated.

'Why are you apologising for that?' Silas said, giving her a quizzical look as they resumed walking to clinic. 'It must have been caused by stress from the trials, that's all.'

Zoe grimaced. 'Stress? Hmm… How do you feel now?' she asked.

'Well, I banged my head, which doesn't help, but apart from that, everything seems normal.' Subconsciously, he ran his fingers over his eye socket, remembering the image in the mirror. He had looked horrific, like an Unseen freak. Twisted, scarred and broken. He shuddered at the memory.

'What are you doing over the season-break?' Zoe's abrupt change of subject brought him out of his dismal reverie and back to the present. However, the topic she chose did little to lift his mood.

'Season-break? Don't mention it,' he groaned, 'Dad's been on at me about that already this morning. It seems that I'm not allowed to have any time off. He wants me to choose between a training camp, or I'm "volunteering" at Bio-health for the whole break.'

'Ouch! That's tough.'

'Tell me about it. What are you doing?' he asked, more out of politeness. He expected Zoe's plans would be equally, if not more, boring.

'We're going to visit some friends of Nana's,' she said, trying to sound matter of fact, but Silas could hear the undercurrent of excitement in her voice. Immediately, his interest was piqued.

'Oh, right. The Community, is it? How long are you going for?' he asked as coolly as possible.

They were walking side by side. Silas had his head down and his feet were dragging along the floor, kicking the occasional loose stone. Zoe's shorter legs were moving at a faster pace to keep up with him, but at his words she stopped altogether. Silas looked at her to see what the problem was. Her face was a picture of concern, and she looked over her shoulder to check no one was in earshot.

'How do you know about the Community? You aren't supposed to mention them. Who told you?'

Taken aback by her aggressive tone, he frowned and thought about where he had heard about it. Then it dawned on him. It was while he was accidentally eavesdropping on Zoe, before he even knew her, when she had been in the Uninhabited areas.

'Um… it's just something I overheard once. I don't know anything about it really.' However, now he was even more intrigued. 'What do you know about them? Who or what is the Community? Can't you tell me?'

'It's not for me to say,' she replied primly, and then added, 'You could ask Nana – she might tell you.'

'Fine! I will,' he responded, as they resumed walking to clinic. He felt even more curious now.

'Though you'll have to be quick if you want to talk to her,' Zoe added. 'We leave tonight, and Nana usually stays there for as long as possible. I doubt we'll be back before the end of season-break.'

'Tonight?' Silas asked, surprised. 'But I thought… I mean, Nana didn't mention it yesterday.' He had been planning on visiting Nana over the season-break to glean more information about his mother. That was the only thing that was going to make this next month bearable. His shoulders slumped as he contemplated how disappointing this news was. Nana had promised to tell him more, and now she was leaving the city for the whole break!

As they arrived at the clinic gates, they saw other students arriving in twos and threes. Out of habit Silas hung back, still not wanting to be associated with Zoe.

'Uh, you go on, I've got to check something with …' He waved a hand towards a cluster of the other students.

'Yeah, sure.' There was hurt in her voice, but he squashed down his sense of guilt. He still had a whole year to survive at clinic, this time without the protection provided by Marc. He needed to play it safe.

As he watched her walk through the front door, he remembered that he still hadn't asked her about the trials. She must think I'm such a selfish, spoilt idiot, he thought. But why do I care what she thinks? However, as he walked away from the front door, choosing to go the long way round to the warm-up room, he couldn't shake the uncomfortable sensation that he was beginning to care very much what she thought.

Chapter 10

'Listen carefully because I don't say this often... I am impressed!' A ripple of relieved laughter ran around the room. 'You have surpassed my expectations, and for that I congratulate you... Silver 5!' This time the students let out cheers and hollers of excitement, and a hint of a smile flickered at the corner of Coach Regan's mouth.

'Yes!' Silas punched the air. At last he was out of Bronze and he knew that his own brilliant climb must have really pushed the combined scores up.

'Individual results can be accessed through your ID code. Corelle, Vernon and Chan, please remain behind. The rest of you, for the last time as Bronze 1, you are dismissed.'

No one even spared a second to glance at the three remaining students as they bundled out the door, chattering excitedly. Silas looked at Zoe and shrugged when he caught her eye. He didn't know why the three of them had been called to stay behind. Dexter Chan was by far the best athlete in the level, and he knew it. A long-distance runner by specialism, with a tough and wiry physique, he was an arrogant piece of work and ordered people around like *he* was the coach.

'First things first. Dexter, your results from the trials are exceptional. You are the only student in Bronze 1 to have performed well enough to be moved up by two levels. As of next season, you will be starting in Silver 4.'

Dexter seemed to swell up with self-importance and stuck his chest out so much that he looked like an overexcited pigeon. Smirking at Silas and ignoring Zoe, he said, 'Thank you, Coach. I knew I'd been the best this year, but I didn't expect this.' His voice was so oily and creepy that even Coach Regan recoiled in distaste from him.

Silas felt an inappropriate bubble of laughter rise up inside him and fought to suppress it. Out of the corner of his eye, he could see Zoe's shoulders twitch with silent giggles.

'Ha!' He couldn't help it; the sound shot out of him like a bark, and he quickly coughed to try to disguise it. 'Sorry, ha... happy news... for you, Dexter! Well done.'

Dexter glared at Silas, recognising the insincerity in his voice. Zoe's face had gone bright red with the exertion of not laughing, and Silas knew that if he caught her eye he would be completely unable to contain his mirth.

'Yes, well, congratulations, Chan. Go and find Coach Disley in Silver 4 warm-up room. He's expecting you.'

As Dexter left the room, Coach Regan turned to face Zoe and Silas, and as suddenly as a drop of water extinguishes a flame, all levity was equally doused with one fearsome frown. 'Veron!' Zoe jumped slightly. 'Mixed news for you. Your results were impressive for a misshapen lump, and it would have placed you in Bronze 4, but yet again the manager has insisted you stay in Bronze 1. It's not for me to question, but, have no doubt, I will make next season tough for you. You will know pain, and there will be no mercy.'

Zoe wisely kept her mouth shut and her expression blank.

'Well, go on, then, Veron. Crawl back to... wherever creatures like you live during season-break!' Coach Regan shouted at her. After casting one pained look at Silas, Zoe swiftly left the room. Coach Regan watched her go with a scowl of intense dislike on her face, then she turned her attention to her next victim.

'Corelle, Corelle. How did you spring from the same genetic pool as your brother and father?'

Being less wise than Zoe, Silas felt the need to defend himself.

'I did a great climb in trials, Coach. I won in my heat, by a massive margin...'

'Don't interrupt me!' she bellowed. 'The judges ruled your climb "Disallowed".'

'What? It wasn't. I did everything right!' he couldn't help but shout back.

Suddenly, Coach Regan lunged forward and grabbed Silas by the wrist. She flicked his arm round and under and held it tight up against his back, forcing him against the wall.

'I said, don't interrupt,' she growled.

This time he was silent. He could feel his shoulder and elbow joint beginning to give.

'Your climb was disallowed because you failed to follow correct safety procedures. You strayed out of your designated lane and in doing so, you could have caused injury to yourself or others. As such, you will not be moving up to Silver 5 with the rest of your level. You also will have me breathing down your neck for another whole season.'

Just as the pain was getting too much and he was sure his muscles would tear, Coach Regan suddenly released her hold and Silas cradled his aching arm.

'But, Coach, I don't understand...' He flinched backwards as she moved menacingly closer to him again.

'You have nothing to understand except that you... have... failed. Spend your season-break working hard. You still have the mid-season assessments, and if you don't mess them up you might just get a sniff at Silver before you leave clinic. Get out now, and when I see you next season, you'd better be ready to succeed!'

Feeling like a whipped dog with his head bowed, Silas backed out of the room.

He couldn't believe it. After all that hard work, his brilliant climb at the trials was being disallowed. The pain from his twisted shoulder receded but what replaced it was a dull ache in his stomach. What was his dad going to say? He would be on Silas' case all season-break. He'd probably insist they did training together. It was going to be awful.

All of a sudden, the overwhelming desire to flee came over Silas. He just had to get out. Get out of clinic, get out of Prima, and get out of Marc's shadow and the impossible expectations placed on him by his father.

Blinded to all else but the need to escape, Silas pushed through the front door and ran down the white stone steps of Vitality Clinic. He thought he heard someone call his name but didn't even glance back. Picking up speed, he turned down a narrow alleyway between two houses and, finally, the pressure of frustration and disappointment building in his chest found release in a yell of pure rage.

The cry echoed and bounced off the walls of the alley. Every nuance of pain and anguish amplified in an acoustic interchange of echo and counter-echo.

He was heading for his one place of refuge, his favourite hiding place – the old tree. He didn't slow his pace as he criss-crossed through the narrow back alleys of the Inhabited district, until he reached the comfortably familiar dilapidated roads of the Uninhabited area.

There, with no one to watch him, he jogged steadily down the overgrown drive to the ruined white cottage. Then, speeding up again, he ran full pelt at the vast trunk of the tree and leapt to grab his first handhold.

He had just pulled himself into the lower branches when he heard the unmistakable thud of heavy footsteps and the rasp of laboured breathing.

Who was disturbing his peace now? Had someone seen him and followed him? Cautiously, he peered down through the branches.

'Zoe!' he said in surprise. 'What are you doing here? How...?'

'Silas!' she gasped through ragged breaths, 'Are you OK? Don't do anything stupid!'

'Of course I'm OK. Why did you follow me?' Silas looked down at the dishevelled sweaty figure beneath him, and he felt a smile pull at the corner of his mouth. What was Zoe up to?

75

She'd chased after him all this way. It was an impressive run for someone in such poor condition.

'I was worried... Ow!' she exclaimed, suddenly bending over double. 'I've got a stitch. I have never, ever run that fast.'

Silas shook his head in confusion. 'You were worried?' he repeated. What did she have to be concerned about? She was escaping the city, heading off on an exciting adventure by the sounds of it. He actually felt jealous. Jealous of Zoe! That is what my life has come to, he thought bitterly. 'What do *you* have to be worried about?' he asked, unable to disguise the envy in his voice.

'You!' Zoe barked back at him. 'I'm worried about you! What on earth did Coach Regan say to you? You shot off from clinic, didn't wait when I called after you and then that noise you made, that shout... like your world had come to an end! I thought... well, never mind what I thought. Please come down so we can talk properly. I'm getting a neck ache to match the ache in my side.'

He had been seeking isolation, and the thought of company did not appeal, especially here at the tree, but Zoe had been concerned about him – enough to chase after him. He didn't know why she would be bothered, but it was comforting to know that she was. Maybe someone to talk to would be nice.

'Why don't you join me up here?' he asked impulsively.

'You want me to climb a tree?' Zoe looked incredulous.

'Yes.' He couldn't help but smile at her. She looked ridiculous with her skin deep red from running and her hair plastered down with sweat. 'I *need* to be up here. If you are so desperate to talk, then you'd better climb up and join me.'

At his challenge, her mouth pressed into the thin line that had become familiar to him as an expression of her determination. She ran at the tree and leapt for the lowest branch and completely missed. Undeterred, she walked around the vast trunk and dragged an old fallen branch to stand on, but with no easy handholds within reach, she gave up and stared back up at Silas.

'A little help wouldn't go amiss,' she said crossly, causing Silas to laugh. Surprisingly, he found he didn't want to be alone any more. He was glad Zoe was here, and he lowered himself from the branch and dropped down to land by her side.

'Only if you say please,' he said, smiling broadly.

She grinned back. 'Please.'

He braced his back against the tree with his knee bent to make his thigh into a step and patted it.

'Stand here and then you should be able to reach the first branch. This is the most difficult part, I promise.'

'Hmm, famous last words.'

Silas chuckled, and then tensed his thigh to accommodate the extra weight, as Zoe used him as a human stepladder.

'OK, what now?'

'Follow me.' Silas clambered to stand on the lower branch.

'Err... how high are we going? I'm actually not great with heights.' But he had already moved up to the next branch, and she was sitting on her own. Gingerly she stood to her feet and, clutching the trunk, looked up. A hand appeared between the foliage. It pointed to a broken branch and then a cleft in the trunk. A voice accompanied the pointing. 'Put your feet here and here and grab hold of the branch above your head.'

With painstaking slowness, Zoe inched her way skywards and before long was sitting on a thick bough, hugging the trunk for all she was worth.

'You're in the best spot in the whole tree. You can see everything from here. Watch this.' Silas was a bit further out on the same branch, dangling his legs. As he spoke, he lowered himself onto the limb below to allow the panoramic view of the whole city of Prima to unfold before her. The Inhabited areas cropped up like islands of order among the chaos and disarray of the Uninhabited districts.

Nearby, the gleaming white edifice of Vitality Clinic shone out in the bright morning sun, and in the far distance the myriad glass walls of the Spire reflected a rainbow of light onto the surrounding buildings.

'Wow!' she gasped. 'That is incredible. The city looks beautiful. No wonder you like being up here.'

'Yeah. I think so too,' Silas agreed, pleased that she appreciated the view. 'Can I ask you something?' he said, as he clambered back up to Zoe's branch.

'Of course,' Zoe said, still looking past him at the scene below them.

'You told me not to do anything stupid. What did you think I was going to do?'

Zoe looked directly at him, and then bit her lip thoughtfully. They remained gazing at each other, and Silas was reminded of the unusual vision from the previous night when she had seemed beautiful to him. He looked deeply into her eyes, trying to get a glimpse of that Zoe again.

'Well?' he prompted, when she didn't answer.

Eventually Zoe broke eye contact and gave a rueful smile. 'It seems I overreacted, Silas. I'd never seen you like that. I thought you were going to hurt yourself. I don't know... When you were shouting your head off down the alley – well, I assumed the worst. I had to check you were OK. I guess Coach didn't have good news for you?'

Silas shook his head. 'I'm not moving up either,' he said simply. He still couldn't believe it. How could his climb have been disallowed?

'Oh, Silas, I'm so sorry. What are you going to do?' Zoe said, her voice full of genuine concern for him.

'There's nothing I can do,' he answered, trying to stop the panicky feeling of failure from overwhelming him again. He managed a faint smile in an attempt to ease her concern for him. However, deep down he was touched that she had cared enough to follow him all this way, to seek him out. She had even climbed up a tree to talk to him, when it was obvious by the way she was still gripping onto the trunk that she was very uncomfortable with her high perch.

This was what a friend does, he thought. This was what Zoe had needed him to be and he had let her down. I'm little better than Taylor or Marc, he realised with a sudden clarity of insight. 'Thank you,' he blurted out, 'for checking up on me. You needn't have worried, though. I wasn't intending on doing anything more stupid than escape for a bit... hide out here.'

Over his time at clinic he had become so used to being a loner... but he no longer wanted that. Surely having one friend was better than having none, even if that friend *was* the most unpopular person at Vitality.

He looked at her again and was struck by how good it felt to have someone to talk to; someone he could trust.

'When Coach said all that stuff, I was so angry. I just needed to get away. I should be moving up to Silver, Zoe. I don't remember straying out of my lane. But my dad, and Marc, my brother ...' He paused, feeling the weight of his father's disappointment and Marc's hatred already crushing him. 'What is my dad going to say? I just needed to get away. I can't face them.'

They sat in silence, each lost in their own thoughts.

'What if you came with us?' Zoe said hesitantly, letting go of the tree trunk for long enough to rest a hand on Silas' arm.

Pleasantly surprised by her touch, Silas didn't pull away. 'Came with you, where?' he asked.

'With Nana and I, to the Community, although I can't promise anything until we've spoken to her about it.' She smiled encouragingly, though, obviously keen for him to say yes.

His immediate reaction would have been to decline, but as he thought it over, it seemed like the perfect solution. He could avoid his dad's anger and the gruelling season-break he would have to endure accompanied by Marc's perpetual torment.

Also, if he went away with Zoe and Nana, it would give Nana the chance to fulfil her promise of telling him more about his mother. Spending time with Zoe was now starting to feel much more appealing too. Maybe this was just what he needed... a change, an escape and an adventure.

Chapter 11

I've made a huge mistake! Silas thought, although it was a little late for self-recrimination. His blindfold had slipped a bit and was covering his nose. It stank of oily damp animal. An attempt to limit the smell by breathing only through his mouth meant that now he could also taste it.

The truck they were travelling in hit another pothole and he lurched sideways, colliding with another body, before bouncing back the other way.

I've made a mistake. I should not have come here! he thought again, but then a soft hand slid into his and gave it a reassuring squeeze.

'I don't think it's much further,' Zoe said.

'This stupid blindfold stinks!' Silas complained, unable to suppress the tremor in his voice. He was exhausted, disorientated and scared. The long sleepless night of train travel had been bad enough, but this final stage of the journey was almost more than he could bear.

'It'll be worth it,' Zoe murmured, her calm tones contrasting sharply with the edge of panic that had crept into Silas' voice. He felt her fingers move as she started to withdraw her hand.

'Don't let go,' he whispered, his voice tight with fear.

Without saying another word, she renewed the pressure of her grip. By focusing on the sensation of her warm hand in his, Silas felt his terror begin to recede.

The concept of being blindfolded is unthreatening when you are discussing it in daylight, with your eyes open, with people you know and in familiar surroundings. The reality of having itchy, reeking wool wrapped over your face by two of the Unseen, before being shut in the back of a truck in a remote Outerlands town, was the most frightening experience of Silas' life. If it hadn't been for Zoe, calmly enduring the same unpleasantness, he would have turned tail, run non-stop back to the city, and begged his father to sign him up as a volunteer with the bio-brats.

It had all been drilled into him the previous afternoon.

Nana had seemed surprised but very enthusiastic about Silas joining them on their trip.

'I'll sort it out with Anton,' she had said in a no-nonsense voice when Silas had shared his concerns over his father's earlier insistence that he should attend a training camp.

The other risk to what Silas now felt was his 'escape plan', was that his father may have already heard about Silas' disastrous trials results. If that were the case, then Silas knew he would be going nowhere. He would be spending his entire season-break stuck in the workout suite.

However, Nana seemed to have no trouble gaining Anton's consent, though she was deliberately vague when Silas tried to pin her down as to the details of their conversation.

'He said yes,' she'd announced triumphantly, entering the nutrition area. She had only been on the com-link for a few minutes.

'Really?' Silas' eyebrows shot up his forehead. 'Does he know it's not a training camp?'

'Yes, I didn't lie; I said that Zoe had asked for a friend her own age to accompany us on our trip to visit family friends in the north. That seemed to be enough for him.'

Silas could understand why. Zoe's name had been the magic word that had so easily persuaded his father. He must still be working with Esther Veron at Bio-health, and anything that kept the daughter happy would keep the mother happy.

'Did you tell him any more than that?' Silas asked. A part of him was hoping that his father might have expressed a little concern.

'I didn't need to, Silas, he didn't ask,' Nana responded.

'Oh!' Although glad to be getting away from the city, he had been left with the faintly bitter taste of disappointment that his father still hadn't shown any interest beyond what suited his work life. He had felt dispensable, an inconvenient problem that had now been neatly solved for the season-break.

'We'll need to catch the evening train and we haven't got long,' Nana said, 'but before you go and pack, Silas, I need to explain a little about the Community. My friends who live there will welcome you, but you must be aware that they have chosen to live *outside* of governmental assessments.'

'What do you mean?' Silas asked.

'Hmm… if they lived here, in the city, or in one of the Outerlands towns, most of them would not be classified as Seen citizens,' Nana explained slowly, and he could see she was gauging his reaction.

'Seriously? How is that allowed? How come they aren't monitored?' Silas couldn't imagine why anyone would want to live that way.

'It is not illegal, yet… It's just not recommended.' Nana was choosing her words carefully and Silas realised she was unsure of how much to tell him. 'The Biocubicle network has not been installed at the Community, and they would very much like to keep it that way. For a variety of different reasons, many Unseen and Seen have chosen to make the Community their home, but… how shall I put it?' Nana frowned and thought for a moment. 'How they live is *not* in line with how our government would like them to live.'

'What do you mean?' Silas asked, struggling to think of another way of living that didn't involve the Biocubicles.

'The people in the Community have a different approach to valuing each other that doesn't involve Health Targets,' Nana said cryptically.

'I don't understand,' Silas said, shaking his head.

'It's hard to explain,' Nana admitted. 'You are better off experiencing it.'

'What?'

'Never mind,' Nana smiled, but then she peered intently at Silas. 'The important thing to remember, Silas, is that not many people know of the Community's existence.'

'So why are you telling me?' Silas asked, and then with sudden insight he immediately answered his own question. 'My mother must have known.'

'Yes, Ellen knew of it, but never had a chance to visit, and so somehow it feels right to include you in this part of her life. However, Silas, this has been a home for my friends for the last 15 years, and to protect it, the location must be kept secret. You must not talk about your visit there. Even I don't know the exact whereabouts of the site. When we leave the train, my friends will drive us the last stretch. We will all be blindfolded. Is this going to be a problem for you?'

'No.' He shook his head to emphasise the point. He was now more desperate than ever to reach the Community if his mother had known of it, and keeping secrets was not a dilemma. Who would he tell anyway? Dad? Marc? Not likely!

The old truck continued to bump and rattle through the dark night. Despite the uncomfortable nature of the transport, Silas found his head beginning to grow heavy, and he tried resting back and closing his eyes. The adrenaline that had sustained him thus far had worn off, but he didn't think he would be able to sleep, not with two Unseen still driving him further into the middle of nowhere.

Zoe's hand still rested in his, and she gently stroked the back of his fingers with her thumb. He didn't know if she was even aware of what she was doing, but it was incredibly soothing.

He relaxed a little more and started thinking about Nana and Zoe. They were, by far, the oddest people he had ever met. They didn't seem to quite fit into normal society, or do the usual things expected of a Seen. Nana didn't even have her own Biocubicle and Zoe was... well... still physically so different from all the other students at clinic. And yet, every moment he had spent with them challenged his perceptions. Even the conversation on the train journey had left him with more questions than answers.

The sense of escaping the city as they left Prima on the high-speed Subterranean had initially been exhilarating, but the train journey itself had proven to be incredibly dull. Zoe had curled her legs under her and had fallen asleep immediately. Nana had advised him to do the same, before settling back and drifting into a heavy slumber.

However, her instruction to sleep had the opposite effect, and Silas was left gritty-eyed, unable to relax sufficiently even to doze. After four hours of frustrated wakefulness, it was time to change train in an Outerlands town that he had never heard of. Nana woke up suddenly, as if her own internal alarm clock had gone off. It had made Silas jump; he had just been on the brink of nodding off. Nana roused an irritable Zoe.

'Time to move now – don't forget the boxes.'

Although Nana had insisted they pack only a few personal essentials, she had subsequently laden them down with a huge rectangular wheeled case each. The one Silas pushed off the train steered fairly easily, but Zoe's crate seemed to have a mind of its own, and she accidentally banged into Silas' legs with it as she tried to push it up the slope.

'It would be rude to turn up empty-handed,' was Nana's only comment in response to Zoe's complaints, as she had marched them out of the Subterranean network, and across a deserted platform.

The Overground branch train was a relic from former times, and rattled its way at a snail's pace through the dark, forbidding night.

Zoe, at least, had stayed awake this time, though Nana was out cold again before the train had pulled out of the station.

'That's uncanny!' Silas grumbled. 'Being able to switch on and off like that. Is she really asleep?'

'Yeah, I think so,' Zoe giggled, as they both surveyed the inert form of her grandmother.

'So what's it like then, the Community? Have you been before?'

'It's extraordinary. I've been a few times, but that was before Mum took me to live on the ship. Nana goes at least twice a year. She's got loads of friends there. She takes them supplies, medicines and vitamins.'

'Is that what's in these massive cases?' Silas rubbed his bruised shin, then kicked one of the boxes absent-mindedly with his foot.

'I guess,' Zoe shrugged. 'She also gets stuff in return, though – herbs and real vegetables to cook with.'

'Mmm… stew!' He patted his stomach, unable to remember the exact flavours, but knowing they were good.

'Ha!' She laughed out loud, making Nana twitch in her sleep, then continued in a quieter voice, 'You'll be sick of stew by the end of your stay. You'll be craving protein bars and carboflakes!'

'Never!' Silas grinned.

They had sat for a while in companionable silence, isolated in a bubble of light lumbering through the endless dark.

'But what about the people?' Silas finally broke the silence with the topic that had been preying on his mind. 'I still don't understand why they would want to live so separately. I mean, no Biocubicles. Why don't they want to know if they're meeting their Health Targets?'

Zoe thought for a moment before answering hesitantly. 'I only know a little about it… so …'

'I can tell you,' Nana's voice cut in, startling them.

'Great,' Silas said eagerly. But then he had to watch impatiently as Nana slowly stood up, rubbed her lower back and rolled her shoulders, before settling again onto the lumpy seat.

Finally, she seemed ready to talk. 'Do you know much about the health issues of the last century?'

'Oh, yeah! What was it? Speed food… No, that wasn't it… fast food! And obesity, oh, and no exercise… history!' He made a face at Zoe and she smiled.

'Yes,' Nana nodded. 'That was part of a huge problem. It was as if the nation was dying out. Heart and lung disease, cancer from toxins in the food and drink. Then fertility rates dropped off the scale, and for those who could have a child, abnormalities in newborns were suddenly much more common. No one could work out why. GM crops? Radiation exposure from mobile communication devices? Air pollution? All these were gradually eliminated but with no discernible effect.'

Silas looked at Zoe, shrugged, and silently mouthed, 'GM?'

'Tell you later,' she whispered back.

Lost in her story, and oblivious to his confusion, Nana continued, 'There was widespread panic, but in all the turmoil, there was one voice that had strategy and purpose.' Her tone became like that of an excited sports announcer, but her eyes looked saddened by the memories. 'A bright new future, strength, life, cures for all… Viva! The political party that promised to work for the health of the nation.'

Nana dropped her voice back down to normal and continued with her tale. 'Viva brought in the Well-being Mandate. It was an attempt to improve the fitness of the population by positive reinforcement. Only people who fulfilled the Healthy Lifestyle Protocol were permitted to work, earn, and receive health care. You name it; it all became linked to how physically healthy you were. Everyone else effectively became excluded. Those who couldn't manage the Health Targets were suddenly unemployable and unworthy of aid.'

Nana paused and looked out of the train window at the darkened landscape rolling by. 'Fear will rule, if you let it. And *everyone* let it; fear of being on the outside, fear of being ill, fear of being physically imperfect and not meeting your targets. Fear of being dragged down by those around you if you tried to help them. The excluded ones became known as the Unseen.

Allowed out, but only at night, to limit any interaction with the healthy citizens, the Unseen were hidden, ashamed and more than anything else, feared.

'The Unseen were not the cause of the health problems in our nation, they were just a product, but they were blamed nonetheless. The dread among the Seen escalated so much that if someone saw an Unseen in daylight, they were immediately removed by Health Enforcers. The Unseen were required to wear coverings to conceal their physical shortcomings. Occasionally, groups of the Unseen would protest and riot, but these protests were brutally quashed. That's when the Citizen Safety Monitors were installed. Any Unseen interacting with a Seen, without a permit, would be arrested, and they would just disappear. There were a few of us, a brave minority of the Seen who tried to stand against the injustice. The Unseen were human beings who needed help; they were not the enemy. We did what we could, like the nutrition provision that Ellen and I were involved with.'

At the mention of his mother's name, Silas listened more intently. It was as if there were two different Ellen Corelles. The isolated and lonely woman who had raised him, and the brave and generous woman that Nana knew.

'Then Biocubicles were introduced and, in many ways, life got easier for the Unseen. If they had a stable "illness", they were permitted to work. But only at night, doing the invisible jobs, like cleaning or working in the nutrition factories.

'But the concern among some was that the cubicles would become another tool to control the nation. Ellen was one of the first to become uneasy with the way Biocubicles were going, but what could she do? She loved your father, and this was his life's work. She loved her sons and wouldn't leave you.'

'What do you mean about my mother being uneasy? Uneasy about what?' Silas was fascinated. He had never heard any disagreement between his parents.

'Ellen was the kindest woman I knew, and she loved people, Seen or Unseen. She saw beyond illness; she saw beyond the outside to the person inside. Do you understand what I mean by that?' Nana's piercing eyes were suddenly fixed on his face. He felt this was some kind of test, and he wasn't sure of the correct answer.

'Um... maybe?'

'It's fine,' she sounded a bit flat, and he felt he had let her down in some way. 'I won't overload you, Silas. Ellen was uneasy because Biocubicles reinforced the belief that worth was linked to health; that the only way to measure an individual's value was by their physical ability. What your father had effectively done was to produce a completely accurate health price tag for every person.'

Her tale seemed to be slowing down, yet Silas felt that so few of his questions had been satisfactorily answered. 'The Community, Nana, how did that come about?'

'Oh! Yes, that was some kind of a miracle!'

'A miracle?' he asked sceptically.

'A rumour started going round of a place in the north where "What was Unseen could be Seen". It was a tiny glimmer of hope for people who had almost given up on living. A group of my friends, both Seen and Unseen, set out to trek overground, across the Outerlands. They avoided the towns and factories for fear of being reported and taken back to the city. By then, the Health Authorities were keen that every citizen was classified as Seen or Unseen and were regularly monitored for a change in status. It wasn't against the law to refuse, but there was no access to housing or nutrition and health care unless you had a classification. To survive, you either were healthy enough to be a Seen, or you accepted your status as an Unseen.

'Looking back, it seems incredible that such a journey was even attempted, but they believed that they could make a life for themselves. It took them weeks, and they were half-dead when they stumbled on the area they now call the "Community".'

The ancient Overground train gave a sudden jolt and a squeal as it started to slow, and Nana gathered her bag on her lap, ready to stand up. Undeterred, Silas persevered with his interrogation.

'And was it what they thought – was it a place where they could all be Seen?' He had been riveted during the account. He had never spared the Unseen a second thought, had barely classed them as people at all, and yet they had fought to survive, and his own mother had helped them.

'It wasn't quite what they expected.' Nana's intense gaze fell on him again as the train came to a juddering halt. Silas felt unaccountably uncomfortable as Nana continued to stare keenly at him. 'But yes, Silas, all that was hidden became seen.'

Through the window of the train, Silas had caught a glimpse of two sinister shrouded Unseen. Despite all that Nana had told him, they still filled him with an overwhelming terror, and a shiver of apprehension ran down his spine.

Now, sitting in the back of the truck, unable to see because of the disgusting blindfold, all Silas could do was replay his conversation with Nana in his mind. Her explanation still wasn't enough to satisfy him. Question after question chased around his brain. He wanted to know more about his mother and her involvement with the Community. His questions, however, would have to wait as he still felt far too inhibited by the presence of the two Unseen.

Eventually Silas' many thoughts merged into his dreams, as neither the uncomfortable truck bench, nor the itchy blindfold, the fear of the Unseen, or even Zoe's soothing touch, could prevent Silas from drifting off to sleep.

Chapter 12

'Wake up, Si.' A hand was sliding his blindfold off. He straightened up and looked into Zoe's face. A night of travelling had not done her any favours; her hair stuck up at odd angles, and her features were puffy and blotchy.

'You look rough,' she said. 'What happened to your face?'

'You don't look so great yourself!' he retorted angrily, immediately on the defensive. He felt sick with tiredness and just wanted to be left alone to sleep.

'I mean, you've got a rash on your face, where the blindfold was,' Zoe explained brusquely, sounding irritated in turn by Silas' grumpiness. 'Are you allergic to wool?'

'Seriously?' He could feel raised bobbles under the skin around his eyes and over his cheeks. 'Well, isn't that perfect! What a rubbish end to a rubbish night. What am I doing here? What was I thinking?'

They glared at each other furiously.

'You didn't have to come. No one forced you,' she hissed back.

Nana poked her head into the truck. 'Stop fighting, you two. You're acting like children. Come and see this.'

Zoe climbed out, crossly muttering under her breath. Awkwardly clambering over the seats, Silas also emerged from the truck and straightened up. His face started to itch like a hundred tiny needles were pricking his skin, and he fought to suppress the overwhelming urge to scratch.

'Stupid… rubbish… pointless…' His grumblings were cut short as he was presented with the most incredible panorama.

They were standing on a cliff edge, and the first light of dawn was breaking through the dark grey of the night. Beams of sunlight raced across the black bowl at their feet, transforming it into a palette of greens, blues and browns. As the sun rose further, more detail was revealed, and Silas could make out the shape of the terrain before him. They were looking down into a massive basin.

The cliff edge he was standing on ran in an enormous curve, all the way round to the far distance. He stepped forward gingerly and peered over the edge. The drop was huge, way higher than anything he had climbed, but from this angle it was difficult to make an accurate guess. It must be well over 100 metres; the trees at the foot of the cliff seemed puny by comparison.

He could see the thin line of a river cutting almost directly through the centre, leading the eye into the distance where it became swallowed up by a dense, dark green forest.

They stood in silence, admiring the wonder that was displayed before them. A flock of birds rose up from the canopy as if to greet the new dawn, and across the stillness Silas could just make out their raucous calls.

'Isn't it incredible? It's a natural crater, about 15 kilometres across.' Zoe moved to stand next to him. She seemed to have forgotten their squabble, and her voice was full of excitement. His own mood had lifted now as he absorbed the sights before him, and he felt ashamed for his grumpiness.

'Look, I'm sorry for what I said in the truck. It's not your fault. I was being rude. It's because I am so sleep-deprived. But this is amazing. Is this it, then? Is this the Community?' Silas asked.

'It's OK,' Zoe smiled at him, 'I feel pretty awful too. A shower and somewhere to sleep that is flat and still is all I care about now. But even that can't happen quite yet. We've got to go on foot from here. The main dwellings are all in the forest.'

'What?' Silas looked aghast. 'That's got to be at least a couple of hours' trek!'

'Oh dear. What happened to your face?' Nana had turned away from her silent contemplation to see what they were talking about. Silas had been aware of the skin around his eyes beginning to feel incredibly tight, and the itchiness was intense.

'He's allergic to wool, I think, Nana.'

'Hmm, I think I may have just the thing to help you.' She opened her bag and handed a plastic tub to Zoe. 'Put this all around his eyes, where the rash is; nice and thick, no need to scrimp, I've been told there's lots more in the trunks.' She pointed at the heavy supply boxes. 'I've just got to have a quick chat with Maxie and Val before they go.'

Zoe opened the jar and they looked at the lumpy green paste inside, then tentatively she held it to her nose.

'Disgusting. Oh no! Smell it. It stinks like... ugh, armpits and old trainers!' Zoe shoved the pot under Silas' nose, and he got a full whiff of the dreadful concoction.

'This had better help,' he muttered, as she dabbed the muck onto his face. 'Who are Maxie and Val, anyway?'

'The drivers, you idiot... the ones who blindfolded you.'

Somehow the innocuous names did not correlate with the sinister Unseen who had met them at the train station last night.

'Those Unseen are called Maxie and Val?'

'Didn't you pay any attention to what Nana has been saying all night? The Unseen are just people, and mostly really nice people. Maxie and Val live near the station and help drive visitors to the Community. Without them, the walk would have been loads longer. You should be grateful. Now stay still.'

From what he could tell, the slime seemed to have done the trick, and the skin on his face no longer felt so inflamed. At Nana's instruction, they dragged the extra supplies into a cluster of bushes.

'Will they be safe?' Silas asked.

'They'll be fine, Silas,' Nana said. 'Some of my friends will rig up a pulley and lower them down. It'll save carrying them.

Right, this way!' She set off at a brisk walk, head high, showing not the tiniest sign of fatigue.

'Is she actually a machine?' Silas whispered into Zoe's ear. 'All the signs are there, the sleep trick, the robot walk. It would explain a lot.'

Zoe snorted with laughter, then pushed him away. 'Wow! Not too close. Your face smells really bad.'

'I've got used to it now, hmmm, cheesy sweat... smells like... Clinic. Ah, Coach Regan, how I miss your sweetly abusive tones,' he joked.

Nana led them off the cliff top and down a perilously narrow path. Even with his climbing expertise, Silas found the drop intimidating; the cliff was sheer and smooth.

'Are you OK?' he asked. Zoe had slowed and with her back against the cliff, was sidestepping along the trail, her eyes fixed on a point in the far distance.

'Fine... I think. How could I have forgotten about this bit? I swear the path is narrower than last time. And I really hate heights.'

'Can I help?'

'No! Yes! Stop talking to me and let me concentrate.' Her mouth settled into the recognisable line of stubborn resolve, and Silas grinned silently to himself as he leisurely followed her.

Above the crunching of their feet on the loose stones, he could just make out a faint hissing noise. As they moved steadily around an outcrop on the cliff face, the sound jumped up in volume.

'What's that noise? Is that water?'

'Yes, it's a waterfall,' Zoe said, more confident now as the path widened. 'It forms the river you saw from the crater edge. The path leads us right past it. It's a torrent after the rains have come, but even in the dry season it's impressive.'

By the time they reached the falls, the noise was deafeningly loud. An astonishing cascade of water roared past them. Looking up, Silas could see that the waterfall was spilling from a cave halfway up the crater wall, like a giant gaping mouth on the flat rock surface.

He stood, mesmerised by the continuous thundering of water, terrified and exhilarated. The haze of fine spray created by the pounding falls drifted up in misty clouds, occasionally catching the light to generate a cluster of miniature rainbows.

Silas turned to make a comment to Zoe about it, but she had already moved further down to a flattened rocky ledge overlooking the waterfall. She was cautiously peering over the edge at the sheer drop to the rocks below.

Suddenly a movement caught Silas' eye. A figure was stealthily moving up the path towards where she was standing. It was a man, tall and thin and wearing grey baggy clothes.

There was something jarring about the way he moved, something unnatural. That's it! Silas realised. His body was all out of proportion. His head was too big on his thin shoulders, and his limbs were incredibly long and spindly; well, three of them were. One of his arms was a tiny little stump that swung in double time compared to the rest of his body.

Zoe was still looking over the drop, oblivious to the figure approaching her. Silas tried to cry out a warning as the man crept nearer and nearer to her, but the roar of the waterfall drowned out his voice. With a couple more steps, the man was directly behind her, towering over her. He raised his good arm with his palm facing out and suddenly pushed forward.

'Zoe!'

The scream felt like it was tearing Silas' throat in half, but even as he started to yell he realised that the man had quickly grabbed the back of Zoe's shirt to prevent her from falling. Silas started running headlong down the steep path to help her. Careless of his own safety, his only concern was for her. He saw her swing round and punch her assailant hard in his stomach and then, astoundingly, she started laughing.

By the time Silas arrived, they were hugging. Zoe's head didn't even reach the gangly giant's ribcage, and his peculiarly elongated fingers were stroking and patting her hair.

'What was that? You idiot! You could have killed her,' Silas was furious, and the rush of blood to his face had made his skin start to itch and tingle again. Squaring up to the newcomer, he realised that despite his abnormal height, they were probably the same age.

'Calm down, Si, I'm fine!' Zoe intervened, stepping between Silas and the newcomer.

'Oh fairest of maidens, who is this bizarrely masked hero that springs to your defence?' the stranger asked Zoe. His voice was deep and resonant, and he accompanied every word with a dramatic pantomime of movement.

Zoe started laughing again. 'It's not a mask; it's a medicine because he's allergic... actually, Si, it does look like you are wearing a mask...' Then her sentence collapsed into an uncontrollable fit of the giggles. Silas scowled at them both.

'I'm Silas,' he said reluctantly when he realised Zoe wasn't able to introduce him for laughing. 'I'm Zoe's friend from clinic. What were you thinking to pull a stunt like that?'

'I am Jono, sweet Zoe's *oldest* and *dearest* companion.' He emphasised the words, as if reinforcing his claim on her friendship, and simultaneously discounting Silas'. 'Parted by a cruel world that forbids us to truly express our love, and yet, "Come what sorrow can, It cannot countervail the exchange of joy, That one short minute gives me in her sight".' Jono drew the back of his hand across his forehead in a play-act of despair.

'You're a clown and a fool, and it's so good to see you again! What *have* you been reading?'

Zoe was still wiping tears of mirth from her cheeks as Jono dramatically fell to his knees before her, bringing them eye to eye. He winked and whispered loudly, '*The Complete Works of William Shakespeare*. I'm borrowing it from Thomas.' Then he added in his over-the-top acting voice, '"Love looks not with the eyes but with the mind. And therefore is winged Cupid painted blind."' He paused again and then ran his grotesque fingers down the side of her face. 'I see you have grown more beautiful during our enforced severance, but you have branded me a fool and therefore I shall take the fool's way out.'

With another theatrical movement he leapt to his feet, staggered to the edge of the precipice and with a final exaggerated bow, flung himself headfirst over the edge.

'No!' This time it was Zoe crying out in alarm. They dashed to the edge in time to see Jono's head resurface from the deep plunge pool. He blew them a kiss, and then, floating on his back, he let the river carry him around a corner and out of sight.

'Good riddance!' Silas said bitterly. 'Who was that freak? He looked like a spider with half its legs pulled off.'

'You can be very cruel sometimes, Si, did you know that? You have got to stop judging people on what they look like.'

The heat in Zoe's words stung, and Silas recoiled from her. He couldn't believe it. She was angry with him? He wasn't the one who had nearly pushed her off a cliff. He had been the one trying to save her. She was so stuck up and self-righteous sometimes. Ugh! She got on his nerves. And as for that skinny monster Jono, all flailing limbs and prancing about, what did Zoe find so hilarious about him?

They walked in frosty silence until they reached the crater floor where Nana was waiting for them.

'Where's Jono? He said he had a surprise for you.'

Zoe's laugh was a bit forced. 'He certainly surprised us!'

'Idiot,' Silas muttered under his breath.

Zoe shot him another scowl, then turned back to Nana. 'It's so great to see him again. He's such a lot of fun,' adding, so only Silas could hear it, 'unlike some people I could mention.'

'Indeed! You just remember last time, young lady. He'll lead you into all kinds of mischief, if you let him.'

Silas pricked his ears up, eager to hear something negative about Zoe's friend. 'What mischief?' he asked. 'What happened last time?'

'None of your business,' Zoe snapped at him. Then, turning her back, she linked arms with Nana and set off along a lush grassy track, following the broad river towards the dense forest ahead.

I've made a huge mistake, Silas thought for the hundredth time as he angrily plodded along behind them. I shouldn't have come here.

Chapter 13

The air was thick and oppressive; sweat was pouring off him but doing little to cool him down. He could have done with a splash in the river, but the path had veered away as they left the grassland.

'We're here at last!' Zoe groaned with relief, dropping her small bag onto the leaf-strewn ground.

'Where?' Silas looked up but could see nothing but dark, unending forest.

'The Community!' She pointed and now, as Silas looked around him, he could make out the shapes of two rough-hewn log huts, camouflaged among the trees.

'Is this it?' Silas couldn't help sounding disappointed. He was expecting something much bigger and more organised. This was pathetic. After all the secrecy and mystery and the blindfolds, all they were protecting were a couple of rundown shacks in a forest.

Zoe rolled her eyes, but before she could answer, they were interrupted by a voice calling from inside one of the huts.

'Is that you, Eva?' The voice was deep and loud, and it reminded Silas of Coach Evans, the biology coach, and immediately made him feel nervous.

But when the owner of the voice stepped out from the hut, Silas could hardly believe his eyes. The man, if that's what it was, could only have been a metre tall. The most lined and wrinkled face Silas had ever seen topped a miniature body with little matching childlike arms and legs: a toddler-sized old man. Silas nearly laughed out loud at the trundling way the old man moved, more of a waddle really, with an exaggerated side-to-side sway.

'It *is* you!' The shrivelled creature spoke in his overly deep voice, making Silas want to laugh again. 'I see you, Eva. And you, Zoe, welcome back. It's been too long since you last came here. You are no longer a child, hey?' He paused and looked carefully at Silas, 'And, I see you, stranger. Be at ease; you are welcome here.'

'Bubba Gee! I see you,' Zoe cried, running up to give the diminutive figure a hug. He looked like an ugly dolly, but that didn't stop her planting a huge kiss on the side of his prune-like face.

Standing beside Silas, Nana let out a little giggle and said, 'I see you, Bubba Gee. Have you missed me?'

Silas realised with horror that she was acting coy and a faint blush had stained her cheeks.

'Zoe,' Nana said without turning her gaze from Bubba Gee, 'would you take Silas up to the guest hut so you kids can get cleaned up? I'm just going to catch up with all the news.'

'Whatever, Nana,' Zoe laughed and bent to retrieve her bag. 'You take as long as you need. We'll see you later!' Zoe led Silas further into the forest. He looked back at Nana, holding hands with Bubba Gee as she ducked her head to enter his hut.

'Even I admit that's a bit gross,' Zoe said, as she weaved her way through the trees. 'Old people flirting.' She wrinkled her nose up. 'Eww!'

That wasn't the thing that I found gross, Silas thought, remembering the squished-up face Zoe had just kissed, but he let the matter slide. He could do without another telling-off.

They saw no one else as they made their way through the close-set trees. Occasionally Silas identified a hut or cabin, nestling camouflaged behind a trunk. Once Zoe stopped and pointed upwards. 'That's Jono's place.'

High above their heads, set in the boughs of a huge cedar, was a palatial tree house, strong and secure, with a wooden tiled roof. It even had a balcony.

He thought back to his sanctuary overlooking the city, and how pathetic it was by comparison. Swallowing down his jealousy, he looked at the thick rough trunk.

'There are no easy branches. How does he climb up there?' he asked.

'It's quite something to watch so I won't spoil the surprise. But he has a rope ladder for visitors, if you want to see it. I don't like it up there; he hasn't got a rail on the balcony and it's such a long drop.' Zoe shuddered and Silas found himself feeling pleased that there was something about Jono that she didn't like.

'So where is everyone?' he asked. 'From what Nana said, I imagined there would be a few more people around.'

'Working,' came the simple reply.

Silas opened his arms and slowly spun around. 'Working where? We are in the middle of nowhere!'

'There's all sorts of stuff to do here. We'll be allocated our share later on; fishing, hunting, gathering fruit, gardening, washing, preparing food…'

She reached the door of a cabin, partially concealed by a bushy conifer tree, and opening it, stepped inside. Her continuing list of jobs was promptly swallowed up, and all he could hear was an indecipherable drone. Silas lingered outside for a little longer. Fishing and hunting, they sounded great… All part of his season-break adventure. But washing? And making food? Those were jobs for the Unseen. There was no way he would be washing anyone else's sweaty underpants. No thank you!

'You'll be in here. Nana and I will share the little room,' Zoe explained as she disappeared through one of the two doors in the back wall. He looked around with a heavy heart at the dingy space that was to be his home for the next few weeks. Words like 'basic' and 'unhygienic' were some of the politer ones to circle around his mind.

Half of the room was taken up with a nutrition area, with a wooden table and chairs. They were set next to a cast-iron stove, and sink. A haphazard arrangement of tin pots and utensils were piled on a shelf that ran the length of the wall. A large black bug scuttled out of one of the pots and, quick as a flash, slipped behind the stove. Silas shuddered with disgust.

The remaining half of the room was to be his bedroom. Hanging from the ceiling was a thick brown curtain that could be pulled the length of the room to provide an illusion of privacy. Pushed up against the wall was a mattress on a low bed frame. Silas dumped his bag on the nightstand next to it. I'll never get a wink of sleep on this, he thought.

He wandered over to the other door and opened it to reveal a miniature washroom. A cracked screen separated a feeble single-headed shower from a toilet. Something didn't smell right, and lifting the lid of the toilet reinforced the unpleasant odour of rotten grass and sulphur. There was no flush, and he stared at it, nonplussed. How does this work? he wondered. I am going to look such an idiot if I have to ask how the stupid toilet works! He dropped the lid back into place to minimise the smell and went back to flop heavily onto his bed. All manner of clunks and rattles were coming from Zoe's room, but she failed to reappear. Silas lay back on the lumpy mattress.

He snapped awake, heart pounding. It was dark. Not the pitch black of night when, on opening your eyes, you fear you have been struck blind, but the heavy grey of dusk where colours are non-existent yet outlines are still discernible. After a moment of disorientation, Silas recalled where he was. The back end of nowhere, he thought bitterly.

It had been a noise, he remembered; a noise had woken him. He lay still, trying to breathe shallowly and slow his thudding heart, straining to hear the sound again. He felt vulnerable and alone. Who knew what creatures roamed through the forests? Wolves? Bears? Was it that freak Jono, trying to mess with his head?

There it was again... a drawn-out scrape by the front door. OK, maybe it's not an animal; there is no growling or padding noise, he rationalised. It's got to be Jono. That idiot doesn't know when to quit. I'll give him a fright instead, he thought, smiling grimly.

Moving as quietly as possible, he stood up and tried to inch his way silently to the front door. He failed completely, every single movement produced a corresponding groan, creak or rasp from the uneven wooden flooring. Giving up on his attempt at stealth and marching boldly to the front door, he swung it wide open to find no one there.

Screeck… The branches from the fir tree had started to sway in the gentle evening breeze, causing one sturdy bough to scratch along the outside of the cabin. Shaking his head, he retreated back inside the cabin and closed the door. Ha! So now I can add 'scared of trees' to my list of fears! First thing in the morning, I'm breaking that off… in fact, maybe I can get an axe and chop the whole thing down. As he mulled over the correct level of punishment for the culpable conifer, a hand tapped him on the shoulder. He screamed and whirled around to face his assailant.

'Woah, steady! It's only me.' Zoe's round face stared up at him through the gloom.

'You crept up on me!'

'Not intentionally. Nana suggested I wait for you to wake up and then take you to the initiation,' she explained with a placating tone.

'Initiation?' He mentally scrolled through the memories of past conversations with Zoe. 'No one said anything about an initiation. Who's being initiated, and into what?'

The expression on her face said it all, and Silas backed away.

'Me?' He collided with the wall, causing the pots on the shelf above his head to rattle alarmingly.

'No need to get worked up. It's fine, but it is necessary. It will help you adjust to being with the Community. Everyone goes through it.' Using her most soothing voice, Zoe reminded him of the house computer at bedtime, but it failed to help him relax.

'I don't like the sound of this! What's going to happen?'

Zoe paused, apparently unsure where to start. 'It's hard to explain. Do you remember the night of the trials?'

'Yes, it was only two days ago ...' He was suddenly struck with how much had changed in his life over such a short time. 'Only two days,' he slowly repeated.

'OK,' Zoe continued, 'after dinner we listened to music.'

'Yeah...' Suddenly grateful for the darkness surrounding them, Silas felt a blush creep up his neck. He vividly remembered how wonderful Zoe had seemed that night.

'When you saw what you saw ...' She hesitated, trying to find the right words before bluntly adding, 'It was not a hallucination.'

'What? I saw some weird stuff that night.' He could clearly recollect his own hideous reflection in his bathroom mirror. 'It wasn't real, what I saw? It couldn't be... there were things inside my face... Ugh!' He felt a flutter of panic at the memory.

'Like I said, it's hard to explain without you going through with the initiation, but it will become clear. Please trust me.' She started ushering him to the door.

'What have I let myself in for by coming here?' Silas asked desperately. 'Did you do it – the initiation – on your first time here?'

'Yes. Like I said before, everyone does it. It's OK, honest!' though her voice betrayed a rapidly concealed nervousness.

'If you went through it, I guess I can too,' he said, resignedly, 'but can I get a drink first? I am so thirsty.' He could feel his tongue clacking around in his dry mouth.

'Better not yet, but there will be plenty to drink at the ceremony. Come on, everyone will be waiting.'

Eh? From where did the words 'ceremony' and 'everyone' spring? Silas considered the possibility that he was still asleep. This was the kind of circular, nonsensical conversation one had in a dream. He shuffled forward in the dark and stubbed his little toe. Not asleep then...

'Ouch! Do we have any form of light?' he barked crossly.

'That's what I'm doing. Stand still.' Zoe was clicking with something at the table, and then a warm glow spread out from her hands. 'Here you go.' She handed him a round sunstorer. 'There are no spares of these, so it's up to us to remember to put them out to recharge tomorrow.'

'Sure.' He looked down at the orb of light cradled in his hands. It fitted comfortably in his palm. He manipulated the blocking cover to reduce the amount shining up into his eyes and to focus the beam on where his feet were going to tread.

He hadn't played with one of these for years. When he and Marc were small, they would hide in the windowless store cupboard. They would switch the lights off and try to scare each other by using sunstorers to make shadows on the wall creating Unseen monsters from the spare bedding. But that was all just childish bravado; they would never have had the courage to play with the sunstorers outside, in the dark of night, where the real Unseen were.

He caught sight of Zoe's face in the glow from her light and realised that she had washed and brushed up. Then he remembered his face, still covered by the gunk Nana had given him, and he tentatively sniffed his shirt and got a whiff of his own sweaty stench.

Zoe noticed. 'Let's get your initiation over with, then you'll have loads of time to sort yourself out.'

Chapter 14

'I'm not doing it!' He grabbed Zoe's hand to hold her back and slid the blockers closed on the sunstorers, plunging them into darkness once again.

They had stopped just inside the cover of the tree line. A few more paces would have brought them out onto a clear area of shore, scattered with scrubby bushes and clumps of long grass, and beyond that stretched an expanse of black water. With the cool of the night came a gentle breeze that stirred the surface of the lake, creating a million dancing ripples. Each movement reflected and multiplied the light from a hundred sunstorers.

The scene would have been magical, had it not been that the light was emanating from the hands of a huge crowd gathered on the shore. And such a menagerie of the monstrous and misshapen – Silas could not believe what he was seeing. The skeletally thin ranging to the incredibly fat, bow-legged, long-armed, hunchbacked, barrel-chested, men and women... and some of indeterminable gender, and even indeterminable species... one man had a normal-looking body, but the whole of his face was covered with a thick growth of hair.

Silas could see quite a few people who probably would have been classified as Seen had they been in the city, but they were by far outnumbered by the many, many Unseen.

All of them stood in a loose circle, whispering and muttering to each other. A palpable undercurrent of excitement and anticipation filled the air.

At the far side of the ring, nearest the lake, still holding hands, were Nana and Bubba Gee. Nana kept stooping down to catch remarks from Bubba Gee, then smiling and whispering back.

Near them, head and shoulders above the rest of the crowd, was the unmistakable figure of Jono. The light from his sunstorer shone up to create a death's head mask of his oversized skull. The skull face was scanning from side to side, watching, looking out. A shudder of dread ran up Silas' spine.

In the centre of the crowd was a tree stump, carved out to make a rough throne, with a cluster of ten sunstorers surrounding it. That was reserved for him, he realised. His initiation was to sit in the middle of all those Unseen and do what, exactly? He had trusted Zoe and Nana, and they had led him to this nightmare.

He was frozen to the spot; all of his fears had coalesced to paralyse him. So many of *them*… and so much worse than his imagination had ever been able to produce!

'Si, you need to do this!' Zoe turned to face him.

'No!' He looked across at the crowd again, his eyes wide with fear.

'Please!' she entreated, clumsily reaching for his other hand in the dark to reinforce her plea. In doing so, she accidentally knocked the closed sphere out of his hand, and it landed with a dull clatter. As it rolled out of reach, the blockers popped open, and a shaft of light, like a searchlight beam, played across the surrounding trees before coming to rest on them.

'There he is!' Jono sent up a cry. 'Our waiting is at an end!'

With a few effortless bounds, he was at their side.

'What took you so long, Zoe?' Jono bent down to retrieve the fallen sunstorer, and as he straightened up he stared at them both. The light in Jono's hands was directed fully in Silas' face, and he squinted in its blinding glare. Jono seemed to only need a moment to take in the scene before him, and then, much to Silas' annoyance, Jono tutted.

'"Of all the wonders that I yet have heard, It seems to me most strange that men should fear …"' he solemnly declared.

That served to galvanise Silas more than Zoe's gentle persuasion.

'I don't know what that is supposed to mean, but I am not frightened!' he growled, his anger momentarily eclipsing his fear. There was no way he was going to let this crazy Unseen ridicule him.

He marched to the makeshift throne, the crowds parting neatly to let him through, and sat down.

The waiting throng drew closer to him, all eager to get a good look at the new arrival. The minuscule burst of courage that Jono's quote had produced suddenly shrivelled back down to nothing. He could actually feel the beginnings of a scream start to build, deep in his chest. Hold it together, he told himself. Zoe did this, so can you!

'Who brings this initiate among us?' Bubba Gee's deep voice carried across the waiting horde, as he toddled up to stand on one side of the chair. Even though he was sitting down, Silas still seemed to tower over him. Ridiculous! he thought, which made him feel braver inside. The whole set-up is ridiculous! He looked around at the physical wrecks encircling him. I could be Gold Standard among this batch of outcasts. I'd be their Flawless Leader!

'I bring the initiate,' Nana came to stand on his other side. 'Silas Corelle …' at the mention of his full name, the volume of excited murmurs among the watching crowd rose like a wave. And he could make out his mother's name, 'Ellen' among the animated hubbub.

Surprised, Silas looked at Nana.

'Your mother helped lots of these people while they were still Unseen. Some of them owe their lives to her.' Nana smiled encouragingly at him as she waited for the noise to subside. 'Silas Corelle… drink and fully see, even as you are fully seen.'

Zoe stepped up, carefully carrying up a plain metal bowl full of liquid, and Nana dipped a cup into it. She passed it to Silas. 'Drink,' she nodded encouragingly. Silas looked apprehensively at the clear fluid in the cup and took an experimental sip.

'It's only water!' He sounded relieved and thirstily drank the contents, then held out the cup for more. Nana refilled it and again he swallowed it down. Oh, that felt so much better, but what a weird place if the height of entertainment is watching someone else drink water, he thought, relaxing a little.

Thirst quenched, he gave the cup to Nana and in return, she handed him a rather ornately gilded vanity mirror. He looked quizzically at her.

'Watch and wait, Si. Remember, you are not alone, we stand with you.'

He looked at his reflection. What a mess! Crusty green blobs were stuck haphazardly across his forehead and the bridge of his nose – the rash from earlier appeared to have subsided, though. His hair! He nearly attempted to flatten it before he remembered the hundred pairs of eyes watching his every movement. He looked up at them all. I wonder how long I have to sit here. I wonder how long they will stand there, watching me sit here.

After a few moments he decided the crowd were definitely winning the waiting game. He was beginning to feel excessively fidgety. Maybe he could try to pick some of that muck off of his face. Raising the mirror, he peered once again at his reflection.

Individually, the sunstorers didn't provide the brightest of light, but the cluster around him were doing a good enough job... so why was there shade across his face?

With a lurch in the pit of his stomach, he understood. The darkness wasn't coming from the outside; it seemed to be coming from the inside. Shadows were accumulating and spilling out from his rapidly darkening eye sockets. Unable to look away, he felt he was being sucked into his own dreadful nightmare. He was deformed and broken. He was becoming an Unseen!

The mirror suddenly weighed a ton; his arms were trembling with the effort of holding it. Then there were other hands, encircling his own.

'Look at me!' a voice commanded. With a huge amount of effort, he dragged his eyes away from his hideous image and looked up.

'Zoe.' He whispered her name with what felt like his very last breath. She crouched before him, radiant and glowing in the light of the sunstorers. The same magnetic draw that he had experienced the other evening returned in full force. If he could just stay looking at her, everything would be all right. His chest relaxed, and he drew a ragged breath in.

'What's happening? My eyes, my face... Zoe...'

'What you have drunk... we call it Soulsight. It enables you to see what is unseen; to see what is normally hidden. Your body is just a shell, an outer casing. It is what is inside, the soul, the real part of you, that is what you are seeing now.'

'How do I stop the darkness? The shadows, I'm hideous... do you see it? I don't want this! Zoe! Help me!' He tore his eyes away from her to stare in horror at his twisted reflection.

'I can help you.' Her voice was low and soothing. 'When I saw myself, for real, for the first time, it was similar to this. Silas, I am going to ask you something, but when you answer you are going to have to be honest with me, totally honest.'

'OK, I'll try.' Leaning closer, Zoe lowered the mirror, and with her free hand lifted his chin so that he looked up into her face again. Immediately, he felt calmer.

'There are things that gnaw away at you, Si. They wake you up in the night and they keep you awake. What are they?'

Easy! He knew exactly what she was talking about because when he was looking at Zoe, he felt them retreat and fade away.

'You want me to list them?' It was a genuine question asked with sincerity. His world had shrunk down to the two of them, forever, in this moment. The crowd surrounding them, watching and listening, had faded to insignificance.

'Yes.' She was steadily holding his gaze, and he felt the floodgates in his mind unlock. He wanted to tell her everything.

109

'Fear! Zoe, I am scared… all the time. I'm frightened of the Unseen, of becoming an Unseen, I'm scared of failing at clinic and what my dad would say. I'm even scared of the dark!' he paused to draw breath. 'I'm jealous. It burns me up sometimes – Marc has everything, always getting the best and being the best. It drives me mad.' He knew there was more, but he was reeling from the things he had already said, recognising the absolute truth in them and rapidly trying to process his own outburst.

'Look around you,' Zoe said softly.

'I don't want to, I just want to look at you!' Now he had started being honest he was finding it difficult to stop. 'Is this stuff a truth drug too?' he asked, suddenly aware of his openness.

She chuckled. 'No, Si, you see me, and you can trust me. I am trustworthy.' There was no gloating in the way she spoke; she was just stating a fact. 'You'll get used to it, and I won't hold anything you say against you!' she gently teased. 'Now look around you.'

He did as he was told. This is a different crowd! he thought. Someone has swapped them – or moved me! He took a closer look, feeling confused. No, it's the same crowd, the same misshapen, haphazard bunch of humanity… But now he could understand what Zoe meant by the insubstantial, shell-like nature of the body; such a fragile casing concealing such treasure. Nana and Bubba Gee were smiling at him. He could not only feel the love they had for him, he could see it like waves of visible warmth billowing over him.

The Community, which had seemed so intimidating at first, was now brimming over with care and acceptance. They *like* me… no, more than that… they *love* me! The realisation was so sudden, and so shocking, that he felt like he had been hit in the chest and had all the breath knocked out of him. His face was wet, and he raised his hand to his cheeks.

'I'm crying!' he said in surprise, but even as he said it, he knew that it no longer mattered.

'Look in the mirror again,' Zoe urged, helping to lift it up. With a feeling of utter peace and release, Silas could see that the deep green of his eyes had begun to replace the flickering shadows.

'It will take time,' she said, and taking hold of his hand, she pulled him to his feet. Then she lifted her other hand to her eyes, briefly touched them and then extended the same hand to lightly brush against his eyes, 'I see you, Silas.'

'And I see you, Zoe,' he responded, copying her gesture. Still holding tightly to his hand she led him to Nana, who embraced him with tears in her eyes.

'I see you, dear, dear boy,' she whispered in his ear, lightly touching his face.

'I see you, Nana.'

The Community had formed a long queue stretching away from the lake and back into the forest. One by one, Zoe led him down the line. He looked intently into each person's face, repeating the greeting and the accompanying eye-to-eye hand sign. From some he got an overwhelming emotion or mood.

One emaciated old lady positively exuded something that he could only describe as joy. Silas found himself laughing till his stomach hurt. Then, picking up her skinny little body, he twirled her round and round while she giggled furiously. Some faces had subtle hints of darkness in them; traces of anger and bitterness were commonly visible; but then again, he reasoned, not everyone could be as beautiful as Zoe, and he found his eyes drawn to her, totally distracting him from the row of people before him. Zoe shook her head in mock despair and continued to lead him further down the line.

The last one, standing like a sentinel by the doorway to the guest hut, was Jono. Gone was the joking and play-acting. The clownish behaviour had been replaced by an unsmiling seriousness that Silas found intimidating. They stood wordlessly observing one another until Silas broke the silence.

'You don't trust me!' He could see the suspicion like it had been tattooed on that oversized forehead.

'I am, by nature, wary of outsiders,' Jono acquiesced, with no hint of an apology in his voice. 'What else can you see?'

Silas stared intently, trying to make sense of it. Jono was a swirling mass of complex, often contradictory characteristics, and Silas hardly knew where to start.

'Um… loyalty defines you… towards those who have earned your trust, especially for those you love.'

At the mention of love, Jono's eyes flickered automatically to look at Zoe. If Silas hadn't been looking directly at him, he would have missed the telling glance.

'*Especially* for those I love,' Jono repeated in a threatening tone.

That couldn't be clearer, Silas thought, wondering to what extreme acts such deep loyalty could push someone, particularly if they were as unstable as Jono. But he was so buoyed up by the events of the evening, he chose to ignore the undercurrents of aggression.

'Safe to say, I see you, Jono.' Silas did the now familiar eye-to-eye hand gesture, stretching his arm to full length to even get near Jono's face.

'And I see you, Silas Corelle, do not doubt it!'

Turning away sharply, Jono stalked off into the night. Silas watched him disappear and decided his best approach to Jono was avoidance; it was a technique that Silas had perfected during his long years at clinic, and there was no reason why it wouldn't work just as well here.

Chapter 15

'It's a shame the cabin doesn't have a soul,' he declared to Zoe as he walked into the bare wooden shack. 'Maybe, underneath, it's a luxury mansion with its own workout suite and swimming pool.'

'Maybe,' Zoe laughed. 'You did great tonight, Si. How do you feel?' She placed each sunstorer into its own clear cage, suspending one from a hook in the ceiling of the cabin, and passing the other one to Silas. The light spilled over them, and again Silas was bowled over by Zoe's brilliance. She was incredible, even in comparison to the others in the Community. She outshone them all; it made it difficult for him to think clearly when she was near.

'I feel like I am flying!' he eventually stuttered. 'It's utterly amazing.'

She smiled broadly at him. 'You already look loads different. At last I get to see the real Silas Corelle.' Zoe gave a light-hearted laugh, and Silas felt his heart constrict almost painfully. He could not remember having ever experienced such open acceptance from anyone. She wasn't judging him on his failings; or trying to change him into something else. He could see that she simply loved him for who he was.

'I've been so blind, Zoe,' he confessed, still unwilling to look away from her. 'All that time at Vitality, I avoided you ...' At last the shame of how he had behaved forced him to lower his eyes. He felt utterly unworthy of her. 'I was no better than Taylor or any of the others.'

'Hey!' Zoe reprimanded. 'I see you, Silas,' she reminded him, tilting her head to catch his eye once again. 'I remember that even without Soulsight you were the only one in the whole clinic to speak to me like another human being. You helped me on my first day… and I know you used to follow me to check I got home safely. Nana told me.' He would have corrected her misinterpretation, but she carried on. 'I endured clinic, but only because I knew my worth wasn't wrapped up in my physical appearance, and I think you knew that too; maybe without ever knowing you knew it.'

Silas laughed. 'OK! You've lost me. I don't know what I used to think, Zoe. But I can tell you this now. You are quite incredible,' he said sincerely. He could have stayed there all night just admiring her, but all of a sudden Zoe yawned and sat on the edge of Silas' bed.

'Silas, we can talk some more, but first you need to do me one favour.'

'Yes, anything!'

'Have a shower,' she grinned, impishly. 'You still need to take care of the outside!'

'Yes, Coach! Your wish is my command,' he said, once more aware of the rank smell emanating from his clothing.

'Oh, and Si, if you are wondering about the toilet, there is no water in it. Everything drops through to a composter …'

'I knew that!' he lied unconvincingly, causing Zoe to smile.

'You get a shadow flare when you tell lies,' she chuckled sleepily.

'No way!' He wiped his eyes with his hands in a futile attempt to rub away the telltale stains.

'It's the same for everyone. You'll find that the Community can be an uncomfortably honest place sometimes.' She pointed to a pile of clean clothes. 'Go and wash,' she instructed. 'I'll wait here for you.'

A scratchy bar of soap was lodged in the corner of the shower, and he scrubbed his face and hair, delighting in the sensation of clean skin. Watching the dirty water spin down the drain was satisfying, but it was nothing compared to the sensation of being clean *inside* that Soulsight had produced.

He felt transformed by the evening; for as long as he could remember there had been a knot of anxiety and fear growing inside like a cancer. He had worked to suppress it, but it had been his constant companion, weighing him down. Now he felt an inner calm and stillness like never before, as if a bubble of peace had expanded in his chest and dispersed the chokehold of terror.

But now, fatigue was creeping up on him. Trying to resist it was futile, and he opened his mouth wide in a lengthy yawn. He didn't want to be tired; there was too much to talk about, and he was reluctant to waste a precious moment of his new-found visual abilities with his eyes shut, asleep.

Hurriedly drying himself, he dressed in the plain linen drawstring trousers and baggy shirt that Zoe had given him and burst into the main room of the hut with the first of his long list of questions.

'How does it…?' His query petered out into silence as he surveyed the situation before him. 'I guess the Q and A session will have to wait,' he muttered.

Zoe had fallen asleep sitting on his mattress, leaning forward onto the low nightstand. Her arms had formed a pillow for her head, and her hair had fallen like a curtain across her face. A strand was gently stirring with each breath she took.

Although he desperately wanted her to wake up, he found himself unwilling to be the one to break into her rest. Stepping as carefully as possible across the creaking floorboards, he stood over her and gently moved the hair off her face. He understood how Jono could have such fiercely protective love for her. Goodness flowed from her – pure wonderful and completely irresistible.

His heart wanted him to stand there all night watching over her, guarding her, but his weary body had other ideas, and as his knees began to buckle with exhaustion, he considered the dilemma before him.

Carrying her to her own room was not an option; he wished he was stronger, but he reckoned that Zoe had a better chance of lifting him. Waking her would be unkind, as would leaving her to sleep in such an uncomfortable position. So as gently as possible, he cradled her shoulders in his arms and carefully lowered her head onto the pillow.

The thought crossed his mind that maybe he could sit on the end of her bed for a while; just to stay close and protect her, he reasoned. However, he knew that he wouldn't be able to stay awake, and what would she think of him if she woke and found him on her bed? And what about Jono? Silas recalled the thinly veiled aggression in Jono's voice, and the complicated swirl of conflicting passions that made up his soul. He's probably spying on us! Silas thought, peering up at the tiny window by the front door. I wouldn't put it past him... the guy is unhinged.

The memory of Jono throwing himself into the waterfall was replaced with the mental image of Jono throwing Silas off the cliff. Hmm, play it safe, Si, he thought, as casting one long, last look at Zoe's serene face, he retreated to the separate room.

The little bedroom contained two small beds. They were so close that there was barely enough room to walk between the two bed frames.

One of the beds had Nana's bag on it. The other one Zoe had claimed as her own by liberally strewing her belongings all over it. There were scrunched clothes and bottles of cleansing fluid. Silas gingerly swept it all into the bag that Zoe had left near the door, then pushed it under the bed. Simply being in their room felt like an invasion of privacy, and he looked once more at the twin beds. On the scale of weirdness, how weird would it be to share a bedroom with Nana? he thought, noticing again how close the beds were to each other. Nana may have been a good friend of his mother's, but she was still practically a stranger to him.

He nearly marched out to wake Zoe. But, he hesitated; Nana wasn't back yet, and if she carried on acting like an old-age teenager, she may not return to the cabin at all. Then, almost of its own volition, his body decided it didn't care, and he toppled, heavily, face down on the bed.

'Please present yourself for assessment.' The house computer chimed the familiar spiel.

Eyes still gummed shut with sleep, Silas rolled over sluggishly. His feet found the floor, and he eventually stood up. Blearily, he stumbled between the beds to where the Biocubicle should be and walked smack into the closed door of the tiny bedroom. He yelled in pain and sat down abruptly on the end of the other bed.

Rubbing his bruised head, he looked around the room in confusion, trying to find the Biocubicle until he realised he had been dreaming. There were no Biocubicles here, no assessments, and no clinic. This was the Community and thanks to his initiation, he was now a part of it.

'You are sitting on my feet, dear,' came the muffled comment from under the blankets. Silas yelled again and shot upright. He couldn't believe it; Nana must have come back and got into her bed while he had been sleeping in Zoe's. How embarrassing.

Horrified, he started babbling, 'Nana! I can explain… I'm so sorry …'

Nana's tousled grey head emerged, her eyes blinking owlishly. The love-light that shone so brightly from her at his initiation was still clearly visible to Silas, and he immediately relaxed, and began to laugh at the awkwardness of the situation.

'I noticed that Zoe pinched your bed. Go and wake her up; I'm going to get some more sleep. Someone's snoring kept me awake last night!' She looked pointedly at him, but he could see the comment was shrouded in affection and good humour, and so, apologising once again, he backed out of the room.

117

As he quietly closed the door, it occurred to him that the effects of the Soulsight hadn't worn off yet.

Zoe was already up and busy in the nutrition area, and Silas was thrilled to still be able to see her properly. She was so beautiful that he felt he could happily spend all day just looking at her. He still felt so ashamed of all the times he had avoided her when they were at clinic. How blind he had been!

She looked enquiringly at Silas as he sat down at the table, having obviously heard the commotion in the other room..

'Don't ask!' he groaned.

'Sorry about crashing out on your bed last night,' Zoe apologised, sounding embarrassed. 'I was waiting for you so we could talk, and, well…'

'Nah,' he said, waving his hand as if to brush away the need for an apology. 'The bed, I can forgive. The talk, you can make up to me now.'

'And I shall, with some breakfast.'

'I usually have a protein shake.' He pulled a face of mild disgust, and then struck a classic wrestler pose with his arms. 'Not my favourite, but it's supposed to build up my muscles.'

Chuckling, Zoe played along with the parody. 'As you can imagine, our state-of-the- art nutrition facilities have provided us with the highest-grade protein meal available – eggs. Do you like them fried or scrambled?'

There was the briefest second of hesitation before Silas responded, 'Scrambled.'

'I don't believe it! You've never eaten eggs before, have you?'

'How did you… Ugh! The Soulsight!' Taking a deep breath, he added, 'No lies. I can do this. No, I have never eaten eggs.'

Zoe gave a short laugh. 'You get used to it, the truth thing. What do you want to talk about?'

'How long have we got?' Without waiting for an answer, he ploughed on, 'What exactly is Soulsight?'

Zoe was mixing some yellowy gloop in a tin pot that was cooking on the stove. She continued steadily stirring as she pondered the question, then replied, 'It's a plant.'

Looking confused, Silas thought about the clear liquid he consumed at the initiation. 'Last night I was just drinking water. I hadn't eaten any plants.'

'The waterfall, on the crater wall, that's just normal water, you can drink it and it will just quench your thirst, but... ' She paused and started scooping wobbly yellow lumps onto two plates. Suppressing a sudden hankering for protein shake, he bravely smiled as she put the plates on the table. Picking up a spoon, she pointed it at Silas, 'There is a second cave with a small waterfall. The large one conceals it, but the waters merge to form the river which then becomes the lake. The second cave is where the Soulsight plant grows. The whole water system here is saturated with it. Everything you drink at the Community has Soulsight in it.'

'So... as long as we are here, the effects won't get a chance to wear off.' Silas smiled to himself. He had been worrying about that. Now he understood what he was seeing in Zoe, he didn't want to suddenly lose it again.

'That's right,' Zoe said. 'You can eat the dried plant and get the same effect, though. Nana has a supply at home, as you well know. I still can't believe she spiked your drink!'

'Your nana!' Silas shook his head. 'I'm glad she did, though; it helped me see the real you...' He tailed off, hearing how soppy he sounded. Zoe seemed not to notice as she started talking more to herself than Silas.

'I wonder what the Soulsight chemical actually is? Odourless, tasteless, definitely soluble, heat-stable, colourless, of course, must be carbon-based... Hmm... I'd like some fresh samples to take back so I can study it properly...'

While she muttered, Silas swallowed down the eggs. Not unpleasant, a bit rubbery perhaps. He squashed the last lump flat with his spoon before scooping it into his mouth, then asked the next logical question that came into his mind. 'How does it work? How does it change the way we see?'

'I don't know. I intend to find out, though.' She tapped her spoon on the table and started thinking out loud again. 'It must act on a dormant area of the brain, maybe a subsidiary of the visual cortex. If the compound could be isolated and reproduced... I wonder if Mum brought the Analyser and Duplicator off the ship.' Zoe looked up and, seeing Silas' empty plate, seemed to remember where she was and started eating her own breakfast. Between mouthfuls of scrambled egg, she continued explaining. 'I'll have to ask Jono to get some for me. The cave is too difficult and dangerous to climb to. Jono can do it, and he gets a little for Nana to take home each time she visits. He says the Soulsight covers all the surfaces and hangs off the cave walls and ceiling in thick curtains. The cavern is almost choked with it, apparently. He also says it is utterly beautiful.'

She scraped the last of the egg from her plate and then neatly stacked the dirty dishes. 'I've longed to see the caverns for myself so, last time I was here, I begged and pleaded with Jono for him to help me get up to the cave and show me the Soulsight. Eventually he gave in, and we skipped our tasks one morning and set off for the waterfall. He climbed up and lowered a rope for me. I got halfway up before the rope became too slippery and I fell. I hit my head and was knocked out. I've still got the scar.' Here she paused in her reminiscence and lifted her dark hair from behind one ear to show a long, thin, white patch of bald scalp. Silas winced in sympathy. 'That's how Jono discovered the plunge pool was deep enough to dive into. He didn't think twice and just jumped straight down to get to me. He carried me for over an hour before I regained consciousness. Nana was furious. I wasn't allowed out of her sight for the rest of our stay.'

Irritated by the mention of Jono in such heroic terms, Silas tried to steer the conversation back to himself, and asked the next question that had been bothering him.

'How do I get rid of the darkness inside *me*? When I look at you there are no shadows at all! Even compared to everyone else here, you are something special.'

While he spoke she watched him, head on one side, then instead of acknowledging the question or the compliment, she said, 'Don't be jealous of Jono.'

'I'm not! Why would I be jealous of him?' The words popped out of his mouth without a thought, but then the realisation dawned, and he was shocked at how automatically the lie had come. For that is what it was: another lie. How many times a day did he twist the truth? How much were his habitual untruths nibbling away at his soul, creating and feeding the darkness within? He sighed heavily, causing Zoe to reach across the table to hold his hand.

'I think I've just answered my own question,' he said gloomily. 'I don't think I'll ever get close to looking as good as you do. The lies, the fear, the jealousy... I think that's always going to be there, and everyone is going to be able to see me for what I really am.'

'It's a process, Si. And it won't happen overnight. When I think back to the twisted reflection I saw when I first took Soulsight...' She shook her head at the memory, and seeing Silas' sceptical expression continued, 'It's true! I was much younger, eight or nine, maybe, but bringing me to the Community was a last resort for Nana. I was a seething mass of anger and selfishness, and I hated everyone. I'm glad *you* never saw me like that!' Smiling warmly at him she stood up, pushing the chair back with her legs. 'It's time to get our task allocation. We can talk more later.'

Silently following as she led the way to the lake, he mulled over her comment. She's glad I never saw her like that. Why? She likes me liking her... so does that mean she likes me? Does she more than like me?

Only a short time ago he would have been horrified by the idea, but now he found he was craving her approval. He knew he was overanalysing one throwaway comment, but the thought that she liked him, even though she'd seen all that was worst in him, was enough to dispel his earlier gloom and set a small spark of hope burning in his chest.

Chapter 16

They emerged from the tree line in exactly the same place as they had for the initiation the previous night. This time, instead of Silas being the central attraction, a cluster of people were gathered around a woman. She was reeling off a list of instructions, while simultaneously jiggling and shushing a crying toddler in her arms.

Instinctively, Silas trusted the woman, and he realised that he was getting used to discerning what the Soulsight revealed to him. She was easy to look at; there were no conflicting passions in her. Internally she was as steady as a rock, fair-minded and just, and he knew he would do whatever task she set him.

In stark contrast, however, the small boy in her arms was a maelstrom of selfishness and rage. This was the first child Silas had seen using Soulsight, and he was alarmed at how ugly it was. How could any parent raise such an unlikable offspring?

In an instant, like the flicking of a switch, the appearance of the boy transformed. A pair of bright blue butterflies danced their way through the air in front of him and the delight and wonder that now emanated from him was infectious. Briefly, he found himself sharing in the boy's awe at the simple beauty of butterflies, before they flew away and, like an inescapable storm, the tempest inside the boy resumed.

As they stood at the periphery of the group, Silas realised he had not noticed a thing about her physical characteristics. The outer shell that made up external appearance was becoming increasingly difficult to perceive, eclipsed as it was by the individual's true nature.

He narrowed his eyes to try to reduce the Soulsight's influence, and was eventually able to make out that the woman looked strong and healthy. She didn't have obvious physical limitations, and he wondered why she had come to live at the Community.

Then a man approached from behind her, and Silas had to suppress a shudder. His face was the stuff of nightmares. Terrible scarring ran from his forehead to his chin and one of his eyes was a milky-white colour. Shiny red skin twisted his features so his mouth formed a permanent sneer. The rest of his body was thankfully covered over, but from the way he limped, Silas assumed the damage was more extensive than just his face.

'Dada!' the toddler cried, his tantrum ceasing once more as he saw the scarred man. The woman smiled, looking relieved, and handed the child over.

Intrigued, Silas stopped trying to block the effects of Soulsight. Gradually the broken exterior of the man was eclipsed by a warmth of love and care for the child. And the child responded in kind. As the man carried his son into the forest, Silas could see the last faint traces of rage leave the boy as he gazed in pure adoration at his father.

Silas' attention returned to the group in front of him, and it was then he noticed the unmistakable figure of Jono. He had his back to them and was talking to someone who was blocked from Silas' view by the crowd. Silas saw a parcel exchange hands and then the two parted company.

To Silas the whole thing looked suspicious and as Jono turned to face the group, and the man strode away into the forest, Silas strained to get a better look at him. A deep, palpable sorrow marked the stranger out, something he hadn't seen displayed in the others. He concentrated again to get a look at what physical deformity could have caused such weighty grief. He only got a brief glimpse of his face before the trees swallowed him but, with a start, Silas realised he recognised who it was. He pointed and made an alarmed choking noise to Zoe.

'Atkins!'

Zoe glanced along the direction of his outstretched arm before lowering it with her hand.

'Thomas,' she corrected.

'No! Coach Atkins, the history coach from clinic. He's here!' he explained.

Yes, I know – Thomas Atkins – I saw him.' Ignoring Silas' open-mouthed expression, she approached the woman who had been holding the child.

'I see you, Frieda. What needs doing today?'

Silas was still trying to understand what Coach Atkins was doing at the Community to pay too much attention to the conversation between Zoe and the woman called Frieda. How could someone who worked at Vitality Clinic and pursued perfection tolerate being at the Community? Maybe that was what was making him so miserable! What was his slogan again? 'To achieve success by learning from our mistakes; to achieve perfection by never repeating them.' Yet here he was with the biggest selection of human mistakes and imperfections you were likely to see.

'Fishing.'

'Eh?' Silas came out of his reverie with a jolt.

'Didn't you hear a word I said? Frieda has allocated us for fishing duty, which is perfect – a gentle introduction for you, and a reminder of the ocean for me.' Zoe was smiling broadly, and the concerns about Coach Atkins fell from his mind. He smiled back at her, thrilled at the prospect of a day in her company.

'Oh, and Jono's coming too. It will be great, just the three of us.'

His smile transformed into a grimace, but Zoe was rummaging through a pile of equipment so didn't notice the change. Jono did, though. He had padded up at the end of the conversation, and Silas saw a dark twist of something ugly flare

125

up in his face. Unwilling to be the one to back down, he held Jono's gaze in a silent battle of wills, until Silas saw Jono's anger abruptly subside. What replaced it was a softer, more open expression. Silas was still wary, but Jono nodded slightly as if they had reached some kind of unspoken agreement. Then he bent down to help Zoe with her task.

Silas released the breath that he didn't know he had been holding, and ran his hands nervously through his hair. It wasn't easy, seeing exactly what made other people tick; all their positive and negative traits exposed. He almost preferred the relative blindness of life before Soulsight, when all you had to go on was superficial appearance and deceptive words.

Then, as quickly as the thought formed, it was dispelled as he looked at Zoe. To have never seen what treasure lay within, to live his life unaware of her true nature, would have been half a life at best. Soulsight *was* a gift, a complicated one, but definitely a good one, and he resolved not to shy away from it. There must be some way to work things out with Jono, he decided, for Zoe's sake, even if not for his own.

Chapter 17

Sweating profusely, with countless stinging lacerations over his arms and chest, he couldn't believe Zoe had described fishing as a gentle introduction.

Three hours of sporadic conversation – mainly between Zoe and Jono about people that he didn't know – interrupted by frenzied wrestling as another monstrous eel was hooked and pulled on board, was not what Silas considered gentle.

It had forced them to work as a team, though; each eel took all three pairs of hands to hold it down, or two and a half pairs of hands, Silas thought meanly, glancing at Jono's useless miniature arm. The tricky part of removing the hook from the tiny serrated jaw was left to Zoe, while the other two maintained their grip. But its long snake-like body would writhe and twist the whole time, and invariably one of them would lose hold, causing the fish to flail around the bottom of the boat in a desperate attempt to reach water, it's spiky, abrasive scales tearing at their exposed arms.

In the green gloom created by the heavy overhanging branches, the fate of each eel was decided. Too small, and it was returned to the water, to be caught when it reached a more impressive size. Too large, and Jono would pronounce it good for breeding, but inedible. But every now and then, Jono would shout 'Keep', and they would force their thrashing victim into the long overboard keepnet.

Not a whisper of a breeze could penetrate the cover of the ancient willows at the lake edge, and fat mosquitoes whined around their ears in the still, humid air, effortlessly dodging their feeble swatting hands.

The fish had stopped biting and the conversation had long since ceased flowing, when Jono declared them finished for the morning. Parting the veil of slender drooping branches, the prow of the boat emerged. Silas rowed with a renewed energy, eager to escape the confines of the green prison that had contained them.

It was late morning, and approaching the hottest part of the day. A light wind was blowing across the lake, which reduced the searing heat from the sun to a tolerable level. After the oppressive, muggy stillness under the willow branches, Silas almost felt cool as the sweat rapidly evaporated off his skin.

'Let's deal with the catch and then eat,' Zoe suggested. Jono nodded in agreement. Silas decided he didn't care what they did, as long as it involved being in the fresh air.

The main shore was deserted as, following Jono's instruction, Silas beached the boat. All three clambered out, then part-carried, part-dragged the heavy net a few paces to a grove of trees.

The eels were struggling less, tired from their hours of fruitless escape attempts. Silas watched Jono grab one deftly from the net, and swiftly smash its head on a flat rock. It continued wriggling but, undeterred, he forced the back of its head onto the first of a line of long steel hooks, conveniently protruding from the tree branches. It carried on writhing, although its head was completely misshapen by the blow, and Silas thought it must surely be dead.

Jono left it hanging there and went to perform the same act on his next victim. Zoe, too, was reaching into the net while happily chattering away to Jono about the smoked eel they had eaten last time she was with him.

I've never killed a living creature bigger than a fly, Silas wanted to say to them. But he found himself unable to, in the face of their efficient slaughter. I've never eaten one either, he added silently.

All the food he had ever consumed, barring Nana's stew and the scrambled eggs at breakfast, had been produced in the

Nutrition factory; synthesised and grown in vats, vitamin-enriched, calorie-adjusted, then presented in perfect portion size.

He didn't know what he should think about killing to eat. It wasn't as if he felt any sympathy towards the eels. The cuts over his arms and chest had effectively removed any concern for their welfare. It was just that it was so brutal, so messy.

Silas took a deep breath and plunged his hand into the net. He got a good hold on the head of one but, as if recognising weakness, it flicked up its spiny tail and entwined its serpentine body around Silas' arm. Yelping in revulsion, he swung his arm down fast, and the eel's head hit the rock with a resounding wet smack. Well, I've done it now, he thought... and it was strangely satisfying.

He hung it next to the others, feeling oddly proud of his achievement, which was reinforced when Jono clapped him on the shoulder with his massive hand. Looking up into his face, Silas could see a shift in Jono. The spiky exterior of distrust had softened and the reassuring depth of loyalty was much more obvious. That must be the Jono that Zoe sees all the time, he thought, and he began to understand why she liked having him around.

'Good work.'

Just two simple words. They weren't patronising. Jono was being genuine with his praise, and Silas recognised the extended olive branch of peace. Could that be enough of a foundation to build trust on? Yes, he decided.

'Thanks!'

Jono watched him closely for a moment, before laughing and clapping him round the shoulder again with his huge palm.

'Good work,' he repeated, but this time Silas knew he wasn't talking about the fishing. He felt strangely vulnerable again, for he had forgotten that his inner self was just as exposed to observation.

Ten minutes later, 20 fat, glistening eels were hanging by their heads from the hooks.

'We need to skin and gut them quickly, before they dry out. They taste weird if they are left too long.' Jono handed out knives with his instructions and he and Zoe set to work.

Silas watched, repulsed, as Zoe grabbed one of the dead eels by the head as it hung from the tree. Steadying it with one hand she nimbly cut a neat circle below the gills to form a roll of skin. Passing her knife to Silas she then gripped the skin flap with both hands and pulled sharply downwards, stripping the skin from the carcass in one piece. The skinless eel corpse gave a final shiver and then hung still.

'They are dead,' she said to Silas when she saw his look of distaste. 'It's just muscular spasms. The autonomic nervous system continues to fire. When I lived on the boat we used to catch saltwater eel. The salt would keep the electric pulses flowing. So if you didn't rinse them thoroughly, they'd still be thrashing about for ages, even after you'd chopped their head off and gutted them …'

'Not helping!' he interrupted her vivid description, queasily feeling saliva pool in the back of his throat.

'Sorry,' she said in a conciliatory voice, but he could tell she was amused by his discomfort. 'Take one of the still ones, and I'll show you how to gut it.'

The skinless eel corpse was cold in his hands and thankfully gave no further spasms as he unhooked it. Laying it on a flat rock, Zoe put the tip of the sharp knife into the ventral opening, then ran it swiftly up the eel's long belly to the head. Pushing the glistening innards to one side, she ran her blade deep inside the newly formed cavity, along the backbone, and the worm-like gut neatly fell out in a shiny pink pile. Taking a broader blade, she beheaded the creature with two swift strokes.

It wasn't as bad as he feared, and he managed five by himself before Jono and Zoe had skinned, gutted and removed the heads of the others. Jono took a basket from the boat and gathered up the severed heads.

'For later,' was all he would say to the questioning look from Silas.

Walking in single file along a narrow path winding through the forest, Jono started singing. His voice was deep and pleasant, bouncing off the trees and startling the birds that chattered out a scolding response.

Hung over their arms, and in Jono's case around his neck, were the carcasses from their morning's work. Not something to sing about, really, decided Silas, as slime mingled with eel blood dribbled down his clothes, but the tune was catchy and the lyrics comical, and he smiled as he listened.

Alone, in a lake, sat an eel.
Am I fish? Am I snake? What's the deal?
But eel beware,
For I do not care,
Whether reptile or fish, you're my meal!

For slippery and quick you may be,
But no one's as patient as me.
I'll wait and I'll wait,
Until you take the bait.
Then I'll skin you and gut you for tea.

All three were laughing at the silliness of the rhyme and from nowhere, Silas found a voice that he had never used in song. The words sprung into his mind, and before he could stop himself, he had started on his own verse.

There was a poor boy from the city.
Whose soul was not terribly pretty.
But skinning an eel
Was such an ordeal,
It taught him at least to feel pity.

His voice sounded reedy and thin compared to Jono's, but they roared with laughter at his contribution, and he felt a wave of pleasure at their approval. They sang through the song again, getting increasingly raucous with each verse.

Jono was still leading the way, but Silas soon realised that they were not heading to the guest hut, or even to Jono's tree house.

'Have you taken a wrong turn?' Silas eventually asked, as it became obvious that Jono was leading them towards a dead end. The crater wall rose up solidly through the trees ahead, towering ominously over them, blocking the way.

Jono guffawed and took a few hopping dance steps forward.

"'I'll lead you about a round, Through bog, through bush, through brake, through brier.'"

Silas rolled his eyes at Jono's antics. 'So do you, or don't you, know where we are going?'

"'If thou follow me, do not believe. But I shall do thee mischief in the wood.'" Jono laughed again as he caught sight of Silas' annoyed expression.

'Come on, Jono, enough is enough,' Silas said, trying to remain patient. 'Just give me a straight answer, will you?' But Jono merely responded with a mad cackle and a few more skipping steps.

'Why am I following you? You are actually a lunatic.' Silas' tolerance had run out. His arms ached from the disgusting burden of the dead eels, and he just wanted to go back to the hut. It would be nice to spend some time alone with Zoe, he thought, without Jono dominating everything. He turned around to start heading back to the shore. From there he knew the way to the guest hut.

'Why have you stopped?' Zoe called out. Possessing neither Jono's giant stride nor Silas' speed, she had fallen behind. 'We're nearly there.'

'But it's the end of the path,' Silas complained, and stepped to one side to let her see the crater wall. 'Jono's just messing

132

around with us. Maybe carrying eel corpses is his idea of a fun day out.'

'Follow Jono,' she insisted, rapidly catching up with him. Muttering to himself in irritation he looked back, but Jono was nowhere to be seen. Confused, he walked on, and reaching the foot of the cliff he saw the path turned abruptly to run adjacent to the wall. Stepping around the sharp bend, he saw Jono still prancing and dancing along the shaded path.

Ahead of Jono, he could just make out other tracks that merged until the whole sheltered under-cliff path broadened into a thoroughfare, each new track spewing forth clusters of people bearing the fruits of their morning's labour.

Silas heard a noise behind him and turned to see a man whistling merrily to himself. Draped over his shoulders were the carcasses of four fat rabbits. Joining the procession from another track were two children carefully carrying a bucket of eggs between them. The ones, twos and threes coalesced and slowed. There were a lot of 'I see you' greetings bouncing back and forth down the line and an infectious sense of camaraderie in the unhurried group.

Soon they entered a vast, high-domed cavern. An assortment of empty containers were clustered by the entrance and, following Zoe's example, Silas gratefully dropped the slimy eels into a bucket. Freed from his dripping burden, he stared around with fascination. The cave opening was huge, but as his eyes adjusted to the dim light inside, he realised that it also extended much further back than the sunlight could penetrate. The ground was level and sandy, and running down the middle of the cave floor was a clear stream. Beyond the stream a large firepit was belching out heat and smoke. From the light of the flickering orange flames, Silas could make out the soot-blackened far wall. Near the fire, Nana was handing out packages to the slow parade of people travelling through the cave.

'It's the nutrition hall,' he said with a dawning realisation.

'Yes.' Turning to him, Zoe grinned. 'Aren't you hungry?'

Until she asked, he hadn't noticed how ravenous he was. Hunger was an unfamiliar and unpleasant sensation; the perfectly balanced meals he usually consumed were designed to avoid it.

'Yeah! Starving!' he grinned back and headed towards Nana, nearly tripping over the two children, who, having delivered their burden of eggs, were now rushing across the cave. His eyes followed them as they sat down with a group of kids, and to his surprise he saw Coach Atkins in the middle of them. The vast sadness that flowed out of him didn't seem to put the children off as they huddled around him, hanging on his every word.

'So what's the deal with Atkins?' he muttered under his breath to Zoe.

'Poor Thomas – "The weight of this sad time we must obey. Speak what we feel, not what we ought to say. The oldest hath borne most."' Jono sighed heavily, stooping over them to join in their whispered conversation.

'I don't understand half the stuff you say, Jono!' Silas said, frowning, and he deliberately turned his back on him.

'I can tell! "The common curse of mankind, folly and ignorance, be thine in great revenue!"' Jono doubled up with laughter at his own joke, causing Silas to feel angry and embarrassed. Who was Jono to make him feel foolish?

'Jono,' Zoe said sharply, cutting short Jono's hilarity, 'don't say things like that when Silas isn't looking *at* you!' The exasperation in her voice surprised Silas and he swung around.

Trying to stand his ground, Silas stared up at Jono. At once he could clearly see that there was no enmity in Jono. There was genuine warmth, and that deep, strong loyalty that he had seen earlier on. Silas relaxed.

'Ah …' Jono said in surprise, as if realising his mistake. 'I apologise most fervently,' he declared in his over-the-top manner.

'Me too,' Silas sighed. 'It seems I misjudge you, even when I'm using Soulsight. I take back the lunatic comment.' He smiled sheepishly at Jono.

'Great!' Zoe linked arms with both of them and steered them towards Nana and her rapidly dwindling supply of food parcels. 'Now that's sorted, let's get some lunch and get cleaned up.'

Chapter 18

Silas couldn't remember a time when he had felt happier. The afternoon had been as near perfect as possible. With their bundle of provisions, they had returned to the boat. At Zoe's suggestion, they had rowed across the water to a steep rocky outcrop, protruding from the lake surface like a giant stone iceberg.

Before they had even moored, Zoe kicked off her shoes and leapt fully clothed from the boat, diving smoothly into the water. Her head surfaced, and then she swam a swift lap around the island.

'That feels so much better!' she shouted, before swimming under the boat and resurfacing. 'Eel slime stinks!'

Following her example, they enthusiastically jumped in. Jono turned his jump into a comedy routine, by pretending to trip over the gunwale and performing a clumsy somersault before hitting the water with a splash.

What followed was an escalating series of jumps, stunts and dives from the sheer edges of the rocky island into the deep lake below. Silas watched, fascinated, as Jono, with utter recklessness, climbed higher and dived deeper than the others. Part of him longed to be so unconcerned, to throw himself off the highest points with such freedom, but it went against all he had been taught. The body was to be nurtured and developed; to achieve its full potential, it *must* be protected from harm.

Having draped their wet outer clothes over the rocks to bake dry in the hot sun, they shared out the lunch of bread, eggs and fruit.

After they had eaten their fill, Zoe had fallen asleep and Silas probably would have too – his belly was satisfyingly full and his mind was pleasantly empty as he watched the treetops sway gently in the breeze – but Jono started talking. Initially Silas wasn't sure if Jono was talking to himself. 'They guessed my age.'

'Hmm?' Silas murmured sleepily.

'Three, or maybe four… I could barely speak, but I'd survived for months. Naked and filthy, rummaging in the city waste pit, like an animal. Thrown out by my parents; discarded because I wasn't perfect. My arm had stopped growing, but the rest of me was growing too much. I would never qualify to be Seen, so they tossed me out. Some Unseen found me, and I was smuggled here… the first child at the Community.'

Wide awake now but not knowing what to say, Silas sat up and stared at Jono. No wonder he was so complicated to look at, his loyalty to the Community so strong and his anger and distrust so evident. Jono was not lying, Silas could clearly see that all of it was true; but what kind of parent treated their child like a piece of rubbish? He thought of his own father. He was disappointed in Silas – that was obvious even without Soulsight – but what if he were to become an Unseen? Would he experience such outright rejection?

Breaking the silence once again, Jono shifted position, rolling onto his side, and addressed Silas directly. 'You wanted to know about Thomas Atkins?'

'Yes!' he answered eagerly, appreciating the change of subject to a topic less raw and painful. 'How did he get involved with the Community? You know he's the history coach at my clinic?'

Jono nodded. 'Yes, I know. Thomas loves history. It's his obsession, but it's also his burden.' Jono paused before asking, 'What does he teach you?'

'Nothing much, as far as I can tell!' Silas laughed, but when Jono didn't, he added more soberly, 'Stuff about the turn of the millennium, obesity, falling population. That kind of thing.'

'What about before then?'

'Before when? Before the millennium? What about it?' Silas' brain was still too preoccupied with the image of a discarded child living off rubbish to really engage with Jono's question, but as he let it sink in, he was surprised at how little he knew about anything... at all. He rephrased his question, 'What do *you* know about it?'

'What's your motto?' At Silas' blank look, Jono continued, 'Your clinic motto. Zoe told me, something about perfection?'

'Oh yeah,' Silas pulled a wry face. 'Achieve Perfection, Achieve Success.'

Jono shook his head with the impossibility of the slogan. 'Perfecting the body may be achievable for some people. You, for instance, and the others at your clinic.' Silas nearly laughed again when he considered how far off Gold Standard he was, but Jono carried on. 'Thomas changes it, doesn't he?'

Thinking back to the coach's droning mantra, Silas mimicked, 'To achieve perfection by learning from our mistakes; to achieve success by never repeating them.'

There wasn't even a flicker of a smile from Jono who, ignoring the impression, continued talking.

'It's not just the mistakes to do with our great-great-grandparents' lifestyle. They seemed intent on destroying themselves by their own actions, but those faults are easy to see and fix. The mistakes that we should never forget came before that. They are the ones that resulted in the death of millions.

'We have forgotten the past, where people destroyed each other because of insignificant external differences, because they looked or acted differently. Skin colour, languages, customs and even different clothing were enough to provoke fear, discrimination and attempted annihilation among our recent ancestors. But we've lost all that remembering, all that learning from our mistakes.

'Thomas believes he can see it happening all over again. This time with the sick, the broken, the damaged... the ones like me. The Unseen. Those are the ones separated, marginalised and, he fears, eventually eliminated.'

Silas frowned. Up until now he had always believed that the separation between Unseen and Seen was completely necessary and right... but now Soulsight had turned all that on its head. He didn't know what to think any more. With Soulsight, he had looked like an Unseen, and Bubba Gee, and even Jono, had looked like they should be Seen.

'Has Coach Atkins shared his thoughts with other people – the manager at clinic, maybe?' Silas asked.

Jono nodded. 'He tried, but of course, none of the Seen would listen to him. His ideas sound crazy, almost against what the government stands for, and he has been belittled and ridiculed. Everyone is focused on the future and no one wants to hear about the past.

'So he gave up on trying to educate the Seen and secretly asked around, among the Unseen, and eventually found the Community. We saw the weight of the truth he was carrying. He'd come to warn us, to prepare us. He says that people don't change, and history proves it. People are afraid of anything or anyone who is different, and fear turns men into monsters. He wants us to learn to protect ourselves... he thinks that eventually there will be a battle, a war, if you like, on people like me, on the Unseen.'

'War?' Silas spat out in disbelief. Suddenly he could understand why no Seen would take Coach Atkins seriously. 'Nonsense! People killing each other? No! I don't believe it.'

Jono shrugged. 'It's what Thomas believes,' he said matter-of-factly.

'But the government is all about health and life... rebuilding the population again. They wouldn't allow conflict. There is separation, Unseen-Seen, but that's just to protect the health of the whole nation,' Silas said forcefully. 'Coach Atkins must be wrong!'

Silas felt unsettled by the conversation. It all seemed too far-fetched, but obviously Jono believed what Thomas had told him. But if Coach Atkins were correct, then that would make the Viva party and the Flawless Leader some kind of threat, and that was laughable.

Then Silas remembered something and relaxed a little, for he had information Coach Atkins and Jono didn't. He knew that the government was pouring money into Biocubicle development, for the Unseen too, and it was all aimed at getting *everyone* healthier. The Flawless Leader was ensuring that the Unseen were going to get more and more help, not less. Thomas Atkins' fears were unfounded. Silas was convinced of it.

'Will you show me where the Soulsight grows?' Silas asked suddenly.

'It's a difficult climb,' Jono replied after a small pause, 'and last time I took someone up there… well, let's just say it didn't end so well.'

'You mean Zoe? She told me about her accident. But I'm a good climber. I'd like to see it for myself.'

He didn't know where the desire had sprung from, but it seemed everything was shifting and changing. All that he had once understood was being shaken and challenged. He needed something tangible, something he could touch and hold on to. His eyes had been opened to greater things, and it had all started when Nana had given him Soulsight at her house… when he had first seen Zoe for who she really was.

'I shouldn't take you there,' Jono said eventually, holding up his hand to stave off argument, 'but I will… though not yet. I saw your fear as you watched me jump off this little rock. If you freeze halfway up the climb…' he shook his head, 'I won't be able to help.'

Ignoring the warning, Silas stood excitedly. 'Why can't we go now? From what Zoe said, it is an incredible place. This may be my only chance to see it. I'm not scared. I was just surprised by your… recklessness.' He knew he sounded like a petulant child trying to justify himself. 'Like I said, I'm good at climbing.' I'm bound to be better than you, he thought to himself. How can you climb anything with only one functional arm?

'The Soulsight cavern is spectacular and I promise, one day I will show it to you but... not today. Today we still have fishing to do!'

Silas grimaced. 'Fishing for what? Not more eels, please no!'

Ignoring him, Jono leaned over Zoe and gently stroked her hair. 'Time to wake up,' he whispered. His whole appearance had shifted again. It was pure adoration radiating from him now, and it transformed him, wiping away all traces of anger and mistrust.

I wonder if I look like that when I look at her? Maybe everyone does. It's what she draws out of people. She must get used to it, Silas decided.

He watched closely as she opened her eyes and focused on Jono as he crouched over her. The intensity of her affection increased when she looked up at him and their eyes met.

Suddenly feeling as if he was intruding on their private moment, Silas quickly averted his gaze. This was something he had no part of. Although he felt captivated by Zoe, what she had with Jono was obviously something special. Trying to suppress the flash of jealousy that shot through him, he turned his back on them and busied his eyes and hands with packing the bag with the remnants of their lunch.

'Are you all right?' He felt the pressure of someone touching him on his shoulder and looked up. Zoe took his breath away! How could he have resented her friendship with Jono? Of course the poor fool was in love with her! How could anyone look at her and *not* fall head over heels in love?

'Yes, fine, thanks.' He felt warmth uncurl in the centre of his chest, dispelling the bitter envy. All was right and good when he could be with her. She made him feel safe and secure.

'"Once more unto the breach, dear friends"!' Interrupting them, Jono adopted his dramatic voice and started ushering them towards the boat that was bobbing gently on the lake.

'Eh?' Annoyed and uncomprehending, Silas looked at Zoe for help. 'Translate for me?' he whispered.

She understood right away and groaned. Turning to face Jono, her shoulders sagging, she threw her hands together in mock supplication, 'No! Not more monster eels. Spare us!'

Jono chuckled. 'I will have mercy on you, fair maid. This will be easy monster fishing!'

And it was... incredibly easy. It was almost as if the beasts wanted to be caught. At a sheltered spot by the riverside, as it broadened to become the lake, they loosely tied the boat.

Producing a net bag and rope from under one of the seats, Jono upended the basket of eel heads into the bag. Slime and blood oozed through the netting leaving sticky blobs over the bottom of the boat. He threw in a couple of rocks and dropped the whole lot over the edge. It fell quickly through the slow-moving water and, satisfied it was on the riverbed, he looped the rope around the oarlock and sat down on the wooden bench.

'And now we wait.'

'For how long?' said Silas, wondering why all three of them had to be stuck in the boat again.

'Not long,' Jono replied unhelpfully.

A few minutes later, he unhooked the rope and, looping it under his feet, he slowly pulled the net up. Even before it broke the surface, Silas could make out rectangular shapes attached to the bag. He got a better look at them when Jono dumped the whole lot in the middle of the boat. About 15 centimetres long, the creatures looked like oversized beetles, similar to the ones he found scuttling around the abandoned areas in the city. Their hard case was reddish brown and each bug had ten spindly legs and two fierce claws. About 20 were clinging to the bag and its disgusting contents.

'Crayfish!' Zoe said enthusiastically, and set to picking them off the netting and dropping them into a basket.

'Why do crayfish never share?' Jono asked, grabbing one by the top of the shell.

'I don't know,' Zoe replied.

'Because they're shellfish.'

'Oh that's dreadful!' But she laughed when he poked his tongue out at her. 'What's the best way to catch a crayfish?' she asked mischievously, looking at the big one she had just picked up. Then, without giving the others a chance to speak, she suddenly flung it at Jono and said, 'Have someone throw one at you!'

He dodged to one side, and it sailed past his head to splash into the river, rapidly sinking to the bottom, out of sight.

'Ha! That's your share gone!'

'No chance,' she argued back, 'that was your one! You didn't catch it, so you don't get to eat it.'

A sharp yelp from Silas drew their attention. 'It's got me! Get it off! Ouch! It's drawn blood!'

'Si! Keep still, you'll make it hold on tighter,' Zoe shouted, alarmed.

In his pain and horror, Silas was flailing his hand about in the air with the fiercely determined crayfish still gripping the base of his thumb.

'Just hold your hand in the water,' Jono calmly instructed. 'It will prefer its freedom to your digits, don't worry.'

Wide-eyed with panic, Silas immediately leaned over the edge and thrust his arm deep into the cool stream. To his relief, he felt the crayfish begin to loosen its hold. Then it let go completely and drifted to the bottom to go and join the other escapee.

'There goes your share too,' Jono commented drily.

'Fine by me,' Silas muttered, inspecting the small, bleeding gash in his thumb.

Zoe and Jono hauled up another two net-loads, filling the basket with 60 or so crayfish. Refusing to touch another one, Silas sat nursing his injury, resentfully staring at the ever-growing catch. Crawling over each other in a jumble of spidery legs and bug eyes, they were disgusting to look at, and surely impossible to eat.

Chapter 19

Yet it was whoops of delight that greeted them when they returned to the cave that evening. The crayfish were admired and fussed over and then promptly dropped, live and still wriggling, into a pot suspended over the firepit.

'Is this everyone?' Silas whispered into Zoe's ear as he gazed around the cave.

'Everyone who?' she whispered back, quizzically.

'Everyone who lives here, at the Community?' he said, impatient at having to spell it out for her.

'I guess so,' she shrugged, 'there are about 200 adults and a dozen or so children, I think. You'll have to check with Bubba Gee. He knows exactly.'

Two hundred people didn't look like many when spread out across the vast sandy floor of the cave. They sat in groups, passing bowls of food around. The children ran, unchecked, weaving past the seated adults, grabbing handfuls of whatever food was in reach.

The whole set-up bothered Silas, and he struggled to locate the word to describe his unease. 'It's all very …'

'Different?' she volunteered

He shook his head. 'No… unregulated!' He finally found the word he had been looking for. 'How do you make sure that everyone is getting the right amount?'

She seemed confused by the question, and Silas thought he hadn't asked it clearly enough.

'The correct amount of nutrients? Carbohydrates, protein… why are you looking at me like that?'

'Like what?'

'Like I'm stupid!'

'I'm not!' she answered hotly, then softened her voice a little. 'I just forget how strict your life normally is. Here, at the Community, you eat when you are hungry and you stop when you are full,' she spread her arms wide, as if laying out the people for inspection, 'and everyone thrives.'

Seeing himself through her eyes was disconcerting. He had never considered his way of life as anything other than normal; to improve his health and strength by doing the recommended amounts of... well... everything. It wasn't strict; it was just necessary. It was important for the nation that everyone should strive for health; wasn't that what it was all about?

But looking around, he could see she was right, the Community was thriving. Even though Soulsight made it tricky, masking the external with the internal, he squinted past it, minimising its effect. It wasn't the pure health he was used to at Vitality, for most of the Community would be classed Unseen anyway, but an unmistakable air of life emanated from the relaxed, laughing groups of people. It was good, he decided, and pushed his reservations aside as they sat together on the sandy floor.

Or at least, it *was* good, until Coach Atkins settled in next to them. He was carrying a large bowl of freshly cooked crayfish, which Jono and Zoe immediately dived on and started messily breaking into pieces, pulling out the soft grey innards. Gingerly, Silas picked one up and inspected it closely before returning it, intact, to the bowl.

'I see you, Corelle,' Coach Atkins grumbled in his dull monotone, his features marred by the misery he exuded. It was contagious, and Silas felt his own spirit sag and become weighed down. It would have made it impossible to stay near the coach for long had it not been for his redeeming feature. Silas recognised it from Bubba Gee, and Nana and, of course, Zoe. It was love, pure and simple, mingling with his deep sorrow. The combination was compelling, and Silas

145

remembered seeing the children flocking around him earlier in the day. 'I heard you were initiated last night, congratulations.'

'Er, yeah… thanks.' Silas squirmed uncomfortably, forcing himself to add, 'I see you, Coach Atkins.'

Silas was cringing with embarrassment. To bump into any coach outside of clinic was weird enough. But for it to happen here, at the Community, which was supposed to be secret… And to both be using Soulsight! Seeing what made Coach Atkins tick… Ugh! It felt too private. Like catching him in the bathroom, or getting changed. Unbearable! And worse, to know that his own soul was exposed and visible – and Coach Atkins wouldn't stop staring at him!

'Thomas. When we are here, you may call me Thomas,' he said.

Worse and worse, thought Silas. 'Thomas, right.'

'You're not as messed up as some I've seen,' Coach Atkins continued to stare unblinkingly at Silas' face.

'No?' Silas said, inching backwards, trying subtly to move behind Zoe.

'Hmm, a bit of fear… jealousy. Yes, but there are good things too. Compassion, love… faithfulness.'

Disturbed by the intimate dissection of his soul, Silas pushed himself further away from Coach Atkins, trying to disengage from the unwelcome conversation. Not even Zoe felt it was appropriate to list all that she could see in him, and he felt she had more right than anyone.

As he tried to shuffle further back, he nudged sharply into Zoe. She was dipping into another bowl now, and passed Silas a thin skewer with pinkish-grey chunks impaled along its length. Eager for an excuse to avoid talking to Coach Atkins, he took it.

'It's the eel. Try it,' she encouraged.

He turned it over in his hands. It looked safe enough, better than the crayfish anyhow; a little like the gelatinous protein cubes that were sometimes served up at clinic. He half-heartedly gripped a bit with his teeth, pulling it off the stick,

146

and started chewing. It broke up easily as he pushed it around his mouth. The taste was subtle and a bit muddy, but with a hint of sweetness to it. He set to work on the rest of his eel with renewed interest. He could hear Coach Atkins talking to Jono now, and he half-listened in while reaching for another eel stick.

'... nothing left to hope for, Jono. Listen to the warnings from history. I believe it was the great historical figure, Gandhi, who said, "A nation's greatness is measured by how it treats its weakest members."'

Silas felt far less ignorant about not knowing who Gandhi was when he also saw confusion flitter across Jono's brow, but Coach Atkins continued to drone on, oblivious to his bewildered audience. 'I don't think that a little haven like the Community has much chance of staying hidden for much longer, do you?'

Zoe immediately chipped in, 'What was that? Thomas, what have you heard?'

'They are going to pass a new law. Mandatory daily bio-assessments, for every citizen,' he answered expressionlessly. 'The Flawless Leader slipped it in as a clause of her "Future Health" edict.'

'No!' Zoe sounded shocked, but Silas couldn't understand her dismay. Surely almost everyone in the city did that anyway. A daily Biocubicle assessment was as much a part of Silas' life as the morning stint in the workout suite was.

'Have you told Nana and Bubba Gee?' Zoe asked.

'That was the purpose of my visit here, but I don't know how long this place will last. Bubba Gee has always been very careful about staying unnoticed. No big buildings, no power source. But I managed to discover them, so others could track the Community down. And there are Unclassified children here. Healthy children. They would qualify as Seen, but as for the rest of the Community... the Unseen runaways, those Seen who want to opt out of the system ...' Here Thomas paused and looked directly at Zoe.

'What would happen to them?' Zoe asked a little breathlessly.

'Who knows. Unseen, then never seen again… like in the bad old days.'

A worried frown creased Zoe's brow as the potential repercussions sank in. Coach Atkins turned back to Jono and continued talking. 'Viva will not tolerate blatant disregard for its policies. Once a law is passed, Flawless Leader Steele will find some way to enforce it. They will have kept records of the Seen and Unseen who have disappeared over the last decade. The government will be searching for the runaways. I fear for the Community.'

Listening to Coach Atkins' dreary voice reminded Silas of clinic and home, and he suddenly remembered Marc, his brother, strutting proudly around the house in his shiny uniform. Would the new Health Advisor squad that the Flawless Leader had created be charged with enforcing this law? Silas shuddered to think how a bully like Marc would abuse that kind of power.

'All this has happened before, you know,' the coach continued. 'History repeats itself. Have you been reading the books that I found for you? You'll soon see what I mean. People don't change.'

Jono muttered something about Shakespeare and Coach Atkins talked over him, his dull voice draining any passion out of his words. 'Shakespeare? That's just fiction and froth. The truth is in the other books. Have you read them?'

Silas thought he was getting used to Jono's appearance, the depths and conflicting nature that was revealed by Soulsight, but when Coach Atkins eventually stopped talking, Silas saw something new and shocking. The dark, twisting shadows that had characterised his own image on that first night were creeping into Jono's expression. They obscured his light brown eyes, causing his eye sockets to take on that empty, hollow appearance. The choking tentacles of fear were distorting and clouding Jono's face.

Arrogance, recklessness and suspicion were all part of Jono's emotional repertoire. But fear was a new addition, and it didn't suit him one bit.

'Are you all right?' was the only question Silas could think to ask, even though he could see Jono was far from all right.

'I need some time to think,' Jono said abruptly, and made to stand up. Zoe noticed his distress and tried to hold him back.

'Wait, we'll come with you!'

'No!' he snapped, and brushed off her hand. He stood, towering over them, bits of crayfish leg and shell scattering around him, and without another word strode from the cave.

'How have you managed to make him so scared?' Silas turned aggressively on Coach Atkins.

Unperturbed, Coach Atkins only shook his head, a picture of sorrow and misery. 'I merely told the truth.'

'Your version of the truth, maybe! You've frightened him. I've seen him dive backwards off a sheer rock face without batting an eyelid, yet you spend ten minutes with him and terrify him out of his wits!'

Unflinching in the face of Silas' verbal onslaught, Coach Atkins started slowly explaining in his infuriating way. 'Jono, for all his appalling infant-hood, has grown up completely sheltered. He has never left the confines of the crater. He has always used Soulsight, and he relies on it to relate to and understand those around him. His fear emerges when I address the idea of a future without these safety nets. No Soulsight for him would be like you, or I, being physically blinded. Can you imagine such a terrifying idea? That, more than the threat of being formally classified as an Unseen, is what frightens him the most. I am merely trying to prepare him for the future, to get him to face his fears now, before they are upon him and overwhelm him.'

Too angry for coherent speech, Silas jumped to his feet. What a pompous, arrogant... What does he know anyway? A history coach – useless!

People were turning to stare; such outright anger was a rare sight. Zoe started to say something to calm the situation, but Silas didn't want to calm down. As he had watched the fear grow in Jono, he knew something had changed. He wasn't watching an enemy, or even a rival, suffer under Coach Atkins' cruel 'truths'. He was watching a friend being beaten down, and he wouldn't stand for it. He was furious with Coach Atkins, and he wanted to let the anger course through him. Without a second thought, he ran out of the cave. He needed to check Jono was OK, and to try to undo some of the damage that Coach Atkins had done.

Chapter 20

Assuming Jono would head back to his tree house, Silas set off at a slow jog, trying to remember the way along the criss-cross of woodland paths. He had always thought he had a good sense of direction, and had relied on it when he used to explore the Uninhabited areas back home. However, he soon realised that city paths were laid out in an easy grid pattern, even if some were broken up and neglected. But in the woods, paths bent and twisted, then deteriorated into overgrown dead-ends filled with brambles.

After a while, the anger that had motivated him began to dwindle, and with increasing alarm he discovered that he was lost. He stopped dead, and let his heart settle. The roaring of blood pounding through his ears was all he could hear initially, and then the noises of the forest took over.

The light was beginning to fade. Late afternoon was becoming early evening, and the forest began to change. All Silas' fear of the dark came flooding back as he heard creaking and whispering in the lengthening shadows around him.

Suddenly, a primitive terror overwhelmed him, and he started sprinting, heedless of direction, careless of the whipping branches that cut across his face and hands. The path had vanished, and he was now pushing through thick undergrowth. The forest had become a trap and he was fighting, desperate now. He had to get out!

His chest felt tight, making it difficult to breathe. Spots were beginning to dance before his eyes, and a rushing noise seemed to be coming from inside his head.

Unexpectedly, the ground went from under his feet, and he fell, twisting and rolling down a short slope. Instinctively, his hands shot up to protect his face, and when his body had stopped moving, he lay in a shallow gully. The wind had been knocked out of him and he remained motionless, his mouth open in a soundless cry until his lungs remembered the correct procedure and sucked in a ragged breath.

He felt confused and disorientated as the rational part of his brain took over and suppressed the animal urge to run. Think, Si, he said to himself. Are you injured? No? Good. Get up!

Sitting up, he brushed the dirt off his clothes. There were twigs and leaves caught up in his hair, and he roughly pulled them out. He squinted as he inspected the latest cuts on his hands. Dad would be furious if he knew how many injuries he was getting. He would have to be more careful from now on, or there would be too many questions when he got home.

The light was getting in his eyes and annoying him as he pulled a large splinter from his palm.

The light!

Forgetting his wounds, he clumsily stood. Golden shafts of sunlight were penetrating through the close-set trees ahead. He had found the edge of the forest! Sobbing with relief, Silas staggered forwards and broke through the tree line, and the wind ruffled his hair like a friendly welcome. The last rays of the sun were individually extinguished as it dropped behind the crater rim.

He was standing at the furthest end of the lake. Along the shore, he could see the shape of the boat they had spent the day in, dragged up, fully out of the water. Feeling relieved, he walked towards the boat. He knew his way back to the cabin from here. He was safe.

Just then, the boat changed. Silas thought it was the fading light playing tricks, as the boat outline seemed to squirm along its top edge.

'What the...?' he muttered, feeling the desire to flee rise up in him again. Then, the outline shifted again, and the single, monstrous shadow split, to become an ordinary boat, and the familiar silhouette of Jono.

Of course! Jono! In his panic to escape the forest, he had forgotten why he was in the forest in the first place. He wanted to help his friend. It was a strange idea to consider Jono in that way. But there was no other word for it. Even though he was often exasperating, and Zoe seemed to be in love with him, seeing the vulnerability that Coach Atkins' words had produced had fully tipped the balance for Silas.

Friends were not a common feature in his life. Even his brother, Marc, had always taken the role of a competitor. As for the other kids at clinic, not one of them would call him a friend, even if he wanted it.

'Hey, Jono!' he shouted, waving his arms to draw attention to himself. But Jono either didn't hear, or didn't want to hear, and loped away from the lake, back into the forest.

Silas pulled his shoulders back and rolled his head, trying to loosen up his bruised body. Do I bother trying to catch up with him? he wondered. No, I'll leave it; he'll be all right. If he can survive out here, in the middle of nowhere, I'm sure he'll work it out. Like me, he's used to being on his own.

Just as he had decided to make his way to the cabin, his conscience prodded him. Zoe had sought him out on the last day of clinic, had followed him all the way into the Uninhabited areas. And he had needed her. He didn't know, at the time, how lonely he was, but now he could see how much good she had done him.

It was no use... he couldn't allow himself just to go back to the cabin now, not without at least *trying* to talk with Jono. Cursing under his breath, he heaved a sigh. The darkness beneath the trees was forbidding. What was it Jono had quoted at them when they didn't want to do any more fishing? Ah, yes...

'"Once more unto the breach, dear friends",' Silas boomed in his best Jono impression, thinking he must ask Zoe what a 'breach' was. Then forcing his aching legs into a run, he plunged back into the thick forest.

Crashing along the more familiar track, he could make out Jono's tree in the gathering gloom. He skidded to a halt, his brain trying to make sense of what he was looking at.

Silas had seen that tree in daylight, and he knew there were no handholds for the first six metres at least. And yet, clinging like a three-legged gecko to the bark of the tree, and crawling steadily upwards, was Jono. How was he doing it? Silas stared, open-mouthed, looking for a rope, or ladder. As he took a step forward to get a closer look, he stumbled over Jono's shoes. Like the rest of him, they were oversized – massive black boats, scuffed and well worn. They made Silas' feet look dainty in comparison. Why has he taken his shoes off? Silas wondered.

Looking up again, he watched Jono reach the first level of branches, bend his leg up, and use his toes to grip onto the nearest one. Once he reached the larger tree boughs, Jono scampered up the rest of the distance to the flat underside of the tree house. Then he let go with his hand and for a moment hung, suspended by one foot, before twisting his upper body to swing over the small overhang formed by the platform base.

Rendered speechless, Silas stood with his mouth hanging open. What was that? If he could climb like that, he'd be in Silver already, maybe even in Gold. He snapped his mouth shut and moved closer to the tree. He tried to get a grip on the bark. Slipping his fingers between the rough grooves on the tree trunk he could hold his weight, but there was nowhere for his feet to go. He slipped his shoes off and tried again, barefoot. Hopeless!

'Jono?' He shouted up into the dark. 'I know you're there. I just saw you climb. How did you do that?'

There was no answer, and Silas felt self-doubt begin to creep in. He wants to be alone, he thought. I know that feeling. At least I tried to talk to him. He stood for another moment, undecided. Just as he was about to turn away, he heard the swoosh and whistle of falling rope, and leapt backwards just in time to avoid being hit by a rapidly uncurling ladder.

From the light of a single swaying sunstorer, Silas examined the sturdy platform on which he now stood. Smooth wooden planks stretched across two of the largest branches. The veranda was small and excessively cluttered. Logs, tools, old pots and broken baskets littered the floor. There was a single path through the debris leading to the front door of a tall hut.

Nestled against the trunk of the tree, the flat-roofed, rough-edged hut was no picture-book cottage, but to Silas it was a thing of beauty. What an incredible place to live, he thought, inaccessible to everyone else, the perfect hideaway. He thought back to his own tree and wondered at the possibility of building something there. A platform at least.

Jono appeared in the doorway. His eyes were still lost under a layer of shadowy fear. Silas felt his heart go out to him in sympathy.

'Hi,' he said uncertainly, still not entirely sure of his welcome, as Jono remained silent, apparently lost in his terror.

'I've never seen anything like this before,' Silas persevered, gesturing at the tree house. 'Did you build it?'

At Jono's nod, Silas let out an appreciative whistle.

'This is incredible!'

Jono began to alter at Silas's open admiration and stepped forward into the light. The fear was still there, but more of his old self was emerging.

'It is,' he said, a touch arrogantly. 'It's taken four years, though,' he looked at the mess around him, 'and it's not finished yet. I'm going to put a second level over there,' Jono pointed to another substantial branch of the tree, 'and then I'll have space for a workshop.'

He led the way inside the hut, still describing his plans for improvements and alterations. Caught up with his enthusiasm, Silas eagerly followed him. Jono now seemed delighted by Silas' interest and started describing in detail the way the hut had been built. Most of the technical terms went straight over Silas' head, but he gazed around admiringly.

Everything was perfectly proportioned to fit Jono, and Silas had the unusual experience of feeling like a dwarf in a giant's home. The bed must have been three metres long and filled the whole of the back wall. One intricately carved chair sat in the middle of the floor, and when Jono indicated that he should sit, he found his legs were swinging, unable to reach the floor. Half-finished wooden carvings, tables, stools and bowls were heaped in a corner, and there was a fine layer of sawdust over everything.

On one of the finished tables was a pile of yellowing books, like those he had seen at Nana's house. Slipping off the high chair, he started leafing through them. Next to them was a parcel. It seemed to be the same one that Thomas had handed to Jono that morning, when they were on the shore with Zoe and Frieda, receiving their tasks for the day. It had looked suspicious then, but now he could guess the contents.

'More books?' he asked.

Jono took the parcel and with a degree of hesitation, began to unwrap it. Two thin, fragile books were inside, the name 'Primo Levi' printed in bold lettering down each spine. Jono added them to a growing pile on the shelf.

'Thomas is attempting to prepare me. He only recently discovered these writings, and they now seem to be his favourite. Each time he visits, he brings me another book. Persecution, discrimination, extermination... I preferred the Shakespeare.' He gave a faint shrug, and Silas saw the flares of fear exert their dominance in his features again. 'Tell me, what is it like in the city... Unseen, Seen? Clinics... Biocubicles?'

Where to start? Silas didn't know what to say. The silence between them stretched for longer and longer until he couldn't stand it any more.

'Before I came here, Zoe and Nana tried to tell me things about the Community and Soulsight, but I didn't understand. How could I? In many ways, my life in the city has been so limited.' He struggled to explain more clearly. 'I had to experience the Community for myself.' He probably wasn't helping, but he persevered. 'Jono, you won't be found here. I'm sure Bubba Gee and the others know what they are doing. The Community will be safe. And if by some unlucky chance you are discovered, it won't be as bad as Coach Atkins thinks. He doesn't know *everything*. My dad says that the Flawless Leader is aiming for better health for all. She wants to help people reach their optimum health. Viva have poured millions into Biocubicles just to ensure that the separation between Unseen and Seen won't be forever.'

If Jono took any consolation from his words, he didn't let it show, but Silas felt he had done his best.

'Thanks for showing me your cabin,' he said.

Lost in thought, and seemingly oblivious to Silas' comment, Jono sat on his huge bed staring at the new additions to his book collection as if frightened to even handle them.

'See you tomorrow?' Silas added, but seeing there was unlikely to be a response, he climbed down the ladder.

An unpleasant pounding had started up in his head and a couple of times he nearly lost his footing as he descended the ladder. He stumbled through the dark, and more by luck than judgment, he found the guest hut.

A sunstorer hung outside and he sighed with relief, muttering, 'Thank you, Zoe.' Then he tiptoed into the cabin and gratefully stretched out on his bed.

Chapter 21

Too hot!

Silas kicked the cover off in a sudden flurry, then moments later his teeth started chattering. Shivering violently, he reached around with his hand and grabbed his blanket, pulling it right up to his chin.

He was on the train, with Zoe. It was moving so fast that the landscape was a blur. But she was pushing him out of the open door, while he held on to the door frame, the cold wind whipping around him. Then his hands slipped, and he was falling, screaming, over a cliff edge into a freezing pool of dark water. He was swimming for the shore when he felt something brush against his leg. A huge eel was wrapping itself around his calf. Then it began to drag him down. Where it touched him, he could feel searing heat until his whole body was burning and the water in the lake began to boil.

He kicked the covers off again, and his flailing arm caught the nightstand. It fell with a loud crash which, in his fevered dreams, became Jono's tree house tumbling down, and, in slow motion, Jono fell with it, turning his fall into a dive, as if hastening towards the solid ground and certain death. 'No!' Silas tried to shout, but no sound came out.

A freezing cold blindfold had been wrapped around his eyes and then Coach Atkins was there. He forced more and more books into Silas' hands, saying, 'Prepare, prepare.'

'I can't see the words with a blindfold on. How can I prepare?' But again, no actual words would come out.

'He's burning up. Get me another wet cloth... I can't believe you let him get so burnt!' Silas felt water dribble through his hair as Nana continued speaking. 'And he's as dry as a bone. Did you make him drink plenty?'

'I am so sorry! I forgot how pale his skin is. It was the Soulsight, Nana. I stopped paying attention to the outside.'

Silas recognised Zoe's voice and tried to hold onto her words, but his brain was sluggish and couldn't make sense of them. He was unable to open his eyes either, and then he realised they were held shut by the heavy wet blindfold from his dreams. The weight lifted off his eyes for a second, and then a cooler, wetter cloth replaced it.

'It's no good blaming the Soulsight. Poor boy! Look at his chest!' He suddenly felt a soothing coolness spread across his boiling hot skin as another cold cloth covered him.

'Nana! He's awake.'

'What's going on?' is what he wanted to say, but a hoarse croak came out instead.

'Si, it's going to be OK, we're here with you. You've got a severe heatstroke.' He tried to listen to Nana, but his delirium was sucking him back under. 'Drink a little before you go to sleep.'

He felt a dribble of water spill into his mouth. It was delicious, and he drank thirstily, water spilling out of the sides of his mouth and down onto the bed.

'This will help to keep his temperature down, but he shouldn't be left alone. He could still have convulsions.' Nana sounded serious as she continued sponging Silas' arms with cold water.

'Nana, it's my fault. I should have looked after him better. I'll stay awake with him. You go back to bed, and I'll call you if he gets worse.'

Silas struggled to stay conscious as Zoe and Nana talked over him, but their words had taken on a distant quality, as if they were talking in another room.

'You must watch him, Zoe. No drifting off to sleep. This is important.'

'I promise,' Zoe said, and even through his hazy concentration he could tell that Zoe was close to tears as she took over from Nana.

'I was distracted... you've changed so much... I'm so sorry,' she was whispering as she replaced the cloth over his chest with a fresh one, and he was sure he felt a gentle kiss on his burnt cheek as he finally succumbed to the welcoming embrace of unconsciousness.

A teardrop fell heavily onto his face and, in his dreams, he lifted his head to catch the first drops of a light refreshing rain.

'Hey, Si.' Someone was gently smoothing his hair and softly calling his name. He pulled fragments of memory together to form a mental image of where he was, and who was touching him, before he committed to opening his eyes.

'Silas,' the voice was calling him again. Ah, yes. I know who that is: Zoe. Definitely open your eyes now. He did so, but it was like dragging sandpaper across his eyeballs, and he winced as he forced his lids apart. It was worth it as he looked up at Zoe. His vision was blurred, but even through that she was so beautiful, a sight for sore eyes... literally.

He blinked again to try to get some tears to ease his discomfort, and as his vision came into better focus he noticed how tired she seemed. Her movements were slow and her shoulders drooped.

'You need to drink again. You're still dehydrated.'

Obediently, he tried to open his mouth, but his dry lips and swollen tongue were uncooperative.

'Here, let me help.' Zoe supported his head and lifted a cup to his lips. Greedily he drained it, and with his immediate needs catered for, his body allowed other sensations to filter through to his clouded brain.

The first thing he noticed was how tight his skin felt. It was like it had shrunk and was suddenly two sizes too small for his muscles and bones. He shifted slightly to reach for the freshly filled cup and the sheet dragged across his exposed chest. He let out a strangulated cry. That hurt! His back, his chest, his arms… in fact, the whole of his upper body was tender and the slightest touch was agony.

'What happened?' he eventually managed to croak at her.

'It's all my fault, Si. We were out in the sun yesterday, and your skin got very burnt. You had fevers all night. I'm so sorry…' She tailed off, looking anxious and upset and Silas wanted to reassure her, but as he moved, his skin cried out its objection, and pain seared over his arms and back.

'Nana's left me some of that green stuff. The cream. It's good for burns too.'

'Anything!' he winced, as he tried not to move. Even the slightest brush of the sheet on his red, raw skin was painful.

Passively he let her gently smooth the disgusting-smelling cream onto his back and chest. It was agony, and it took all his self-control to prevent himself from screaming at her to stop.

After she had finished, he felt exhausted and weak. His eyelids were already drooping closed again, but Zoe wouldn't allow him to sleep before carefully feeding him a little bread, and making him drink. Then he couldn't help himself but drift off, though this time his sleep was easier.

When Silas next awoke, daylight was streaming through the cabin window. The green muck had worked its magic on his skin, and he felt little pain, even though the sheet had stuck to him, and he had to peel it off. More water had been left within easy reach, and he swallowed it down in thirsty gulps.

He thought he was alone, but Zoe appeared from her bedroom carrying a fresh set of sheets. Her face lit up when she saw he was awake.

'How are you feeling?' She fussed over him, touching his head with the back of her hand.

'I'm loads better now.'

Truth be told, he was feeling stronger, but he was quite enjoying all the attention. He was tempted to play the sick role a little longer, and this time be well enough to enjoy it. But she was genuinely worried, and he couldn't add to her concern.

'I feel so responsible.' She was looking down at her feet, as if she was ashamed.

'Why?' he asked, confused. '*You* didn't burn me!'

'I know, but you're not used to…'

'What?'

'Well… having to make decisions for yourself.' Hearing the clumsiness of her own statement, she tried to elaborate. 'What I mean is that you get told what to eat and drink, what to wear, how much to exercise. I guess it wouldn't occur to you to think about those things for yourself. So that's why I should have reminded you about the sun, and drinking plenty.'

She was smiling at him with affection, but Silas suddenly saw her kindness in a new light. She thinks I'm a big baby! A baby that needed to be dressed and fed because it doesn't know how to look after itself. I thought she really liked me, maybe even something more than that… but she just wants to mother me! At that moment he couldn't think of anything worse. She was everything to him; he had never felt like this about anyone. And Zoe… she loved him, that was clear in her gaze, and the way she had cared for him and watched over him as he had slept, but she loved him like a big sister loves a dim-witted kid brother.

Interrupting these thoughts came a noise from outside and the creak of footsteps across the veranda.

Not Jono! Please don't let it be Jono, Silas silently pleaded. He didn't want to witness Zoe and Jono's special relationship play out before him, especially now his own hopes had been crushed.

He breathed a sigh of relief when Nana elbowed her way through the door, her arms laden with boxes and bags.

Closely behind her was a strangely shaped woman with a huge round stomach who waddled heavily into the room and plonked herself down unceremoniously on the end of Silas' bed. He felt the frame move and creak in protest, and hastily

162

pulled his legs from under the covers and got up before the bed gave way completely.

'Silas!' Nana hugged him tightly and it hardly hurt his chest and back at all. 'You are up and about. That's wonderful. You had me worried last night!'

'I'm much better, Nana,' he said. Though, now he was on his feet, he felt a bit shaky and made his way to the table to sit down.

'I can't believe Zoe let that happen to you,' Nana carried on, unwittingly hitting a raw nerve in Silas.

'It's not her fault. I can look after myself you know,' he answered huffily, refusing to make eye contact with any of them. As he said it, he immediately knew that it was nonsense. He had not been able to look after himself. That was obvious; otherwise they wouldn't have to be wasting their time nursing him back to health. Nana merely raised an eyebrow at his remark, reinforcing the absurdity of the comment. But the newcomer, sprawled across his bed, laughed outright and said, 'It doesn't look like that from where I'm sitting, poppet!' And then she cackled again before clutching her enormous belly with both hands and saying, 'Oh, don't make me laugh! It hurts.' This made Nana and Zoe giggle as well.

Silas ground his teeth in irritation and embarrassment. They're laughing at me, he thought, and he was suddenly desperate to get out of the room. He got ready with an excuse about needing to use the washroom when Nana said, 'Si, Zoe, this is Bonnie. She's been part of the Community for – how long would you say – five months now?'

Bonnie nodded, then suddenly, as if remembering her manners, added, 'I see you, Si. I see you, Zoe.'

'I see you, Bonnie,' Zoe replied, warmly.

'I see you, Bonnie,' Silas muttered. Then he forced himself to get over his annoyance and look at her properly. Yet again the Soulsight surprised him.

She was so rich to look at, a feast for the eyes. Not beautiful, like Zoe, but he felt his heart begin to swell with complicated emotions when he looked at her.

He struggled to find the words to describe Bonnie. Love didn't seem to be an exact fit. Zoe, Nana, even Coach Atkins had love, but if Zoe was like the bright morning sun, raw and bold and unrestrained, what came from Bonnie was like the full golden warmth of late afternoon, where colours begin to change and deepen.

It unsettled him, and he was left feeling a little transparent and insubstantial next to her.

'Bonnie's going to look after you tomorrow,' Nana explained, reminding him that, to them, he was still a child that needed babysitting. 'I want you to stay out of the sun for a couple of days until your skin is fully healed. Bonnie will show you around the cave, and you can help her with the food preparation.'

Resigned to the fact that he was a useless burden to them all, Silas didn't even attempt to argue. He just nodded feebly and rested his head in his hands.

'Give me a hand up, would you, Zoe?' Bonnie suddenly said. 'I want to get to the cave. I'm starving. Eating for three is hard work.'

On hearing her comment, Silas glanced at her distended belly again as she levered herself upright, and the penny dropped. Her huge cumbersome body wasn't caused by an illness, or a result of being unhealthy or Unseen. Instead, she was pregnant.

Silas looked at her with a mixture of horror and intrigue. He had never seen a pregnant woman up close. In the city, the HE-LP team cared for most mothers-to-be to minimise all risk to the unborn child. They were most definitely kept as far away as possible from potentially germ-laden teenage boys.

It dawned on Silas, as he squinted past Soulsight to stare at the huge roundness of Bonnie's belly, balanced precariously over two insubstantial-looking legs, that her situation was far

164

more unusual. Bonnie said she was eating for three… so she must be carrying twins. That was very rare and, to Silas' limited understanding, far more risky.

His fascination with Bonnie's pregnancy remained overshadowed by the inescapable fact that he was to be looked after by this woman. He was so useless to Nana and the rest of the Community that for the next couple of days he was going to be stuck in some kind of crèche.

'Wait a moment, Bonnie. Zoe and I will walk with you,' Nana called after her as Bonnie cumbersomely swayed her way to the door, the floorboards of the cabin groaning under her weight. 'Silas,' Nana turned back to him, and he lifted his head from his hands. 'I didn't think you'd be up to eating in the cave tonight, so I brought you some food.'

He mumbled his thanks and then resumed sulkily staring at the table until they'd left. Not even Zoe's gentle goodbye was enough to persuade him to look up.

When he was alone, he opened one of the containers from Nana. Steam rose up and warmed his face. Stew! He inhaled deeply, the rich aroma was almost a meal in itself, and then started to eat it straight from the pot. As it settled in his stomach, he felt warmth flood his whole body. His mood lifted, and he began to feel ashamed of his earlier grumpiness. He knew that if he wanted Zoe to stop thinking of him as a child, he had better stop acting like one.

Resolving to apologise to her first thing in the morning, he pushed the pots aside and, grabbing a chunk of bread, lay down on his bed, eating, and thinking about Zoe. With her face in his mind's eye, he drifted off into a deep sleep.

Chapter 22

'Was I wrong in encouraging him to come here?'

'Why do you say that, Nana?'

The voices were merging with his dream. It was the familiar recurring dream, which felt dull but comfortable after the frenzy of his feverish nightmares. The empty wasteland, but this time, the words were adding colour and texture to it. 'What would happen if he caused some serious damage to his body? Let's say he broke a leg or cracked his skull, like you did last time.' Nana's anxious voice had caused the empty sky to fill with dark clouds and the dusty bare ground was now covered in long green grass. 'How would we explain that to his father? It could expose the whole Community. Maybe I was just being selfish, but he reminds me of his mother. Having him here is like being with her again.'

Silas emerged out of his dream and lay in the dark. He was fully awake now, but with his eyes closed, still and silent, trying to work out where the voices had come from.

'What was Ellen like?' Zoe was talking quietly, but in the silence of the cabin the sound carried. No wonder the noise had broken into his usual dream. At the mention of his mother's name, his eyes shot open. Light was spilling out from under the door to Zoe and Nana's room, seeming unusually bright in the otherwise pitch black of the night.

'She was an inspiration.' That was Nana's voice. 'I've never met anyone quite like her. Bonnie is close, I guess, full of that self-sacrificial love.'

Catching hold of the unusual term, Silas mentally pocketed it to think about later. Then he resumed listening in.

'But Ellen, she would give away her last credit to help someone who needed it.'

There was a pause and a shuffling noise from behind the door. Silas wondered if they would open it. Should he feign sleep? He wasn't intentionally eavesdropping, and it was his family they were talking about, but somehow it still felt wrong to listen in.

Then came a creaking of a wooden bed frame and Nana continued. 'She was tireless, working every night, figuring out a system of how to smuggle out the Unseen that wanted to leave, visiting the sick, making food, and sourcing medicines.

'But then it all became complicated. I didn't know that she had stopped her recommended exercise routine, skipped her health assessments and body scans, and that's how her aneurysm got missed. One day, without any warning, it burst.

'Because her records were out of date, and she hadn't worked to maintain her health, her death was classed as self-inflicted. Like it was suicide!' The noise of a heavy sigh filled the room and Silas realised it had come from him. There was a pause in the conversation in the other room. Had they heard him? He lay still again and tried to breathe quietly.

'Poor Si,' Zoe said.

'Yes, poor Si,' Nana echoed, 'Ellen didn't kill herself; far from it… and now the memory of her life has been tainted, and even her own family is ashamed to talk about her. It must have been a dark time for Silas' father and the boys. Can you imagine? The man who had been called the "Saviour of the Nation", unable to save his own wife.' Nana lapsed into silence, and after a few moments the light from their room was extinguished and soon steady breathing was all that could be heard.

Silas lay in the dark, his head full of the things he had overheard. Self-sacrificial, that was the word he had needed to describe Bonnie. The richest and purest kind of love. How he wished he had seen his mother with the benefit of Soulsight. She must have been so beautiful. She gave up her time, her

167

health and eventually her life for a group of people that no one else could care less about. Could you get any more self-sacrificial?

His memories of her were hazy from having been suppressed for so long, but he remembered her eyes, a mirror image of his own, set in her pale face. 'The eyes are the window of the soul, Silas.' She must have known of Soulsight. Had she used it and seen into his soul? Maybe. He smiled at the possibility of a shared secret that connected him with his mother and let that thought carry him back to sleep.

The next time he was woken up, it was by the sound of running water and clattering pots. Zoe was up and clearing away his mess from the previous evening.

'Leave it,' he tried to say, but only managed to produce a phlegmy rattle. He cleared his throat and tried again. 'Leave it, Zoe. I was going to sort it out.'

She smiled as she looked at him, her face sparkling. His heart did the familiar lurch inside his chest.

'I don't mind, Si. I'll do it. You've not been well.'

'But I'm better now,' he insisted, keen to prove he wasn't completely useless. 'I am able to clean up after myself.' He stood and started stacking up the pots.

'If you insist.' Zoe put down the cup. 'I'll go and get washed first, then.'

'What are you doing today?' Si asked as nonchalantly as possible, hoping beyond hope that she had been allocated some duty or other in the cave with him.

'Jono and I are going to collect waterberries. They're just about ripe, and there's a massive patch near the waterfall.' Recognising the jealous flickers that against his best efforts, stained his features, she added, 'It's going to be boiling today so you will be much better off in the cave. Maybe we can do something in the forest tomorrow. I'll ask Frieda to find us a sheltered job, OK?' She disappeared into the washroom, and then he heard the shower start up.

Silas was unsure whether to feel relieved or disappointed that she hadn't understood the real reason for his jealousy. It was not about picking fruit; it was about her being with Jono, alone. He desperately wanted to spend the day with Zoe, just the two of them. How could he tell her that, though? She obviously didn't feel the same about him.

He did the best he could with the pots. He had never washed up as much as a cup before, and the stew was particularly hard to remove as it had dried into a crusty layer overnight. Just as he was finishing up, he heard the washroom door open and Zoe go into her own room, shutting the door behind her.

Gathering up his towel and clothes, he headed to get cleaned up too. He smelled disgusting, a mixture of feverish sweat and cheesy lotion, and he gratefully stood under the running water, letting the stench dissipate. As he began to methodically wash the muck off his arms and chest, a strange thing began to happen. The green layer of lotion was rinsing away easily enough, but with it came a ballooning layer of white. He pulled at a bubble of it on his arm, and it came off in his hand, tearing down the length of his forearm. With a sickening sensation deep in the pit of his stomach, he realised the bubble of white was a layer of his own skin. He was vividly reminded of the eels being stripped back of their skin, like removing a layer of clothing, showing muscle and guts underneath. Gagging, he noticed the same white blisters on the other arm. This was bad! Pincering it between his finger and thumb, he pulled, feeling it separate from the rest of his body.

'Aargh! Zoe! Help!'

The rising hysteria of panic audible in his voice, he leaned against the shower wall, a long string of skin dangling from his fingers.

Through the fog of his horror, he heard her slam out of her room and, with a sudden moment of clarity, remembered he was completely naked. Grabbing the towel, he let go of the ribbon of skin and watched it wash away with the force of the

169

water. He awkwardly tangled the towel around his waist just a second before Zoe burst through the door.

'What is it? Are you all right? Are you… What are you doing?'

She looked at him standing under the full force of the water with a drenched towel clutched around him.

'I thought you were better. Si, did you know that you're showering with your towel on?' she asked in a confused and concerned tone.

'Well, yes.' Silas shuffled his feet and reached to turn the shower off without dropping his sodden towel. He peered down the drain hole but the white skin layer had been irretrievably swept away.

'Why?'

'Zoe, I didn't call you in here to look at my towel. Something really bad has happened. Look at my skin.' He pinched a bit on his chest, and alarmingly another whole layer came away in his fingers. He pulled and it spread out to form a large thin sheet of translucent skin. This was getting worse and worse – the problem was spreading all over his body. 'And?' Zoe said, shrugging.

'Well, what's going on? Is it a side effect from the green stuff, or from the Soulsight? Zoe – my skin is falling off!'

'Are you being serious?' she asked, although the bemused smile on her face faded as Silas scowled at her. 'Si, you're peeling,' she explained in her soothing tone. 'It happens to pale skin after the sun burns it. It's fixing itself.'

'Oh. Peeling? And that's normal?'

Her gentle nod and amused smile said it all, and he immediately felt exceptionally stupid. He knew nothing about anything, and everything he did just reinforced to Zoe how dim he really was.

To add to his humiliation, Zoe suddenly let out an undignified snort of poorly suppressed hilarity that rapidly deteriorated into laughter.

'Oh, I am so sorry.' She tried unsuccessfully to stop laughing as she backed out of the bathroom. 'It's not funny. I'm not laughing *at* you, it's just that the expression on your face!' As she shut the door firmly behind her, she let rip with full-blown hysterics, occasionally shouting 'Sorry!' as if that would make up for it.

After the incident in the shower, Silas didn't want to face Zoe again that morning. Cringing with embarrassment, his mind kept forcing him to relive the scene. He was just peeling! It was normal. And he'd called her in when he was naked in the shower. What an idiot!

He pulled the heavy curtain across his corner of the room and sat, fully dressed, on his bed, waiting for her to leave.

He didn't have to wait long, for soon there came a double knock at the front door with Jono calling out.

'Good morrow, fair maid.'

Giggling came from Zoe's room.

'Be out in a minute.' She sounded so pleased to be going out, Silas thought dejectedly. Probably glad to be getting away from me, the fool who showers with his towel on.

There was a ripple of movement by his curtain.

'I'll see you later, Si.' Just by the sound of her voice, he could tell she was still close to laughter.

'Yes, see you later.' He couldn't help an element of self-pity creeping into his voice.

'Are you going to be all right today?' she asked, pressing closer to the curtain, forming an indent as her forehead leaned into it. He reached up with his hand as if to stroke her face through the brown fabric, but then she stepped away and the curtain swung back into line.

'I'm fine,' he said, trying to inject some enthusiasm into his voice. 'I'll be fine,' he repeated. He was suddenly grateful for the barrier between them, which hid the telltale shadowy flares of his lies from Zoe.

'Listen, I'm really sorry about the shower thing …' she started to say, but then, from outside, Jono's voice interrupted them,

'"Shall I compare thee to a summer's day? Thou art more lovely and more temperate …"'

'Look, I'd better go. I'll see you later. Bye.'

He heard her leave the cabin, laughing in delight as Jono continued loudly reciting poetry to her.

'Bye,' Silas said to the now empty cabin.

Chapter 23

With a heavy heart, Silas looked around the cave. The large fire still roared in the back corner, belching out heat and smoke. There were figures dotted here and there, all focused on their particular tasks.

'Hi, Silas! Over here!' Bonnie's voice cried out from the darkness at the back of the cave. He squinted, waiting for his pupils to adjust to the low light, and then walked across the sandy floor in the vague direction of the voice.

'Did you sleep well?' she asked as he approached, then without giving him space to answer, continued talking. 'I can't wait for a decent night's sleep. These little fidgets kicked me to death, from the inside out. All night long, I tell you. It'll get worse when they're born, I guess. But at least I'll be able to roll over in bed again!' She kept rubbing her oversized belly. Silas tried not to stare, but it was huge.

Swaying heavily, she led the way into the black depths of the cave, her continual chatter acting as an auditory beacon. The roof above their heads began to slope sharply downwards, and soon Silas was able to raise his arm and run his fingers on the damp stone ceiling. He shivered in the cold air, and felt a tiny flicker of claustrophobia course through him.

'So what's up with you?' Bonnie asked. 'You're very quiet.'

'I'm fine.' He was going to say more, using his poor sleep as an excuse for his silence, but Bonnie cut across him.

'I guess you don't want to be stuck in here with me, when your girlfriend is off enjoying herself in the sunshine.'

'She's not my… girlfriend,' Silas interjected, the sudden rush of blood to his skin providing a temporary surge of warmth.

'Don't even bother telling me she's not. I know you two are together, even if you don't know it yet.' She laughed merrily.

'We're just friends,' he murmured, missing his footing, and stumbling slightly in the dark. 'She doesn't like me like that,' he admitted, unable to keep the disappointment out of his voice.

'Meaning that you *do* like her "like that". Don't need to tell me, I can see it. Right,' she said, suddenly coming to a stop, 'this is your quick guided tour, so if I need something, you can run and get it for me.'

She clicked open a sunstorer. In front of them were three secondary cave entrances. Gulping down a feeling of foreboding, Silas stared at the grey wall and its three pitch-black openings. They looked terrifying, like three options of doom: fear, dread or horror...

'Storage caves. First one, cooking equipment,' Bonnie said, and Silas fought down his nerves and quickly popped his head through the entrance as she shone the light in. There were shelves and shelves of pots, knives and bowls, all neatly stacked and gleaming in the light. The contents were incredibly mundane for such a sinister doorway. More death by boredom than anything else, he thought to himself.

He still stayed close behind the light source as she showed him the middle cave. 'Medicines. Dressings, vitamins, painkillers,' Bonnie listed. 'It's a regular hospital in there.'

Silas' eye fell on two large boxes, shiny and rectangular and very familiar.

'I recognise those,' he said, walking up to look closely. Yes, definitely the same cumbersome boxes. He still had bruises on his shins from those corners. 'We brought them with us on the train.'

'Good old Nana. She keeps us well stocked up. She has a contact that works for Health Emergency-Life Preservation who gets all the drugs that are headed for the incinerator. It's all quality stuff; her contact just keeps it off the record. I haven't got round to sorting through them yet.'

'What's in the last cave?' he asked.

'Food store. Got to be careful of vermin, so we keep storage to a minimum, but we keep our emergency rations in there.' The light fell over a couple of dozen crates, all bearing the Nutrifarm stamp. 'Carboflakes, protein mixes, all the essentials, if we ever hit a bad spell, you know.'

Silas nodded, as if he understood what she was talking about.

Emerging once more into the relative brightness of the main cave, Bonnie clicked the sunstorer closed and handed it to Silas.

'You keep hold of this, so if I need anything from storage you can run and get it for me, OK?'

Silas nodded and slipped the sphere into his pocket.

'Now, let me tell you about the river,' Bonnie said as Silas followed her across one of the many rough wooden bridges spanning the central stream.

'The rules are simple,' Bonnie said. 'The water is fresh and clean. It runs from the lake and heads through the cave on its way out of the crater.' Bonnie waved her hand towards one of the deep recesses of the cave. Silas stared into the darkness and, following the line of the river he thought could make out a dim light under the curve of the cave roof. Before he could ask about it, Bonnie was drawing his attention to the wide cavern opening. 'Water for cooking or drinking is collected from the cave mouth.' Turning his head, he shielded his eyes from the brightness of the light and could make out the silhouette of a woman busily filling a variety of containers with water.

'Today,' Bonnie continued, 'you will be preparing food, which happens here,' she indicated a spot closer to the enticing morning sunshine. 'Washing pots happens there,' she drew his attention back towards the heart of the cave, 'and washing clothes happens right down there.'

Silas stared once more into the dark depths. The faint glow must be coming from a sunstorer, and he thought he could make out two figures squatting down by the inky black river.

Silas shuddered and suddenly felt glad he would be working closer to the light.

'I'll leave you to get on with your task for today. These need to be washed thoroughly – make sure you get all the dirt off.' She indicated a large pyramid of what looked like muddy fist-sized rocks piled at the edge of the stream. 'At least in here you'll be able to keep nice and cool, hey?' She slapped him firmly on the back, causing a shudder of pain to run down his body. His burns were improving, but not completely better yet.

Bonnie ponderously swayed off towards the fire, leaving Silas at the water's edge. Washing mud off rocks... Silas sighed inwardly. What's that got to do with food preparation? he wondered. Still, he consoled himself, it shouldn't take too long, and then maybe he could catch up with Zoe later.

Although his hands were numb from the cold water, Silas' task was unchallenging. The pile of mud concealed vegetables, not stones, and it was hypnotic, watching the dirt swirl off in the clear stream, revealing the shiny orange or beige skin underneath.

He lost count after his hundredth vegetable when, from out of nowhere, he suddenly became distracted with the thought of Zoe... out with Jono... exploring, laughing together. What else? Flirting? He sat up a bit straighter. What if Jono's making a move on her? I bet he's been waiting for a chance to be alone with her, ever since he came to 'surprise' her at the crater edge on their first day. He hadn't expected me to be there. He's never really accepted me, and there I was, beginning to see him as a friend, Silas ruminated with a growing sense of outrage. But he's wanted rid of me since day one!

All the tolerant feelings he'd had towards Jono evaporated as he imagined them together in the sunshine. Anger started to build in him, and his hands ceased washing and gripped tightly to the rough vegetable as if it were Jono's neck. His fingers began to squeeze...

'Are you having a nice little dream there?' called Bonnie's voice behind him.

'Huh?' With a start, he relaxed his hands and hurriedly resumed the monotonous task of washing. Muddy vegetable in – scrub, scrub – shiny vegetable out.

'What are you thinking about?' Bonnie asked as she sat down on a large flat rock at the edge of the river, just a bit downstream from Silas. It was a complicated process for her, involving a lot of gasps and groans, but eventually she seemed comfortable and, with a sigh of pleasure, thrust her puffy purple feet into the cold running water.

'Nothing much,' Silas answered, preferring to keep those particular thoughts about Jono to himself. However, that wasn't a satisfactory response for Bonnie, who tutted her displeasure.

'People are always thinking about something. Even if it is inconsequential.'

Feeling annoyed by her persistence, Silas said sharply, 'You seem to be able to read minds, so why don't you tell me?'

She took no offence, just laughed a big, wobbly laugh, then groaned, 'Oh, what did I say about not making me laugh!' then clutched her enormous belly with both hands. 'Fine,' Bonnie said when her discomfort settled. 'I would say that you were thinking about Zoe and Jono.'

Dumbfounded, Silas dropped an orange vegetable in the stream and scrabbled quickly to retrieve it.

'How did you ...? Does Soulsight work in a different way with you? Can you actually see what people think?' He looked at her fully again, and was struck with the incredible depth and splendour of her beauty. His mind went back to the overheard conversation between Nana and Zoe. His mother looked like Bonnie, full of that beautiful, golden, self-sacrificial love. How he wished he had seen her properly, with Soulsight. But then what would she make of me? he thought. What if she was disappointed in me? That would be awful; my father

177

disappointed in my physique and my mother in the state of my soul!

Bonnie was still holding his gaze, and she smiled at him.

'No, I can't read your mind, and Soulsight works the same on everyone. But your jealous streak was coming through really strong, messing up your handsome soul.' Bonnie winked. 'It doesn't take a genius to figure out what makes envy like that bubble up.'

Unlike Coach Atkins' painfully clumsy comments when he had seen fit to openly dissect Silas' soul, somehow it wasn't embarrassing when Bonnie did the same thing, and Silas was suddenly eager for her help.

'How do I stop that happening? I don't want Zoe to see me like that! She already thinks I'm just a stupid child, and I don't want her to think I'm a hideous, stupid child.' He was full of self-pity now. He wanted to impress Zoe, and everything he did went wrong. Although he knew he was kidding himself if he thought she would ever feel the same about him as he did about her... Especially not after the episode in the shower... Ugh, maybe he couldn't cope with seeing her at lunchtime.

'She doesn't see you like that at all. No one does,' Bonnie said, emphatically. It did little to lift Silas' spirits. 'Let's look at it this way, Silas. What is the opposite of jealousy?'

Silas was puzzled. 'I don't know. Maybe you can only not be jealous if you don't care about someone. Would that be better? Not to care about Zoe?' He shrugged his shoulders, knowing his words made no sense. He couldn't stop himself from being concerned about her. She was permanently etched on his mind.

Bonnie laughed at him. 'That sounds like an impossible goal!' she said, accurately guessing his thoughts again. 'I would say the answer to your predicament is trust. Which leaves you with this question: do you trust Zoe?'

Silas nodded slowly, mulling over Bonnie's words. Of course he trusted Zoe. That was one of the first things he saw in her at his initiation. He could tell Zoe everything and anything and she would never use it against him.

'Good,' Bonnie smiled, 'so when your old friend jealousy comes back to bite you, you focus on how much you trust her, not only with your friendship, and your heart, but also with how she feels about Jono.'

'But I don't want her to have feelings for Jono,' he interrupted sulkily, making Bonnie chuckle again.

'Oh, Silas!' Bonnie shook her head in mock despair. 'You were making good progress for a moment there. Enough of the "I want, I don't want". You focus on Zoe. Show her that you trust her. Your jealous feelings will wither and die and they won't trouble you again.'

A commotion at the far end of the cave entrance made them both look up. In ones and twos, people were arriving, carrying in the fruits of their morning's work. Half a dozen dead birds, another load of eggs, bucket-loads of fruit and vegetables were all deposited in the empty containers.

'Feeding time already!' Bonnie groaned as she laboriously levered her body upright. 'Si, get those vegetables over near the fire; they can be cooked for the evening. Then grab yourself a lunch pack.'

He did as he was told, but all the while keeping watch over the parade of people coming into the cave. He saw Nana and Bubba Gee hand in hand, followed by Coach Atkins with a cluster of small children around him. Frieda arrived and left again, carrying an armful of lunch packs, and then he remembered that Zoe had promised to speak to her about task allocation for the next day. I wonder if she did, he thought, as he munched through his food. I don't want to be in the cave again tomorrow! He was about to chase after Frieda to double-check, when Bonnie called to him.

'Si, could you give me a hand? I am melting here.'

Bonnie was standing by the firepit, stirring one of the huge cauldrons of food. Sweat was pouring off her brow, and she fanned herself ineffectively with her spare hand.

Suddenly she took a little unsteady step backwards, blindly feeling for the cave wall behind her.

'I don't feel well,' she said in a small voice. Her legs seemed to suddenly give way, twisting awkwardly as she slumped against the wall, causing her to slide into a sitting position.

Silas' first instinct was to reach for the HE-LP key, but then remembered there was no Biocubicle here, and there was no Emergency team at all. Thankfully, he hadn't been the only person to witness Bonnie's sudden collapse, and shouts of alarm had brought people running from all over the cave. Nana was first there.

'Si, help me. We need to lay her down and get her onto her left side!' Nana's shout galvanised him into action.

He tried to manoeuvre her, but it was next to impossible. She was immense. He may as well have been trying to shift a boulder. Then other hands were there, helping him, and between them they managed to manhandle her to the correct position. The colour began to return to Bonnie's face within seconds of her lying down, and shortly afterwards she opened her eyes. She remained still and silent as Nana shooed away the helpers.

'Thank you, everyone, that's all we need for now. Bonnie will be better soon; she just fainted. Let's give her some space now.'

Silas started to sidle away as well. Seeing Bonnie faint brought back unsettling memories of finding his mother dying. Like Bonnie, her eyes had been open, but they had been unfocused and unseeing. As her damaged brain shut down, her active body stopped functioning, and she lay inert, a slumped heap of tangled limbs.

'Silas, good, you're still here.' Nana beckoned him over. He took a reluctant step closer to Bonnie, almost frightened of what he might see.

'Nana,' Bonnie whispered, 'the babies …'

Shushing her, Nana patted her arm, then rested her hand lightly on Bonnie's belly. 'I'll check now,' she murmured reassuringly.

'Si, did Bonnie show you where the medical supplies are?' Nana asked, her voice calm and matter-of-fact as she prodded and squeezed Bonnie's stomach.

'Yes, in the storage caves.' He tried to match her composed demeanour, though a little tremble of anxiety caused his words to sound high-pitched and childish. He cleared his throat. 'What do you need?'

'On the shelf at the back wall there is a black case containing a scanner.' She lifted her hands from examining Bonnie and held them up in the air in an approximation of its size. 'It's not very big and it should be labelled. You'll also need a power pack, which will be on the shelf next to it. But if that has been used, then there will be spares in the big boxes that we brought with us.'

'OK.' Silas started to jog towards the back wall of the cave, keen to help, but relieved to have a task to do that was far away from where Bonnie was recovering.

Pulling the sunstorer from his pocket, he clicked it open as he entered the narrow passageway at the back of the cave. It flickered a little in the dark; it must be nearly out of charge. He shook it firmly, which did nothing to improve the strength of the dim glow it was now emitting. The fading light gave extra urgency to his task, and he hurried into the medical store. Skirting around the silver boxes, he came to the back shelf. There were a variety of square cases and boxes, the colours all fading to grey in the low light from the sunstorer. He ran his hands over them, looking at the labels. At last he found the scanner, and as the light faltered and went out, he saw the chunky rectangle of the power pack snuggled in next to it. He grabbed both, and then, drawing on his spatial memory, started inching back towards the entrance. His knee caught one of the bulky boxes and, suddenly thankful for them, he used them as a guide and followed the edge to the cave entrance. His eyes were adjusting now, and the pale black arch of the doorway was clearly visible. Within moments he was back in the main cave. The light seemed unnaturally dazzling, and he blinked to counteract the brightness as he hurried over to Nana and Bonnie.

Bonnie was still lying down but was properly awake now. The glazed look in her eyes had gone, and her voice carried across the cave as she argued with Nana.

'I fainted because I stood for too long by that boiling hot fire, that's all. I've just felt the babies kick. Look at that, you can *see* them kicking.' She pulled up her shirt, exposing the pale pink balloon of her stomach just as Silas arrived with the scanner. He stared in shock. Her belly looked awful. Vivid purple wounds ran from her navel to her flanks, radiating out like the legs of a monstrous spider. As he watched, he saw her whole abdomen suddenly wriggle and shift, and under the skin a new bulge appeared and glided smoothly across the top of her stomach, then disappeared under the rib cage. Silas made a thick choking noise in his throat, causing Nana to look round.

'Great! You found it. Let's have a look, then, Bonnie. We may as well, now Silas has brought us the scanner.' Without waiting for confirmation, Nana took the box from Silas and clicked it open. Picking up a rectangular screen, she connected the power pack to the side and held the scanner over Bonnie's exposed stomach. Silas was riveted to the spot. He felt emotion flood through him. It was like seeing with Soulsight for the first time. Bonnie's pregnancy-ravaged belly, so damaged and bloated, concealed two miniature human beings. The two babies were facing each other, but their heads were low in Bonnie's pelvis so they could only see the shoulders and neck of each one. A small fist suddenly appeared in the picture, the tiny fingers uncurling slowly.

'Both are head down, Bonnie, that's good news, hey?' Nana said conversationally, then she pushed a button on the scanner, causing the image to change, and there were two tiny hearts beating almost in unison. 'Good,' Nana muttered, and then flicked the image back.

'How's the boy?' Bonnie replied, biting her lip, obviously anxious.

'I can't tell which is which yet, but they look the same size, so he must be growing.' Nana moved the scanner up to hover over Bonnie's navel. The image showed the back of one of the babies. The perfect curve of its spine concealed the other twin behind it. Unexpectedly the smooth skin surface altered and Nana held the scan over an uneven lump at the base of the spine. Nana moved the scan up even further and watched the baby's legs kick a couple of times.

'The boy is here, at the front. He seems to be using his legs well... despite the lump.' Moving the scanner to one side, Nana ran her hand up the front of Bonnie's stomach. 'Let's roll you this way and get a good look at the girl.'

Bonnie obediently moved onto her side and Nana repeated the slow scan. This time there were no lumps or blemishes to see. The second baby looked perfect.

Handing the equipment back to Silas, Nana helped Bonnie to sit upright.

'You need to go home and get some rest, Bonnie,' Nana said.

'I'll do no such thing!' Bonnie retorted. 'You've seen the babies are fine and I'm better now. It was just a faint. Anyway, there is too much to do here.'

Nana shook her head without arguing back until Bonnie added, 'All right, all right! I'll take it easy. Just sitting here. Keeping an eye on things. OK? But don't make me "rest". I'll go mad doing nothing! Silas is here. He's a good lad. He'll help me, won't you Si?' she pleaded, looking directly at him, and leaving him no option but to say, 'Of course... I'll help.'

Chapter 24

With her feet raised on a cushioned box, and her back and head resting against the cave wall, Bonnie seemed to recover full use of her mouth at least. She kept up an almost constant flow of conversation, interspersed with a barrage of cooking instructions for Silas. He had to admit he had started her off, though, by asking the simple question of, 'Why?'

'Why what, Si?'

Silas waved his available hand around the dingy cave, while his other hand continued forcing a ladle through the thick gloop in the cooking pot. 'Why did you come here? I mean, you are a Seen, right? You could have your twins in a health facility, couldn't you? All safe and clean?'

Bonnie nodded in agreement. 'It's true.'

'So, why ...?'

'Pass me that knife and a pile of those potatoes, will you? I may as well use my hands. I'm sure Nana can't object to that, now, can she?'

She continued talking as he carried the equipment and a huge pot of the freshly scrubbed vegetables to her.

'I found out I was pregnant and I was ecstatic. Ten years we'd been trying for a baby... and then when it was twins! It was the best news ever. But the early assessments showed a problem with the little boy. Did you see it on the scan?'

'Yes,' Silas admitted, 'a lump, on its back.' He held up his thumb and finger to form a small circle in the air.

'Everyone was pushing me to have a selective termination. Even my husband insisted that it was the logical choice. But I couldn't do it. I didn't want to. When the day came for the procedure I just walked out of the HE-LP clinic. I had started to feel movements. I tried to explain it to my husband, but he was having none of it. "I'm not going to be responsible for bringing another Unseen into this world," he said. Fifteen years we'd been together and suddenly he was like a different man. He left me, and I let him go.' Bonnie shook her head sadly, then seemed to recollect who she was talking to.

'It's OK.' Silas gave a weak smile. Although he felt embarrassed by Bonnie's openness, Soulsight showed him how deeply hurt she was. Inseparable from the wonderful golden love she radiated was the pain of the decision she had made.

'Anyway, my babies were growing bigger, and I still had a difficult decision to make. I didn't really know what to do,' Bonnie continued. 'I didn't want one twin to grow up being Seen, and for the other to be Unseen. I want both my children to know what it feels like to have the sun on their face, and to grow up with people who accept them for who they are, not how healthy they are.' She handed a pot of finely chopped vegetables to Silas. 'Add that, and keep stirring... don't let it burn!'

'I am stirring,' he defended himself, as he tipped the fresh ingredients in.

'You have to get the spoon right to the bottom or it all sticks. Look, let me do it.' Bonnie started the complex procedure of trying to stand, which caused Silas to show renewed vigour in his cooking.

'Sit down, Bonnie. I'm doing it! Nana will send you home if she catches you standing up again,' he threatened. 'So how did you end up here, with the Community?' he added, trying to distract her with another question.

Bonnie reluctantly settled back against the wall, watching Silas' every move with a sharp eye.

'I knew Nana from years back, and she's always known what to do. She's very wise. She suggested this as a third option. It's risky, I know that, but... it's the best chance my boy will have.' She craned her neck to try to peer into the pot.

'Lift it off the heat now and stick a lid on it; it can simmer for a while.'

Silas turned a handle at the side, and the pot lifted out of the firepit.

'That's perfect, it will keep nice and warm now,' Bonnie said, then pointed to a giant metal lid, which Silas carefully slid over the pot.

'Good. Now go into the storage cave and get the big metal bowls. There should be about ten of them, and we'll need spoons and knives.'

By the time the rest of the Community returned to the cave for their evening meal, Silas had made over a dozen trips into the storage caves, toing and froing, fetching and carrying, and he was glad his day's work was nearly over. He watched eagerly for Zoe and Jono, or to be more accurate, he watched eagerly for Zoe and slightly reluctantly for Jono.

Yet as the strip of sky visible from the cave faded to dusky purple, and the shadows outside deepened to black, and everyone else was settled in small groups, dipping hunks of bread into bowls of vegetable mush, his impatience became concern. Where were they? Was Zoe all right? He knew how reckless Jono could be. What if she'd become injured in some stupid stunt or game of Jono's? He was on the brink of sharing his fears with Nana or Bonnie when, eventually, they arrived.

Although their return to the cave was unnoticed by everyone else, to Silas it was like the whole evening had lit up. Zoe's face was as radiant as ever; she seemed to illuminate the whole cavern. Even from across the other side of the cave, she filled his vision and caused his pulse to start racing. Behind her, Jono towered like an ever-present, loyal guard dog.

Amid the return of his earlier paranoia about Jono, Silas watched them carefully. They weren't holding hands or gazing into each other's eyes – that was a good sign. Then he noticed that Zoe was scanning the groups of people seated around the cave floor, as if looking for someone, until eventually she spotted him. She immediately smiled and waved, sending his pulse galloping triple-time, and he grinned at her from across the room. Zoe started to move towards him, and he had to restrain himself from leaping across to her. The 12 hours apart seemed to have lasted a week, and he wanted to tell her all about Bonnie, and hear about her day.

Their reunion would have been sweet and touching, had it not been for Coach Atkins performing an incredibly slick intercept by grabbing Zoe's hand as she passed close by where he was sitting. Zoe cast an apologetic glance at Silas and then allowed herself to be seated between Coach Atkins and Nana.

Now Silas faced a dilemma. To go and talk to Zoe would also mean having to sit near Coach Atkins, and he wasn't sure he had the energy for another lecture. He stood watching Zoe immerse herself in Coach Atkins' conversation for a few moments until a tall figure blocked his view.

'We missed you today.'

Looking suspiciously up into Jono's face, Silas saw only a statement of fact and was pleasantly surprised.

'Thanks, Jono! I missed being with you two as well. Did you get the fruit?' he asked.

'Loads! We filled the cart,' Jono said proudly.

'What cart?' Silas strained his eyes to see into the darkness outside.

'I'll show you, come on.' Jono started to lead the way out of the cave. Looking over his shoulder, Silas tried to catch Zoe's eye, but she was now fully engrossed in her conversation and didn't notice him leave. Reluctantly, he followed Jono outside and came face to face with the most depressed-looking animal he had ever seen.

'Silas, meet Terence the donkey,' Jono said with mock formality.

Laughing, Silas bowed and then did the Community eye-to-eye greeting of 'I see you, Terence the donkey.'

Chuckling, Jono gently stroked Terence's long ears. The donkey gave no sign of appreciation, but stood stoically, as if he was enduring the affection. He raised his nose briefly when Jono produced an apple, which was dispatched with two rapid crunches, then resumed his patiently disinterested waiting.

'Round here, look.' A rickety cart was hitched up to the back end of the donkey, and it was piled high with crates full of fist-sized blue fruits. 'Waterberries,' Jono said, proudly.

'Jono! That is loads. You must have worked all day!' As Silas walked around the cart, inspecting the piles of fruit, he felt relieved. For Jono and Zoe to pick all this, they must have picked fruit flat out, with no time for the romantic scenarios that his suspicious mind had created.

'Try one, they're good to eat,' Jono encouraged.

Selecting a dark blue fruit, Silas turned it over in his hands. The skin was shiny, like it had been polished to a high gloss, and completely smooth, except for a dimple and a stalk. He sank his teeth into it, and the juice spurted out, flooding his mouth with sweet, fragrant water. He wiped the juice off his chin and took another bite. He could understand where the name 'waterberry' came from. They were a drink and a fruit all in one.

'Bubba Gee will take the most, though. Waterberry rum tastes even better than waterberry fruit.'

Halfway through wiping the sweet, sticky juice off his face, Silas looked up in surprise.

'Rum? You mean alcohol?'

'Only on special occasions, mind you. Births, weddings, funerals ...' Jono caught sight of the surprise on Silas' face.

'But alcohol is banned. It's very unhealthy; you may as well drink poison! Surely you know that?'

Jono waved his hand dismissively in the air. '"Come, come, good wine is a good familiar creature, if it be well used: exclaim no more against it"!'

'That's your old buddy Shakespeare again, I suppose. Well, I wonder how long he lived for, eh?' The question was rhetorical but Jono answered promptly.

'He only reached 52… and he probably died of syphilis… but look at what he achieved in his life. Here we are, nearly 700 years after his death, still quoting him!'

Silas rolled his eyes, reluctant to concede his point, adding, '*You* are still quoting him.'

'Grab a couple of crates for everyone in there, would you?' Jono angled his head towards the cave, then grasped Terence's bridle. 'I'm going to take the rest to Bubba Gee's.'

Pursing his lips with disapproval, Silas lifted a couple of boxes off the back before Terence pulled the cart away into the dark. This was the first difference he had encountered at the Community that really bothered him. Living without Biocubicles and health assessments was risky, but that was understandable if your only other option was to be classed among the Unseen. The unmonitored nutrition was another unwise but unavoidable side effect of living so remotely, but choosing to poison the body, actually making alcohol to drink… that was plain stupid.

'Guess who?' It was Zoe's voice; she had crept up behind him, and covered his eyes with her soft hands. They smelled of the sweet waterberry juice. Silas tried to think of the most unlikely person who would initiate a guessing game.

'Um, Coach Atkins? Is that you?' Silas said, as innocently as he could, hoping to make Zoe laugh. She let out a surprised squeal of amusement and took her hands off his face.

'No, that was Zoe,' came the coach's unmistakable monotone. Horrified and embarrassed, Silas spun around; Zoe was bent double in silent paroxysms of laughter. Coach Atkins stood behind her, his all-pervasive gloom unruffled by the awkward humour of the situation.

'Zoe and I have come to help you carry in the waterberries. The children love them. Have you tried one?'

'Yes. Thanks, Coach… I mean, Thomas. They're lovely.' Silas stumbled over his words, attempting to cover up his discomfiture. 'Here,' he hefted one of the crates and handed it to Coach Atkins, who took it into the cave. Picking up the other one, he turned to scowl at Zoe, who was just about recovering her composure.

'You could have told me he was standing there!' he hissed at her.

'How was I to know you were going to "guess" him, of all people? I love you, you are hilarious!' Wiping a tear from her eye with the back of her hand, she turned to follow Coach Atkins.

Standing alone in the dark, holding a heavy crate of waterberries, Silas' heart did an ecstatic dance of victory. She *had* said it – his mind replayed her parting comment. She'd said, 'I love you'!

Chapter 25

'I'm nervous. Are you nervous?' Zoe whispered into Silas' ear, her warm breath pleasantly ticklish.

'A little,' he admitted, also keeping his voice to a whisper.

Her face was so close to his, and he gazed into her eyes, momentarily lost to all else except Zoe.

'Shh!' Jono hissed over his shoulder. 'They'll hear you and run, and then we'll have to start all over again.'

'Sorry,' Zoe whispered back contritely, and then rolled her eyes at Silas, making him want to laugh.

Reluctantly, Silas inched his way forward on his belly away from Zoe. Her excited giddiness was contagious, and he didn't want to mess up his chance to be involved with the hunt.

'Take a look,' Jono passed him a chunky black box. It had a viewfinder and two switches.

'What do these do?' Silas whispered, pointing at the brightly coloured buttons.

'Don't touch those… yet!' Jono flinched and angled the box to point away from them. 'It's a disruptor,' Jono said, as if that explained it. 'Just start by looking through it.'

'OK.' Silas raised the box to his eyes and squinted through it at the herd of deer a couple of hundred metres away. They were beautiful. A handful of stags, the largest sporting an impressive set of antlers, kept careful watch over 50 or more females. They were grazing, and the whole herd was steadily moving towards the long grass where Jono had chosen to lay in wait.

Although he had barely moved a muscle for over an hour, Silas' heart was racing so much he felt like he had run a marathon. The adrenaline coursing through him was intense. He handed the scope back to Jono.

'They need to be closer for the target lock to work,' Jono murmured.

The three of them lay silent, still and watching.

Over the past couple of weeks they had become inseparable.

It was helped by Silas' decision to follow Bonnie's advice and replace his jealousy with trust. In doing so, his relationship with Zoe and Jono had deepened and matured. His fervent love for Zoe hadn't abated, but his cautious friendship with Jono had developed into a brotherly affection far stronger than he had ever experienced with Marc, his real brother.

Every job that Frieda suggested, they requested to do together, from cleaning out the composting toilets, to egg collection and milking the herd of temperamental goats. The long mild evenings were spent watching the sun set behind the crater rim from the rocky outcrop in the middle of the lake, or gathered around the fire in the large cave talking and laughing with others of the Community. Silas had never known such acceptance, and he savoured every moment.

'Here they come.' Jono passed the bulky binoculars back to Silas. 'You do it,' he encouraged.

'Really?' Silas said with excitement, then, realising he was making too much noise, lowered his voice to a whisper again. 'What about you?' he asked Zoe, not wanting to get in her way. After all, it was her first hunt too.

'Not a problem – I'll take my turn after you miss,' she said teasingly, grinning at him.

He grinned back, then dragged his eyes away from her to concentrate on the deer in front of him.

'You want a young doe. They give the best meat. There is one right at the edge of the herd.' Jono muttered instructions as Silas gazed through the scope.

'Got it,' he muttered back.

A tiny pang of regret formed in his mind. Down the magnifying lens of the disruptor he could see that the doe was beautiful. Its large black eyes were framed with long, elegant lashes, and its soft, dusky brown speckled coat shone in the sun. Could he do this? He didn't have to. Jono and Zoe wouldn't think any the less of him. He didn't need to prove himself to anyone. But then, the Community had to eat. They didn't have a supply of artificial protein to keep them strong, so animal protein was the only option, and this week the source of the protein was fresh venison.

'When you've got the cross hairs over the deer's head, press the Target Acquired button. The blue one.'

Silas suppressed his reservations and followed Jono's instructions.

'Try not to wobble.' Jono helped hold the scope steady. 'Now press the red Disrupt button.'

The doe didn't even flinch, and Silas thought he had missed. He kept staring through the viewfinder as she suddenly, silently crumpled to the ground, her legs folding up neatly beneath her. The remainder of the herd continued grazing, utterly unaware and undisturbed by the disaster that had befallen one of their own.

'Whoa!' Silas let out one long breath and turned the scope over in his hands. The warm sun rapidly evaporated the wet sheen of his two sweaty handprints.

'How does this work? It didn't even make a noise.'

'The disruptor is one of Thomas' little gifts to the Community, should we need to defend ourselves.' Jono rolled his eyes at the improbability of Coach Atkins' doom and gloom prophecies ever coming true.

'Talk about overreacting! This is deadly. What does he expect you to do? Kill people with it?' The incredulity in Silas' voice made them all laugh. The noise did the job that the doe's death had failed to do, scaring away the rest of the herd of deer. They scattered, leaping and zigzagging, into some nearby trees.

'Who knows,' Jono shrugged. 'But it is a useful bit of kit for hunting. You don't even need a very steady hand. The scope locks onto the target brain stem signal, disrupts it and,' Jono clicked his fingers, 'painless brainstem death. Just like that. No blood or gore… very tidy.'

Suddenly nervous to be holding such a deadly item, Silas hurriedly returned the scope to Jono.

'The trick is to be in range. It can't lock on over 100 metres.' Standing up and brushing grass and dirt off his clothes, Jono started to walk over to where the deer lay.

Swinging from side to side with each step they took, the body of the doe hung heavily upside down from a long sturdy pole. Its legs had been securely lashed together over the top, but its head lolled down, occasionally grazing the floor, until Jono looped a coil of rope behind its neck to tuck the head between its forelegs.

Silas was in the lead, the pole resting on his right shoulder. To keep the height even, Jono had to carry his end hooked in the crook of the elbow of his good arm. Though Jono seemed to experience no discomfort, after a while the pole dug in to Silas' shoulder, and it caused his whole arm to become numb.

'This is heavy! Weights never were my speciality subject,' he complained.

'I'll take it for a bit.' Zoe shuffled next to him. 'I've got more padding, and you're too bony, so no wonder it hurts!' she teased. Between them they moved the pole across for Zoe to carry.

As he massaged his shoulder and neck, the feeling started to return in the form of intense pins and needles. Silas groaned and waved his arm around, attempting to shorten the duration of the tingling.

Abruptly he stopped and stood completely still, blocking the path.

'What's wrong?' said Zoe. 'I nearly walked into you.'

'Hush!' Silas waved his arm around again, but this time in an attempt to silence her. 'Did you hear that?'

'What? Come on, this is heavy! Or have you already forgotten that?'

They had walked for an hour from the deer's grazing area and had just reached the edge of the forest. The shady cool of the trees was beckoning so, deciding he must have imagined it, Silas started walking again, only to suddenly come to a halt once more.

'There!'

This time they all heard it. A guttural moaning emanated from behind a tree that stood beside the dusty path. Someone sounded like they were in pain. Jono and Zoe gently lowered their burden and stood near Silas.

'Hello?' Silas edged forward.

'Help!' a weak voice responded, rapidly altering to become another wordless groan.

Immediately recognising the voice, Silas threw off any caution and quickly stepped around the large tree trunk.

'Bonnie, what are you doing? Are you hurt?' He knelt beside her. She looked pale and sweaty, and gritted her teeth in pain as she let out another animal groan.

'Si...' she gasped, as she got her breath back. 'It's my time. The babies are coming.'

'Now?' He jumped up in alarm. 'Here?'

'Yes. Unless... Help me up, and I can try to get home.' She stretched both her hands out to him. Between them they got Bonnie on her feet, only for her to hunch over in crippling pain.

'Oh, it hurts!' she hissed through clenched teeth.

'Shall I get Nana?' Silas asked, feeling totally out of his depth.

'Hasn't she gone away for a few days?' Bonnie forced the words out as her pain subsided.

Silas had forgotten about that. Coach Atkins had persuaded Nana to leave the Community and visit their friends in the local town with him, to find out more about the proposed 'Future Health' laws. He had been irritatingly insistent, interrupting most evenings with his paranoid ramblings. Perhaps Nana had thought it easier just to do as he requested, rather than tolerate another session of nagging. The man was insufferable! Great timing from you, yet again, Coach Crazy! Silas thought.

'Well, who else can I get for you?' Fighting the panicky urge to run, he let her drape her arm around his shoulders and took the burden of her weight as she leaned heavily on him.

'Frieda. She said she'd help. If Jono could find her?' she said between gritted teeth, as another wave of pain seemed to crash over her.

Jono nodded. 'Of course. I'll bring her to you. I'll be quick.'

'Si, go to the medical stores ...' Another pain made her stop walking and she groaned again. '... And get the scanner, and the labour pack. It should be in one of the big boxes. Nana promised she'd request one.'

'Sure!' Silas said, as Zoe stepped in to support Bonnie. 'Will you be all right?'

Zoe nodded, and he turned his back on them and ran as fast as he could towards the cave.

Chapter 26

It was only mid-afternoon, and at first glance the cave seemed deserted. Although Silas knew the way to the storage caves easily enough after his day helping Bonnie, he wouldn't be able to search through the cases without a light. There must be someone here with a sunstorer.

'Hello? Anyone?' he called, his voice bouncing off the high cavern roof.

A movement near the fire caught his eye. The light from the flames flickered, casting a huge shadow on the back wall… A nightmarish grotesquery of the human form; elongated and distorted by the fluctuating flames. Then, to Silas' relief, the shadow compressed to a less alarming size, then it shrank down again to become a perfect fit for the figure of Bubba Gee.

'Bubba Gee!' Silas shouted, running to him. 'Bonnie needs our help. She's giving birth now!'

'Silas, I see you!' Bubba Gee boomed at Silas as he approached.

'Yes, I see you, too,' Silas responded, rushing through the greeting. 'Can you…'

Bubba Gee interrupted. 'What were you saying about Bonnie? Has she gone into labour? Oh, Eva will be livid to miss the birth!' He toddled with his peculiar childish gait away from the fire, and sat on a low stone. 'She's the one you need, really. I've got no idea when it comes to babies and the like. I don't think I can be much help to you, son.'

'No, no! Jono is getting Frieda for all that stuff.' Silas suppressed a shudder at the idea of being in charge of birthing a baby, momentarily losing his train of thought.

'Oh, good.' Bubba Gee sounded relieved. 'That's very good. Frieda is best for that. So, what help do you need from me, young man?'

With a start, Silas was reminded of the urgency of his task. 'A sunstorer! Have you got a sunstorer? I need to find a scanner and a labour pack or something. It's in the storage cave.' Silas was talking faster and faster, frustrated now by the conversational sidetrack.

'Now, that is something I can assist you with, Silas,' Bubba Gee said, nimbly getting to his feet and trundling over to the fireside. 'I've got two!' He triumphantly held up his hands, his stubby fingers barely reaching around the circumference of the silver sunstorers. 'Let's look for the things you need together.'

'I can't see it. It's not in here!' Silas was bent at the waist inside the storage container in the medical supply cave. Bubba Gee stood beside him, his head just peeking over the top of the box. Under one arm he had tucked the scanner and battery pack, and his other hand held the sunstorer as high as he could to cast sufficient light for Silas to find the elusive labour pack.

'Suture kit, analgesics. No way... Bone saw!' Silas continued to search through the contents of the crate. 'Definitely not in this one,' he declared, standing upright.

Bubba Gee was already fiddling with the clasp on the second case, and as the lock released, Silas lifted the lid upwards.

'Aha!' Sitting on top of the pile of medical booty was a clearly marked package: 'Labour pack.' Silas triumphantly lifted it out and was about to drop the lid closed when something caught his eye.

'Bubba Gee, what's that?'

Wedged behind a multipack of the malodorous green lotion, which Nana favoured as a heal-all, was a slim, grey case. It was

198

the size of Silas' palm, and he wouldn't have noticed it, except it had just started emitting a light.

Silas picked it up for a closer look. The case appeared seamless, there was no catch or opening mechanism, and it had a solid, weighty feel to it. The light pulse was faint and came from within the device. Had it not been so dark in the cave, the weak glow would barely have been visible.

He passed it to Bubba Gee, who was stood on tiptoes, peering into the large supply box. A gossamer thread trailed from the gadget and, following it with his fingers, Silas traced it to the edge of the supply box.

'It's attached here, Bubba Gee, look.' The thread was firmly fused to the solid metal rim. 'What is it?' Silas asked.

Turning it over in his hands, Bubba Gee frowned. 'I don't know exactly, but it looks like some kind of beacon... a transmitter.'

They locked eyes and, with a jolt, Silas saw the first flicker of shadow emerge in Bubba Gee. Fear, dark and primitive, ever lurking, ever present, ready to paralyse and consume, as the full implication of what the device may mean started to sink in.

'Where did it come from? Why is it in with the medical supplies?' Silas asked, unsettled by the change that had come over Bubba Gee.

'It appears to have been placed quite deliberately, and designed to start transmitting only when the supply box was opened,' Bubba Gee said as he twisted the fine wire in his fingers.

'By an Unseen?' Silas asked hopefully. 'Maybe someone wants to join the Community?'

Bubba Gee shook his head. 'I think not.' With a sharp tug he snapped the thread and held the grey box away from the supply crate. It continued to pulse with the same faint light. 'I expect this was placed here by the Health Authorities,' he said grimly.

'What?' Silas stared. His brain seemed reluctant to allow Bubba Gee's comment to sink in.

'From what Thomas has been saying, it sounds as if the government is pushing forward with its new "Future Health" laws. There won't be space in this nation for a place like the Community. There are too many unregulated health issues here.'

'But, I mean, how…' Silas' head was spinning. 'Bubba Gee, if the Community has been discovered, if…' He paused, trying to make sense of it all. 'If Coach Atkins was right, then this is serious. What are you going to do?'

'I don't know,' Bubba Gee admitted, looking at the transmitter and then glancing back at the medical supply box.

'We should destroy it,' Silas said suddenly, looking around him for a heavy enough tool to smash the beacon with.

'That will only serve to pinpoint our location more precisely, I fear,' Bubba Gee said slowly. 'What we need to do is get this thing as far away from the Community as possible. I have an idea,' he said, and began swiftly moving around the supply cave gathering an odd assortment of items.

'What's your plan?' Silas asked, watching Bubba Gee in bewilderment.

'The river that runs through the cave can carry it away, and keep it underground to suppress the signal, maybe take it as far as the open sea.'

Bubba Gee had wrapped the beacon in a double layer of plastic and then placed it into a smaller lightweight box. It was a snug fit, but the lid closed tightly over it.

'Tip the lotion out of these.' He handed Silas four pots of Nana's green cream. Obediently he started emptying them onto the floor of the cave.

'Nana won't like this,' he muttered, flicking a blob off the end of his finger. He sniffed his hands, the familiar odour causing his eyes to water slightly.

Bubba Gee gave a short laugh. 'I'm sure Eva will understand that this small sacrifice is for the greater good.'

Grabbing the four emptied pots, he tied them securely around the box. Two on top and two underneath, then the whole mess got another plastic outer coat.

'Let's hope it floats.' Bubba Gee grabbed a sunstorer and headed towards the main cave. 'Don't forget the things for Bonnie!' he shouted over his shoulder.

Bubba Gee's improvised boat seemed to do the trick, and the scanner was swept quickly out of their sight, bobbing and dipping on the fast-moving stream as the darkness swallowed it.

'Tell Jono there's to be an emergency gathering this evening. He needs to get as many here as possible. And remind him, there is no place for fear. Perfect love drives fear away.' Looking once again deep into Bubba Gee's eyes, Silas could see no sign of the earlier darkness, only the bright, radiant love that typified him. Drawing reassurance from that, Silas left the cave and Bubba Gee's steady hope, muttering under his breath, 'No place for fear…'

'You were quick! I've only just arrived with Frieda,' Jono exclaimed. He was standing under a large tree that sheltered Bonnie's small wooden hut.

'Quick?' Silas was surprised. The events in the cave with Bubba Gee, and the momentous discovery of the beacon had skewed his perception of time. In retrospect, it had only taken minutes for Bubba Gee to arrive at a solution and send the transmitter floating down the dark, underground river and hopefully far away from the Community.

'What's going on?' Jono took a step closer to look at Silas more intently. 'You are all over the place, my friend! Something bad has happened.'

Silas nodded. Obviously the 'no place for fear' mantra hadn't quite done the job. He looked down at the equipment in his hands. 'I've got a message for you, from Bubba Gee…'

Jono looked at him even more keenly, '... but first, let me just take these in for Bonnie.'

'Er...' Jono moved his body to block the way. 'I would not go in there! Firstly, you will not be welcome, and secondly... just don't go in!'

'Right, sure...' Silas said stepping round Jono. 'I'll just slide this round the door, then, shall I?'

'That's for the best... trust me!'

A scream emanated from Bonnie's hut as Silas approached. It was frighteningly loud, even through the closed door, and he looked back at Jono in alarm. Jono made an impatient movement with his arm, obviously eager for Silas to drop the supplies and pass on the message.

'Hello?' Knocking tentatively at the door, Silas gently pushed it open a fraction. 'Zoe? Frieda? I've got the pack and the scanner...' Kneeling down and placing the equipment on the ground, he was about to push it into the hut as another scream rent the air.

Suddenly the door swung wide.

'Thanks,' Zoe said.

From his kneeling position, Silas looked up at her.

'Zoe,' he said, clumsily scooping up his precious packages and handing them to her. 'How's Bonnie? Do you need me to help?' he found himself asking, despite Jono's warnings. 'I can stay with you... if you want...'

I'm digging myself a deep hole, he realised. I don't want to go in and help. What am I saying? It was the effect Zoe had on him; she blinded him to all else but the need to be with her. He rapidly tried back-pedalling. 'I mean, I'm probably not the best to have in a "baby being born" kind of situation... what with my immense squeamishness and fear of blood, illness...'

She laughed, but it was cut short when another blood-curdling scream emanated from the recesses of the hut.

'Hmm... I'd better go. I don't think you should come in, Si, but stay close by, will you?' She pushed the door shut with her foot, and Silas stood on the doorstep, simultaneously relieved and disappointed.

'I'll be right here,' he whispered to the rough wooden door.

'And I'm certain the door appreciates your show of solidarity, but come on, tell me what's going on,' Jono's voice called out impatiently.

Chapter 27

As Jono left to spread the word about the emergency meeting, Silas began his vigil. At least the sounds inside the hut had lessened. He assumed that was a good thing – maybe there had been a painkiller or knockout drug in the labour pack.

Sitting alone in the stillness of the woods, with no way to judge the passing hours, meant that time had begun to take on an unreal quality. It seemed as if he were in stasis while life was progressing at its normal rate outside of his bubble of isolation. Dissociated from the drama unfolding both in Bonnie's hut before him, and from the new crisis now affecting the Community, nothing could touch him; nothing could disturb this eternal moment.

With his back propped up against a sturdy tree trunk, Silas stared vacantly into the shadowy depths of the forest. Everything was completely still, frozen in time. He felt so heavy, so drowsy.

All of a sudden, the sun emerged from behind a cloud, sending a beam down through the heavy canopy. The lifeless gloom was momentarily illuminated, revealing a myriad of flying insects that glittered and danced in the light. They'd been there the whole time; he had just been unable to see them.

With a jolt, his senses kicked back in, like his mind had rebooted. He shook free of the hypnotic state his prolonged wait had induced. Just because he wasn't with his friends at that precise moment didn't mean that their struggles had ceased. Far from it! Lives hung in the balance, both in Bonnie's house and in the gathering in the cave.

Bonnie! he thought with a guilty start, and strained his ears to hear any noise from the hut. Only the occasional murmur of voices – no change there yet.

He thought about Bubba Gee. Had he started the emergency meeting? Had they made any decisions? Would the Community have to go somewhere else? Now he was mentally alert, all these questions crowded round his head. What about Jono? What would he do?

He let his mind revisit their conversation. As unpredictable as ever, instead of being scared, as Silas expected, Jono was phenomenally calm as Silas explained what had happened. There was not a hint of the frightened boy who ran and hid when Coach Atkins was discussing the theoretical possibility of discovery. Instead, Jono had radiated peace. Now that the danger was real and present, he seemed to become steady and mature, almost serene. Silas was impressed. Sharing Bubba Gee's reminder of fear having no place, and perfect love driving it away seemed unnecessary.

A faint mewling cry broke through the silence, followed closely by another. The duet got stronger and stronger. Bonnie's babies – their first cries! He was hearing new life! Silas jumped to his feet, emotion rushing through him. Even his scalp began to tingle with excitement.

'Bonnie?' He tapped gently on the door. 'Zoe, Frieda…? Can I come in?'

The crying babies were getting louder by the second, exercising their new skill of breathing air. No one came to the door, and deciding they couldn't hear over the noise inside, he cautiously stepped in.

The warm, sickly sweet stench of blood hit him immediately. The air was thick with it, and he could almost taste it. Piled on the table were bloodied towels and sheets, and blood-smeared metal implements sat in a shiny tin bowl.

With his head starting to spin, he felt a growing sense of trepidation. The twins were still crying for all they were worth, but what about Bonnie? Was she OK? Had she survived? He swallowed nervously and called out again, this time louder and more urgently.

'Bonnie? It's Si... hello?'

He hurried to the bedroom door just as it opened, and Zoe emerged holding a tiny screaming bundle.

'Good timing.' She unceremoniously thrust the little parcel into his hands. 'Hold this one, would you?'

It was surprisingly light for the amount of noise it was making.

'How's Bonnie?' Silas asked, trying to look into Zoe's eyes for the truth he feared to see.

'Frieda had to sedate Bonnie in the end.' Zoe ran a hand across her brow, inadvertently leaving a smear of blood across her forehead.

'Um... you've got blood...' Silas began to say, but saw that Zoe was beyond caring. The pure and uncomplicated beauty that typified her was ruffled, like it was shifting in her, changing, deepening. 'Zoe, what went on in there, during the birth? You look different.'

Without warning, Zoe burst into tears and buried her face in her hands. Silas stood, uncertain what he should do, a crying baby in his arms, and a crying girl in front of him. Awkwardly, he cradled the baby with one arm and reached his other arm around Zoe's heaving shoulders. He would secretly have loved the opportunity to throw both arms around her and be the one to comfort her until she stopped sobbing, but encumbered by Bonnie's baby, he could only manage a clumsy one-handed patting.

'What happened? Is Bonnie... is she going to be all right?'

'Yes.' Zoe sobbed again, then drew in a steadying breath but stayed close in Silas' one-armed embrace. 'Sorry... I didn't mean to... I never usually cry... it's all been too much for me. The pain, the blood, and then the moment the babies were born...' Her voice was muffled by her hands, and her breath caught again as she tried to steady her emotions. 'Bonnie is still asleep. She's weak, but Frieda said she'll be OK.'

'That's good… hang on, the baby… I've never held one before and I don't want to drop it!' Hurriedly letting go of Zoe, he adjusted his hold of the infant and looked down into its tiny wrinkly face for the first time.

The child had stopped howling because it had managed to push its skinny fist into its mouth and was sucking furiously.

'Would you look at that!' Silas gazed in wonder at the baby. Such a valuable treasure encased in such a fragile body. A whole beautiful life packaged in flimsy skin and bone.

Staring open-mouthed at the newborn infant, it dawned on him that Soulsight was working its usual magic. Here was something brand new, an original creation, an eternal soul brimming with untold potential. He would never have placed such value on a baby, but suddenly it felt like this little one was so vital, so important, not just to Bonnie but also to him. He felt a sense of responsibility towards this little life. It was a priceless gift to protect, to cherish, to nurture and value.

'I didn't understand…' he started to say, and then faltered; he didn't even know how to put what he was feeling about the child into words, '… how special…' Adjusting his hold, he pushed the blanket off the baby's scrawny little arms. His thin skin was red and crumpled and covered with fine, downy hair.

'Shall I take him?' Zoe had recovered sufficiently and, wiping the tears from her cheeks, reached forward to reclaim the newborn. Wrapped up in the intensity of feelings the baby had evoked, Silas' immediate instinct was to hold the bundle in his arms closer to his chest.

'No! He's fine with me!' Surprised at the strength of his own response, Silas looked up. 'Sorry! I didn't mean… you can have him back.'

Zoe raised her hand. 'No, that's all right, you seem to have bonded. I never knew you were so paternal.'

'I'm not normally …' he began, and then he saw the ghost of a smile on Zoe's face.

'Only teasing,' she said. 'It's overwhelming, though, isn't it? The powerful need to protect him? It's got to be because of Soulsight.'

Silas nodded, looking again at the infant. If this was the boy then it was the baby with the defect on his back. The one who would become an Unseen... His mind boggled at the conflicting concepts. That this miracle in his arms would be declared Unseen because of a physical abnormality – it seemed beyond comprehension.

'I need some air,' Zoe suddenly announced. 'The smell is making me feel a bit sick.'

'What about him?' Silas looked down at the baby in his arms.

'We'd better get him back to Bonnie. If she wakes up and he's not there, she'll be worried.'

Reluctantly, Silas handed the child back to Zoe, and she carried him into the bedroom. He could hear a muted conversation between Frieda and Zoe, and then she emerged, her arms loaded with more bloodstained cloths. She added them to the growing pile on the table, then led Silas outside into the cool early evening air.

'I've got to stay nearby, just until the others come. Talking of which, where is everybody?'

'In an emergency gathering.' Silas said, suddenly nervous of explaining to Zoe. It was irrational, but he was concerned that she would hold him responsible, that she would blame him; after all, it had been him that opened the supply box. Also, she still looked so unsettled from having to be involved in Bonnie's labour; he didn't want to add to her worries. But it was too late now. She had that determined look. He would have to explain it all, and the Soulsight would mean that she would know if he failed to tell the whole truth.

'What emergency gathering? What's happened?' Zoe's voice was getting more and more insistent. So, taking a deep breath, Silas started explaining.

Chapter 28

'This doesn't feel right.' Silas looked around the hut that had been his home for nearly a whole month. Such a short time, but one which had taken his ideals and values and shaken them all up until he could barely remember the terrified boy that had arrived at the Community. 'We shouldn't be leaving.'

'I know,' Zoe looked as downcast as Silas. 'It is like we're abandoning our family. I feel dreadful. I don't want to go. This feels more like my home than the city, or even the boat.' She sighed and sat on the edge of Silas' little bed in the corner of the guest hut. Silas sat next to her, too subdued to enjoy her physical proximity.

'It won't be as bad as Bubba Gee thinks, will it? I mean, we can come back next season and see everyone, can't we?' Silas said hopefully.

'I'm sure you are right. Jono said it is just a precautionary measure.' She repeated the message that had been passed onto them the previous night. It did little to comfort either of them, and they sat in silence in the bare room.

Jono had found them immediately after the emergency gathering finished. The decision had been made, he told them. The Community would go into deep hiding. The cave network behind the main cavern was extensive and there were enough provisions in the nutrition store to last them a couple of months if necessary. All guests and friends – which, with Nana and Coach Atkins still away, meant Zoe and Silas – were to return to the city, and a message would be sent via Maxie and

Val when the danger of the Community being discovered had passed.

'Look, it's only temporary. Just until it's safe,' Jono said; he had been trying to encourage them. 'And, I get to walk with you to the crater rim tomorrow. Maxie and Val will be returning with Nana and Thomas tomorrow night. We can explain the situation to them, and Maxie and Val can take all four of you back to town, and you can catch the Overground to the city.'

'Are *you* going to be all right, Jono?' Zoe asked him, though Silas hadn't seen the need for that question. Jono was obviously fine; he was buzzing with drive and excitement.

'I prefer it when I can do something. I can't handle all the theory, the "what ifs", the uncertainty. At least now the threat is real, not just imagined,' he said.

'You'll be safe, won't you?' Zoe had persisted. 'Don't do any mad stuff. Stay hidden, in the cave, for me…' She had looked at Silas, then included him in her plea, '… for both of us.'

Jono had smiled. 'I will.'

Zoe packed up Nana's few belongings with her own, and they took one last look at the guest hut before heading to Jono's.

'Did you sleep well?' his booming voice called down to them. He was in the process of lowering a heavy bag down on the end of a slender rope. As the bag hit the ground, he let go of the rope, and it hissed down through the air to land in a coiled heap. Then he swung his long body over the edge of the platform and effortlessly climbed down the tree trunk. He shoved the rope in the bag and slung it over his shoulder.

'I didn't sleep at all last night,' Silas grumbled, answering Jono. Zoe didn't say anything.

Jono looked at them both.

'We don't want to go,' Silas said. 'We belong here too.'

'That's not possible.' Shaking his head, Jono said, 'I have promised to stay safe for you, and you must at least return the favour by staying safe for me. You belong with your families. Anyway, if you two Seen went missing …' Jono shrugged.

Zoe and Silas didn't need it spelling out. They knew the search would be so thorough that eventually the Community would be discovered, and then all Bubba Gee's precautions would have been in vain.

'We'd better go, then,' Zoe sighed, and Jono reached out to hold her hand. The old familiar feeling of jealousy suddenly sparked inside Silas, but he immediately squashed it. After all, it would just be him and Zoe until they could next visit the Community, but the thought provided little comfort. He didn't want the three of them to separate.

'I'm going to miss you, Jono,' he blurted out before he could stop himself.

'And I you! "Absence from those we love is self from self – a deadly banishment"!' Jono responded, looking at Silas over the top of Zoe's head.

'Is that so?' Silas burst out laughing, the sound of which caused all three of them to giggle, and their dark mood lifted as they followed the forest path towards the distant crater rim.

As they approached the edge of the wood, it occurred to Silas that this was the same path they took yesterday after their hunt, but where was the deer carcass? They'd abandoned it to help Bonnie, so surely it should still be there. Were there wildcats or bears in the crater, despite Jono's assurances?

'I forgot about the doe, with all the concern over Bonnie,' Zoe piped up, her mind obviously recalling the previous day's events as well. 'Did you come back for it? It would have been such a waste to leave it.'

'I got Sim and Shay to come back and collect it,' Jono answered, mentioning two of the stronger men in the Community. 'I couldn't leave it to rot. It's just as well now; it might be the last bit of fresh meat we see for a while. I've got a treat for you, though.' Releasing Zoe's hand, he patted the big bag slung over his shoulder. 'I selected a few nice cuts for us, for later.'

It was nearly midday as they neared the steep wall of the crater. They had ambled along enjoying each other's company, with no desire to reach their destination and split their small group. The sound of the waterfall reached them across the plain, getting steadily louder and louder as they followed the river upstream.

'Shall we climb the cliff path now, then we can eat while we enjoy the view?' Jono asked.

'Sounds good to me,' Silas agreed. Now he had explored the base of the crater he was keen to see it again from the edge.

'But this is the perfect place to stop. I don't want to leave just yet. Let's eat here,' Zoe pleaded.

Silas looked at Jono and shrugged. 'I don't mind,' he said, with a smile. 'I'm sure the view will still be there later on.'

'Then, Zoe, here is a *very* good place to stop,' Jono declared, throwing his bag on to a flat area of grass that formed a bank of the deep, burbling river. A very fine spray from the nearby waterfall carried through the still air, providing a gentle cooling mist before the hot midday sun burnt it away. Zoe dropped her bags next to Jono's and flopped onto the grassy bank.

'I told you,' she said. 'Perfect.' Zoe closed her eyes, basking in the warmth of the sun.

'Let's get a fire going first, lazy, and I'll roast some venison for your lunch,' Jono chided.

At the mention of food, Zoe jumped back up again and started breaking off sticks from an old dead tree that leaned precariously over the water's edge.

In no time at all, Jono had a neat fire burning within a rocky circle. Twelve sharpened sticks, each with a cube of meat skewered on the end, were resting on the edge, angled into the flames.

Following Jono's example, Silas tended to his skewers by continually turning them in the flame. As they browned up, droplets of fat and juice dribbled into the fire, causing the flames to hiss and spit. The aroma of cooking meat filled the air, and Silas' stomach growled approvingly. His mind wasn't quite as appreciative, though, for as he watched the dripping meat, he kept picturing the beautiful doe that he had killed, replaying its death, over and over, the way its life had been so silently extinguished. It hadn't even had a chance to escape.

'Don't let it burn!' Zoe leaned over and twisted the wooden sticks in Silas' hands. 'You're struggling with this, aren't you?'

'Yes,' Silas winced. 'All I can think about is that this was a living, breathing, beautiful animal, and I ended its life. I killed it.'

'I know,' Zoe agreed. 'It's somehow worse than eating fish. I mean, they're cold to the touch even when they're alive – I refused to eat meat the first time I came here. Do you remember, Jono?'

'That's why I always sat next to you. So I could eat your share too!' Jono smiled, and started biting into a lump of brown meat. Greasy juice ran down his chin.

Zoe laughed. 'That was the *only* reason, was it?'

'Yup… what, did you think I liked you?' Grinning, he wiped his face with his sleeve as he started on his next skewered portion.

Zoe laughed and stuck her tongue out at Jono. Then she turned her back on him and resumed talking to Silas, although her choice of words made him feel like a child once again. 'You don't have to eat it, but you are going to get very hungry later on. Why don't you just try it?' She moved back round the fire to tend to her own lunch, and Silas looked at the sizzling chunks of meat. Again his stomach grumbled in anticipation. Maybe if he just pretended it was a simple protein cube…

He nibbled at it cautiously, and a strand of muscle fibre came loose in his teeth. Immediately, he was reminded of dissection in biology class and the blobs of worm flesh dangling from the ceiling. Suppressing his gag reflex as best he could, he forced the memory out of his head and tried to think he was eating a new vegetable.

That was easier, and as he tentatively chewed, he let his senses actually experience what he was eating.

The flavour was complicated and strong. It set Silas' taste buds tingling, and even after he had swallowed his first mouthful, the meaty tang lingered. He nearly reached the point of enjoying the meat, until his brain rebelled during his second portion and reminded him exactly what he was eating.

Without needing to be asked twice, Zoe and Jono swiftly dispatched the last two pieces, casually tossing the sticks onto the ground around them.

After they'd cooked and eaten all the meat, Jono slipped his hand into his bag and produced a slim flask. He stood to his feet and with great ceremony started speaking, flamboyantly gesticulating, as if addressing a huge audience.

'On this auspicious day, we have both great cause for celebration, and also great cause for melancholy. A day when we have seen new birth in our midst, which increases us; and yet a day when friends are parted, which diminishes us.'

'Get on with it!' Zoe heckled, throwing a charred skewer at Jono.

'Madam!' Jono remonstrated. 'A little decorum, please.'

Zoe laughed and Jono raised his flask above his head, 'To long life and lifelong friends!' he shouted to the sky, then upended the flask and took a hearty swig.

'To long life and lifelong friends!' Zoe echoed, as she took the proffered flask.

Silas followed their example, enjoying the sense of solidarity, and took a large swig from the flask, assuming the contents to be the usual Soulsight-infused water. As the sweet fire of waterberry rum filled his throat, the shock of the astringent alcohol forced the liquid up his sinuses. He did a combination sneeze-splutter all down his shirt and jumped to his feet.

'Was that alcohol?' he shouted when he got his breath back, though his eyes were still watering and his palate was burning. 'What are you trying to do? Are you trying to poison me?'

Zoe and Jono looked at each other in alarm.

'Si, I'm sorry,' Jono said. 'I didn't mean any harm. I thought you knew what a toast was ...' he finished lamely.

Silas wasn't listening; he had stretched out over the edge of the grass bank and was washing his mouth out with scoops of water from the deep river below.

'I hope I didn't swallow any!' Silas muttered crossly, then resumed rinsing and spitting out water.

'It won't damage you, honestly. Not such a small amount,' Zoe said in a subdued voice.

Silas looked at his two friends and shook his head. 'I would have thought you had more sense, Zoe. We've got to return to our normal lives. Playtime is over, the Biocubicles await!' Suddenly the anxious thoughts that had been building in him since he learned of their return to the city overwhelmed him. 'What happens if you go home and the Biocubicle detects an illegal substance in your blood? What if all this unregulated food has damaged us? What if we've dropped off our targets? What then, hey?'

Sitting up, Silas tried to sponge the rum off his shirt and trousers, leaving big wet patches down his clothes. The three of them sat in an awkward silence, their shared bonhomie completely extinguished.

As he looked at his wet clothes, he could feel the anger welling up in him. This was all Jono's fault. By the sounds of it, he always led Zoe into risk-taking behaviour... he wasn't going to change. He didn't have to. He could stay here in his precious Community, protected from the harsh reality of life in the city, where you always had to stay on top of your game, always striving to maintain health, and relentlessly seek perfection.

'Don't be scared.' Zoe quietly sat beside him, and took his hand in hers.

'I'm not scared. I'm angry! Can't you see that?' he hissed fiercely back at her, and snatched his hand away. 'Why do you always assume I'm scared?'

'Fine,' she said flatly, obviously hurt, and hurriedly got to her feet.

Silas immediately felt ashamed. Why was he lashing out, and at Zoe of all people? He knew she was right.

I *am* terrified and it is making me angry. How mixed up, he thought to himself. I was so scared when I came here, and now I'm scared to leave. Get a grip, Si, he told himself firmly. You've got no fears compared to Jono and Bubba Gee; it's not your home under threat.

'Jono, Zoe… I'm really sorry. What's the matter with me, eh? You are completely right Zoe, I am scared…'

'Shh!' Jono sharply cut across his apology and gestured for him to be silent.

'I'm just trying…' Surprised, Silas persevered with his explanation.

'Listen!' Jono instructed, cutting across Silas again. Tilting his huge head to one side, Jono's expression was one of intense concentration.

Chapter 29

The other two strained to make out the noise that Jono had heard. They stood holding their breath and listening. The gurgling river was the loudest sound, and the waterfall, gushing and rushing in its perpetual torrent, added to it. Then, just when Silas had reached the point of thinking that Jono was making it all up to distract them, he heard it.

A low bass hum, almost so deep as to be out of the range of normal hearing. And it was steadily getting louder, vibrating through Silas' bones until he felt he wasn't just hearing it with his ears, but with his whole body.

'What …?' Silas started to say, but Jono was staring, open-mouthed, at a spot above Silas' head. He lifted his good arm and wordlessly pointed. Almost too afraid to turn around, Silas reluctantly looked up at the crater wall.

A huge white aircraft was inching its way over the edge. The sun gleamed off its hull as it hovered weightlessly, dwarfing the mighty cliff.

The dull thrumming growl of the flight system got louder as more of the craft slowly glided into view. It was absolutely immense, and its bulk cast a long black shadow down the cliff face as it steadily eclipsed the sun.

The three friends stared at the craft. It seemed to defy all logic, and they were unable to comprehend its existence, their brains unwilling to process what they were seeing.

As they watched, a strip of crimson appeared, running from one side of the vessel to the other, as if the blunt nose had been gashed across its base. Then with an audible buzz a fine arc of red light shot out from the underside of the huge vessel.

It illuminated the ground at the top of the crater rim, and the horizontal beam began descending the cliff wall as if chasing the edge of the aircraft's dark shadow. The thin ray briefly highlighted every rock and shrub, and the waterfall ran scarlet as the light hit it and was refracted through the multifaceted cascade.

With a start, Silas became conscious that Jono was shouting instructions at them.

'... been discovered. It looks like they're scanning for us. We must hide. Quick!'

'Where?' Silas hollered over the brain-numbing rumble from above.

'Cover the bags and get in the river!' Jono shouted. Then he stamped out the remains of the fire, and kicked the stones to spread them around the grassy bank. Grabbing hold of Zoe, who was still rooted to the spot by the dreadful appearance of the craft, he started dragging her by the hand to the water's edge.

Quickly shoving their belongings under a scrubby thorn bush, Silas glanced across the grass. It was obvious they had been there; a circle of scorched earth remained where the fire had been, and the ground was littered with meat skewers. They wouldn't need a scanner to detect a human presence. Too late to do anything about it now, though, the red beam had reached the base of the cliff wall and was making its unremitting progress towards them.

Jono helped Zoe into the water, and Silas heard her gasp with the shock of the cold. He joined them, lowering himself over the edge of the bank. The water was chest-deep on Silas and nearly neck-deep on Zoe, who was struggling to keep her balance in the fast-moving river. Jono had submerged his head completely, but when he surfaced the water level only sloshed around his waist.

'What do we do? Will the water shield us?' Silas shouted. The red ray of light was inching closer and closer.

Jono shrugged. 'We just have to hope it's some kind of a heat sensor.' They both looked at Zoe, whose teeth had started to chatter from the cold. 'What do you think, Zoe? You're the clever one.'

'M… m… maybe,' she stuttered. 'I… if we hold tight together, li… like we are one body, it might c… confuse the sensors.' She shrugged helplessly. 'Maybe it's a th… thermal scan like Jono says… and the cold water will hide us.'

'Right,' Jono barked decisively. 'There is a slight undercut to the bank. Si in first… hold on to the bank… keep us stationary. Zoe, grab onto Si, and I'll try and shield you both, so if the scan picks up anything, it only picks up one body. Yes?'

Silas and Zoe nodded mutely. The beam of light was almost upon them, and with one last glance at each other, they ducked fully into the river. Using the large rocks on the river floor as handholds, Silas manoeuvred himself into the darker water under the bank.

Trailing grass roots and muddy debris clouded his vision, but he flattened his body to the riverbed as Zoe snaked her arms around his chest. There was no additional weight as the river kept them buoyant, but the drag on his arms increased, and he tensed his muscles to accommodate the extra strain.

The cold water stung his eyes, and he craned his neck up to see the river shining red as Jono threaded his long arm around Zoe and Silas. The stress on Silas' biceps and shoulders was almost too much, and he felt his grip beginning to slip. They were going to be washed downstream, and caught in the scanner. He couldn't hold on any longer.

Crimson water churned and bubbled as red as blood, as the scanner beam pierced through to their hiding place. Jono held on tighter, trying to lower his body into the water. Silas desperately gripped on to the rock below. He could feel it begin to loosen and shift on the riverbed with all the increased weight pulling on it. He had to get a better handhold.

He looked desperately for something else to hold onto, but his vision was so obscured by the dirt that was being knocked off the bank by their jostling bodies that he couldn't see any better anchor to grasp.

Then, with a jolt, the large rock pulled free, and a cloud of mud and sand bloomed up in their faces. Instinctively shutting his eyes tight, Silas let go of the useless rock, and forced his hand deep into the muddy riverbank. Things in the mud squirmed away from his grasping hand. His mind flickered back to the crayfish they had caught, with their sharp, penetrating claws. He squashed that memory and pushed harder as his fingers brushed against a deep embedded root, and his hand wrapped tightly around it.

His lungs began to burn and he opened his eyes. From what he could tell, the scanner beam seemed to have halted. We've been seen! Silas thought. I can't hold my breath any more; if we're going to get caught, then let's just get it over with. He angled his head to the side and let out a stream of bubbles to indicate his defeat to the others. Just then, the red hue in the surrounding water started to diminish. It's moved past us, he thought with surprise.

Wriggling free from his friends' suffocating grip, Silas pushed himself upright and broke the surface of the river, gasping for air. Jono and Zoe got their footing and dragged themselves out of the water.

'We need to tell Bubba Gee and the others!' Silas said, turning to retrace their steps along the river path, the beam of red slicing through the sky and earth ahead of him.

'No,' Jono said.

Silas wheeled around to glower at him. 'No? What do you mean?'

'You won't be able to get ahead of the scanner, and anyway, they'll hear the aircraft before you get close enough to warn them about it.' Jono started to retrieve their belongings from under the bush. 'Bubba Gee has been moving people into the caves all morning. We stick to the plan. You and Zoe need to get away, and I promised Bubba Gee that I would get you out safely.'

Silas caught the bag that Jono threw towards him and reluctantly slipped it over his shoulder. Jono was talking sense, but he couldn't shake off the feeling that he was abandoning the Community.

'We need to move fast,' Jono continued, 'before they come looking for us. We are too exposed here. Even if the scan couldn't penetrate through the water, they would have picked up the remains from the fire.'

It only took a few moments for them to run to the base of the cliff – the continuous crashing of the waterfall providing a background accompaniment to Silas' racing heart. Craning his neck, he could just make out the narrow, twisting path that wound up the sheer crater wall.

The massive body of the scanning aircraft was nearly in full view, and it hung in the sky, dwarfing the cliff and making Silas feel very small and vulnerable. He was suddenly overwhelmed with a sense of urgency and picked up his speed as he approached the ascent. The crater itself now seemed like a huge cage, hemming them in. Previously, the walls surrounding them had felt like a secure fortification, but now they were a restriction, a barrier to their freedom.

As he sped around the second bend, Silas looked back at Zoe. She had only just reached the first little turn in the path and was already lagging behind, and it was plain to see that she was struggling with the new fast pace. He could see her chest heaving to draw in breath, and could almost hear the hoarse gasping noise of hungry lungs sucking in air. They'd have to slow down for her. She couldn't keep this speed up, not on the ascent anyway.

'Jono!' he shouted up the slope. Jono continued striding onwards and upwards with his strange lolloping gait, either failing to hear, or possibly choosing to ignore Silas' call.

Fighting against the cramp building up in his calves, Silas performed an uphill sprint that would have even made Coach Regan proud.

'Jono – wait!' he gasped as he reached him.

Jono stopped for Silas to catch his breath, but he was fidgeting the whole time, obviously impatient to get to the top of the cliff and onto clear ground.

'Zoe... can't keep up... slow down.'

'We must hurry,' Jono said.

'I know... but it's a long way up, and we should stick together.' Silas looked up the path ahead of them, following its twists and turns; up past the place where Jono had 'surprised' them, and then performed his stunt dive into the waterfall. How he had despised Jono, and how quick he was to write him off. Silas shook his head, disappointed in his past self. Imagine being so blind...

The shadow of the mighty aircraft cleared the crater edge, and they were once again bathed in the hot midday sun. The warmth of it was a welcome relief, and he realised how cold the wet clothes had made him. Even the heat from his little uphill sprint had dissipated. Silas squinted as he gazed up. 'What's that?' he asked in a puzzled voice.

'What?' Jono said.

'Look – there, at the top of the path!' Silas pointed and Jono saw it immediately. Something was reflecting the bright sunshine, glinting and shimmering in the light. 'Is it Nana?' Immediately the words were out of his mouth he knew the folly of them. It wasn't Nana, unless she had arrived with a 20-strong escort.

'Get back!' Jono said and pressed his back to the dusty cliff wall. Silas did likewise but couldn't resist leaning out for another glimpse.

The figures had started moving down the cliff path. Their bright white uniforms looked familiar, and he stepped forward to get a better look.

'Stay out of sight!' Jono grabbed him roughly by the shirt and pulled him as close to the wall as possible. 'We need to go back down and hide again until they've passed by.'

Silas nodded in assent. He remembered where he had last seen the white uniform. It was on his brother after his final Trials, after Marc had visited the Spire to meet Helen Steele. The Flawless Leader had created a new squad, and Marc had been hand-picked for it. He could clearly recall the initials running up the arms of the suit in stark black lettering.

'GHA – Government Health Advisors,' he muttered, following Jono as they moved as quickly as possible back down the path, sticking close to the meagre shelter afforded by the cliff wall.

Although she was too far away to hear their conversation, Zoe had seen them turn back, and with alarm had looked up and spotted the figures at the top of the crater. She was already waiting at the base of the cliff when Jono and Silas joined her.

'Who are they?' she asked.

'They must have come with the scanning craft. We should wait until they've all passed, and then we can carry on up,' Jono said.

They looked around at the stunted trees and grass. There was nowhere to go that wouldn't involve moving across the open ground and being noticed from above.

'I know where we can hide. Follow me!' Sticking as close to the cliff as she could, Zoe led the way toward the crashing waterfall.

'Of course!' Jono exclaimed. 'Good thinking, Zoe!'

Deafened by the noise of the falls and blinded by the spray that rose from the plunge pool, Silas stumbled after them. He was confused, because as far as he could see, Zoe had only led them around a shallow curve of the cliff. She seemed to be heading towards the churning plunge pool formed by the raging waterfall.

It was a dead end, and the only place to hide was in the water again, and that didn't seem like such a great plan. He shivered, he was already very cold, and now they were fully in the shade again he had to concentrate to stop his teeth from chattering. If the pool were their only hiding place, they wouldn't be able to hide for long.

There was no path to follow now, just a series of large boulders to clamber over, each with a thick coat of slimy green algae that thrived in the permanently damp conditions at the waterfall base. Yet Zoe continued on, clambering and sliding over the rocks towards the thundering cascade.

She turned and said something, or at least, Silas assumed she said something. Her mouth moved, but the roaring din of water falling drowned out all other sound. Miming his utter deafness, she nodded and then did a series of curving movements with her hand and pointed at the waterfall.

'Oh!' Like a light coming on in Silas' head, he suddenly understood. 'We can hide behind it!'

She performed the same 'I can't hear you' mime, and he repeated the curving hand to the waterfall. She nodded and then clambered up the last boulder, steadied herself, stepped into the wall of water and disappeared from sight.

'You next,' Jono mouthed at Silas.

The rocks were now treacherously slippery and Silas could feel his grip fail on the slimy algae. Scrabbling with his hands on the wet rock wall, he regained his balance and looked at the watery barrier in front of him. It seemed almost solid, as the turbulent flow had turned the water opaque, and he could make out nothing on the other side.

Just then, some disembodied fingertips emerged through the white curtain of water, wiggling impatiently. Silas smiled and immediately let go of the wall, put his hand into Zoe's and boldly stepped into the waterfall.

The weight of water was phenomenal, and although it only took a second to pass under the torrent, it was nearly heavy enough to force him to his knees. He staggered, bent-legged, still clutching Zoe's hand, gasping like a landed fish.

The first thing to hit him was the drop in noise. The waterfall still roared its spirited presence, but the sound was muffled, like a door had been closed on the noise.

He barely had time to register much more of the secret space behind the waterfall before Zoe sharply pulled him back into the darker recesses.

'Make room for Jono,' she instructed, as one of his long legs appeared through the sheet of water, and then he was standing with them, shaking his body like a wet dog.

'Brr – Invigorating!'

Refrigerating more like, thought Silas, looking around the damp, slimy alcove that was to be their temporary refuge. Water spray hung around them like an ethereal mist, and a shiver ran up Silas' spine.

Chapter 30

They'd changed into dry clothes from their bags, and like lost lambs, they huddled together for warmth. It seemed to make little difference, and Silas felt the chill in the air begin to seep into his bones. His strength was being sapped away as the moments passed.

The rock shelter behind the waterfall was only a couple of metres wide, but it was deep, and they stood in relative dryness watching the unending body of water falling and crashing, providing a seemingly solid shield.

'I think we've waited for long enough.' Zoe finally broke the silence that had descended over them.

By Silas' calculations they had been hiding in the dingy, damp crevice for hours. It should be nearly nightfall – the continual hammering of the waterfall had induced a semi-somnolence in him as if his body remained awake, but his brain kept temporarily shutting down.

'We've been here well over an hour,' Jono said, to Silas' incredulity – surely it was longer than that?

Was an hour enough time for a whole troop of people to reach the crater floor? He tried to think back to his own descent. They'd stopped to sightsee, and then of course Jono had delayed them…

'The path ought to be clear,' Jono said, 'but maybe only one of us should check first.'

'I'll go!' Silas immediately volunteered, longing to feel the warming sun fall on him and dispel the numbing coldness. He felt he would almost rather be warm but discovered than cold and hidden.

'I think it should be me,' Jono said reluctantly, and Zoe sighed impatiently and shook her head as Jono explained. 'If I'm spotted, I can always lead them away from here, and you can get out.'

'I don't like that idea,' she argued. 'We shouldn't split up. But if we have to, then I should go. Jono, what if you are caught? Who knows where you'll be taken. You may not end up in Prima. How will I be able to find you?'

Zoe impulsively threw her arms around him, and he stooped to kiss the top of her head.

'I won't get caught. It would be worse if they took you. You'd probably never be allowed to leave the city again!'

Their concern for each other, borne out of their obvious love, was so strong and so exclusive, that without further comment, Silas made the decision for them. Quickly and quietly he stepped towards the falling wall of water. He cast one last look over his shoulder at Zoe and Jono. They shouldn't be separated. He would go. It was the most sensible choice, he persuaded himself. Anyway, what did he have to fear? Surely as the son of the renowned Anton Corelle – friend of the Flawless Leader – the worst that could happen was that he would be returned to the city in disgrace. He was already a failure in his father's eyes, so nothing much would change there.

Walking through the waterfall still held a strong sense of stepping blindly into the unknown, and Silas forced his mind not to overthink it. He pictured the green slimy boulder on the other side, put his hand on the rock wall and stepped into the torrent.

Silas didn't think he could get any colder, but his third drenching in icy water that day had finally stolen any residual heat his body had. A loud groan of agony escaped from his mouth before he bit hard on his lip, remembering he was supposed to be quiet. Hoping the waterfall spray was enough to conceal him for the moment, he moved slowly across the rocks, keeping close to the cliff.

Looking around, Silas could see none of the white uniformed intruders. However, in the distance, on the other side of the crater, hovering menacingly in the sky was the scanning aircraft.

It must be over the forest now, Silas thought with a sinking feeling. He hoped Bubba Gee had managed to hide everybody, and that the caves would indeed be big enough to conceal them, even from the searchers on foot.

But Silas had a terrible sense of foreboding. The government seemed to be doing a very thorough exploration, and he didn't see how any of the Community could escape. There were signs of human life everywhere in that forest, with the cabins, the boat, and the huge fire in the cave...

Still, he couldn't do anything about that now. All he had to do was focus on getting Zoe and himself out, and somehow keeping Jono hidden.

The path remained just out of view, as the cliff jutted out a fraction to create a gentle curve, so Silas started inching his way forward, still hugging the wall in an attempt at concealment from any watchful eyes.

The crashing of the waterfall, which up to this point had drowned out all other sound, had lessened, and Silas focused his attention on catching any other noise. There was nothing else; he was certain the squad had moved on. However, he continued his approach with as much stealth as possible.

'Stop!' A woman's voice commanded. It was close and loud.

Silas froze and tried to merge with the rock behind him. He'd been seen! He looked around, his eyes wide with panic. He couldn't work out where the voice had come from. There was no one else around. He knew he hadn't imagined it, but who had spoken?

Then there was the sound of a man's voice, low and entreating. He couldn't make out any words, but the sound carried clearly. There were people just above his head!

Slowly leaning away from the wall, he could see the edge of the path at one of its many twists. It was only four or five metres directly over the place he was standing and, if whoever was up there looked down, he would surely be seen straight away. He held his breath and tried not to make a sound.

'I mean it!' the female voice said again. 'Leave off! We're on duty.'

The voice was confident and clear and Silas immediately recognised it.

'Come on, Taylor,' came the man's voice again, louder this time, 'there's no one else here. Just give me a little kiss, then...'

Silas could hardly believe his ears. That was Marc! No doubt about it. His brother was here – at the Community. Marc and his girlfriend, Taylor, were standing just a few metres above him.

'Marc! I'll stand somewhere else if you can't keep your hands to yourself!' she remonstrated again, to which Marc let out a throaty chuckle. 'I'm serious!' she continued. 'I only got to be part of this squad because you recommended me. I can't be caught messing around – not all of us are the Flawless Leader's favourite, are we?'

'Relax,' Marc said, sounding undeterred by her rebuke. 'We'll get these Unclassifieds collected and processed, and then we can have a bit of off-duty time together, OK?'

'OK,' Taylor agreed after a short pause. 'Do you think there is even anyone out there? How can people survive living in a dump like this?'

'I don't know. They must be riddled with disease. That's why they have to be found and assessed. I doubt we'll find anyone healthy enough to become a Seen, but we can have a bit of fun with all the Unseen ones.' He laughed the familiar threatening laugh that Silas knew all too well. It made his knees feel a little weak with fear. Marc was a threat to any Seen who was less physically strong than he was; what would he do to an Unseen?

'Advisor Corelle!' The new voice sounded tinny and remote, and it pronounced their surname with a distinct rolling of the 'r'... Corrrelle.

229

'Yes, Chief,' Marc responded, his voice brisk and neutral as he answered his communicator.

'We think there may be one or possibly two Unclassifieds in your vicinity,' the voice said.

The crunch of boots on gravel forced Silas to push his back further into the unyielding rock wall, trying to blend into it. A tiny shower of stones sprinkled around him – Marc was standing on the edge of the path, directly above Silas, looking out over the crater.

Don't look down! Silas pleaded silently with his older brother.

'There were some discrepancies on the initial scan,' the remote voice said. 'We will perform a rescan. Maintain your current position.'

'Yes, Chief!' Marc said, with an unpleasantly eager tone to his words.

'They're coming back!' Silas burst through the waterfall, nearly colliding with Jono.

'What did you do? Have you led them here?' Jono shouted, stooping over him, his anger and distress spilling out, making him seem taller and darker than ever, all the old unstable storm of distrust flooding out of him.

'I didn't *do* anything!' Silas shouted back, retreating slightly as if it may be safer outside the cover of the waterfall, with the approaching Health Advisors, than inside with a furious Jono.

'Why did you go? We were worried. I didn't know if you were going to come back,' Zoe joined in with the onslaught of questions.

'I wasn't running out on you. I wouldn't betray you! Do you really think I would do that?' Silas was shocked that she thought he would abandon her. Surely they had seen enough of him to know he wouldn't just leave?

'Look at me!' he challenged. 'I was trying to help.'

Stepping closer to Zoe and Jono, he looked at them in turn, full in the face, then touched his eyes and reached out to touch theirs.

'I see you, Jono, and I see you, Zoe.'

Jono held his gaze and then visibly relaxed. 'I'm sorry. I was concerned... we both were. I see you, Si. Now, tell us, what did you find out? What do you mean about them coming back?'

'That's what I overheard,' Silas said and started to hurriedly explain. 'The scanning ship is returning. Hiding in the water wasn't enough! Also the path up the crater wall is still blocked by ...' He hesitated, still stunned from the unlikelihood of his own brother being so close. 'By Marc!'

'Your brother?' Zoe asked, hope apparent in her voice. 'Will he help us? Do you think he'd let us get out?'

Silas thought about it and then shook his head. As soon as he had known it was Marc and Taylor on the path, his first instinct hadn't been to ask for help, it had been to stay hidden.

'He may be my brother, but I don't trust him.' He knew it was harsh, but it was true.

'Do you know that for sure?' Jono persevered. 'Did you *see* him, with Soulsight? Did he see you?'

'No. I just heard him and his girlfriend talking.' Silas glanced at Zoe. Taylor had systematically ridiculed and tormented her when they were at Vitality Clinic. Though Zoe never let it show, it must have hurt her. 'I wouldn't rely on either of them to help us,' he continued. 'I know that nothing would make Marc happier than for me to be discovered out here, to be caught and humiliated. He hates me.'

Chapter 31

For a while nothing more was said as they shivered in the gloom of the damp shelter. They were going to be discovered, it was inevitable, and yet none of them wanted to say it out loud. If it wasn't mentioned, then they could hold onto the illusion that they could stay hidden. Eventually, Jono cleared his throat, and Silas mentally braced himself, ready for the confession of defeat to break the silence, and end the fantasy of escape.

'There is another way,' Jono said.

They looked at him in surprise. He was gazing far up into the tall narrow roof of the damp cave that stretched up into the darkness. 'Although I hesitate to suggest it as it is very dangerous.'

'Yes!' Zoe came to life, as she appeared to understand what Jono was saying. 'The Soulsight cave. You and Silas can escape that way, and I'll take my chances with Marc and Taylor. Is there a way out, though? Will it take you to the top of the crater?'

Jono nodded. 'I've explored the cave. There is a way through in the dry season, when the water level runs low, like it is now. The underground tunnel network is long and convoluted, but it emerges far enough away from the crater rim. But Zoe,' Jono crouched down to look at her more closely to gauge her response, 'I think we should go together. I will help you up, and Silas said he is a good climber, so he can help too…' He let his unfinished plea hang in the air.

Zoe objected immediately, looking at Jono as if he was mad. 'I cannot do that climb again! Have you forgotten? I fell!' The

232

horror in her voice matched the horror in her face as fear began to exert its dominance. It distressed Silas to see the cold, grey shadows replace the deep brown of Zoe's eyes. He hadn't seen her frightened of anything before. 'I don't need to climb. Maybe the scanning ship won't see me if I stay here. It's far more sheltered than in the river. I'm sure I'll be fine. I can escape later.'

Jono shook his head slowly. 'I don't think so. We were detected through water, and they will have found the remains of our fire. There will be another thorough search. You need to come with me.' He pointed upwards. 'I will look after you, and I won't let you fall. Do you trust me?'

'Of course I do,' Zoe sighed, 'but I still do not want to do that climb!'

'Look,' Jono unwound a length of rope from his huge bag, 'I've got the rope from my tree house. We can tie it around you. I'll lead, you can go in the middle and then Si can follow on.'

Jono looked at Silas for support with his plan, but Silas was torn. On the one hand, he desperately didn't want to be found here, especially not by Marc and Taylor. But on the other hand, he didn't want to make Zoe do something that so clearly filled her with dread.

Then he thought of the Soulsight-filled cavern. He still harboured a desire to see it, and after today he may never get another chance to return to the Community. Soulsight had changed him; it had opened his eyes to the real nature of an individual, to the true beauty of a soul that could be hidden by the plainest of shells.

They were both staring at him; Zoe's face still marred by fear, Jono confident and sure of his plan.

'Zoe,' Silas began, but she interrupted him.

'Oh no! Not you as well! I cannot do this. I thought you'd understand how I feel – I am terrified.'

'I think Jono is right,' he said slowly, as she covered her face with her hands, 'and, let's face it, this may be our last chance to

233

come here. We may never get to see the Soulsight cavern again. This is your only opportunity to get samples.' Although it felt a bit manipulative, he resorted to appealing to the scientific part of her brain, but it did the trick, and her fear seemed to start to recede a little.

'I did want to take some back to analyse it, didn't I?' she muttered, letting her hands drop to her lap.

Silas nodded. 'You did. Also, I have a really bad feeling about being found here – especially if my brother and Taylor are involved. We have to try to get out, and this sounds like the only way.'

Zoe took a deep breath in and out and then nodded once. That was enough for Jono, and he threw the rope to Silas.

'Tie that around you and Zoe. As I said before, I'll lead; Zoe can go in the middle so she gets lots of support. We'll take it steady. We should leave most of our things, but take the sunstorers. I'll collect the bags after all this is over.'

He slipped his shoes off, neatly placed them on top of his bag, and flexed his elongated toes.

'Ready?'

'Yes,' Silas responded, as the familiar rush of adrenaline that accompanied the start of every climb surged through him and dispelled the damp and chill of the cave.

Zoe remained silent, her lips pressed into a thin line, but she approached the rock wall, following Jono's lead, and reached for the first handhold. Then it was Silas' turn.

The damp rocks were jagged and rough on his hands – nothing like the smooth handholds on the climbing wall at clinic – but they were regularly spaced and even Zoe made steady progress upwards. The cavern narrowed at the apex, and Silas was able to lean back against the clammy wall behind him as he waited for Zoe to move up. Soon he felt the tug of the rope around his middle and obediently continued climbing.

The route was becoming increasingly treacherous and for the first time, Silas understood how difficult a challenge the climb would be. The shape of the cliff was changing and Silas

234

began to feel the strain on his arms as the beginnings of a craggy overhang led them into the falling water.

Clinging tightly to the wall, Silas forced his hips close to the rock face, just as Coach Hunter had instructed. If the coach could see me now, Silas thought, climbing with such disregard for safety, he'd have me expelled from Vitality! No proper equipment, climbing through a sheet of water...

Silas froze as the utter insanity of what he was doing suddenly broke through the haze of adrenaline that had thus far fuelled his climb. He couldn't move a muscle; this was madness, and they were all going to die! What were they doing? Surely it was far better to be caught, but in one piece, than to be smashed to death on the rocks below a waterfall? So what if he got sent back down to Bronze 5, or kicked out of clinic altogether!

A tug from the rope around his waist brought him back to the present, but still he was unable to move. His knuckles were white, as his hands remained frozen, gripping the rock face. The water was pounding on his head and his back, weighing him down. I am going to fall – and there is nothing I can do about it. And when I fall, I'm going to pull Zoe and Jono down with me. I'll have to untie the rope!

Just as his fear-addled brain reached, what seemed to him, the only reasonable conclusion, he felt the pressure of the falling water begin to lessen. Looking up to see the reason for this respite from the pounding cascade, he could make out the gangly form of Jono as he nimbly appeared over the edge of the overhang.

With an element of fascination that was dissociated from his paralysing fear, Silas watched as Jono's toes clung to the rocks. His feet were so peculiar, really like extra hands, with each lengthened toe flexing and gripping independently of its companions. No wonder climbing was so simple for him, despite only having one useful arm.

'It's not much further!' Jono shouted down to him. 'Just over the top of this outcrop – Zoe's waiting for you.'

Silas tried with all his might to move up, but his body was still in rebellion at the precarious position it found itself in.

'I can't move!' he shouted back to Jono. 'I am trying... but I'm stuck! Just go, Jono, take Zoe and hide – do it!'

The panic in his voice carried clearly upwards and Jono growled in frustration, then started climbing back up the rock, away from Silas.

Assuming that Jono had understood him, Silas felt inexplicably peaceful. At least he wouldn't risk the lives of his friends when his strength gave out and he fell. The rope went slack. They've untied themselves, he thought, and they've carried on without me. Jono had seen sense. He idly wondered if Zoe had needed any persuasion.

He felt a painful cramp begin to develop in his fingers. It wouldn't be much longer now before the muscles in his hands fatigued completely, and he would lose his grip and fall.

Another noise reached his ears, past the crash of the waterfall: the deep grumble of the returning scanning vessel. The water turned dark grey as the shadow of the ship passed overhead.

I'm rescued! He nearly sobbed with relief. They'll find me. Whatever the punishment, at least I'll be alive.

Without any warning, the rope around his waist slipped upwards as it was stretched taut. It wedged around his ribcage and pulled sharply under his armpits. The discomfort forced him to finally release his hold on the wall, and he grabbed on to the rope as he found himself being winched up and over the outcrop. He could hardly believe that Jono and Zoe were risking their freedom to save him.

He kicked away from the wall with his legs and swung precariously outwards, spinning as he did so and crossing through the waterfall. A view of the crater opened up before him, the panorama overshadowed by the mighty scanner craft. In the few seconds that he dangled outside of the waterfall, Silas could see that the rescan was almost complete. The red beam of light was nearly at the base of the waterfall.

What, moments before, Silas had considered being his rescuers, once more became his enemy, and he willed his friends to pull faster. His muscles unlocked, and he began clumsily climbing the rope as it moved upwards.

As he was dragged, panting and spluttering, over the lip of the cave and onto the wet floor of the Soulsight cavern, he struggled to his feet. Without a word of explanation or thanks, he freed himself from the rope and grabbed his two friends, pulling them away from the entrance. They could all hear the familiar reverberation of the vessel outside, and the shadow it cast over the crater wall made the cave even gloomier.

Dark green swathes of the Soulsight plant covered every surface and choked the stream, giving the illusion that it was a river of viscous mould. Thick moist sheets of it hung from the ceiling, glistening wetly in the dingy light. The cave was small and gloomy and had an unhealthy and unappealing look to it. It wasn't at all like he had imagined, but Silas had no time to feel disappointed. They had to get as far away from the cave mouth as possible. He looked at the back of the cavern. The small stream was emerging from a darkened tunnel. They would have to hide in there.

Pushing heedlessly through cold curtains of the plant, he led them further into the gloom until the cave narrowed, and they had no option but to step into the water. The river bottom was slick and far too slippery to move fast on. He grabbed Zoe and Jono again and, holding onto each other for support, they shuffled upstream.

'Hurry!' Silas said. 'The ship is right overhead. I don't know how deep that scanning beam can penetrate, but we need to get as far away from the cave mouth as possible.'

'I'm trying, but this is impossible,' Zoe said. 'It's like trying to walk uphill on ice!'

All of a sudden, the quality of the light near the entrance began to change and redden in colour. As they turned to look, Zoe lost her footing on the slippery floor of the stream and fell, pulling Silas down with her. In surprise, he let go of Jono's arm, and the flow of the river started to carry Zoe and him slowly over the smooth carpet of Soulsight and back towards the all-seeing scanner beam.

As he struggled to get onto his knees, Silas felt his sunstorer fall out of his pocket and made a grab for it as it bobbed along the surface of the water. His fingers brushed against the silver metal case, but only resulted in pushing the sunstorer further away. Briefly loosening his grip on Zoe's arm, he made another lunge for it.

'Don't let go of me!' Zoe shouted in panic to Silas.

'It's OK, I've got you!' Holding onto her wrist, he watched as his sunstorer got caught in a miniature current and was soon washed over the edge of the waterfall. That's going to be us in a minute, Silas thought, redoubling his efforts to stop their steady drift downstream. 'Try digging your feet in to the riverbed,' he shouted back to her.

He tried forcing his own feet between the rocks, but couldn't get a secure foothold. This is unbelievable, he thought. We're going to be slowly, but surely, swept over the edge!

Then the stream tumbled them towards a soft swathe of the green plant and Silas managed to twist his arm into it. The vegetation seemed to be firmly anchored to the ceiling and halted their helpless progression. His grip remained firm around Zoe's arm, and she grabbed a fistful of Soulsight with her other hand.

They lay in a tangle of limbs and strings of slimy Soulsight, their breath rapid and shallow as, for the second time that day, the scanner beam sought them out. The ray penetrated easily behind the waterfall and the whole front of the cave was bathed in red light.

Although the danger was so near, Silas couldn't help but admire the effect the light had. The glossy covering of the Soulsight plant shimmered and sparkled as the scanner beam hit it. It looked magical, like a secret grotto, filled with diamond-encrusted tapestries. As the light source from outside faded and moved on, the whole cavern continued to glimmer, for the plant seemed to retain and magnify the brief illumination.

The strands of greenery that were still twisted around his arm and over his legs mesmerised Silas. It was as if he were wrapped in strings of flickering light. It was beautiful and incredible that such a slimy, unappealing-looking plant could actually become quite so delightful. As he lifted his arm, the plant trailed off him, looking like a shining wing. Lost in wonder as he admired the effect, he was only reminded that they had been in the process of escaping when Jono clasped him firmly under his arm and hoisted him to his feet.

'That was close. But we did it! We weren't picked up on the scan this time, I'm sure of it. To me, it looked like the angle of the beam wouldn't see past the first couple of metres. Don't you think so, Zoe?' Jono said.

His question fell on deaf ears as Zoe still sat in the river, mouth slightly open, watching the light chase itself in endless spirals around the walls of the cave.

'I said – don't you think so, Zoe?' Jono repeated, helping her to get to her feet.

'Eh?' Zoe said, still looking around her with wide eyes. 'Seeing this was well worth the climb, I agree,' she said, not answering his question at all.

'We would have been caught for sure if we'd stayed at the bottom of the waterfall,' Jono said, amused by Zoe's distraction.

Zoe merely nodded as Jono carefully led the way upstream and then onto a patch of slightly drier ground. The magical light show began to fade, and the Soulsight once more became just a slimy dull-green plant.

'How beautiful,' Zoe sighed, and joined Jono.

'You wouldn't think something so plain could look so lovely. What a transformation,' Silas said, as he lowered himself next to them. It was similar to what he had thought about Zoe when he first saw her with Soulsight. From now on, I'll only be able to see the outside, the plain shell. I'm going to miss seeing her properly, he thought, with a pang of regret.

He ripped off some of the green plant and stuffed it in his pocket. At least he could use a bit every now and then, just so he wouldn't forget.

'I don't think the scanner reached this far into the cave, do you, Jono?' Zoe said, apparently without realising that he had already asked her exactly the same question just seconds before. 'We would have been caught for sure if we'd stayed at the bottom of the waterfall.'

Jono caught Silas' eye and smiled.

'What?' Zoe asked.

'Nothing.' Jono shook his head, then added, 'We're safe, but we can't stay here. We should follow the river through the cave. It leads to a way out. Are you all right? Can you carry on?' The questions were directed at Silas.

Caught up in the relief of escape and the wonder of the Soulsight cavern, Silas had pushed his terrifying experience of the climb out of his mind.

'What happened out there?' Zoe asked. 'Jono had to drag me up the last bit, and then we waited for you. I thought that you'd been caught,' she pointed at the retreating shadow of the scanning craft at the cave entrance, 'and they'd just taken you off the waterfall.'

A shudder ran up Silas' spine as he remembered how powerless he had been to move and save himself. He had been certain that he would fall.

'"This youth that you see here. I snatch'd one half out of the jaws of death",' Jono muttered, more to himself than to the others, but Silas nodded earnestly.

'At last! One of your Shakespeare quotes that I can understand. It's true; you saved my life, Jono. I won't ever forget that.' Silas stood up and stretched, revelling in the movement of his limbs. He was alive and unhurt. He was with his friends, and he was in an incredible cave filled with the mysterious Soulsight. With surprise, he recognised that he was no longer feeling so afraid. 'It's good to be alive and breathing, and I'm ready to keep moving.' He looked into the black mouth of the tunnel that led upstream and away from the waterfall. It was very dark in there. His enthusiasm waned substantially, and turning back to his friends, he added, 'Has anyone else still got their sunstorer?'

Chapter 32

When it comes to Soulsight, Silas decided, everything gets turned on its head. The dark is made light, the frightening transforms into the magical and the plain becomes glorious.

Whatever component of the plant that reacted when the red scanner light fell on it was even more active when the multiple wavelengths of white light hit it. The gloomy tunnel was transformed into a swirling vortex of colour. Each corner that they turned as they followed the underground river became a new luminous wonderland.

They squeezed through a narrow gap in the green-coated tunnel walls to enter a large cavern. Jono opened the blockers on his sunstorer to the brightest setting. It only needed a brief flash of light and the Soulsight plant responded accordingly with a dazzling light show of its own. The illumination shimmered through a full rainbow as it split and refracted across the cave ceiling in multicoloured waves. Tall pillars of Soulsight-covered rock blazed with light, causing the cavern walls to pulse and dance.

Stepping slowly over the floor of this new cave was like walking on a sponge carpet of lights, and Silas tapped his feet on the thick vegetation, causing undulations of colour to spread out from him.

'Look at this!' he exclaimed delightedly, and jumped on the spot. Billows of light flowed from his feet. Zoe copied him and the ripples collided and fused.

'Come on, this way,' Jono called. He was already striding across the cave, the spongy flooring giving his gait an extra bounce. Waves of light streamed across the ground behind him till it resembled the turbulent wake of a boat.

'Spoilsport,' Zoe muttered, adding, 'we want to play,' in a deliberately petulant tone.

'Try to step where I step,' Silas challenged, then set off after Jono, first doing little steps, then leaping in long bounds. Zoe easily followed the marks in the light until they arrived giggling and out of breath on the other side of the cave.

Jono opened the sunstorer and sent another beam of light into the next section of tunnel. 'We should find somewhere to rest soon. That way, when we leave the caves it will be night, and it will be easier to travel without being observed.'

All the concerns of the scanning ship and the GHA squad now seemed far behind them, but deep down Silas knew Jono was right. As soon as they left the safety of the caves, they would be vulnerable again.

'Do you know a good place to stop?' he asked, briefly looking at him in the shifting light of the Soulsight plant. Then he did a double take. 'Wow! Jono, you've changed. Zoe, look!'

'Jono!' Zoe cried. 'Are you all right? Whatever is the matter? You look so angry!'

'No, he doesn't,' Silas contradicted. 'He looks like Bonnie, doing that whole self-sacrificial thing. But, somehow... even more so.'

'OK,' Zoe interrupted, sounding relieved. 'Now you look the same as you always do.'

'Not to me he doesn't,' Silas insisted. 'I'm still getting the "golden glow" view of you. How do you feel?'

Jono opened the sunstorer just a little, and the cave flared once again with light.

'I feel the same,' he said. 'I've not changed. But you two have. Zoe!' He reached out to touch her face, 'You fill me with such hope, and you radiate life.' He shook his head in wonder, his voice filled with awe.

Silas couldn't see that. Of course, her heart still transformed her, making her beautiful and bright, but she didn't look *that* different. Then, before Silas' eyes, her soul blossomed. It was like watching spring turn into summer as she reached a fullness of heart maturity in the space of a few seconds. Hope flowed from her.

Silas felt tears well up in his eyes as he experienced the same awe that he had heard in Jono's voice. He knew, with absolute certainty, that he would give up everything to follow her, for with Zoe there was a future; there would always be something to look forward to.

'Silas, you've gone from completely terrified to utterly peaceful in about ten seconds. What is going on?' Zoe asked.

'I think we might be overdosing,' Jono said. 'We're absorbing pretty concentrated Soulsight.' He pointed to the river gurgling in the far corner of the cave. 'We're breathing it in as vapour all the time. I think we must be seeing what our souls were once like, right up to what they might become.'

'What? Do you mean we are seeing into the past and into the future? Are you sure? Has this happened to you before?' Silas asked.

'I'm always alone when I come here, so it might have happened... but I wouldn't have known,' Jono shrugged.

At that point Zoe altered again, and this time not for the better. As if summer had been overtaken by winter, she seemed to shrink back in on herself, and all the radiant life she emitted was replaced with something much darker. It was as if her soul had rotted away to nothing – all murky and warped with selfishness. She was incredibly ugly, and Silas made a noise of repulsion.

'Oh, great,' Zoe muttered through her twisted lips. 'I take it you are seeing the old me! Now you know why I didn't want you *ever* to see me like this.'

Gradually, the Soulsight fluctuations caused by the overdose steadied. Much to Silas' relief, they stopped seeing the past versions of each other – Zoe's twisted selfishness, Jono's anger and mistrust, and his own dark, shadowy, overwhelming fear –

and were left with the incredible vision of their own potential future selves.

Walking with Jono and Zoe and witnessing all that they would become was beyond anything else that Silas had experienced. They seemed other-worldly... almost magical. And they seemed just as affected by him. They kept moving through the caves, but it was no longer the light show from the plant that distracted them, it was the transformation in each other.

'We can stop here for a while and try and get some sleep,' Jono said a short time later. They had been clambering over the uneven floor of a narrow tunnel, tripping and slipping over the Soulsight-covered boulders. Jono pointed to a low ceilinged, shallow recess at a position where the tunnel briefly widened. The floor of the small nook was the only piece of flat ground they had seen for a while. Neither Silas nor Zoe objected to Jono's suggestion. But then it would have been difficult to contradict Jono, because whatever he said was reinforced by his current appearance. The self-sacrificial love he manifested meant they felt completely secure with his decisions.

'I can't think straight with you two looking at me,' Jono complained as they sat together. He shut the sunstorer, and the lights playing around the little alcove gradually began to fade. 'Just being with you washes away all my worries, but I still know there is so much to do. That scanning ship is still out there. Yet I look at you and you,' he pointed at Silas and Zoe semi-accusingly, 'and all that diminishes, and I feel it will somehow all be OK. I'm losing my edge! If we let it get dark, and I can't see you, maybe I can think clearly again.'

Before the gentle illumination dispersed completely, Silas took another long, admiring look at his two friends. Before he had met Zoe and tried Soulsight, he thought the only way to be perfect was to be a Gold Standard, like Marc and Taylor. But here he was witnessing a perfection, the like of which he had never dreamed existed. Zoe and Jono would need a whole new level of award, he decided. Maybe Platinum Standard for Jono… and Zoe would be a Diamond…

The light died away, and for the first time since entering the Soulsight cavern, they were completely enveloped in darkness.

'That's better,' Jono said. 'It was weird. I've never doubted my Soulsight before, but that was too much.'

'Let's try to sleep, then, and maybe it'll wear off a bit,' Zoe said, and Silas heard her wriggling in the thick, damp cushion of vegetation that covered the floor.

The regular deep breath sounds from Jono should have been enough to lull Silas to sleep, but instead it just annoyed him. It was like his first journey on the train all over again – when Nana and Zoe fell asleep instantly and Silas was left exhausted but, frustratingly, wide awake; however, this time it was Jono and Zoe who had managed to fall asleep in minutes.

Silas rolled over on the thick spongy carpet. The ground was impossible to get comfortable on. It was well cushioned, but Soulsight was a wet plant and although excellent at reflecting light, it was terrible at reflecting heat. He was still cold and damp from his repeated soakings that day, and was unable to ignore his discomfort enough to even nap.

The cave was so dark that Silas' eyes began playing tricks on him. Patches of blacker darkness were visible out of the corner of his eye, like shadows on shadows. But when he looked directly at them, they dispersed and there was nothing there. Closing his eyes didn't help either – the blackness weighed on him, and the flittering dark shapes seemed to get under his eyelids.

It wasn't frightening, but it was making his head ache as his eyes tried to fix onto something. He turned onto his other side and nestled down into the vegetation.

Chapter 33

At first he thought his tired mind had made up some patterns out of the darkness. It looked like fine speckles of dust falling in the distance. Gradually the specks merged, giving the appearance of an approaching cloud of faint silver rain.

Silas sat up and rubbed his eyes. This wasn't an optical illusion. There was light seeping along the winding tunnel, triggering the Soulsight plant in a luminous chain reaction. It was getting stronger by the second. It could only mean one thing…

'Someone has followed us!' Silas shook Jono and Zoe. 'Wake up!'

'Leave me alone,' Zoe grumbled sleepily.

'Jono… Zoe!' Silas was less gentle in his shaking. The illumination was getting stronger and to Silas' light-starved eyes it seemed extremely bright. Whoever was following them must be close.

'What is it?' Jono said irritably. 'Si, did you turn the sunstorer on? It'll run out of charge if we're not careful.'

'Shh!' Silas whispered. 'Your sunstorer is still in your pocket, Jono. The light is coming from someone else.'

Jono sat bolt upright. 'Someone followed us?' He was incredulous. 'I thought we were in the clear.' He stared wildly about him until his gaze fell on Zoe. 'I let my guard down. I put you both in danger.'

'Why are you whispering?' Zoe groggily rolled over and pushed her hair off her face.

'Shh!' Jono and Silas said together.

Silas pointed at the strengthening radiance at the far end of the tunnel. 'We were followed. Quick, we need to go.'

He helped Zoe get to her feet. She was still dozy, and as she tried to lean on the Soulsight-covered wall, her feet slipped on the spongy floor. Silas steadied her and stretched his hand out to help Jono.

'They are getting nearer, Jono. Let's move.'

'Wait.' Ignoring Silas' proffered arm, Jono levered himself upright. 'I don't think the three of us will be able to outrun them now they are so close.' With a sudden sinking feeling, Silas knew that Jono was right. Zoe would not be able to keep up if they had to move at speed. He remembered how far she had fallen behind when they had tried to hurry up the crater wall path. But surely Jono wasn't about to suggest that they leave Zoe behind?

'I've got an idea,' Jono continued. 'I know this cave system. I can lead the person following us to one of the exits, and then double back to you two. We can then take a different route to the surface.'

'That sounds risky,' Zoe whispered, fully awake now. 'We should stick together.'

'The first way out involves another climb,' Jono explained. 'It's an easy climb, not dangerous like the waterfall route, but I'm the fastest and I'll make it seem that I've got away outside the cave. No one would expect me to come back in.'

'What about us?' Silas said, his lack of dispute acting as a tacit agreement to Jono's plan.

'I'll hide you. Just sit tight, and I'll come back for you,' he insisted, and with his large hand, Jono started scraping the thick layers of Soulsight away from the base of the tunnel wall.

'Can't you look more like a rock?' Jono criticised in an undertone. 'Pull your knees up a bit.'

Silas was lying on the cold, muddy floor in a loose foetal position as Jono lowered a wet blanket of vegetation over him. The Soulsight had lifted up easily, and Zoe was already curled up at the back of the alcove, the vibrantly shimmering plant concealing her completely so she looked like just another of the many coated boulders that littered the tunnel floor.

Jono looked over his shoulder. 'I can hear them now. I'll be back as soon as I can.' He covered Silas' head and, through the looser strands across his eyes, he saw Jono's huge bare feet walk away from their hiding place.

The brightness of Silas' Soulsight covering continued to increase as the light source came closer. Through the muffling layer of plant material, he heard a voice that he recognised.

'Corelle here.' Yet again his brother was so close to him – Silas could hardly believe it! He slowed his breathing and tried to remain as still as possible. He wondered how Marc had got into the Soulsight cavern. He couldn't have climbed. Marc had never been much of a climber.

'Yes, Corelle, any sign of the Unclassified?' The voice came through the communicator, the rolling emphasis of his surname causing an uncanny echo around the cavern.

'No, sir... but this cave... the lights. It is... unusual, sir,' Marc replied. Silas could hear wonder in his brother's tone, which was extinguished by the response from his superior.

'You're not there to sightsee, Corelle!' the voice barked, and Silas saw Marc's boots slip on the uneven floor as they passed by his hiding place. 'Health Advisor Price clearly stated that she saw a movement on the crater by the waterfall. The tunnel system has been mapped, and Price is waiting with a team at the other end. Flush them out, Corelle, and let's hope it is someone who can become a Seen. I dislike using valuable resources on a worthless Unseen.'

'Sir ...' Marc's voice dropped to a whisper. 'I see him ...'

'Seen or Unseen?' Came the immediate response.

'Seen... definitely. He's remarkable!' Marc sounded impressed. 'Hey, you!' he shouted. 'Come with me. I can take you back to the city where you belong. We need people like you.'

His voice grew fainter as he chased after Jono, and Silas risked shifting the layer of Soulsight off his head. He looked

249

along the tunnel and saw Marc moving as fast as possible down the glowing passageway, as Jono led him away from their hiding place.

Silas lay still for a few more moments, in case Marc was not the only Health Advisor sent after them, but hearing nothing, he gingerly pushed the wet blanket off his body.

'Zoe? Did you hear that?' Silas whispered urgently.

'I did,' Zoe emerged from her hiding place, pulling strands of the glimmering plant off her face. She sounded panicky, though Silas could still only see the vision of the hope-filled future Zoe that the Soulsight gave him. It was very misleading. 'He's heading into a trap,' she said, her voice full of fear, her appearance one of optimism.

'What are we going to do?' Silas felt completely dismayed. He hadn't worried at all about Jono being on his own, as long as he and Zoe were together. Now Jono was going to be captured, and he would be completely outnumbered. 'Marc must be seeing with Soulsight and thinks Jono is a Seen, but as soon as Taylor claps eyes on him, he's going to be taken away and classified as Unseen.'

'We shouldn't have let Jono go on his own!' Zoe said agitatedly. 'What were we thinking?'

'It's this overdose! It's just like Jono to do something so…' Silas searched for the correct word, '… noble!' he eventually said. 'He looked so magnificent and I found I didn't even *want* to disagree with him. He risked his life to save my neck when I froze on the waterfall climb – I was going to fall, you know – and now I've let him risk himself again. I'm so selfish!'

'We both are, but we can make it up to him now. We have to try to help him,' Zoe said, her words anticipating Silas' next thought.

At least there was little chance of getting lost. The light that was held and reflected in the Soulsight plant left a clear, bright trail along the tunnel and into the next cave. Silas and Zoe paid little attention to their surroundings now. Their only focus was to catch up with Jono and somehow protect him from being caught.

They moved as fast as possible through tunnels and caverns, yet without gaining on Marc or Jono at all. In fact, the opposite was happening. They knew that they were getting further behind because the illumination became increasingly dim and the path grew harder to see.

'I've still got my sunstorer,' Zoe said as she paused to catch her breath. 'I'll retrigger the light.' She felt in her pocket and pulled out the familiar orb. Silas shielded his eyes in anticipation of a blinding glare as she popped the blockers open. But there was not even a flicker emanating from Zoe's hands.

'No!' she gasped breathlessly and closed and opened the blockers again. 'No, no, no, no!' She shook the sunstorer and banged it firmly against her palm. 'This can't be happening. It's out of charge.'

Their eyes met, and a tiny shadow of fear crept into Zoe's face which, given the overdose that Silas was seeing her through, meant that she must have been terrified.

The residual glow from the plant had nearly disappeared when they rounded a corner and were confronted by a towering vegetation-coated rock face.

'That must be the final climb before we can get out,' Zoe said in horror.

Silas stared into the gloom, trying to cram the details of the wall into his mind. He could only see the lower section, but there were regular indents in the Soulsight covering, and that meant there were plenty of handholds. Jono had said it was easier than the waterfall climb, but then he would have climbed it when the whole thing was blazing with light.

'We can't get up there! Not without Jono, not in the dark,' Zoe said and slumped to the ground, letting out a sob of despair. She pulled her redundant sunstorer from her pocket and opened it in the vain hope that there was something left.

'We can't help him – he's going to be caught. Can you imagine what leaving the crater will be like for him? Having to exchange all the freedom he has here for a life of Biocubicles and Unseen robes? He'll hate it.'

Silas continued staring up at the massive obstacle ahead of them as the last gleam faded completely to blackness. Zoe let out another anguished cry and then fell silent.

There was nothing to see and nothing to hear, and yet Silas felt strangely calm. Just one thought ran around his mind and that was the message that Bubba Gee had given to him. The message that was meant to be for Jono after he discovered the beacon that broadcast their location – 'perfect love drives fear away'. In a flash of revelation he understood it. When you love someone enough, no obstacle is too great; you'd risk everything to save them.

'Zoe,' he said, his voice steady and strong in the silence of the cave. 'Jono needs us, and we need him. Maybe we can still help him.'

'How?' Disbelief was clear in her voice, but Silas heard her stand and move towards him.

'We can climb this…' Her sigh of utter hopelessness interrupted him, and she was close enough that he felt her warm breath on his cheek.

Fumbling a little in the pitch black, he felt for her hand and guided it to the rock face. 'I'm going to tie a rope of Soulsight around us and we are going to get up this wall together. The strands seem drier here, away from the river, but I think it would hold us if we fell.'

There was no response but Silas felt the pressure of Zoe's head as she rested it on his chest. He ran his hand over her hair and onto her cheek which, to his surprise, was wet with tears.

'Zoe, shh…' he soothed, as he hugged her tightly to him. 'We can do this… for Jono.'

'For Jono,' she repeated, pulling away slightly. 'Do you think there is any chance we will able to save him?'

'I don't know,' he admitted, as he let go of her and started running his hands across the wall in front of them, 'but we have to try.'

Chapter 34

Silas had no idea how secure his knots were, but the long tendrils of Soulsight seemed fairly pliable as he wound and tied them together. He lashed an improvised lasso of rope around him and Zoe, with the idea that as they climbed to the extent of their first tether, they would exchange it for a fresh one.

'For Jono,' he heard Zoe mutter again, as they slipped their hands under the Soulsight to grip hold of the rocks underneath.

'Ha!' Silas shouted in relief after they had started the ascent. 'This is like climbing a carpeted ladder! No wonder Jono said it was easy. I thought he was just boasting. Can you feel, Zoe, it's even becoming less steep!'

Sure enough, the vertical start of the imposing wall had turned into a more gradual incline, far more like climbing stairs than a ladder, and Silas laughed again. The wall, that had appeared so daunting in the dark, was incredibly simple to climb.

'Hush!' Zoe said. 'Don't go too fast! I still need to concentrate.' But her voice sounded calmer, and she kept moving upwards in the darkness.

They paused as their first rope reached its full limit. Silas steadied himself on the stepped wall and felt among the strands of Soulsight that hung across the rock face. At last, his hand found a thick rope of Soulsight, and pulling it free from the wall, Silas looped it around him and Zoe. He didn't want to hurry and be careless; a fall from this height could still be fatal.

'Are you ready?' he asked Zoe, before releasing the old rope.

The thickness of the vegetation was lessening as they carried on upwards. By the time they had climbed the full length of their second Soulsight rope, they were climbing up bare rock.

'We must be nearly at the top, Zoe. We are going to have to untie ourselves and climb the last stretch without any ropes. Unless you want me to go up first and ...'

'We stick together!' she forcefully interrupted. 'I'm not being left behind halfway up a cliff in the dark.'

'Fine,' he said. 'We do this together.' He loosened the rope and let it drop into the blackness below. It made a faint whooshing sound as it fell back into place. Silas took a deep breath and reached up for the next step. It seemed a lot deeper than the other crags and crevices that he had fitted his hands and feet into. Stretching further, he patted his hand to the left and to the right.

'We've reached the top!' He nearly sobbed with relief, and Zoe let out a high-pitched half-laugh, half-cry.

He helped Zoe over the edge, and they shuffled away from the cliff on their hands and knees before collapsing, weak from the realisation of what they had just done.

'I'm shaking all over,' Zoe said. 'I can't believe we did that... you did that. If it wasn't for you, we'd still be stuck down there in the dark.'

'You were brilliant,' Silas reminded her, 'for someone who hates heights.'

She let out a groan. 'Maybe it wasn't so bad because I couldn't see how high up I was; no, forget that, it was just as bad!' He heard her shifting on the gravelly floor. 'We should keep going.'

'Are we facing the right way?' Suddenly disoriented, Silas had a panicky thought. 'I don't want to crawl back over the edge.'

'It's this way,' Zoe said confidently, and holding onto each other they stood up and began painstakingly feeling their way forward.

'You remember when the light from the plant faded, when we were at the bottom of the cliff?' Silas asked as they blindly stumbled over the dry, rocky ground.

'Yes,' Zoe replied. 'I don't think I'm likely to forget that.'

'I thought it was because Marc and Jono were so far ahead and the Soulsight had used up its light by the time we got to it. But it wasn't that, it was because the thickness of the plant layer had lessened. I don't think we were as slow as we feared.'

'Oh?' Zoe gripped Silas' hand tighter as she understood what he was saying. 'You mean, there is still a chance? We might not be too late to help him?'

'Maybe,' Silas said. He didn't want to nurture false hope in his own heart, let alone Zoe's, but if they could find their way out, then maybe they could do something to help Jono.

The shift in light quality was so gradual that they hadn't noticed it at first. It was only when Silas heard the faint sound of dripping water and automatically tried to pinpoint it visually, that he discovered he could make out the outline of shapes again. He waved his hand in front of his face and saw his dark-black fingers against a light-black background.

'We must be near the surface,' he said to Zoe. He could make out the dark circle of her head, and at that moment, it was the most beautiful sight. 'I see you, Zoe.' He lifted his hand to his eyes and then across the small gap between them to brush against her eyes.

'I don't believe it! I thought this cave was endless. I see you too, Si!' she repeated, and he could hear the smile in her voice as her hand found his face and gently touched his eyes.

Moving as fast and as soundlessly as possible, they pressed on as black became grey, and then the first hint of colour began to dispel the monochrome. There was still no obvious exit, and the tunnel began to get narrower and narrower until they were squeezing through twists and bends of a constricted fissure.

After contorting their bodies around an almost impossible corner, they saw a wonderful sight, the gleam from a slender strip of daylight.

'Is that sunshine?' Zoe asked, her breathing fast and laboured. 'It is, isn't it? I'm not imagining it, am I? We've found the exit!'

In the confines of the narrow tunnel, Zoe's voice seemed inordinately loud and excited and Silas' impulse was to hush her. He was acutely aware that even if Jono had been captured, there still might be a Health Advisor patrolling the area.

'Zoe,' he said quietly, conscious that even his whisper now seemed to create echoes, 'we need to be silent. If we get caught, there will be no way to help Jono. Can you hear anything from outside?'

Zoe silently mouthed 'sorry' and they both stood, intently listening. The roar of blood through Silas' ears deafened him, until he relaxed a little and tried again. He could hear Zoe's breathing, still a little fast after her recent exertion. A faint scurrying noise drew his attention, and out of the corner of his eye he saw the tiny grey shape of a rodent dart across the tunnel floor just in front of him, alarmed by the intruders in its underground residence.

He looked at the tantalisingly close slit of bright light, and listened again. The gentle blowing of a breeze across the surface of the ground produced a barely audible whistle. He could hear no voices, no machinery, nothing else at all.

'I want to take a look outside and see what's happening,' he whispered into Zoe's ear.

She grabbed his arm. 'I'm coming too!' she insisted quietly.

On the final approach to the cave mouth, the tunnel floor began to slope sharply upwards. On his hands and knees and covered in dirt and dust, Silas realised that this end of the tunnel system wasn't going to end in a wide, open mouth on a cliff face or hill; this exit to the cave was simply an easily overlooked, and unimpressive, hole in the ground. It was so constricted that for an awful moment it seemed as if Zoe

257

wouldn't be able to squeeze her large frame through the last section. But soon, both were crouching under a thin lip of cover, where weeds and grass had grown over the edges of the exit. It was a smooth circle of green, except for a few gaps in the grassy rim, where clods of earth dangled, suspended by a few filamentous roots.

'Jono came this way,' Silas mouthed to Zoe and pointed at the telltale damaged edges.

They sat looking at each other as Silas struggled to build up the courage to raise his head above the cave edge. Zoe seemed to be waiting for him to take the lead and scout out the surrounding area. He took a few steadying breaths and was about to move when he felt the restraining hold of Zoe's hand on his arm. She had her finger to her lips and was pointing upwards.

'Get away from me!' The fear in his brother's voice made it sound high-pitched, almost feminine, and Silas barely recognised it as Marc's.

His first instinct was to rush to Marc's aid, but Zoe must have felt the muscles in his arms tense under her hand, as he prepared to charge headlong and help his brother.

'Wait!' she said firmly, her mouth close to his ear.

'Something is after Marc!' Silas responded. 'I may not like him, but he is my brother! I have to help him – you don't understand…' He tried to shake free of her grip, but she held tighter.

'There is someone else out there,' Zoe muttered, tilting her head, trying to catch every available sound.

'What is the matter with you, Marc? Are you ill?' Taylor asked, sounding genuinely concerned. Her voice grew louder as she approached the partially concealed cave entrance, and Silas saw her regulation white running boots just stepping into his line of vision. Her attention was completely on Marc, who was making a strangled whimpering sound of primitive terror. The noise set the hairs on the back of Silas' neck tingling.

Marc started shouting as Taylor moved closer to him and away from the cave edge. 'Get away from me! You're disgusting, foul and rotten… Aagh! Don't touch me; you might infect me! Why are you wearing that uniform? You're not allowed to… you can't be in the squad!'

Listening to Marc's description made it abundantly clear to Zoe and Silas what was going on and they mouthed one word to each other: 'Soulsight.'

'What sick little game are you playing, Marc Corelle?' Taylor shouted back at him, all element of concern apparently extinguished by Marc's insults. 'You were all over me earlier on, and now you are saying this. You got me into the squad, and what now? Am I no longer your girlfriend? Are you finishing with me? What has happened to you?'

'Girlfriend?' Marc's incredulity was audible, even through his fear. 'I would never touch someone like you in a million years!'

'That's it! I've had enough of this nonsense. You are history, Marc. It was me who saw the Unseen escaping up the waterfall, and it was me who was here to tranq' it when you took forever coming out of the cave. What happened? Did you let an Unseen get the better of you? Did it outrun you?' She had laced her words with a venomous aggression that Marc seemed barely to notice.

'Unseen? You're the Unseen! Where are your coverings? You shouldn't even be out in daylight …' His words were suddenly interrupted by the sound of a high-pitched whistle and a dull thud.

In the shelter of the underground cave, Silas looked at Zoe with alarm, shaking his head in denial at the full implication of Marc's sudden silence. Taylor had just shot his brother.

'That's shut you up, you waste of space. You've crossed one line too many,' Taylor growled. 'I hope you feel as wretched as an Unseen when you wake up, and that's more than you deserve – speaking to me like that.'

Silas let out a slow breath of relief… Marc had been knocked out by a sedative, rather than shot dead.

'Advisor Price?' came the voice over the communicator

'Yes, sir?' Taylor responded with calm efficiency, her voice betraying nothing of the drama that had just ensued.

'Did you locate Advisor Corelle?'

'Yes, sir… But there seemed to be something wrong with Advisor Corelle. He needs an emergency Biocubicle assessment. He was behaving in a violent and aggressive manner and tried to attack me. I believed his intent was to cause harm, and so I had to sedate him. Also, I would like to report that he failed to apprehend the Unclassified, who was clearly an Unseen… contrary to Advisor Corelle's classification. And, sir?'

'Yes, Price?' the voice responded.

'In my opinion, Corelle seems physically unfit and mentally unstable, and I would like to question his suitability to be on such an elite squad as this.'

The derogatory analysis flowed without any hesitation from Taylor's lips, and Silas reckoned her dark soul must be flaring and contorting in a terrifying manner. Marc would have been scared senseless, he thought with a wry amusement. Maybe it was just as well he was sedated while Taylor executed her incredibly thorough revenge.

'Your comment has been logged, Advisor Price, and will be investigated accordingly. Arrange for your team to transport Advisor Corelle to the rendezvous at the landing zone. Helen Steele is arriving shortly to assess our progress, and I want the maximum personnel present for her arrival.'

'Yes, sir… the Flawless Leader coming here…?' Taylor sounded thrilled, Silas thought. Maybe she was hoping to become the Flawless Leader's new favourite now that Marc was temporarily out of the picture.

'Bring the Unseen as well; we can put him in with the others until we can transfer them to the city for processing. Hopefully they can learn some useful task, although several of them seem barely human.'

The remote voice of Taylor's superior set Silas' blood boiling. How dare he be so dismissive of the incredible people who made up the Community? Bubba Gee and all the others... physically imperfect but with such beautiful souls... And what would happen to Bonnie and the twins? Her son would now become an Unseen.

All the people that Silas had grown to love and trust, and who, in turn, loved and trusted him, had been rounded up like animals. Silas doubted that any had managed to hide from the scanning vessel that was even able to map tunnels that ran deep underground.

There was a commotion above ground, and Silas returned to worrying about his own predicament. Taylor's team was moving Marc.

'He's a dead weight,' one of them moaned.

'Just shift him,' Taylor said. 'Put him in the back with the Unclassified. That's all he deserves... and hurry. The Flawless Leader is landing soon.'

The complainer fell silent, obviously impressed by the news, and soon the sound of their heavy footsteps faded as they carried Marc away.

Chapter 35

Silas leaned his head back against the damp, earthy edge of the cave entrance and closed his eyes. He felt exhausted and vulnerable. He had wanted to save Jono, and even believed they had a chance to reach him in time, but Jono had walked into a trap, and Silas now understood that he was to blame.

The figure that Taylor had spotted climbing the waterfall must have been me, Silas thought, furious with himself for bringing this trouble down on them. He clearly remembered swinging clear of the water when Jono had to pull him up the last section. If he hadn't been so utterly scared on the ascent, he would have stayed concealed by the falls.

He also felt such a burden of responsibility towards his friends from the Community and yet didn't know how to begin to help them. Even Marc had needed him, and Silas had been unable to help him.

'The sun is setting,' Zoe said, cutting across his despondency. 'We should follow Taylor while there is still enough daylight if we ever hope to find where they've taken Jono.'

She began to pull her body over the lip of the cave and onto the grass and then, lying on her belly, she looked down at Silas. 'What are you waiting for? They've all gone. Now is our chance!'

'It's hopeless, Zoe,' Silas finally confessed. 'We've been tracked, scanned and hunted, and all this running and hiding has been futile. We've tried and we've failed. Jono will have to wear an Unseen robe, and as for us, we will be caught and probably forced out of Seen society… so at least we'll see him during the night shift.'

'You're giving up?' Zoe sounded horrified.

'I'm just acknowledging the facts,' he tried to defend himself, but she was suddenly angry.

'It's up to us now, Si. Our friends still need us, and with or without you, I *will* try to help them, even with my last ounce of strength.' As she spoke, Silas saw her begin to develop a touch of the self-sacrificial radiance that reminded him of Jono, of Bonnie and of how he imagined his mother's soul to have looked. What would my mother have done? he thought, but he already knew the answer. Ellen would give her health and then her life to help the hurting, and the lost, and the lonely…

'All right,' he grumbled, ashamed by his defeatist attitude. 'I'm coming with you. Let's try to find this "landing zone",' he said as he clambered out of the small cave entrance and stood up.

The last rays of the setting sun had turned the sky into a multihued display, the colours ranging from deep purple to dusky orange.

'I think we should try going that way,' Zoe pointed behind Silas.

'What makes you think… ah …' Silas said, as he turned around. 'I see.'

In the distance, across the flat, scrubby plain, the white hull of the scanning vessel gleamed dully like the carapace of a giant insect. A shudder ran up Silas' spine as he looked at it. Even though it had landed, and its deep, growling engines were silenced, it still exuded menace as it dominated the landscape.

In the dusky twilight they could see a swarm of activity around the body of the craft, but it was too far away, and the light was too poor to make out any details.

As he took his first step towards the landing site, Silas' head and his heart began an internal struggle.

He knew the sensible thing for him and Zoe to do would be to turn around and walk as far, and as fast, as possible in the

263

other direction. The chances of finding Jono now, let alone helping him to escape, were so remote and the likelihood of their own exposure so great, that what they were doing was madness. Yet his heart was aching with the overwhelming injustice that was being imposed upon his friends. Their independence was being stolen, and he couldn't stand back and passively let that happen. A new-found fire in his spirit drove him on and overruled his rational mind – pushing him towards the awaiting vessel and the inevitable end to his freedom.

The ground around the landing zone was completely flat, with no natural opportunity for concealment, but by the time Zoe and Silas arrived, the sun had long since set, and the darkness of night provided enough cover. Pools of bright light spilled from the underbelly of the vessel, illuminating 20 or so large rectangular containers. Each box was well over two metres high and twice that long. White-suited Health Advisors moved purposefully from container to container, peering in at the contents and discussing things among themselves.

The Soulsight overdose was still exerting a massive influence, and Silas kept stopping to stare at another distorted figure dressed in tight white clothing. However, some of the faces were nearly beautiful. There were people here who genuinely loved and cared… but invariably fear shadows were spilling out and tainting even the least corrupted.

Zoe and Silas stayed hidden in the darkness as they skirted around the edge of the light, instinctively crouching low every time a Health Advisor passed nearby. But no one saw them. It seemed that they were no longer looking for any more Unclassifieds, trusting the scanner results to be infallible.

'What's in the crates?' Zoe whispered to Silas, as they passed close to one of the oversized containers.

'I don't know,' Silas hazarded a guess. 'Vehicles, supplies…'

As he spoke, an impeccably dressed Health Advisor strolled around the back of the box, rapidly typing notes up as she walked. She leaned against the side of the unit and looked out into the darkness beyond. Her face was a mixture of pity and fear, and Zoe and Silas froze, thinking that somehow she had seen them, but her gaze was unfocused, and she pinched the bridge of her nose before continuing with her typing.

Suddenly, she banged the metal wall behind her with her fist.

'Silence!' she commanded in a stern voice. 'You will have to be sedated if you continue to make noise! Why can't you see that this is all for your own good? We are trying to help you.' She pressed her ear to the crate for a moment, and then crossly she straightened up and walked around the side of the large box and out of Silas and Zoe's view. The sound of gentle hissing filled the air, and then the woman could be seen approaching another Health Advisor near one of the massive crates on the other side of the lit area.

'I had to knock another lot out; they were going wild in there – they're going to hurt themselves!' she called across to him, accompanying her words with a sad shake of her head.

'Are you ready to start loading up?' the man called back, checking something on the screen in front of him.

'Yes, let's get moving, before they all wake up again.'

She spoke into a communicator, and a panel on the belly of the scanning ship opened. Silas tried to see what was inside, but it was too dark, a black rectangle of emptiness, like a wide-open, toothless maw. Then the Health Advisor went from container to container, and with a flick of a switch, each crate began to gently hover and move upwards into the waiting mouth of the ship.

With a sick feeling in the pit of his stomach, Silas understood – packed in the crates like goods to be transported were all his friends from the Community. Those who had welcomed him with love and joy at his initiation; he had seen their acceptance and care for him when he was at his most repulsive and fearful.

'They've caught them all,' Zoe began. 'Bubba Gee... Bonnie... everyone. And they're gassing them!'

'Sedating,' he tried to lessen the horror, 'like Taylor did to Marc... remember?'

She was shaking, but whether it was with shock or rage, Silas didn't know. He looked at the boxes. There were still a few left, and maybe ten to 15 people could fit in each; even if he and Zoe could unlock just one...

But then he saw a container slightly separate from all the rest, the door of which was already wide open. Inside it looked like a large-scale Biocubicle – all stainless steel and flashing lights – but this one contained two figures. Inert, and lying on low stretchers, the first was dressed in the generic white uniform of the GHA. Silas was convinced he knew the identity of the unconscious Health Advisor without needing to get any closer, and he felt a shred of pity for his brother. The second figure was also instantly recognisable. With legs dangling off the end of the stretcher and nearly trailing out of the crate... and what immense feet! Silas had never felt so happy to see Jono's ridiculous oversized monstrosities before.

'Look!' he whispered to Zoe, relieved to offer her some hope. 'Jono!'

Health Advisors were continually crossing from one hovering container to another, occasionally stopping to check on Jono and the other unconscious figure. Silas and Zoe moved through the shadows to get closer to him. As they approached, however, the sinister sound of hissing reached Silas' ears. For a moment, he thought he and Zoe were the target for an attempted sedation, but the sound was subtly different... more of a muted roar than a gaseous hiss.

'We are back where we started,' he murmured in Zoe's ear, and in response to her blank look said, 'We're on the crater edge... above the waterfall.'

Chapter 36

'All personnel …'

The voice echoed around the landing site, causing Silas to jump. An announcement… that's all it was… let's hope it's not about us, he thought to himself.

'The Flawless Leader will be arriving in five minutes.'

The amount of activity that followed the broadcast increased triple-fold, and there were white suits running everywhere, leaving no clear window to get near Jono, let alone to manhandle him away from the container. They waited and watched, hoping for a lull in the commotion, but it got more frantic as the government officials heard the whine of a transport vehicle approaching.

The small sleek craft glided into the space where the containers had been, and the shrill scream of the engines drowned out all other sound as it slowed and gently landed.

From their hiding place in the shadows, Silas and Zoe could see the excitement among the waiting staff as they crowded around the white door emblazoned with the Viva party's emblem of the blazing torch. The door slid open and gasps of delight came from the waiting Health Advisors as the Flawless Leader stepped into the light.

Silas had seen her on the news many times, and her image was displayed around Vitality Clinic to remind the students what perfection looked like and to inspire them to aim high. He knew that she was faultless; her physique always toned and displayed beautifully in the pure white clothing she wore. Her lean brown face was striking and ageless, and her smile, wide and attractive – but what emerged from the transport vehicle was something else altogether.

The creature was the same height as Helen Steele and dressed in the Flawless Leader's trademark pure white, but it was so physically deformed that Silas wondered how it was walking at all. He tried squinting to reduce the Soulsight effect, but the overdose was still too strong.

Its face was completely pockmarked, with bony protrusions bulging through its tightly stretched skin. The fear that flowed from it was so thick it had become pure hate, and it wasn't shadows that spilled from its darkened eye sockets, it was a tarry black liquid. Under the clinging white gown, the creature's body seemed to bulge and wriggle, as if it was bloating and shrinking all of its own accord. The only way he recognised this *thing* as Helen Steele was by the adoration of the Advisors as they struggled to get closer to her.

'She's pure evil,' Zoe whispered, and they looked at each other with utter shock. This was their leader – the woman who promised health for all and a brighter future for everyone. How could she say such good things, and yet be utterly selfish and poisonous inside?

'She's coming this way!' Silas lay flat on the ground, suddenly wishing they had something more substantial than the darkness to hide them.

The awestruck team of Health Advisors had been dismissed by a senior official, who then led Helen Steele towards the open crate that contained the prone figures of Jono and Marc.

'I hope this meets with your approval, Ma'am,' he was saying, and Silas realised that he knew the voice from somewhere. 'I know Advisor Corelle was hand-picked by you, but there was an incident and he had to be sedated. He was a danger to others.'

Of course! Silas thought. It didn't have the same tinny quality that the communicator added, but the unmistakable sound of the rolled 'r' in the middle of his surname gave no doubt that this was Marc's 'chief'. The one who, thanks to

Taylor, believed that Marc was too 'physically unfit and mentally unstable' to be in the squad.

'We've put him in one of the Medi-transports, just while he is recovering from the tranquilliser. It seems to be wearing off now.'

The chief was correct, and Silas could see both Jono's and Marc's feet begin to twitch, and accompanying groans rolled out from the prone figures.

'Flawless Leader, this is Health Advisor Price.' The chief introduced Taylor as she stepped out from behind the container. It appeared that she had been waiting for this moment, and she bowed her head in humble acknowledgement of Helen Steele's outstanding perfection.

Silas felt Zoe shuffle closer to him to get a good look at her arch-tormentor, and he heard her give what he could only describe as a satisfied sigh when Taylor turned her face in their direction. She was utterly ugly, twisted with malice and spite. She wasn't anywhere near as awful as Helen Steele, but Soulsight showed that her interior was almost as wrinkled and repulsive as Bubba Gee's exterior. Silas felt a speck of sympathy towards his brother when he remembered how disgusted he had sounded at Taylor's appearance.

'Ma'am,' Taylor began, her voice resonating with reverence, 'it is such a privilege to meet you. I was involved in the situation with Marc... I mean, Advisor Corelle.' Silas felt mildly impressed at Taylor's acting skills as she added a tremor of emotion to her words. It sounded as if she actually felt grief over Marc's circumstances, rather than delight at the opportunity his fall from grace had given her. She continued to explain how Marc had been utterly useless, all the while painting herself as the hero of the hour.

Helen Steele listened until Taylor, emboldened by the favourable attitude of the Flawless Leader, overstepped her boundaries. 'I think that Corelle should be removed from the Health Advisor Squad...'

'Your task is not to *think*!' Helen Steele spoke the words calmly, but the way she said them was so cutting that Taylor whimpered slightly and then began apologising furiously. 'Your task is to *obey*!' she said, interrupting Taylor's fraught mutterings. 'Now bring *Advisor* Corelle here!'

'Yes, Ma'am...' Taylor stuttered, and backed into the open cubicle. She bent over Marc and injected something into his shoulder. Silas saw his brother suddenly sit up and pull his knees to his chest, backing as far away from Taylor as possible.

If Zoe had been intrigued to see what Taylor looked like using Soulsight, Silas was just as eager to finally see Marc. And the revelation was completely unexpected. He could hardly tear his eyes away, for he had anticipated seeing a repugnant display of unchecked aggression and anger, but what he saw was a heart that was still in its infancy – undeveloped and childlike. Marc looked so vulnerable and so terrified. Fear was clearly visible, but it was blended with a weakness, a frailty, almost.

Poor Marc, Silas thought, he is lost and so afraid. He felt a desire well up in him to protect him, as if their roles had been reversed and now Marc was the younger of them.

With the lingering effects of the tranquilliser reversed, Marc suddenly started shouting.

'Get away! What do you want with me? You shouldn't even be close to me without a permit! Get off – stop touching me!'

Taylor grabbed Marc by the elbow and was trying to pull him to his feet.

'The Flawless Leader is here, you idiot. Get up!' she shouted back at him.

As if the 'Flawless Leader' were the magic words he was waiting to hear, Marc stood and started straightening his clothes. 'Out of my way, creature.' He pushed past Taylor and stepped out of the container to meet Helen Steele.

Again, Silas felt sympathy for what his brother must be going through. At least during his own initiation, the transformation had been the other way. He had been surrounded by love, joy and affection when the Soulsight worked its magic on the Community. Poor Marc was just confronted by fearful monstrosities.

Marc took one disbelieving look at the hideous vision dressed in white before him and with a terror-filled shout, he succumbed to the primitive urge of flight or fight and lunged at her with outstretched hands.

His fingers gripped around her neck and he started to squeeze. Taylor and the chief immediately sprang to their leader's aid, but their help was not needed. With two rapid and efficient jabs of her fist – one to Marc's throat and one to his stomach – she made him loosen his grip and fall to the ground.

Even from his hiding place, Silas could hear the rasp of breath as Marc tried to suck air in through his bruised larynx.

Helen Steele was incandescent with rage, and waves of fury washed out of her. To Silas and Zoe, it appeared that her skin was beginning to bubble and spit, like sizzling meat. He found Zoe's hand and gripped tightly; he was torn between being too afraid to watch, and too afraid to look away.

'He dared to touch me!' she shouted. 'I am the Flawless Leader, and he put his hands around my throat in an attempt to strangle me!' Gone was the calm, measured speech and the last sentence emerged as a scream. Surely everyone from the scanning ship could hear the commotion, but they didn't need Soulsight to tell them to stay as far away as possible.

'Advisor Price, fetch a disruptor.'

'A disruptor, Ma'am?' Taylor asked hesitantly. Silas could see that she had suddenly realised how far out of control her desire for revenge had spiralled.

'Yes. What are you waiting for? Do as I say!'

'But, Ma'am, if I may… I think Marc is sick or something. He's Gold Standard…' Her words dwindled under Helen Steele's glare.

'Yet again you assume you have a right to *think*! Your task is to *obey*, and if you cannot understand that, then perhaps you do not belong with me either. Gold Standard is a childish title for your clinic to award. I expect my elite team to be perfect, and that also means perfect loyalty!'

Taylor didn't need any more persuading and within moments had returned with the chunky black weapon.

Chapter 37

Silas didn't know what to do. Was he really about to witness his brother's execution? He looked at Helen Steele and saw the evil that consumed her. She wouldn't even bat an eyelid at taking another human life. Silas had to do something – he had to intervene.

He was on the brink of leaving his hiding place in the shadows to run to Marc's side. Maybe he could plead with the Flawless Leader on Marc's behalf, to try to explain about the Soulsight. Just then, someone else spoke. The voice held such confidence and authority that everyone turned to look at who had spoken.

'Leave him! He doesn't understand what he is seeing. He doesn't recognise you,' Jono called out from the container. His naturally commanding voice was made more powerful as it bounced off the metal walls. He was standing up in the doorway, his head nearly touching the top of the metal roof. The tranquilliser must still have been affecting him, Silas thought, as he staggered out of the container.

'Be careful!' Marc shouted a warning between erratic breaths. 'Don't let them touch you: they may carry infection!'

It took Silas a moment to realise that Marc, still seeing with Soulsight, was warning *Jono* to take care. 'Run!' Marc continued. 'Go and find the Seen, they will help you. You're too valuable… get away from here!'

Jono took a slow step towards Taylor and Helen Steele, his hand open and low, and his shoulders hunched to minimise his height.

Now Helen Steele had questioned Taylor's loyalty, Taylor seemed desperate to prove her allegiance and assumed the role of bodyguard to the Flawless Leader.

Holding the disruptor up, she pointed it at Jono. 'Stay back,' she warned.

Jono stood still as Marc struggled to his feet.

'No!' Marc said, as he stepped in front of Jono, shielding him from the fatal disruptor in Taylor's hands. 'Please don't hurt him. Can't you see, he is incredible – perfect.'

Silas blinked and looked again at his brother. There was genuine goodness there, and it was increasing the more he tried to protect Jono.

'What is your problem, Marc?' Taylor shouted at him in fury. 'What happened to you in there? You were fine when we dropped you off at the cave entrance, but when you came out, you were acting so weirdly… and now? You attempt to harm the Flawless Leader, and you seem to be infatuated with this freak of an Unseen!'

'Stand down, Advisor!' Helen Steele stepped past her new faithful guardian and, ignoring the revulsion on Marc's face, looked at Jono.

'Did you poison him, Unseen? Have you done something to him to force him to attack his own kind?' she asked, her voice sharp and acerbic.

'He was only carrying this when we searched him, Ma'am.' The chief held out a clear container containing a few mashed and ruined pages of a book, and Jono's sunstorer.

Helen Steele held the bag between a finger and thumb and waved it in front of Jono. 'What did you do, Unseen? I command you to tell me! I am your Flawless Leader. What did you poison him with?'

'I did not poison…' Jono started to explain, but Helen Steele cut him off mid-sentence.

'My squad is loyal to me and me alone. I hand-selected Advisor Corelle. He would not lift a finger against me, so you must have done something to him. I know all things and you

274

cannot lie to me,' she said, her voice rising with her anger, and her pretence at omniscience causing her own exterior to flare and ripple again.

Marc plainly could not bear to stay silent. It must have been as clear to Marc as it was to Silas that Jono was telling the truth, and the monstrous version of the Flawless Leader was spouting lie after lie.

'He's not lying, you are! You twisted, rotten, foul monster – you know nothing!'

The revolting waves of rage rolled over Helen Steele once again, and this time Silas had to look away in disgust.

'I am the Flawless Leader, and you *will* show me respect, and if you are unable to… then, you are of no use to me, and you will be discarded.' The threat-laden tone of the Flawless Leader's voice left no one in any doubt as to her meaning, and as she turned to leave, she flicked her wrist towards Taylor. 'Carry on, Advisor.'

'It happened when we were in the cave. The effects will wear off!' Jono's desperate half-confession persuaded the Flawless Leader to turn back to him.

'You *did* poison him, then?' Helen Steele pounced on the admission.

Jono stared as her wretched soul writhed and twisted, and then he looked again at Marc. That small shift from infancy into maturity was there. Marc's heart was looking stronger by the second.

'That's what *you* say I did,' Jono eventually acknowledged with a heavy finality.

A smug satisfaction oozed from the creature that was Helen Steele and her twisted face leered into a smile.

'Good,' she said, as if a deal had been struck and she had got the best part.

'No, he didn't,' Marc was shaking his head in confusion. 'I don't understand.'

'Bring Corelle with us,' Helen Steele barked orders at the Chief Advisor. 'I believe he is worth trying to salvage.'

'Yes, Ma'am,' the chief said.

'What... what's going on?' Marc stuttered. 'I don't understand. Who are you?'

Choosing to ignore Marc, Helen Steele spoke to Jono. Her voice had softened again, and she almost sounded apologetic. 'I quite lost my temper earlier. It is just as well you intervened. Losing such a fine specimen would have been tragic.' She pointed a gnarled hand at Marc although still addressing Jono. 'And can you imagine the questions from the father... Oh, no. That would have been too messy. I have *him* just where I want him. How strange, though,' she mused, 'a useful Unseen.' Her laugh was quite beautiful, yet hearing it come from the mouth of so vile a creature made Silas flinch.

'Chief!' She briskly rubbed her hands together as if her work was finished.

'Ma'am?'

'Sedate Corelle, and as for this – thing,' she pointed at Jono, 'his crimes are poisoning a Seen, one of my own Advisors, forcing him to act against his will to cause me harm. If it were a Seen it may be worth trying to reclaim, but as an Unseen... it's expendable. Finish it.' She started to walk back to her transport ship, but then turned to the chief, 'And when you have done that, destroy the dwellings.' Her arm swung wide towards where the crater lay in the dark bowl behind them. 'We don't want this place to remain a temptation to any of our new Unseen citizens.'

'Yes, Ma'am.' The chief and Taylor respectfully bowed as the Flawless Leader stepped aboard her personal transport. With a rumble of engines, the craft smoothly glided from under the belly of the scanning craft and up into the dark night sky.

Taylor watched the transport go and then turned her attention back to Jono. With a malevolent darkness beginning to twist her appearance even further, she lifted the disruptor and stared down the viewfinder to get a clear shot at Jono's head. Next to her, the chief loaded a small dart gun and aimed at Marc.

Time seemed to slow down for Silas. He watched, a powerless observer, as Jono and Marc realised that their chance at negotiation had passed. All of a sudden, as if by some unspoken consensus, they split up and started sprinting in different directions.

Marc ran straight across the middle of the pool of light. His speed was impressive, but he didn't stand a chance at outrunning the tranquilliser dart, and he went down heavily onto his face, plumes of dust billowing around him.

Jono took a different approach and zigzagged like a hunted deer, while Taylor tried to get a lock on. Soon he was swallowed by the darkness and Silas could no longer see him.

Taylor was cursing loudly. 'Chief,' she shouted, 'I need light over here, I can't see a thing.'

'He can't go far, Price,' he called back, 'that's the cliff edge!' Nonetheless, he barked into his communicator, 'Control, increase light at the vessel stern.'

There was a blaze of additional light and Silas and Zoe found they had to scurry backwards to avoid being caught in it. The edge of the cliff was clearly illuminated now, but Jono was nowhere to be seen.

'He got away!' Zoe breathed. 'I forget how quick he is.'

'How… where? We have to find him.' Silas whispered back. There was nowhere for Jono to go but over the edge. And from what he remembered, the cliff was utterly sheer.

'He'll be scuttling down!' Zoe said, her fingers twiddling in the air like a spider. It wasn't dissimilar to what Jono actually looked like. 'You've seen him on that tree of his…'

'Did he do the job for us and fall over?' the chief called to Taylor across the landing area, and he laughed as she peered over the cliff edge. With a shout she dropped to her belly and wriggled her head and shoulders over the void.

'Impossible! Chief, he's climbing down!'

'Well, shoot him, then!' The chief left Marc in an undignified heap in the middle of the dirt and ran to join Taylor.

Silas willed Jono to climb faster as Taylor lifted the disruptor to her eyes and her thumb hovered over the blue Target Acquired button. 'He's fast! It's unnatural, like an insect... a bug... a huge spider!'

'Why haven't you acquired him yet? He's nearly at the waterfall. Don't let him get out of range. I don't want to have to scan this miserable hole for a third time today.'

'Got him.' Her thumb pressed the blue button, and shifted to hang over the red Disrupt button. Silas felt his throat constrict, and he struggled to his feet. He had to get that disruptor out of Taylor's hands! But before he could take a step, the chief gave a cry of triumph as Taylor's thumb firmly depressed the Disrupt button.

'Well done, Price! For a moment there, I thought you were going to let him escape.' The chief stood up and dusted down his clothes. Taylor pulled the scope away from her eyes and wriggled back onto the plateau. She was wreathed in grey shadows. They were twisting and pulling her body and face, as if she were undergoing some kind of metamorphosis.

'Did you see the way he fell, Chief?' Taylor lifted one grey wreathed arm and let her clenched fist suddenly drop, smacking into the palm of her other hand. 'Like a stone!'

'There's going to be a nasty mess... a fall from that height,' the chief laughed. 'That bug should be grateful that you killed him painlessly, before the rocks at the bottom smashed him to pieces.'

'Yes, Chief,' Taylor said. She peered back over the edge, a twisted smile on her hideously distorted face, before following the chief to where Marc lay. They dragged him into the last empty container and closed the door behind them. The box started to lift off the ground, and silently moved towards the open belly of the ship.

'No!' Zoe grabbed Silas' hand as he sank back in horror. She was digging her nails into his flesh, but he hardly felt it past the searing agony in his heart.

'Jono!' Zoe suddenly screamed his name, but her voice was lost in the earth-shaking sound of the ship's engines as it ponderously lifted off the ground.

Silas could feel his teeth vibrate with the sheer volume of the noise, and he rolled into a ball on the dusty ground, desperately trying to escape from the reverberation in his skull.

The sound dropped out of the painful range as the ship rose higher, and Silas looked up to see Zoe running towards the cliff edge. For one horrific moment, Silas thought she was going to throw herself off the cliff after Jono, but instead she fell to her knees at the crater edge and shouted his name down into the blackness. Over and over again she called, as the scanning ship rose higher and the circle of white light grew wider but fainter until it dispersed completely.

The ache in Silas' chest was almost too much to bear. He wished he could scream out his agony like Zoe, but he felt crushed by the weight of his distress. No words or sound could express his anguish. He couldn't believe that Jono was gone… dead. Killed by the same people who had promised life.

High in the sky the thin cloud cover began to break, and almost hesitantly, the cold light of the moon shone down on their despair.

Silas could make out Zoe's form in the faint moonlight and unsteadily moved towards her. His legs were slow and heavy, as if he had forgotten how to walk, and he stumbled when he stepped onto an object on the floor. He flicked it away with his foot before realising it was the bag containing Jono's belongings – his sunstorer and his ragged book. He knelt on the stones, feeling in the dark with his hands until he found the plastic case. Opening it with shaking hands, he reverently cradled the sunstorer like it was a precious relic. The orb glowed bright and strong, and Silas carried it to the cliff edge and stood in mute tribute to his friend.

The rumble from the scanning ship engines was still audible as it made its way across the crater. It halted over the forest, and with a hideous icy premonition, Silas knew why. Beams of searing blue light fell from the ship like lightning bolts, and as Silas blinked away the after-image, he saw the forest respond with bursts of orange and yellow.

At last he found his voice and screamed a primal howl of loss. They were burning the forest! Dozens of individual huts were blazing like torches, burning brightly like beacons scattered in the dark. But fire is never satiated, and it spread from hut to tree, and from trunk to canopy, until the whole forest was a roaring firestorm.

Chapter 38

Drawn by the faint glow from the sunstorer, Nana found them. Zoe was sitting bolt upright, completely still and with her eyes closed. But her lips were silently mouthing one name over and over: 'Jono... Jono...'

Silas was on his hands and knees, rocking backwards and forwards, groaning as if in physical agony.

The forest was still a blaze of orange flame, and the hungry fire had spread onto the dry grasslands. The acrid stench of burning tainted the air.

'Silas, Zoe, are you hurt?' Nana repeated the question over and over, but neither seemed able to answer coherently. One at a time, Nana helped them to their feet and guided them to the waiting truck.

Silas took one last look over the crater. He didn't want to remember it like this, a place of smoke and fire and death. He tried to picture the first time he had seen it, as dawn broke and light chased the shadows away. But he couldn't do it; all that came to mind was the moment the huts exploded in flame – Bubba Gee's cabin, Jono's tree house – all destroyed.

He was beyond exhaustion, emotionally and physically, and so the ride in the truck with Nana was little more than a blur, though he recalled the moment when the Soulsight overdose began to wear off. It came as a relief in some ways, for Zoe's grief was so raw it was like looking at an open wound ripped in her heart.

He wished he could have protected her from this. He should have been able to help Jono... if only he had been faster, and less concerned for his own skin, he may have been able to save him. So what if he'd been caught? And now Zoe was in so much pain that it was as if she had gone into some kind of mental shock. She was awake but stayed rigid and silent and completely unresponsive to Nana's gentle voice.

Nana tried speaking to Silas as well, but he couldn't get her words to make sense. Eventually, his tired brain understood one question. 'Are they all dead?' Her voice was full of anxiety, and she kept asking, 'Silas, are they all dead?'

He just managed to muster the energy to whisper, 'No...' and Nana sat back on the bench with her eyes closed and let the tears fall unchecked down her cheeks.

Much later he awoke, disorientated and confused, in a firm bed in a simple, tidy room. Then he remembered he wasn't at the Community any more, and it all came flooding back, and with it, the urge to howl and scream.

Nana was swiftly by his side. He didn't recognise her at first and pulled away from the old woman with the severe face.

It was another loss, and he wasn't ready for it. He had become used to knowing Nana by what the Soulsight showed him – mainly by her generous, loving nature – and he hated the limitations of just seeing her physical shell.

'How's Zoe?' was his first question, and when Nana didn't immediately answer, he grabbed her hand. 'I want to see Zoe,' he insisted, his voice beginning to edge towards hysteria.

To calm him, Nana let him peek through Zoe's door. She was sleeping, and he watched her for a moment. He didn't think it was possible to feel any more pain; his heart was already in pieces, but looking on her plain face, so ordinary without Soulsight, made him feel robbed and cheated.

'She won't speak – to anyone,' Nana said, sounding worried. 'What happened, Silas?'

'Jono... he...' The words stuck in his throat, and he found he couldn't admit to the horror of the truth.

Nana quietly shut the door to Zoe's room. 'Come, we can talk through here.' She led him down a corridor into a dimly lit lounge area. The windows were dark, and Silas was confused. Was it still night, or had he slept through a whole 24 hours?

'Have I missed a day?' he asked.

'No,' Nana pressed a button on the side of the window and the opaque glass grew a shade more transparent and a muted sunlight filtered through. 'This is Maxie and Val's house. They drove to the crater to help me search for you. They sleep in the day, because they are Unseen... remember?'

Silas nodded and then, copying Nana, he sat on a hard bench by a basic food dispenser.

'Water, protein sticks, carboflakes,' she listed into the machine.

'So, I'm in Maxie and Val's house?' He digested the fact and looked around the simple room. His mind went back to the terror he had felt when they had blindfolded him on his trip out to the Community. All those precautions of secrecy and concealment... it had all been for nothing.

'How did you know where to find us? And where's Coach Atkins – I mean, Thomas?' Silas asked, looking down at his hands while he waited for his nutrition to be dispensed.

'Thomas returned to Prima two days ago. While we were at the crater, the new law came into effect. Bio-assessments are now mandatory and no one is exempt. He wanted to talk to some of his friends in the government to see how the law would be enforced so he could accurately assess what threat the Community would be under.' Nana's voice shook a little. 'If he had waited an extra day he could have seen for himself.' Nana sighed. 'Oh, Silas, when I saw the scanning ship go over the town I knew the Community was at risk, but I couldn't understand how they had found us so quickly.'

'It was the medical supplies, Nana. There was a transmitter. The Health Advisors must have been waiting, ready to investigate as soon as the device was triggered,' Silas said. He could hardly believe that only two days ago the Community had been secure, a safe haven, and now it was gone.

'It has all happened so fast,' Nana looked shaken. 'Poor Bubba Gee, I wish I had been with him, but Maxie and Val couldn't get to the truck until evening, and by then it was too late. *I* was too late. I assumed they would round the Community up for processing, but when I saw the fire in the distance, I thought they'd burnt the forest and everyone in it.'

It was as if the weight of her fears had aged Nana, and she sounded vulnerable and afraid.

With a click and a whirr the dispenser interrupted them, and Nana looked at the portions of nutrition. 'You need to eat now, Silas,' she instructed.

Obediently, he went through the task of swallowing the familiar nutrition, and reluctantly, he began to feel it was doing him good. His strength started to return, and he felt more able to cope as Nana started questioning him again.

'Did you see Bonnie and Bubba Gee get taken?'

'Everyone was taken.' Silas did his best to describe the Health Advisors, the containers and the awful sound of the sedating gas, but he felt guilty under Nana's gaze, like he had escaped at the expense of the people that she loved.

'Will you be able to find Bubba Gee? Is there some other place he can go, so he won't have to stay an Unseen?'

'I don't know, Silas,' Nana admitted.

'I want to help… in any way I can. I'll help you look for him,' Silas said.

'Thank you. I'll see what I can find out first. I have a contact who works for HE-LP. He may know where Unclassifieds get processed. Also there is Thomas. He needs to know what has happened.' She smiled. 'Don't worry, Silas. We won't abandon our friends. We will find them.' Nana looked thoughtful. 'But first, tell me what else you know. What about the Health Advisors? Who are they?'

'A new elite squad,' Silas explained, 'that's what my brother said. He was there – hand-picked by Helen Steele herself.'

Nana's expression grew more and more stern as Silas recounted how his brother had followed them as they had tried to escape through the Soulsight caverns, and the way Jono was captured.

'Helen Steele was there and Marc stood up to her. He tried to protect Jono, but it wasn't enough.' Silas thought of the bubbling skin and the hate pouring from her. 'She was far and above the most distorted out of everyone. I don't know, Nana… she was like a nightmare. She killed Jono; she ordered his execution.'

'Oh, Silas,' Nana's eyes filled with tears. 'What happened?'

His voice faltered as he described Jono's final moments. 'The Flawless Leader told one of the Advisors to destroy him, and he tried to get away. Then they shot him with a disruptor as he was climbing down the crater wall. He fell…'

Later in the afternoon Nana came to find Silas again. Her voice was hoarse as if she had been crying.

'Zoe is awake, and she's asking for you.'

Silas had been lying on his bed, trying to clear his head, trying to sleep. However, his mind wouldn't allow it. Instead, he seemed stuck on an imagined replay of the horror of Jono's body falling off the cliff and smashing onto the rocks below. His limbs would have shattered. His head would have caved in. There would have been blood, irreparable damage… death.

There was no escaping his tortured thoughts and he almost didn't want to, as if imagining Jono's death over and over again would somehow make amends for his failure to save him.

Consequently, it took a moment for Silas to register what Nana had said but, when he did, he jumped to his feet and seconds later, was knocking on Zoe's door.

'It's me, Silas,' he said.

'Come in,' Zoe's familiar husky voice called.

Seeing her without Soulsight wasn't so bad the second time. She was sitting up in bed, her dark curly hair an unruly mess of tangles. Her cheeks looked swollen and her eyes looked small and lost in her round face. He had forgotten that she had freckles, and the darker brown splotches looked like dirty marks across her paler brown cheeks.

'I'm glad you're awake,' he said, half-closing his eyes and trying to imagine her beautiful loving heart shining through.

'Who are…?' Zoe hesitated, appearing confused. 'Oh… Silas.' Then she sighed heavily. 'Silas without Soulsight… I miss that already.' She seemed more affected by Silas' altered appearance than he was by hers, and stumbled as she spoke to him, as if she struggled to remember exactly who he was.

'Hey,' Silas gently remonstrated, 'it's still me… in here.' He pushed his dark hair off his forehead and pointed at his green eyes. 'Just look a little deeper.' He tried to coax a smile from her, but the eyes that stared back into his seemed distant and empty.

'I didn't dream it, did I?' she asked uncertainly, and Silas shook his head. He didn't need to ask what she meant because he had awoken with the same hope… that the previous night's horrific events had been a nightmare.

'No. You didn't dream it.'

'It's all gone?' she continued, frowning at Silas as if she were trying to look for lies in his answers.

'Yes,' he said, his voice thick with emotion.

'And Jono …'

Silas couldn't make a sound. He just nodded and looked away, ashamed, as if he had been the one to have pressed the Disrupt button.

'Jono's dead,' she said flatly, and then repeated the statement as if she couldn't quite believe what she was saying. 'He's dead, and it's my fault.'

'What do you mean?' Silas asked, looking in surprise at Zoe's round face and noticing the heavy dark bags of puffy flesh under her eyes.

'I didn't want to leave,' she said in a small voice. 'I was too slow. I held you back. We could have been up and out of the crater before the scanner ship arrived, but I just wanted to stay that little bit longer.'

'What?' Silas said. 'No, Zoe! If that is your reason, then we are both to blame. I got stuck on the waterfall... Taylor saw me and sent Marc chasing after us. You are not going to carry the guilt for this. Maybe we both let Jono down, but it was Helen Steele and Taylor Price that killed him.'

Zoe shrugged, as if whatever Silas said would make little difference.

'I wish I'd died out there too,' she whispered in an almost inaudible voice, and at her words, Silas felt a rush of numbing fear, so powerful, so awful.

'No!' he said urgently, longing to reach out and simply hold her. 'Never say that.' Suddenly, the haunting mental picture of Jono's broken body at the foot of the cliff was replaced with that of Zoe's. 'Zoe, please don't ever say that again, don't even think it. We have each other. We can get through this, together...'

Silas didn't know if she was listening to him any more. He had never known her so lost, so hopeless.

'Zoe, I...' he was about to continue, but she silenced him by stretching out her arms in mute appeal. Unhesitatingly, he wrapped his arms around her and they clung to each other, united in their shared grief and pain.

Silas only let go when he heard Nana moving around in the next room.

'I should probably let you rest. You still look exhausted,' he said, noticing for the first time a greyish tinge to her pale brown skin. He stood up to leave, but Zoe held on to his hand.

'I do feel tired,' she said, 'but I don't want you to go.'

'I'll sit here,' Silas said, reaching for a chair to pull it closer to the bed. 'You sleep now, Zoe.'

She continued holding his hand as she lay down and closed her eyes.

'You'll stay with me?' Zoe murmured, her speech slurred and drowsy.

'I'll stay,' Silas promised.

'We'll get through this, won't we?' she whispered.

'Together,' Silas reassured her. He watched her until he saw her body relax and felt her grip on his hand loosen. He watched her until his own eyelids began to grow heavy and, despite the uncomfortable chair, he too drifted off to sleep.

He woke with a start an hour or two later and immediately knew something was wrong. Zoe's breathing was laboured and rattling, and when he brushed his fingers across her brow, they came away damp with sweat.

'Zoe?' he said, gently shaking her shoulder. Her eyelids fluttered, and he could see the whites of her eyes stained pink by a fine network of inflamed blood vessels.

'Jono...' she muttered. 'Don't leave me.'

'It's Silas,' he said, but she didn't seem to hear and stared straight past him before drifting asleep again. Suddenly concerned, Silas hurried to find Nana.

'It's a mild fever, that's all,' Nana said to Silas, as he fidgeted anxiously beside her. Zoe fitfully tossed and turned in the little bed, muttering under her breath in her sleep.

'Will she be OK?' Silas asked. 'She was just talking to me a couple of hours ago, she seemed fine.'

'Don't worry, Silas. All she needs is rest. As do you, by the looks of it. I'll look after her tonight,' Nana said, guiding Silas to his room. 'She'll be well by tomorrow. You can talk to her more then.'

Chapter 39

By the following morning Silas was feeling physically much better. He had slept a long and dreamless sleep and awoken when he heard Maxie and Val return from their night shift.

His first thought was of Zoe, and he crept along the darkened corridor to her room and peeped in. Nana was asleep, sitting upright in the same hard-backed chair that he had dozed off in yesterday. Beyond her, Silas could see Zoe's hands resting on a smooth sheet. She seemed to be sleeping soundly. Gone were the ragged breathing and fevered movements. Silently, he closed Zoe's door and padded back to his own room.

From downstairs he could hear Maxie or Val coughing, a deep painful hacking sound that travelled through the small house. Now would be the perfect opportunity to meet them and thank them, he thought. They had driven all night to the crater to find him and Zoe, and had generously shared their home, and he had never even spoken to them.

However, another thought occurred to him, and he almost gave up on the idea of meeting them at all. What if he was scared of them? What if seeing them brought back all his old childhood fears... they were Unseen, after all... He wished he could see them using Soulsight because then he would hardly be aware of their physical appearance.

Then he remembered the handful of the Soulsight plant that he had hidden in his trouser pocket; the clump he had taken, more as a souvenir, from the cavern, after Jono had pulled him to safety. Desperately hoping no one had been to clear his room, he rummaged at the end of the bed. He found his filthy trousers scrunched on the floor and slipped his hand into the stiff pocket.

Jono's sunstorer and his water-damaged book fragments were there, and then under that, a damp tuft of dark green Soulsight. There wasn't much there, and Silas hoped that just a little would do the trick. He didn't want to waste it, for if this was all he had, then he had better make it last.

He let a small piece rest on his tongue, hoping that the chemical would still be lingering on the green strand. It tasted of nothing at all and after a moment he removed the fragment. Carefully folding the remainder of the plant into the pages of the book, he placed it on his bed. There was a mirror on the wall, and Silas watched to see if the Soulsight was working by waiting for his reflection to change. It didn't take long, and it wasn't as bad as he thought it would be.

He was still fearful, but his green eyes were clearly visible and bright in his face, despite the lingering shadows. He looked more solid, more vivid, than he had done when he had last seen his reflection, way back, at the initiation. And as he inspected his unfamiliar self even more closely, he could make out hints of his friends reproduced in him, as if they had rubbed off on him. There were elements of Nana and Zoe's immense love, Jono's loyalty, and even a sense of Coach Atkins' sorrowfulness.

His time at the Community had changed him for the better, and taking courage from that, he quietly opened the door and headed downstairs.

Two strangers sat on the bench by the dispenser, sipping cups of cloudy brown liquid.

'Hello,' Silas said tentatively. As they looked up at him, he knew he had done the right thing by taking Soulsight. Two of the kindest faces he had ever seen smiled back at him. Being near them was like standing by the fire on the cool evenings in the crater, when the heat from the flames would radiate through his body. He let their kindness fill him and warm him, as the ice of his grief began to slowly thaw.

'I see you,' he said softly, as if he could break the Soulsight vision if he spoke too loud. He wasn't even interested in knowing what disfigurements their bodies carried as he raised his hand to his eyes in the Community gesture.

'I see you, Silas. I'm Maxie.' The woman, dressed in the long cloak of the Unseen returned the sign.

'And I'm Valentine, but everyone calls me Val,' the man said. 'I see you, Silas.'

In Val, the deep kindness was perfectly blended with love and acceptance. It was the look of approval that he longed to see from his own father, and here it was, unexpectedly, from this Unseen.

As Val stood up, something broke in Silas and, without hesitation or restraint, like a child running to the embrace of his parent, he threw his arms around the man. Unperturbed by the extravagant gesture of his young visitor, Val merely held Silas tight in a strong bear hug.

'You're going to be all right,' Val mumbled in a deep bass growl. 'You are strong inside, and you will take your loss and you will turn it into something beautiful in memory of Jono. I am proud of you, Silas.'

With those words, Silas felt the jagged edges of pain in his chest soften. Val released his hold and indicated for him to sit.

Maxie made room for him on the bench, and as he sat with Maxie on one side and Val on the other, he had never felt safer.

'It is lovely to finally meet you, Silas. You are welcome to stay here for as long as you need to,' Maxie said.

'Nana told us all that happened on the crater edge,' Val said, his large bulk filling up at least half of the little bench.

When he didn't respond, they didn't ply him with questions and seemed happy with the comfortable silence that filled the room. Silas didn't want to talk about the Community or the crater again, and Maxie and Val seemed to understand that.

'Thank you for finding me and Zoe,' Silas finally said.

Val gave a slow nod, but as he tried to start speaking, something caught in his throat and his words were lost in a fit of coughing. Silas looked at Maxie with concern.

'It's his lungs,' she explained. 'They seem to be getting worse at the moment. HE-LP has him on medication, but he needs rest now. Come on, Val.' She helped Val to stand. Still coughing, Val raised his hand in farewell to Silas and leaned heavily on Maxie, as she supported him upstairs.

'Goodnight, Silas, and please make yourself at home.'

After Maxie and Val had gone to their room and Val's coughing fit had settled, Silas had the house to himself. He ordered some nutrition from the dispenser, even though he had no appetite, and forced himself to eat it. Every now and then Nana would appear to get water or food, but mostly he was left with the silence of the house and his own thoughts to accompany him. The roller coaster of his emotions was exhausting enough, as they would swing from overwhelming gratitude that he was alive, to sharing Zoe's desire that he had died with Jono, for at least then the pain would be gone.

Later in the afternoon he tried to get in to see Zoe, but Nana wouldn't let him through the door.

'There's something more serious going on,' Nana whispered to Silas.

Past Nana's shoulder, Silas could see Zoe's face. She was completely still, but now it wasn't the stillness of rest and for one gut-wrenching moment, Silas thought he was witnessing the heavy inertness of death in Zoe's motionless form.

'Is she …?' He couldn't bring himself to finish the question. The words shrivelled up in his throat.

'She's unconscious,' Nana hurriedly explained, seeing Silas' stricken look. 'I need to call the Health Emergency …'

'No!' Silas interjected. 'She was fine yesterday; you said it was just a fever.'

'It's developed into something more,' Nana said. Her voice was surprisingly calm at the idea of getting HE-LP involved, but to Silas it was the equivalent of Zoe being handed a death sentence.

'But what if she doesn't come back,' he pleaded with Nana, 'like my mum…?'

'Oh, Silas,' Nana said, her voice full of compassion, 'I understand. But this is different. The Health Emergency team will be able to help Zoe. I'll be with her, though,' she continued. 'I won't leave her side. I'll make sure she stays safe, OK?'

Nana sounded confident in her decision, but Silas wished he could see her properly. He should have used more Soulsight. The fragment of plant he had taken earlier on had worn off too quickly.

He wanted to see how serious she really thought Zoe's illness was. Nana had never lied to him in the whole of their time at the Community, but what if she was now? What if she was hiding something from him, even if to protect him? He would rather know the full truth now than discover she had deceived him.

'Can I come with you?' he asked, unwilling to be separated from Zoe at all. 'I promised Zoe I'd stay with her.'

'No, Silas,' Nana responded. 'I'm sorry to ask you to do this, but you'll have to make the journey to Prima without us. You need to be home and be with your family.'

'You're my family,' Silas immediately objected.

'You need to go home,' Nana insisted again. 'It's for your safety too. If questions get asked over your whereabouts, then your connection with the Community may come out. And I don't know what repercussions that could have on you, Silas. Be safe, my dear boy, for me and for Zoe. I need to know you are home and, when she wakes, Zoe will want to know that you are waiting for her in Prima.'

Silas gave a reluctant nod. It didn't seem like he had much of a choice. He felt severely disappointed, though. The journey home was to have been his and Zoe's chance to talk some more, to share the burden of grief and find a measure of solace in each other. He wanted to tell her about Val and maybe begin the painful process of talking about Jono. The memory of Jono's death was seared in his brain, but Silas wanted to remember the good things, the quotes and quirks that made Jono so exceptional.

But Silas couldn't share this with Nana. She was burdened enough, so all he said was, 'When do I have to leave?'

'When night falls, Val will take you to the station. He'll travel on the Overground train with you and escort you to the Subterranean connection, but Unseen are not permitted on the Sub, so you'll have to make the rest of the journey on your own.'

Within the hour the HE-LP team arrived and, from the upper window, Silas saw them guiding the stretcher into the squad transport. He couldn't see Zoe's face, just the unmistakable shape of her short, round body, under a silvery blanket. Nana climbed in with her and then the door slid shut, and they were hidden from sight. The craft smoothly lifted into the sky, and he watched it until it became a speck in the distance.

At that moment, there was a tentative knock on the door.

'Come in,' Silas said, and looked up to see a huge man filling the doorway. With an immense barrel chest and large protuberant abdomen, the man had a similar way of moving to Bonnie at the end of her pregnancy – swaying and ponderous.

'How are you doing, Silas?' The man coughed and wheezed a little, and Silas realised that this was Val without the benefit of Soulsight. 'Zoe will be sent home in a couple of days,' Val said. 'They said she had an infection. It is serious, but they can treat it.'

Silas tried to feel encouraged. He wanted to feel relieved that Zoe was going to be OK, but he still couldn't shake his distrust of HE-LP.

'You'll see her again, when you get back to Prima,' Val reassured him. 'Now, if you can be ready to leave by sunset, we'll catch the first Overground train that I have a permit for. I won't be able to stay with you as I will travel in the Unseen carriage, but look for my signal so I can let you know where you need to change trains to board the Subterranean.'

'How do you bear it?' Silas asked, thinking of his friends from the Community who had worked so hard to escape the restrictions of being an Unseen.

'Bear what? Being an Unseen?' Val laughed, which led to another painful coughing fit. 'I've known little else,' he said, when he had recovered sufficiently to talk. 'But it was worse before Viva came to power, when there was nothing for the Unseen, when we were spat at in the streets and starving in our beds. I am grateful for the little things – food and drink, a home for Maxie and I.' He smiled at Silas and rested a heavy hand on his shoulder. 'I get medicine and that keeps me breathing, and I'm thankful for every lungful of air.'

After ordering some new food from the dispenser, Val packed it in a small tub and gave it to Silas to hold.

'Val, I couldn't find your Biocubicle. I wanted to see if I'd dropped off any levels, so I could think up a reason to explain to my dad…' Silas pulled a wry face. He really hoped he hadn't dropped too far. Maybe if he got straight into the health suite when he got home, he could make his results less shameful.

'We don't have one yet,' Val answered. 'We get assessed at the factory. But the Flawless Leader has promised one for every person, Unseen included, by the end of the year. I don't know why, though, the communal ones are perfectly adequate. Thomas Atkins would say it's so that the government will know exactly where everyone is all the time. But that's just Thomas talking.' Val chuckled and Silas joined in, but it occurred to him that Coach Atkins had been right about the Community being discovered. He had been right to try to warn Jono. Maybe they all needed to start thinking a bit more like Thomas Atkins.

Night came and Silas watched Val take the Unseen cloak off the peg by the door. He didn't want Val to wear it. Just seeing it filled him with a childish fear as if, by simply putting it on, Val would transform into a monster.

'Come here,' Val said reassuringly, as he saw Silas' face. 'I don't change because I have to wear this thing. Have you got all your belongings?'

Silas nodded and clutched the small bag tighter in his hand. There wasn't much in there at all, but it was all he had left from his time at the Community. The tub of dispensed nutrition from Val, Jono's old sunstorer that he wanted to give to Zoe next time he saw her, and most importantly, his small supply of Soulsight. It was still wrapped in the ragged pages of Jono's book and carefully placed at the bottom of the bag.

Val gave Silas a strong hug, then pulled the large hood over his face and walked out of the front door into the night.

Silas waited for a moment, then followed the large shrouded figure. He walked alone, for even in the Outerlands, Citizen Safety Monitors were everywhere.

He kept his eyes fixed on Val's back as he turned left and then right to join a busier street. A few more Unseen were emerging from doorways and alleyways like silent wraiths. Feeling increasingly nervous, Silas tried to move closer to Val, but he needn't have worried: none of the Unseen went near him. They saw Silas and immediately moved out of his way, giving him a clear berth all around, like he was surrounded by an invisible force field.

Now his nerves were replaced by sadness, and he remembered his friends from the Community. He tried to smile at the hooded figures, unsure if they were even able to see him through the heavy cloth.

'What are you smiling at? Stick to the day, Seen!' a voice hissed close by, and Silas swung round.

'Who said that?' he challenged.

'The night belongs to us! You don't fit in. Go and hide under your bed!'

Again Silas turned around and couldn't work out which of the Unseen were speaking. He saw the bulky figure of Val waiting at a crossroads and quickened his pace again. A bitter laugh followed him down the street, and he chided himself for his own naivety. Not all Unseen were as kind as Val, just as not all Seen were as twisted as Helen Steele and Taylor.

Silas sat in an empty compartment on the Overground train, unsure if Val was even on it. There had been a press of cloaks and hoods at the carriage for the Unseen. He thought he had seen Val's barrel-shaped body push through to the door, but the Unseen all looked the same in their enveloping robes.

Silas just hoped he wouldn't miss his stop. He had already accidentally dozed off for a few moments, only to wake with the panicky feeling that he was going to be lost in the Outerlands. Eventually, he stood up and paced along the short corridor in an attempt to stay awake.

Pressing his face to the window he tried to see the landscape outside, but all was dark. He was tired of living in the dark, he decided – the pitch black of the cave, the long night after the scanning ship left, then a day in the dark at Maxie and Val's home.

How terrible to live that way all the time; no wonder the Community wanted to stay hidden. For Bubba Gee and for so many of Silas' new friends, a perpetual night was now what awaited them. Maybe Jono was better off avoiding that fate; he wouldn't have coped living like a nocturnal animal.

What am I thinking? Silas headbutted the windowpane sharply to stop his mind going there. Of course Jono should have survived. He would have found a way to make it work. Why couldn't the Flawless Leader and the Health Advisors have left them alone? Why did they have to destroy such a beautiful thing?

The train started slowing and eventually jolted to a halt at a platform. He saw an Unseen cross in front of the window and it beckoned with a veiled hand.

Grabbing his bag, Silas opened the carriage door and whispered, 'Val?'

The Unseen nodded and walked across a deserted platform and pointed down a well-lit tunnel.

'Say goodbye to Maxie for me, please.' The Unseen nodded again and Silas walked away. He looked over his shoulder as the tunnel reached a bend. Val was still there, a hand raised in farewell.

Chapter 40

As the Subterranean pulled into the station, Silas could see that most of the carriages were empty, so he deliberately chose one of those. He didn't feel ready to be around 'normal' people yet. He didn't want to have to hear their meaningless conversations about the mundane trivia of their existence. It all felt so pointless now. How could anything in his old life ever be the same again? How could he go back to clinic? How could he face Marc, knowing what he had been involved in?

Placing his bag in the nearest chair, Silas dimmed the overhead light and leaned back into the cushioned seat. His head was full of unresolved questions. He kept thinking of Zoe. How he wished he were making this journey with her.

Eventually the silence of the carriage soothed him, and Silas drifted off to sleep. However, his dreams did not give him the rest he desired, for in them he was holding a disruptor and pointing at a herd of deer. The picture shifted, and it was Jono in the viewfinder. Without meaning to, he pressed the Acquire button, and his thumb was being drawn of its own accord towards the Disrupt button. 'Run!' he shouted in his dream, but he knew Jono would never be fast enough to outrun the deadly ray. In his viewfinder he saw Jono collapse in an untidy pile. 'No! I didn't do it.' He was explaining to a circle of accusing faces. 'I didn't do it ...'

An external noise broke into his sleep, and he sat up and rubbed his eyes. The Subterranean made very little sound as it raced through the long underground tunnel, so it must have been something from within the carriage. There it was again – a loud, impatient sigh. Someone else was in the same car and was sitting a few rows down. Silas stood up so he could see over the top of the chairs. He could just make out a few wisps of pale yellow hair, shining in the glow from the overhead light.

This was my carriage, he thought unreasonably. There were plenty of other empty ones to choose from. It wasn't as if the night was a busy time for the Seen to travel.

As he leaned further over to get a better look at the unwelcome company, his hand slipped on the seat, and his face hit the cushioned top with a soft thud.

The noise made the newcomer straighten up and turn around.

'Oh good, you're awake.'

A girl stared at him. She seemed young. Her hair was a light feathery mist of gold that provided a frame for her small, pretty face. All her features seemed tiny and sharp, almost feline. A little pointed nose, neat dark eyes and, when she grinned at him, a perfect row of small white teeth. 'You'll wish you were still asleep, though, because all the projectors are faulty in this car. It's going to be a long, boring journey to the city.'

'Thanks,' Silas muttered, slumping back down onto his chair. He decided he would try to get back to sleep as long as that girl was quiet. What was she doing out at night anyway? From her face, she looked pre-clinic age and surely too young to travel alone. Still, it wasn't any of his business; she'd have to look after herself… he wasn't going to babysit her.

Closing his eyes and resting back, he tried to get comfortable again. He heard her moving about in her chair and kept his eyes firmly shut. If he ignored her, she'd leave him alone.

'So, what were you dreaming about? It sounded very dramatic. "Run… I didn't do it!"' she mimicked.

Startled, he opened his eyes. She was hanging upside down in front of him, dangling by her legs from the luggage store above their heads! He pressed back into the chair, trying to escape the proximity of her face.

'Don't do that!' he said crossly and slid into the next seat. 'I'm trying to sleep.'

'Sorry,' she said, without a hint of remorse, and in one graceful move, rotated her legs over and lowered her torso into the seat that Silas had just vacated.

Now that he could see more than just her face, he realised she was older than he had originally assumed. Through her fitted clothes he could see that her musculature was exceptional and her limbs well proportioned. She was slender but tall, and definitely didn't have the physique of a child.

'Kesiah Lightman.' She pushed her hand towards him.

Silas stared at her hand. This girl didn't seem to picking up on the 'I want to be left alone' message he was trying to communicate. He would have to spell it out for her.

'Er… I'm Silas,' he said slowly, ignoring her proffered hand. 'I'm going to move over there,' he pointed at another empty seat further down the carriage, 'and I'm going to go back to sleep.'

'Sure,' she said blithely, following him as he changed seats. 'What's the matter?'

He stared at her with disbelief. Who was this girl? Why wouldn't she leave him alone? 'Nothing's the matter!'

'Hmm,' was Kesiah's only response, but the way she looked at him, with her head tilted on one side and her eyes alight with sympathy and curiosity, suddenly reminded him of Bonnie. Whenever Silas said something blatantly untrue, Bonnie would have that same look. It was almost as if this girl, Kesiah, could see him with Soulsight…

'I see you?' Silas said experimentally, suddenly feeling hopeful.

'That's because I'm sitting next to you, I can also see you,' Kesiah said slowly, laughing at his odd statement. 'That's not a very good game.'

'It's not a game,' Silas said despondently. 'Look, I'd really rather you left me alone.'

301

'OK,' Kesiah said, suddenly standing to her feet and grinning. 'If that is what you truly want, or… we could play a proper game. Something fun.' Kesiah grinned again. Her perfect teeth were quite disturbing, almost fearsome.

'Fun?' Silas echoed, feeling his heart sink. Why couldn't she leave him alone? 'No, thanks! I am not a child. I… just… want… to… sleep! I do not want to play a "game"!' He spat the last word out, hoping to reinforce his disinterest. He didn't know how to make it any clearer, but Kesiah was undeterred.

'Here's the deal: you play one game with me and then I'll let you rest… but only if you win. Otherwise, I will pester you for the whole journey!'

He stared at her with disbelief. 'Look, just go away,' he said, rapidly losing patience.

'One game and, whether you win *or* lose, I'll leave you alone.' She arched her eyebrow and added, 'I promise.'

'Who are you?' Silas cried in exasperation. 'Why are you doing this to me?'

Kesiah smiled and sat down opposite him. 'Because you need to take your mind off whatever was causing your bad dreams.'

'You know nothing about me,' Silas said defensively, but even as she tucked her legs under her on the chair, he wondered. Maybe there were people who could see more than what their natural eyes revealed, even without Soulsight. Bonnie always seemed to see more, to know more.

'So, tell me,' she challenged, still smiling. 'Tell me about you…'

Silas shook his head; he wasn't going to share his heart and his hurt with a complete stranger. Maybe the game was the preferable alternative.

'Fine!' he said suddenly, still not quite believing what he was being sucked into. 'What's the game, then? It had better be quick.'

'Yes!' She cheered triumphantly. 'Right, let's look at you.'

Much to Silas' embarrassment, she reached out her hand and squeezed his biceps.

'What are you doing?' He leapt to his feet and brushed her hand off.

'You've got to be a climber. Am I right?' She stood next to him, still eyeing him up and down. 'Slim build, narrow hips, wiry upper body… speciality climber? Yes?'

'Yes.' Silas backed away. 'Was that the game?' She was really unnerving him, and he wished she would leave him be.

'No,' she laughed and pointed down the carriage. 'This is the game; whoever gets to the end of the carriage wins. But you can only use the luggage compartments and chair tops. The seats and the floor are out of bounds.'

Silas looked down the length of the car. There were 30 rows of well-spaced chairs and over each one an individual shallow metal tray. There wasn't much room between the two, and he would have to squeeze through the gaps, or go over the luggage holds, to make it the length of the car.

'Really? This is your game?' He looked at Kesiah and looked at the carriage again. 'And if I do this, you'll leave me alone?'

'Promise.' She clambered onto a seat back. 'Go!' she shouted and then swung up into the luggage tray.

'Wait, I'm not ready,' Silas shouted, climbing up as well.

'You snooze, you lose!' she called over her shoulder.

The best technique seemed to be to loop over the luggage tray and rest his feet on the seat top and then lean across to grab the next tray. He was slowly gaining on her, but she was fast, and her body seemed to fold effortlessly through the tiny gaps above the trays. He wondered what clinic she went to. He hadn't seen her at any trials before, but she looked like she should be in Gold.

'I win!' Kesiah shouted gleefully as she touched the far wall.

'That wasn't fair,' Silas complained, as he clambered from the luggage tray onto the chair. 'You had a head start.'

'OK, you set the challenge, then.' Kesiah walked back towards him. He noticed her poise, the way she held her head high, making her appear a little taller than she really was. She smiled at him, and this time he smiled back. She wasn't so bad... a bit pushy, but otherwise... OK.

'What's your speciality, then?' he asked.

'Guess,' she challenged with another fierce grin.

'Not another game,' Silas gave an exaggerated sigh and shrugged, 'I don't know... running? Gymnastics? What clinic do you go to, anyway?'

'Gymnastics,' she confirmed and tipped her body backwards onto outstretched hands, effortlessly forming a perfect bridge. Her flexible spine bent like a sapling, and then she kicked her legs up and over, suddenly standing upright again. 'I'm transferring clinics. My parents have just split up.' She puckered her lips, making her little mouth even smaller, and for a moment there was a dent in her overbearing enthusiasm.

'I'm sorry to hear that,' Silas said quietly, wishing he hadn't asked. He'd rather deal with her annoying childishness than cope with her sadness. He had enough of his own worries.

'They hardly saw each other by the end. Honestly, it's better this way.' She shrugged off her momentary gloom with one shake of her head and said, 'I'll stay with my dad in season-breaks; my mum has moved to Prima so I'll be with her during the season. Simple.' She did a forward handstand, but this time stayed upside down and walked towards Silas on her hands. He laughed and started backing up the length of the carriage as she followed after him.

'I've got into Vitality Clinic,' she said, as she elegantly righted herself. 'My mum's pleased; it's supposed to be the best one.'

'Oh?' Silas said in a non-committal tone, then coolly added, 'It's not bad, I suppose.'

'Is that your clinic?' she gasped and then grinned again. 'At least I'll have one friend when I start there, then. You know, I'm more worried about not seeing my friends again than I am about not seeing my dad. Is that bad?'

Silas shrugged. It was how he felt about his dad...

'You never kept your promise,' Silas said to her later.

The journey was nearly at an end. They had raced the car length a few more times, and Silas was now sitting on his chair near the door. He was reluctant to admit it, but he had had fun with Kesiah. She was full of life and lightness. His time with her had been a temporary reprieve from the hopelessness he was feeling.

'What promise?'

'That if I played your game then you would let me sleep.'

'Oh, yes. I'd forgotten about that. Well, do you want to sleep? I'll leave you alone... I promise.' She smiled and looked at the time on the display board by the door. 'You've got 20 minutes until we arrive in Prima.'

Silas laughed. 'I guess I'll survive. You'd better keep me awake now, though. I know, teach me how to do that thing where you walk on your hands.'

Chapter 41

By the time the Subterranean pulled into the main station, just before dawn, he had managed a couple of 'steps' on his hands, and Kesiah jokingly promised she would complete his training when they met at clinic.

She spotted her mother waiting and, without looking back at Silas, was swept into an enthusiastic hug by a petite, fair-haired woman.

Approaching the Autocar bay, Silas could see a few Unseen hurrying to get undercover before daybreak, and he hoped Val had managed to catch the Overground back home.

He pressed his hand to the Autocar sensor and the door slid open.

'Where would you like to go, Silas Corelle?' the simulated voice asked.

'Home,' Silas responded and climbed in. A few options were presented on the screen: clinic, Bio-health labs, the Spire and his home address.

'Home!' Silas repeated and pointed at the correct address.

Ignoring the seat, he chose to stand and watch through the glass.

It was the time of day when the city paused – that short window at sunrise when the Unseen had retreated for the day and the Seen had yet to emerge. How he missed the Community, where there was no such division, where Soulsight brought a whole new way of seeing each other. Where you were free to mix, befriend and even love, regardless of any external appearance... and now that was gone. The Community had become his family; thanks to Soulsight, they

306

knew him far better than his own father and brother... and his family had been taken from him. The girl on the train had distracted him for a short while, but now he felt utterly alone.

The house was silent as he opened the door. Silas guessed his father must have left for work really early. Maybe he was too busy even to come home, especially if there was no one waiting for him. The house had a faint musty, dirty smell to it, and for the first time, Silas wondered if his father was lonely. With his new job, Marc would have more or less moved out, and Silas had been away for nearly a month.

Silas stepped past the Image room and out of habit looked in. Usually Marc would be there, lifting weights and watching sports.

In the confusion and pain of losing Jono, he had barely spared his brother a second thought. Now, though, he wondered how he was coping. Marc had definitely needed putting in his place but having to be tranquillised by your own girlfriend... how on earth would he have explained his strange behaviour?

'Is that you, Silas?' Marc's voice called out of the gloom, making Silas jump.

'Marc! You're home!' Silas peered into the dark room. 'House, lights on.'

The lights came on slowly, to reveal the huddled figure of his brother, sitting on the floor at the far end of the room.

Silas was taken aback. By his appearance, it seemed that Marc had not been coping... not at all! With grey smudges under his eyes and greasy, unwashed hair, he looked a mess.

'Why are you here? Are you ill?' Silas asked. He was genuinely concerned. He had never seen Marc look anything other than in perfect condition.

Marc slowly shook his head. 'Not ill... not in my body... and I don't think in my mind... but I've been suspended from active duty in the Advisor squad... but I'm not sure why.'

Silas thought about his brother attacking the Flawless Leader. Poor Marc. Helen Steele had done something to him to make sure he was no longer a threat.

Silas adopted a gentle voice and stepped closer. 'I'm sorry you've been suspended.' He crouched down near him. Marc absolutely stunk. He was the source of the strange odour in the house, and Silas breathed in through his mouth instead of his nose, to limit the smell. 'Does Dad know? Is he here?' Silas asked.

'I guess, but I've not seen him yet. He's been away, and he's due back tomorrow. I don't know what to do, Silas.'

'What happened?' Silas asked, curious to know how much his brother knew, and intrigued by this new, lost and surprisingly humble Marc; so different from the arrogant bully he usually had to avoid.

'I can't really remember much. It's all so fuzzy. We were rounding up some Unclassifieds in the Outerlands and there were Unseen everywhere, and they were trying to hurt this magnificent Unclassified that would have been a perfect Seen. I tried to defend him… and then it all becomes very mixed up… I woke up and I was back here in Prima. I'm not an Advisor any more. I don't know what I did wrong…' Marc's voice cracked like he was admitting something shameful.

'Can I get you anything from the dispenser?' Silas asked, feeling sorry for Marc. He was obviously really struggling. His life had gone from success and stability to failure and uncertainty, overnight. He remembered the childlike nature of Marc's heart when he had seen it with Soulsight. No wonder he was finding it all so difficult.

'No… but I'm glad you're home, Silas. I don't think I ever told you that I like having you as my brother.'

Silas was so surprised that he nearly laughed outright. His brother had *never* said anything like that before.

'Right,' Silas said, unwilling to let himself be the butt of another of Marc's jokes. There was a strange look in Marc's eyes, and it took Silas a moment to recognise it was sincerity.

'Thanks, Marc. Are you sure you're all right? I mean, you are being kind to me.' Silas let out a half-laugh to break up the tension. But it seemed to have the opposite effect and Marc grabbed his hand to draw him closer. His breath was awful. When was the last time he'd washed? Silas tried to pull away, forgetting that Marc had more strength in his fingers than Silas did in his whole arm. He couldn't budge an inch and was stuck breathing in his brother's fetid air.

'Something in me has changed Silas.' He dropped his voice to a conspiratorial whisper. 'There is *more* to life than achieving physical perfection.' He nodded solemnly.

Silas didn't underestimate the importance of this statement. Marc, who had dedicated his life to honing his body to perfection, was now openly saying that it wasn't enough, and Silas wondered whether Marc's Soulsight overdose was still having lingering effects.

'You've really changed, Marc,' Silas admitted.

'I owe a debt...' Marc muttered.

'What?'

'I don't know, but it's nagging at me... I feel like I owe someone something... and I don't know what or why.' Marc sighed heavily in frustration, sending another foul wave of stale breath across Silas.

This time the smell didn't bother Silas; he knew that Marc was talking about Jono.

'Maybe it will come back to you. You just need a bit of time,' Silas said, trying to ease his hand free from Marc's strong grip. 'It's good to be home, Marc, but I need to get cleaned up before Dad gets back, and you should too. You look terrible. If Dad sees you like this, he'll call HE-LP.'

'OK,' Marc said compliantly, and stood to his feet. 'After you, Silas.' Marc towered over Silas, but for the first time in years, Silas didn't consider his brother as a threat.

The moment of truth! Silas had never, ever felt nervous of his Biocubicle assessment before. He just had to do it, and if the results were terrible… well, he still had a few days to work on that before clinic started.

He took a deep breath and stepped in.

The infrared beams probed and analysed, and he was vividly reminded of the scanning ship. He could hide nothing from the Biocubicle.

'Percentages,' the voice started up. 'Muscle… 40 per cent. Fat… 15 per cent. Blood pressure… 115 over 60… Heart rate 61 beats per minute. Weight… 52 kilograms.'

Silas couldn't believe it; whatever unregulated food he had been eating at the Community had caused him to bulk up! His levels had actually improved. He had more muscle and had gained a bit of weight. He did a few poses in the high reflective wall. He couldn't see much difference, but at least he wasn't getting any skinnier.

With a familiar gurgle and clunk, the dispenser produced the recommended morning shake. Silas drank it without pausing. It was tasteless. He had never noticed before, but the shake had absolutely no flavour. It was like drinking thick, cloudy water. This needs something to liven it up a bit, Silas thought… maybe some waterberry juice.

He was reminded of the toast that Jono had made with Bubba Gee's waterberry rum: 'To long life and lifelong friends.' Why hadn't he just enjoyed the moment when he had shared in the toast?

'To lifelong friends,' he murmured, and then the sharp pain of loss caught him once again, but this time he felt the warm salt of tears finally begin to fall.

Curling up on his bed, he let the emotion wash through him. He cried over the death of his friend and for the destruction of the Community. He wept for Bonnie's son, now condemned to a life of permanent night, and for Maxie and Val, their beautiful kindness forever hidden by their broken bodies.

He didn't know how long he had slept for, but he was woken by the persistent voice of the house computer.

'Please visit the health suite for your recommended exercise,' it said, over and over again. Silas straightened out on his bed and rubbed the dry salt tracks from his eyes. The tears had been cathartic and part of the healing process, but Silas still felt emotionally fragile, as if the slightest harsh word would bruise him beyond repair.

How must Zoe be feeling? he thought, sitting upright. It must be so much worse for her; she had loved so deeply and lost so cruelly. He wanted to remember Jono with her, and be able to talk about him until the memories didn't hurt any more.

He also wanted to see Nana. She would need his help to find their friends from the Community. Clinic would still take most of his daytime, but he could spend every night among the Unseen. He could do what his mother had done and help them escape the confines of the city. The Outerlands were vast and empty. They would find a new place... a new home... Silas felt sure of it.

'Visit the health suite,' the house repeated, and this time Silas was sure he heard an edge to the computer's voice.

'Yes, House. I'm going. Silence now!' he commanded and then reluctantly headed out of his room.

Marc had showered and dressed and was powering along on the treadmill. He looked a different person to the broken man who had been hopelessly cowering in the corner just hours ago. He looked like his old self. Silas couldn't help but feel disappointed. Marc the Gold Standard had returned. So much for there being 'more to life than achieving physical perfection', Silas thought bitterly.

Turning to the screen by the door, Silas looked for his recommended exercise routine.

'Weights?' He couldn't help but voice his annoyance. He had put on muscle already; surely it was time to focus on something else.

Settling onto the machine he tried to empty his mind, but it was impossible. He had changed so much over the past month, and yet he was stuck in exactly the same old rut. What was the point of it all?

'Do you want me to help you?'

Silas sat up so quickly he nearly banged his head on the horizontal bar.

'Marc? What do you… you want to help? Er… yes… sure,' he stuttered.

'You've got the machine set all wrong,' Marc said. Silas stared dumbfounded while Marc started resetting it.

'I figured you were talking sense, by the way,' Marc continued, peering at the dials on the back of the machine. 'I've got to get back on track. Get back out there.'

Silas made a surprised gulping sound. Marc has taken advice from me, he thought.

'Right, that will be better. Now let's build it up gradually,' Marc said, and Silas obediently settled back into the machine and gripped the handles.

With Marc as his personal coach, Silas came out of the health suite feeling the exercise may have actually done him some good. He couldn't believe how different Marc was, though. He had been patient and even encouraging. It was as if he was rediscovering the brother that had been lost to him. It felt good, like his small broken family was mending at long last.

He couldn't wait to tell Zoe about Marc. It was doubtful that she would be home yet, Silas thought, but he could call round just in case. Maybe Nana would be there. They could start looking for Bubba Gee…

'I'm just going out,' he called to Marc, who was still powering along on the treadmill.

'OK, be careful,' Marc replied.

An incredulous smile spread across Silas' face as he closed the front door and set off to Zoe's house. If the change in

Marc was anything to go by, then things were definitely beginning to look up.

Jono's Shakespearean quotes in order of appearance:

Romeo and Juliet, Act 2 scene 6
A Midsummer Night's Dream, Act 1 scene 1
Julius Caesar, Act 2 scene 2
A Midsummer Night's Dream, Act 3 scene 1
A Midsummer Night's Dream, Act 2 scene 1
King Lear, Act 5 scene 3
Troilus and Cressida, Act 2 scene 3
Henry V, Act 3 scene 1
Sonnet 18
Othello, Act 2 scene 3
Two Gentlemen of Verona, Act 3 scene 1
Twelfth Night, Act 3 scene 4